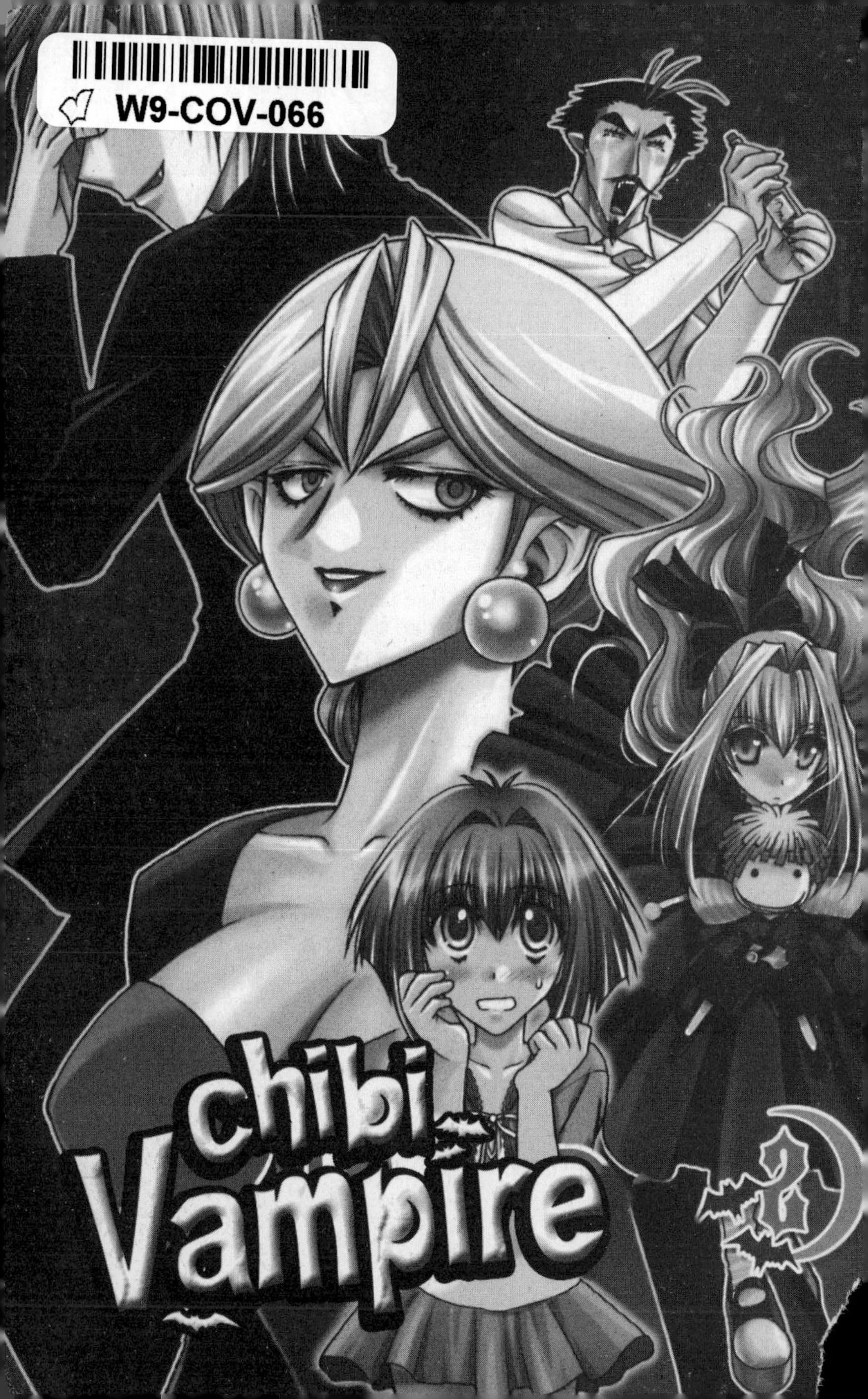
Chibi
Vampire
3

Chibi Vampire Vol. 2
Created by Yuna Kagesaki

Translation - Alexis Kirsch
English Adaptation - Christine Boylan
Layout and Lettering - Erika Terriquez
Production Artist - Jennifer Carbajal
Cover Layout - Kyle Plummer

Editor - Tim Beedle
Digital Imaging Manager - Chris Buford
Production Manager - Elisabeth Brizzi
Managing Editor - Sheldon Drzka
VP of Production - Ron Klamert
Editor-in-Chief - Rob Tokar
Publisher - Mike Kiley
President and C.O.O. - John Parker
C.E.O. and Chief Creative Officer - Stuart Levy

A  TOKYOPOP® Manga

TOKYOPOP Inc.
5900 Wilshire Blvd. Suite 2000
Los Angeles, CA 90036

E-mail: info@TOKYOPOP.com
Come visit us online at www.TOKYOPOP.com

ISBN: 1-59816-323-X

First TOKYOPOP printing: August 2006
20 19 18 17 16 15 14 13 12
Printed in the USA

Chibi Vampire

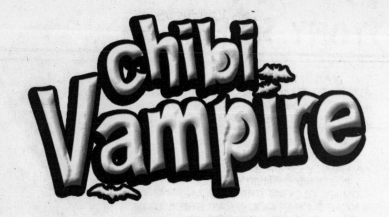

Volume 2

Created by
Yuna Kagesaki

TOKYOPOP®

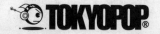

HAMBURG // LONDON // LOS ANGELES // TOKYO

OUR STORY SO FAR...

KARIN MAAKA ISN'T LIKE OTHER GIRLS. ONCE A MONTH, SHE EXPERIENCES PAIN, FATIGUE, HUNGER, IRRITABILITY—AND THEN SHE BLEEDS. FROM HER NOSE. KARIN IS A VAMPIRE, FROM A FAMILY OF VAMPIRES, BUT INSTEAD OF NEEDING TO DRINK BLOOD, SHE HAS AN EXCESS OF BLOOD THAT SHE MUST GIVE TO HER VICTIMS. IF DONE RIGHT, GIVING THIS BLOOD TO HER VICTIM CAN BE AN EXTREMELY POSITIVE THING. THE PROBLEM WITH THIS IS THAT KARIN NEVER SEEMS TO DO THINGS RIGHT...

WHEN LAST WE LEFT HER, KARIN WAS HAVING BOY TROUBLE. KENTA USUI—THE HANDSOME NEW STUDENT AT HER SCHOOL AND WORK—IS A NICE ENOUGH GUY, BUT HE EXACERBATES KARIN'S PROBLEM. KARIN, YOU SEE, IS DRAWN TO PEOPLE WHO HAVE SUFFERED MISFORTUNE, AND KENTA HAS SUFFERED PLENTY OF IT. KARIN DISCOVERED THIS WHEN SHE BIT KENTA'S MOTHER, AN INCIDENT THAT WAS UNFORTUNATELY WITNESSED BY KENTA. NOW, KARIN'S CONVINCED THAT SHE CAN KEEP HER NOSEBLEEDS UNDER CONTROL AS LONG AS SHE KEEPS KENTA HAPPY. AS FOR KENTA, HE JUST THINKS SHE'S WEIRD.

THE MAAKA FAMILY

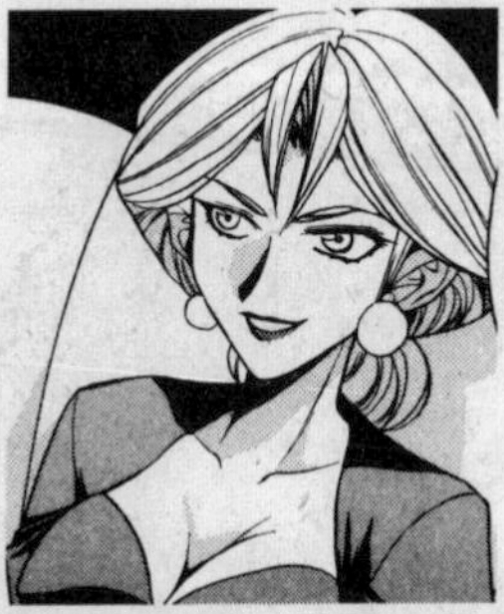

CALERA MARKER

Karin's overbearing mother. While Calera resents that Karin wasn't born a normal vampire, she does love her daughter in her own obnoxious way. Calera has chosen to keep her European last name.

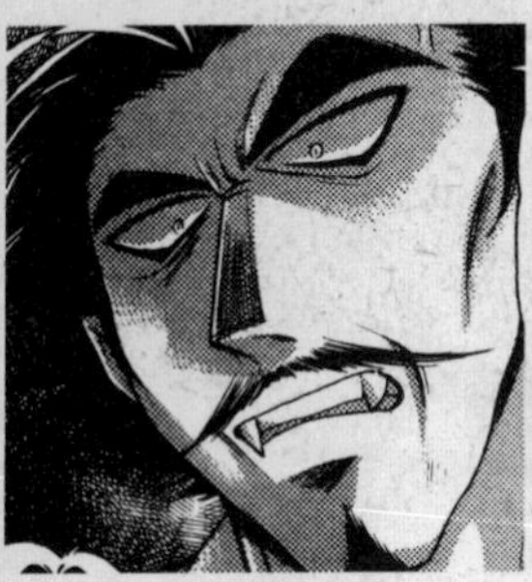

HENRY MARKER

Karin's father. In general, Henry treats Karin a lot better than she's treated by her mother, but the pants in this particular family are worn by Calera. Henry has also chosen to keep his European last name.

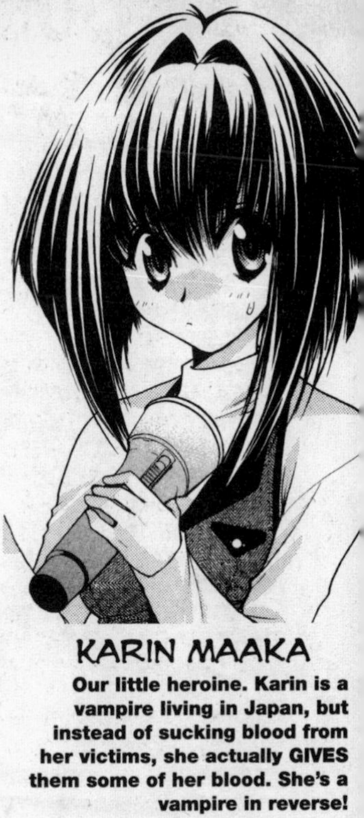

KARIN MAAKA

Our little heroine. Karin is a vampire living in Japan, but instead of sucking blood from her victims, she actually GIVES them some of her blood. She's a vampire in reverse!

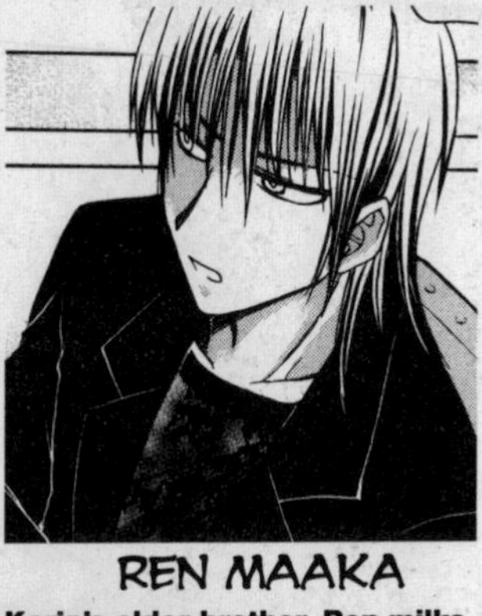

REN MAAKA

Karin's older brother. Ren milks the "sexy creature of the night" thing for all it's worth, and spends his nights in the arms (and beds) of attractive young women.

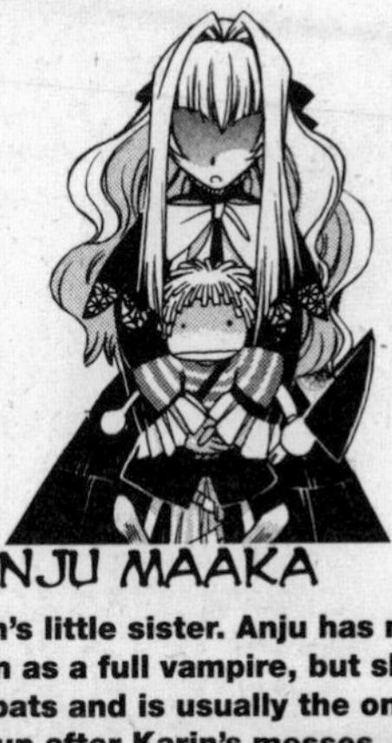

ANJU MAAKA

Karin's little sister. Anju has not yet awoken as a full vampire, but she can control bats and is usually the one who cleans up after Karin's messes. Rarely seen without her "talking" doll, Boogie.

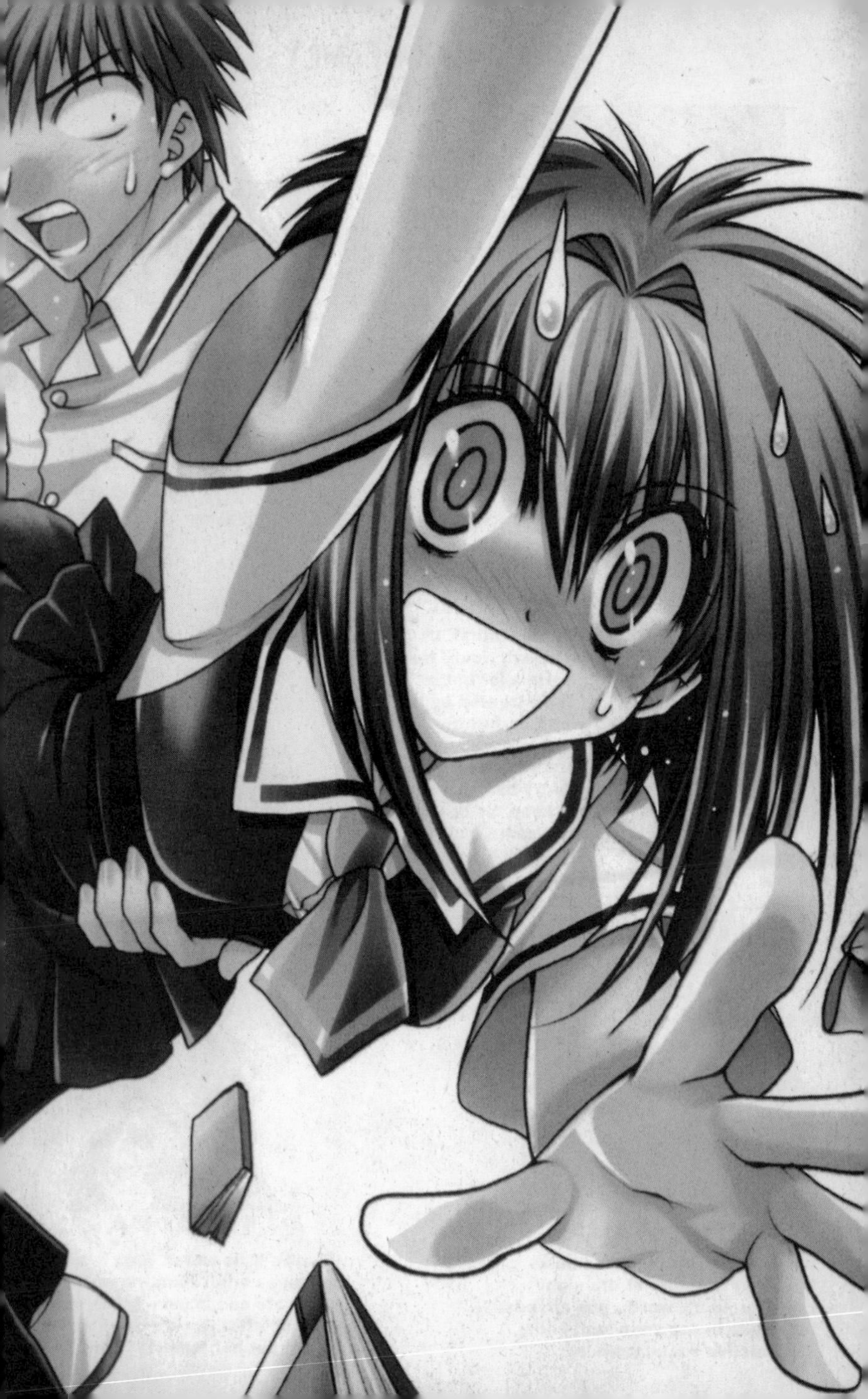

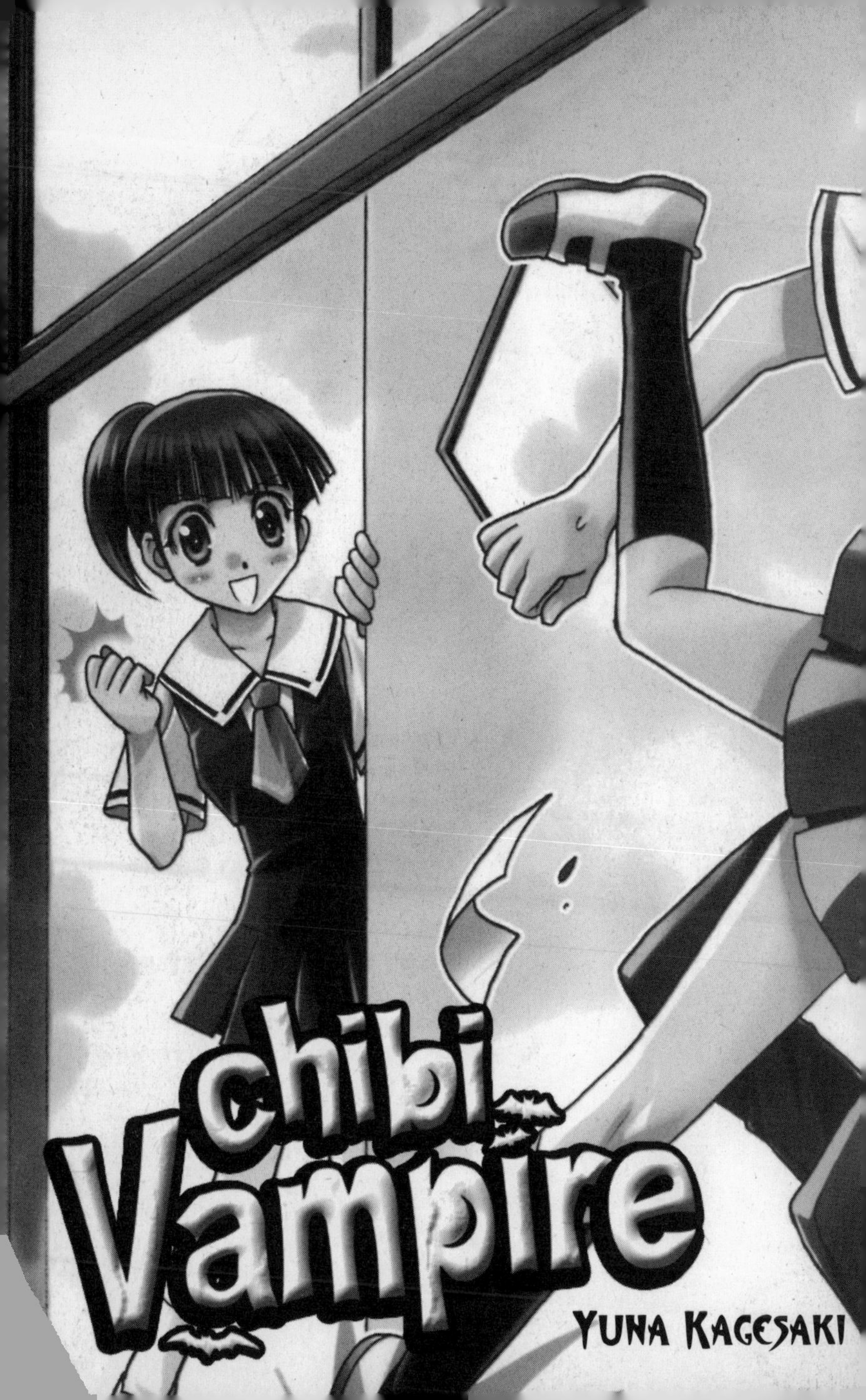
Chibi Vampire
YUNA KAGESAKI

VOL.2
CONTENTS

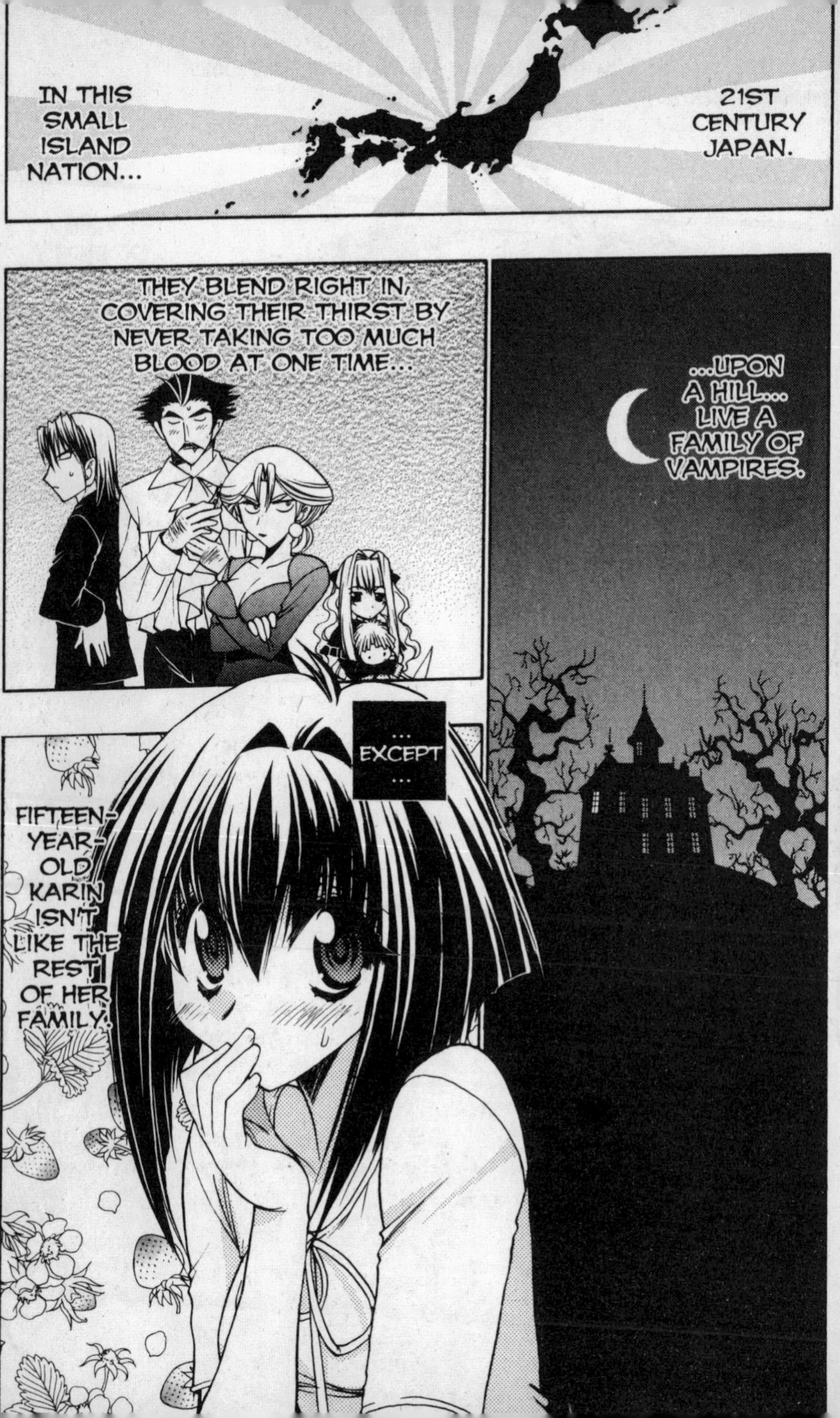
21ST CENTURY JAPAN.
IN THIS SMALL ISLAND NATION...
...UPON A HILL... LIVE A FAMILY OF VAMPIRES.
THEY BLEND RIGHT IN, COVERING THEIR THIRST BY NEVER TAKING TOO MUCH BLOOD AT ONE TIME...
... EXCEPT ...
FIFTEEN-YEAR-OLD KARIN ISN'T LIKE THE REST OF HER FAMILY.

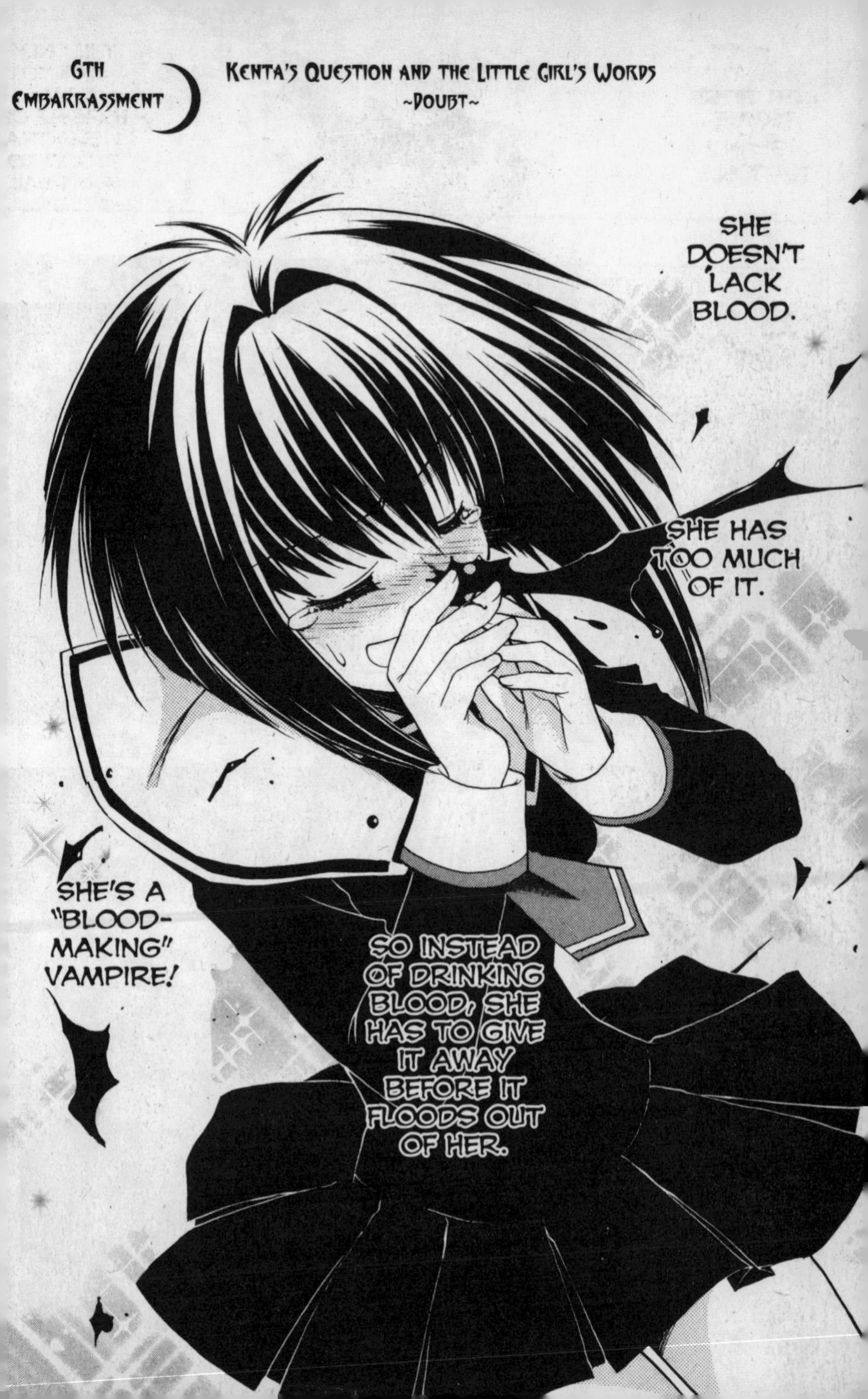
6th Embarrassment
Kenta's Question and the Little Girl's Words ~Doubt~
SHE DOESN'T LACK BLOOD.
SHE HAS TOO MUCH OF IT.
SO INSTEAD OF DRINKING BLOOD, SHE HAS TO GIVE IT AWAY BEFORE IT FLOODS OUT OF HER.
SHE'S A "BLOOD-MAKING" VAMPIRE!

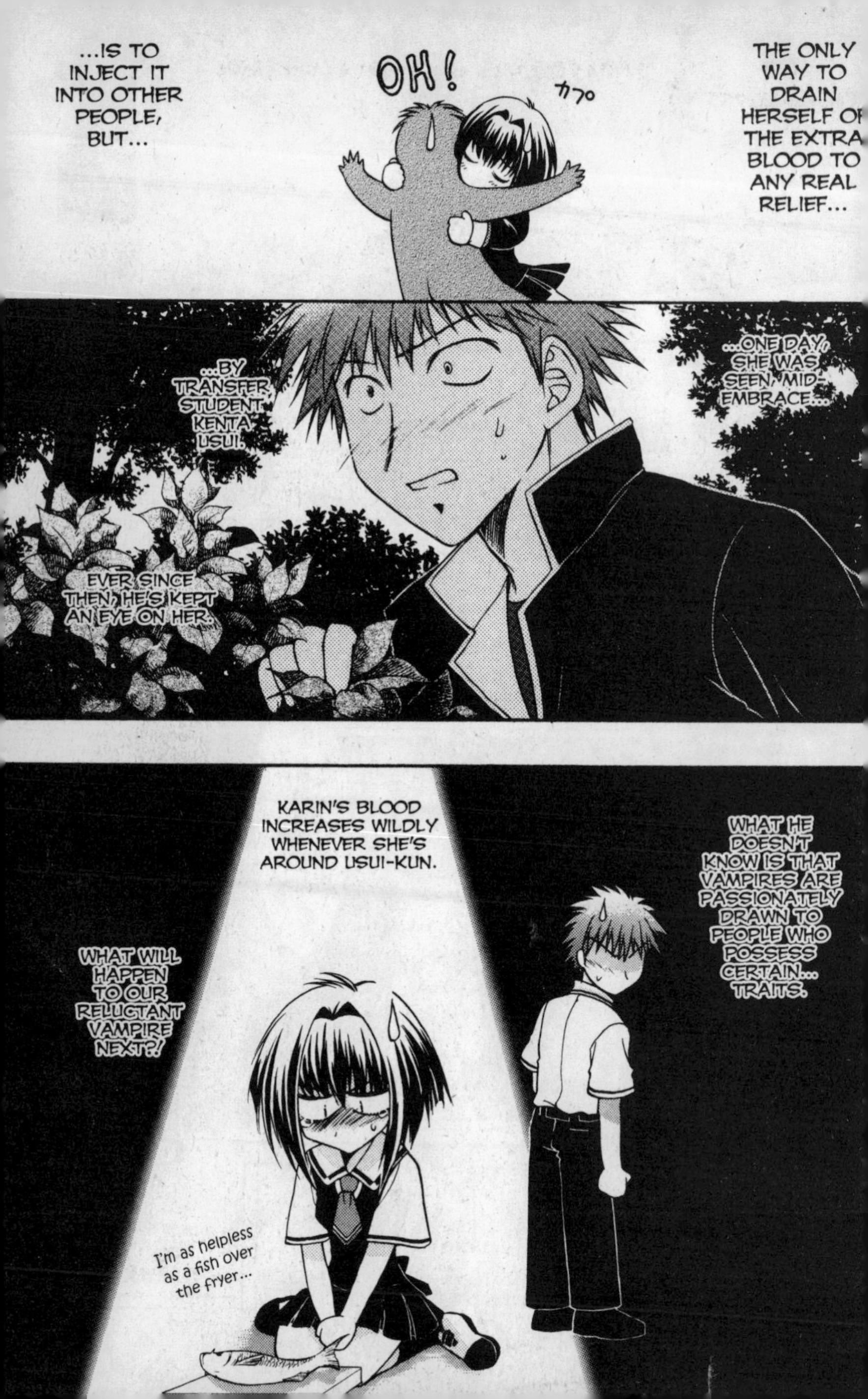
THE ONLY WAY TO DRAIN HERSELF OF THE EXTRA BLOOD TO ANY REAL RELIEF...
OH!
...IS TO INJECT IT INTO OTHER PEOPLE, BUT...
...ONE DAY, SHE WAS SEEN, MID-EMBRACE...
...BY TRANSFER STUDENT KENTA USUI.
EVER SINCE THEN, HE'S KEPT AN EYE ON HER.
WHAT HE DOESN'T KNOW IS THAT VAMPIRES ARE PASSIONATELY DRAWN TO PEOPLE WHO POSSESS CERTAIN... TRAITS.
KARIN'S BLOOD INCREASES WILDLY WHENEVER SHE'S AROUND USUI-KUN.
WHAT WILL HAPPEN TO OUR RELUCTANT VAMPIRE NEXT?!
I'm as helpless as a fish over the fryer...

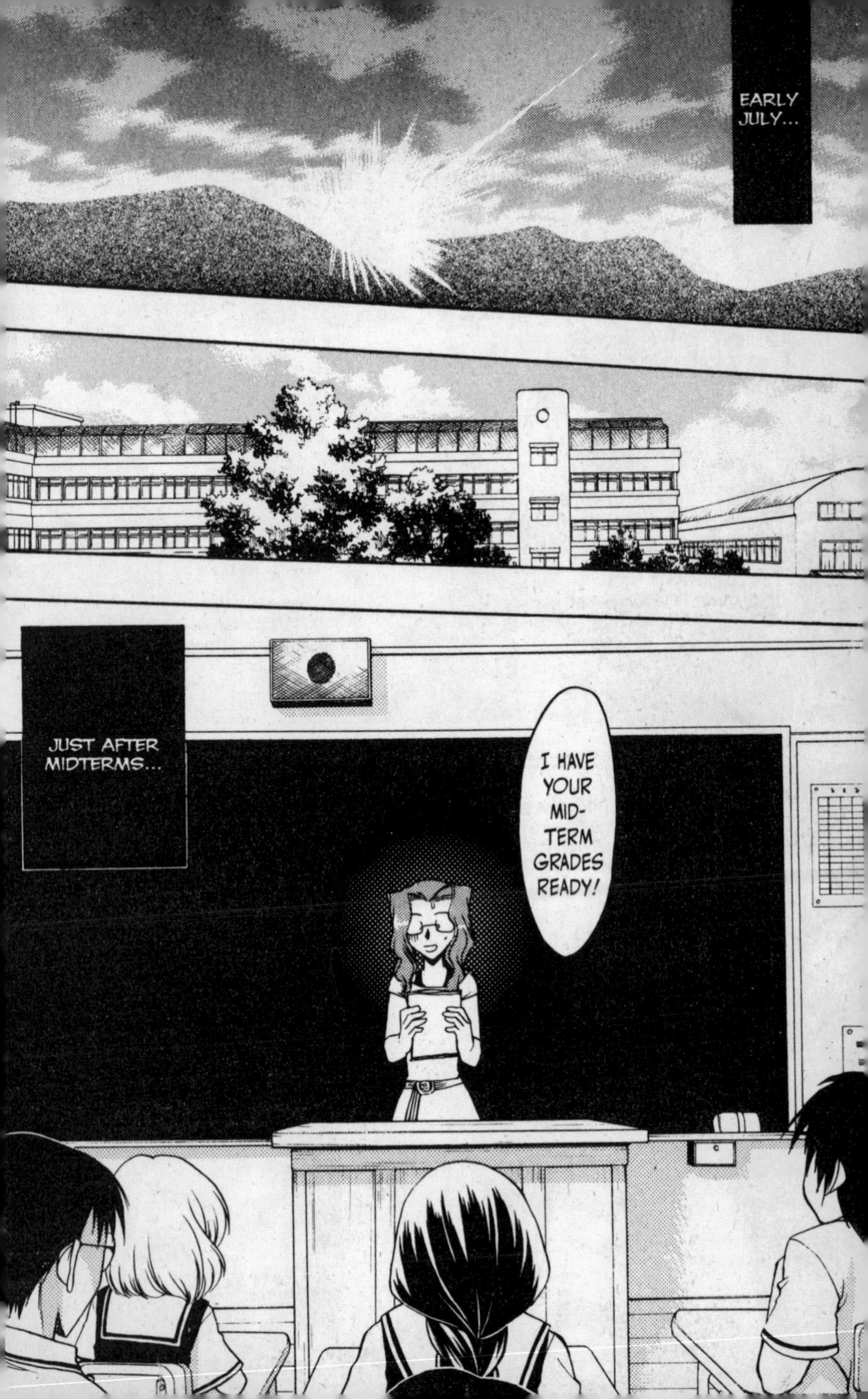
EARLY JULY...
JUST AFTER MIDTERMS...
I HAVE YOUR MID-TERM GRADES READY!

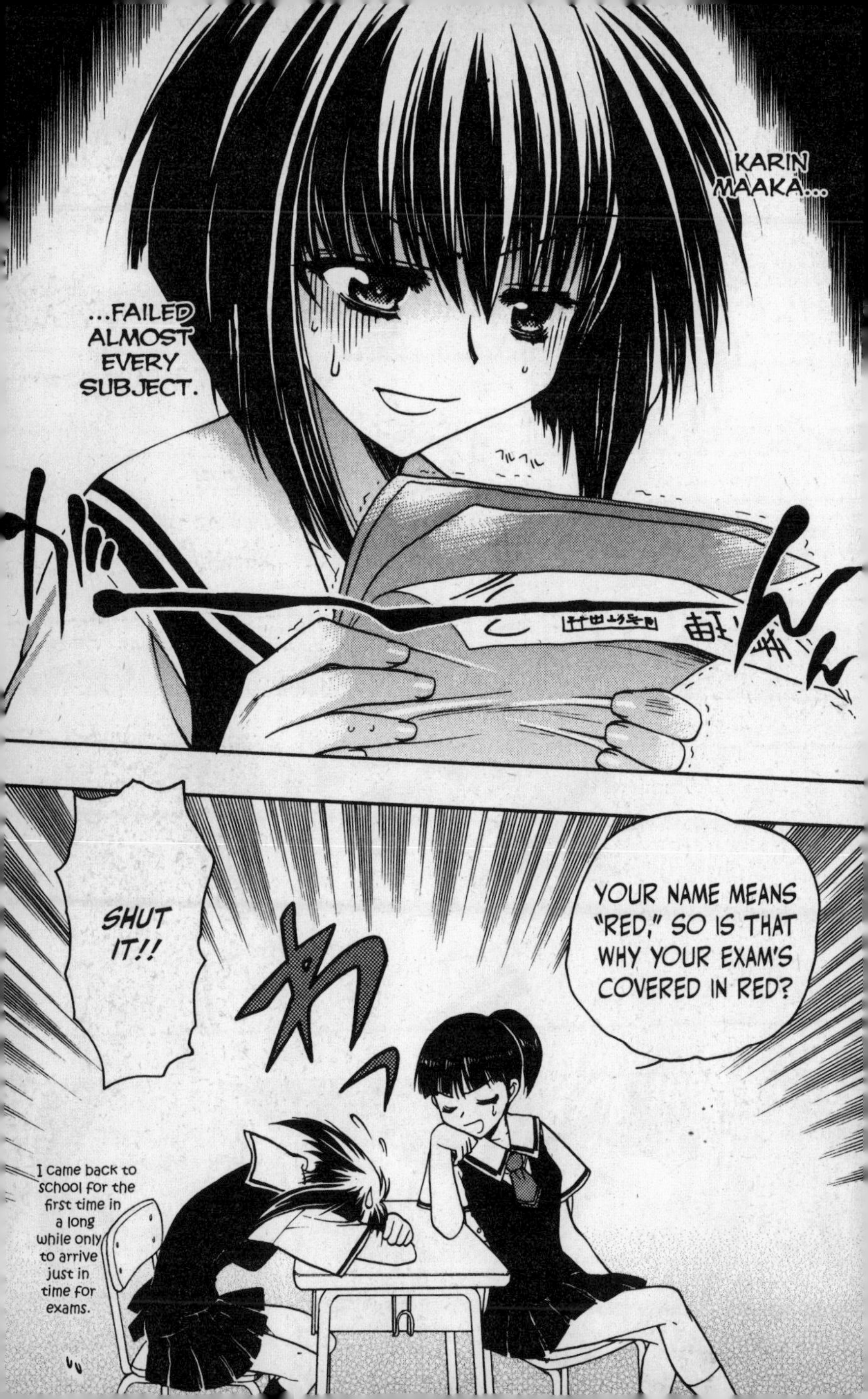
KARIN MAAKA...
...FAILED ALMOST EVERY SUBJECT.
YOUR NAME MEANS "RED," SO IS THAT WHY YOUR EXAM'S COVERED IN RED?
SHUT IT!!
I came back to school for the first time in a long while only to arrive just in time for exams.

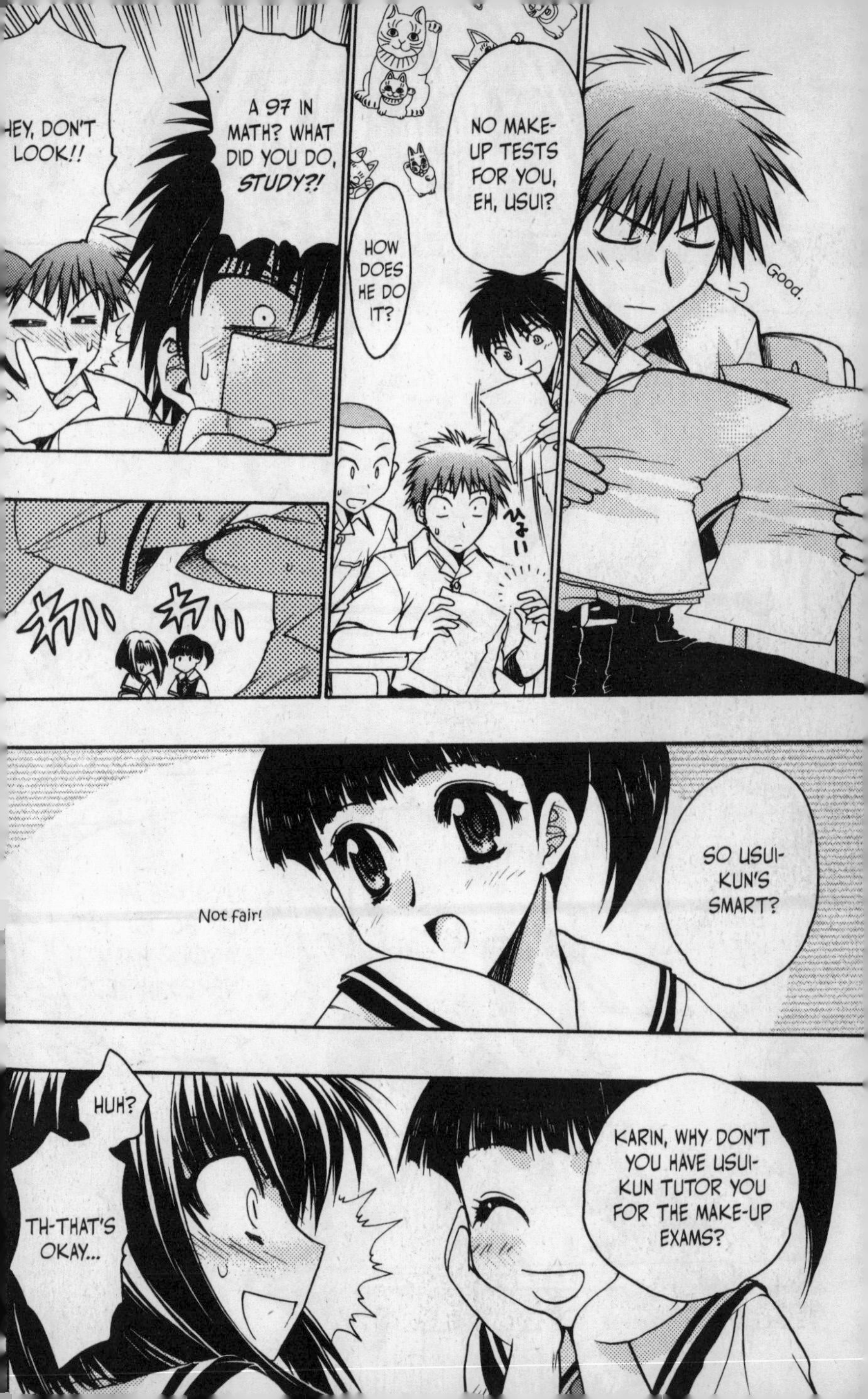
NO MAKE-UP TESTS FOR YOU, EH, USUI?
Good.
HOW DOES HE DO IT?
A 97 IN MATH? WHAT DID YOU DO, STUDY?!
HEY, DON'T LOOK!!
SO USUI-KUN'S SMART?
Not fair!
KARIN, WHY DON'T YOU HAVE USUI-KUN TUTOR YOU FOR THE MAKE-UP EXAMS?
HUH?
TH-THAT'S OKAY...

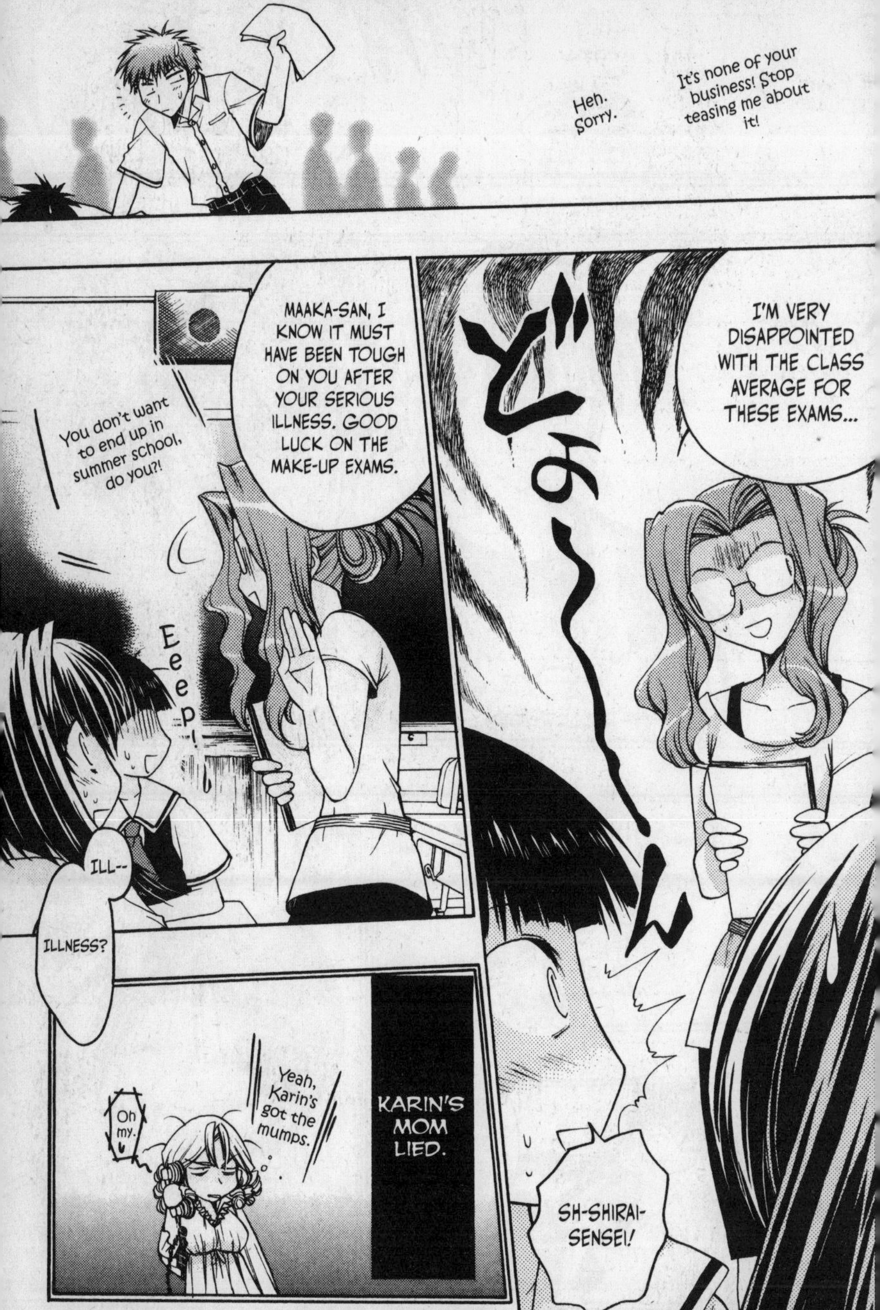
It's none of your business! Stop teasing me about it!
Heh. Sorry.
I'M VERY DISAPPOINTED WITH THE CLASS AVERAGE FOR THESE EXAMS...
どよ~ん
SH-SHIRAI-SENSEI!
MAAKA-SAN, I KNOW IT MUST HAVE BEEN TOUGH ON YOU AFTER YOUR SERIOUS ILLNESS. GOOD LUCK ON THE MAKE-UP EXAMS.
You don't want to end up in summer school, do you?!
Eeep!
ILL--
ILLNESS?
KARIN'S MOM LIED.
Yeah, Karin's got the mumps.
Oh my.

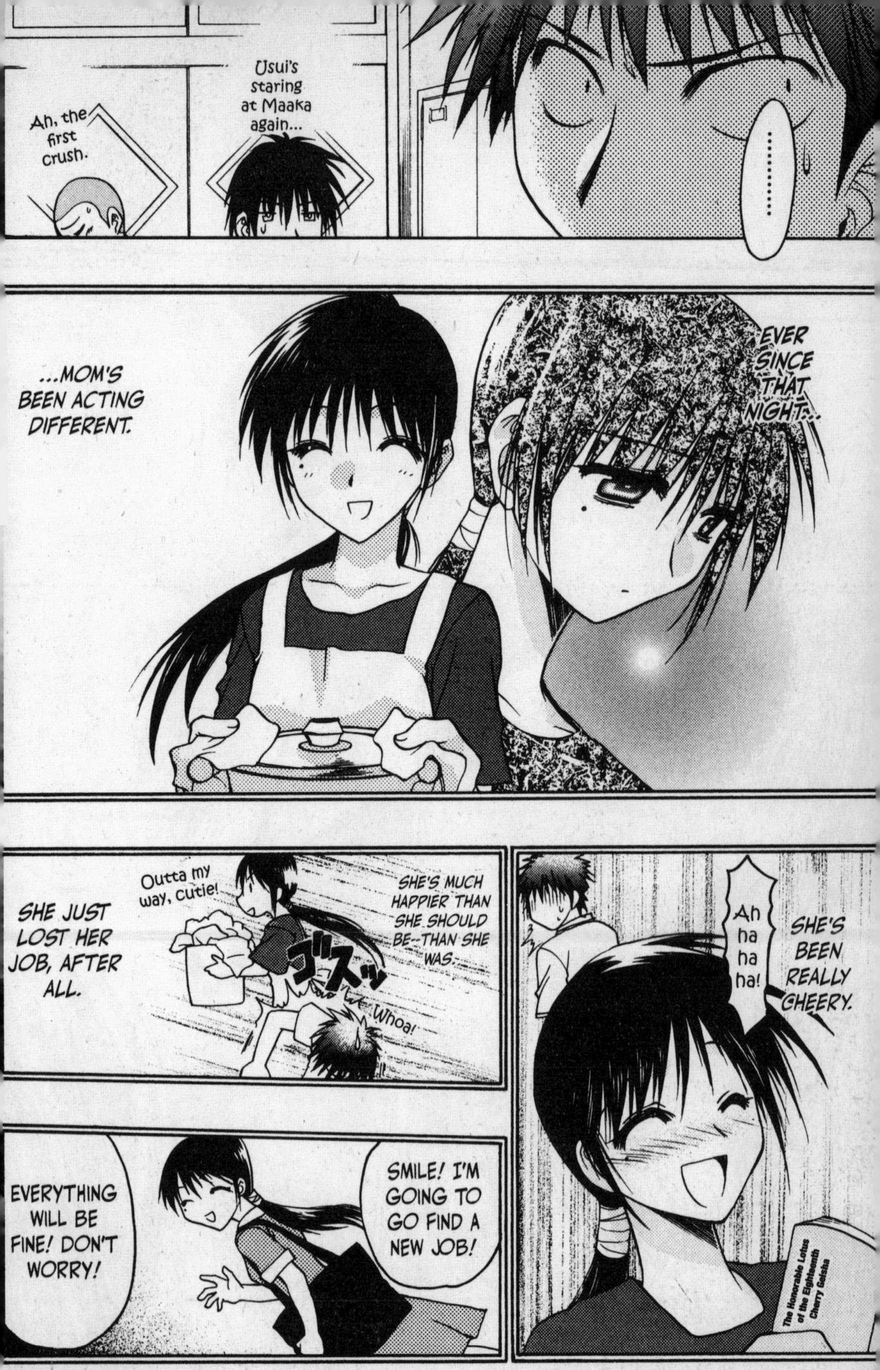

......
Usui's staring at Maaka again...
Ah, the first crush.
EVER SINCE THAT NIGHT...
...MOM'S BEEN ACTING DIFFERENT.
SHE'S BEEN REALLY CHEERY.
Ah ha ha ha!
The Honorable Lotus of the Eighteenth Cherry Geisha
SHE'S MUCH HAPPIER THAN SHE SHOULD BE--THAN SHE WAS.
Outta my way, cutie!
ゴスッ
Whoa!
SHE JUST LOST HER JOB, AFTER ALL.
SMILE! I'M GOING TO GO FIND A NEW JOB!
EVERYTHING WILL BE FINE! DON'T WORRY!

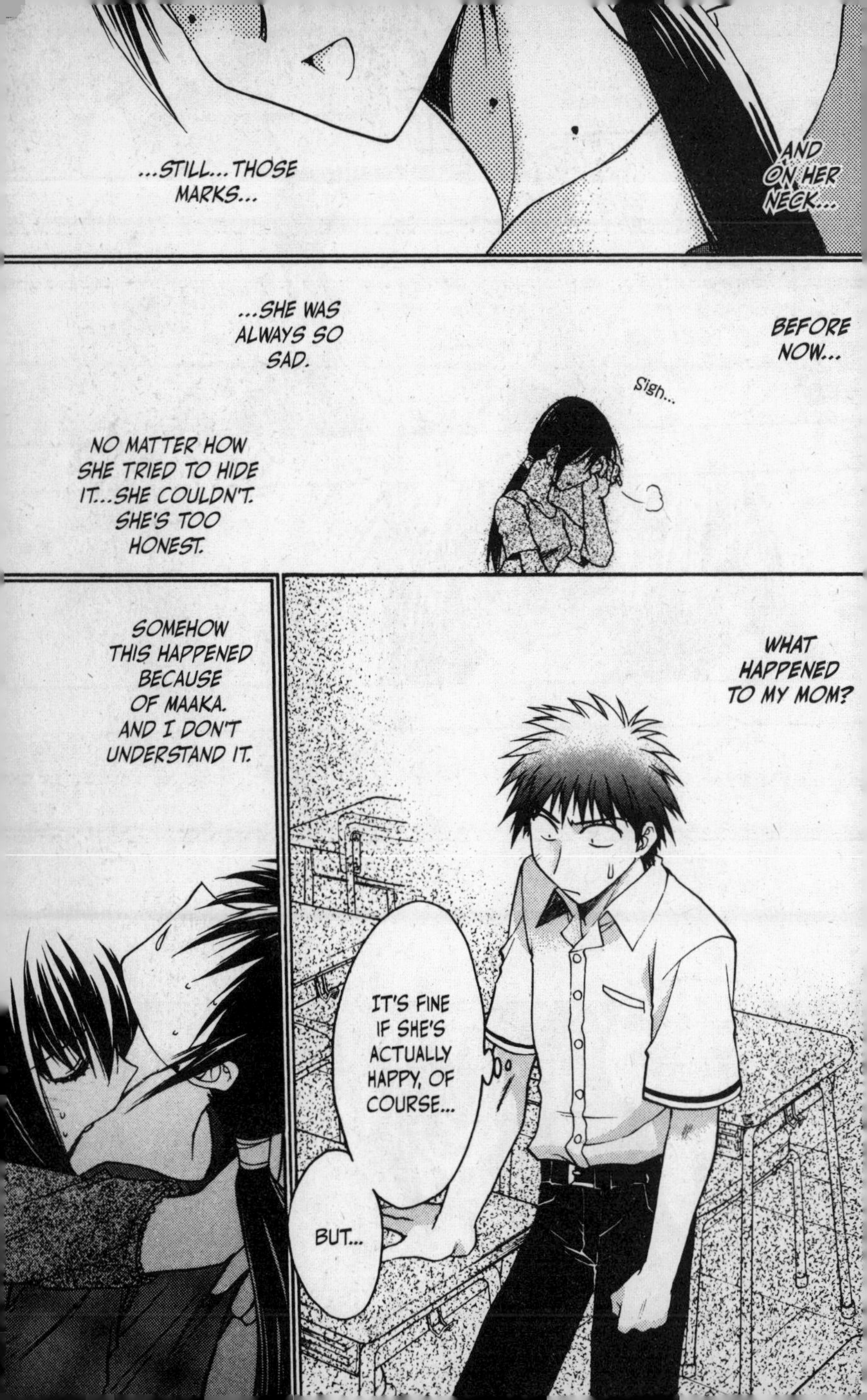
AND ON HER NECK...
...STILL...THOSE MARKS...
BEFORE NOW...
Sigh...
...SHE WAS ALWAYS SO SAD.
NO MATTER HOW SHE TRIED TO HIDE IT...SHE COULDN'T. SHE'S TOO HONEST.
WHAT HAPPENED TO MY MOM?
IT'S FINE IF SHE'S ACTUALLY HAPPY, OF COURSE...
BUT...
SOMEHOW THIS HAPPENED BECAUSE OF MAAKA. AND I DON'T UNDERSTAND IT.

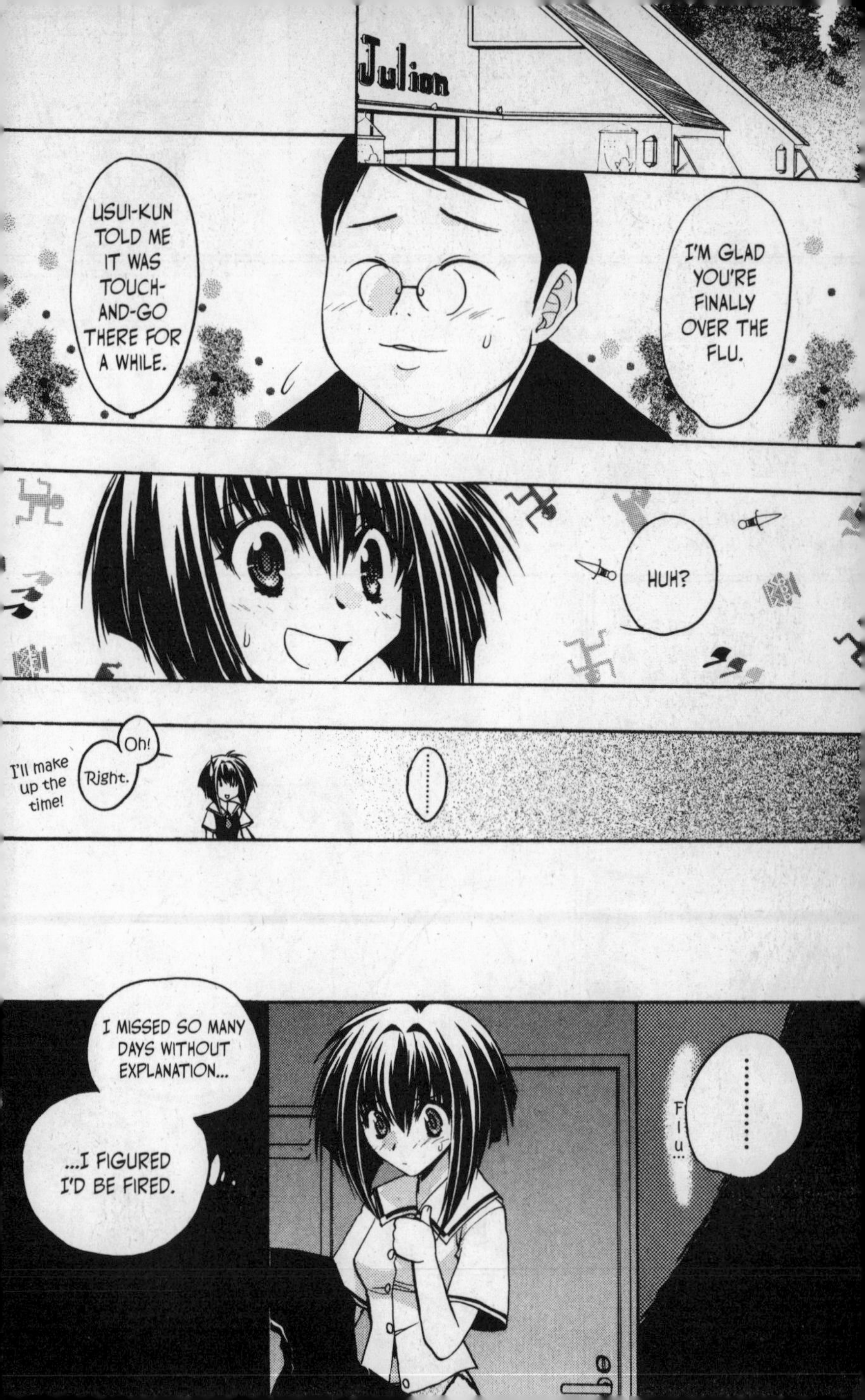
Julion
I'M GLAD YOU'RE FINALLY OVER THE FLU.
USUI-KUN TOLD ME IT WAS TOUCH-AND-GO THERE FOR A WHILE.
HUH?
......
Oh!
Right.
I'll make up the time!
....
Flu...
I MISSED SO MANY DAYS WITHOUT EXPLANATION...
...I FIGURED I'D BE FIRED.

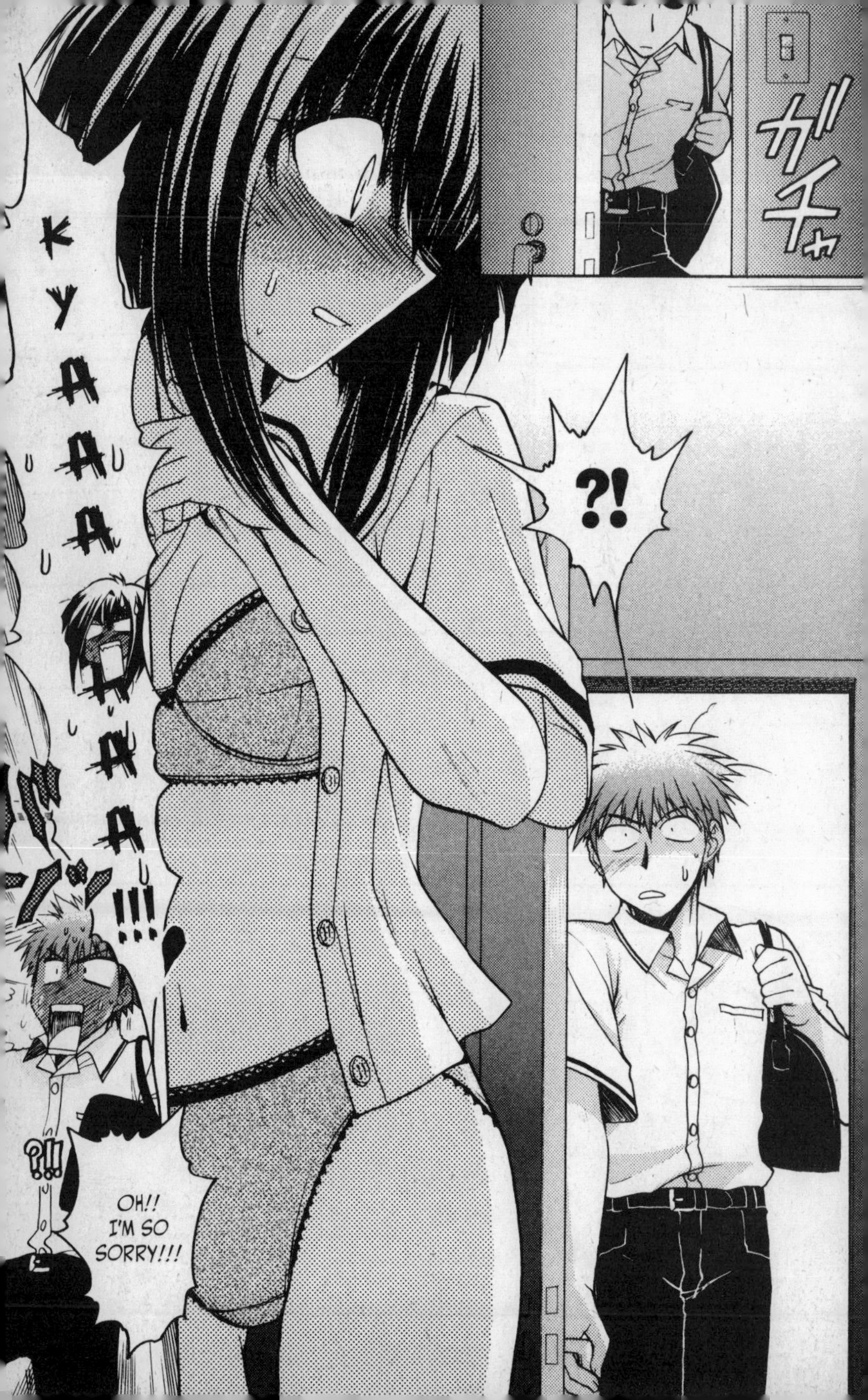
ガチャ
?!
KYAAAAAAAA!!!
?!!
OH!! I'M SO SORRY!!!

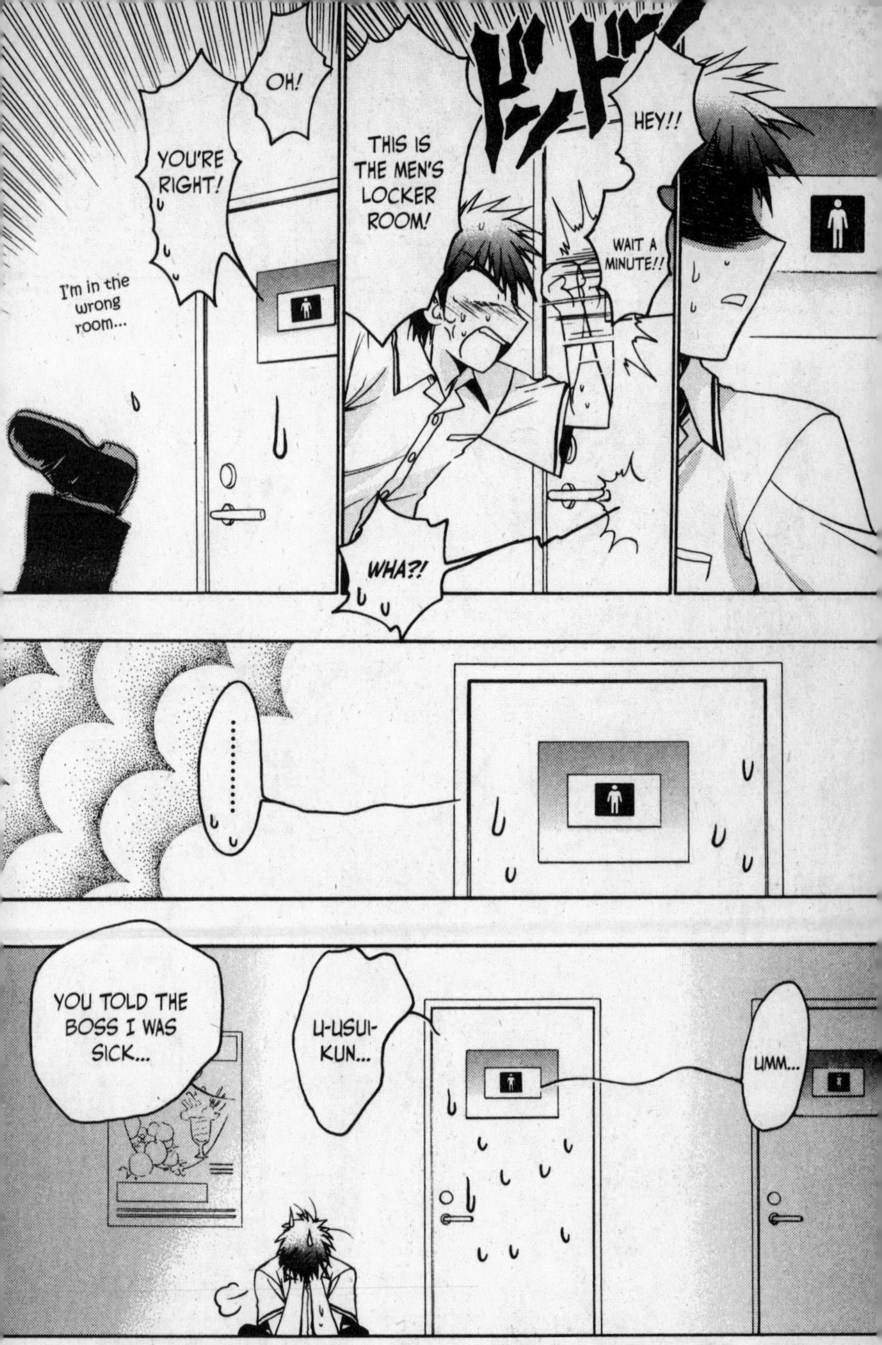

HEY!!
WAIT A MINUTE!!
THIS IS THE MEN'S LOCKER ROOM!
WHA?!
OH!
YOU'RE RIGHT!
I'm in the wrong room...
......
UMM...
U-USUI-KUN...
YOU TOLD THE BOSS I WAS SICK...

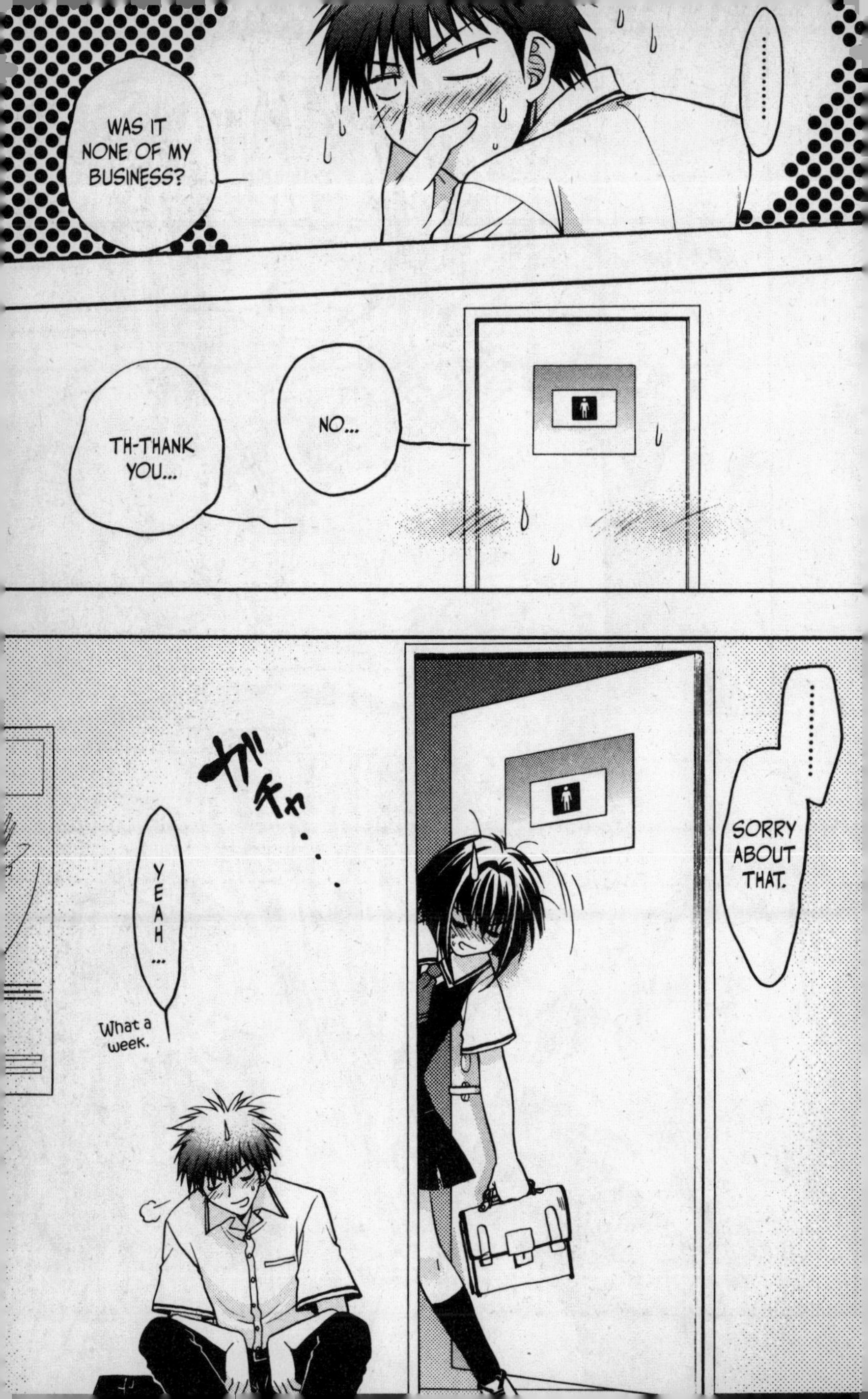
......
WAS IT NONE OF MY BUSINESS?
NO...
TH-THANK YOU...
...... SORRY ABOUT THAT.
ガチャ...
YEAH...
What a week.

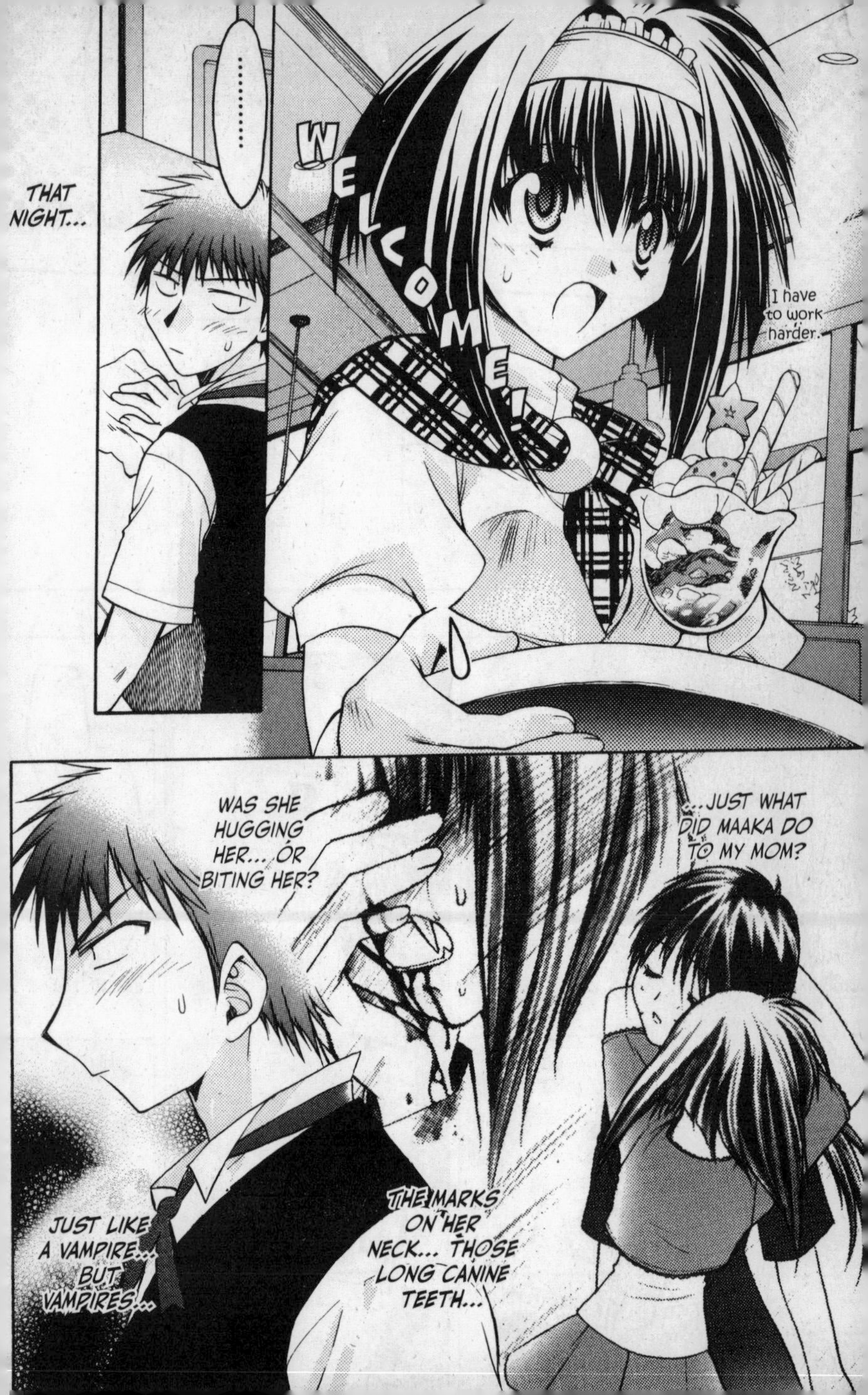
WELCOME!
I have to work harder.
......
THAT NIGHT...
...JUST WHAT DID MAAKA DO TO MY MOM?
WAS SHE HUGGING HER... OR BITING HER?
THE MARKS ON HER NECK... THOSE LONG CANINE TEETH...
JUST LIKE A VAMPIRE... BUT VAMPIRES...

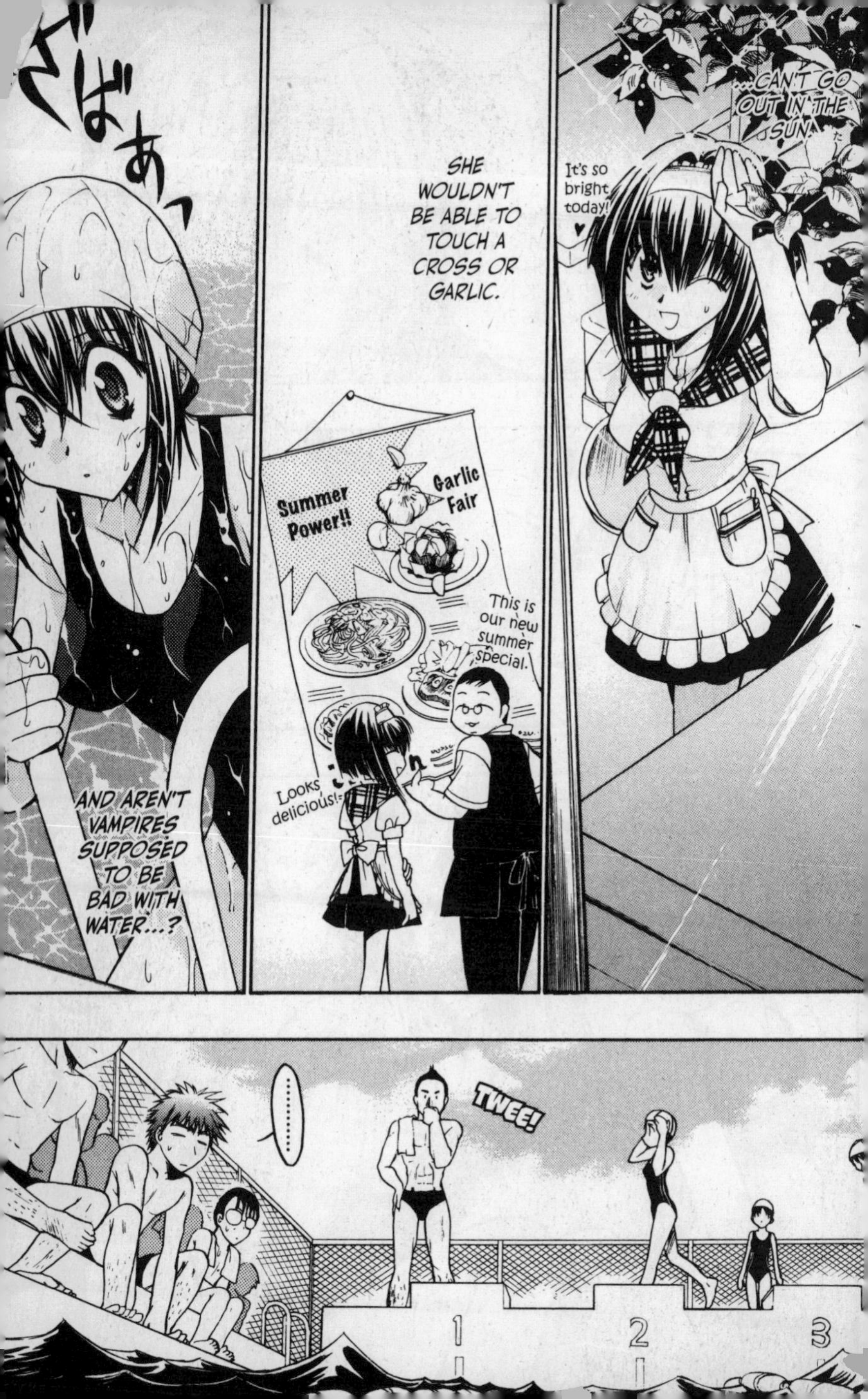
...CAN'T GO OUT IN THE SUN.
It's so bright today! ♥
SHE WOULDN'T BE ABLE TO TOUCH A CROSS OR GARLIC.
Garlic Fair
Summer Power!!
This is our new summer special.
Looks delicious!
ざばぁ
AND AREN'T VAMPIRES SUPPOSED TO BE BAD WITH WATER...?
TWEE!
......
1
2
3

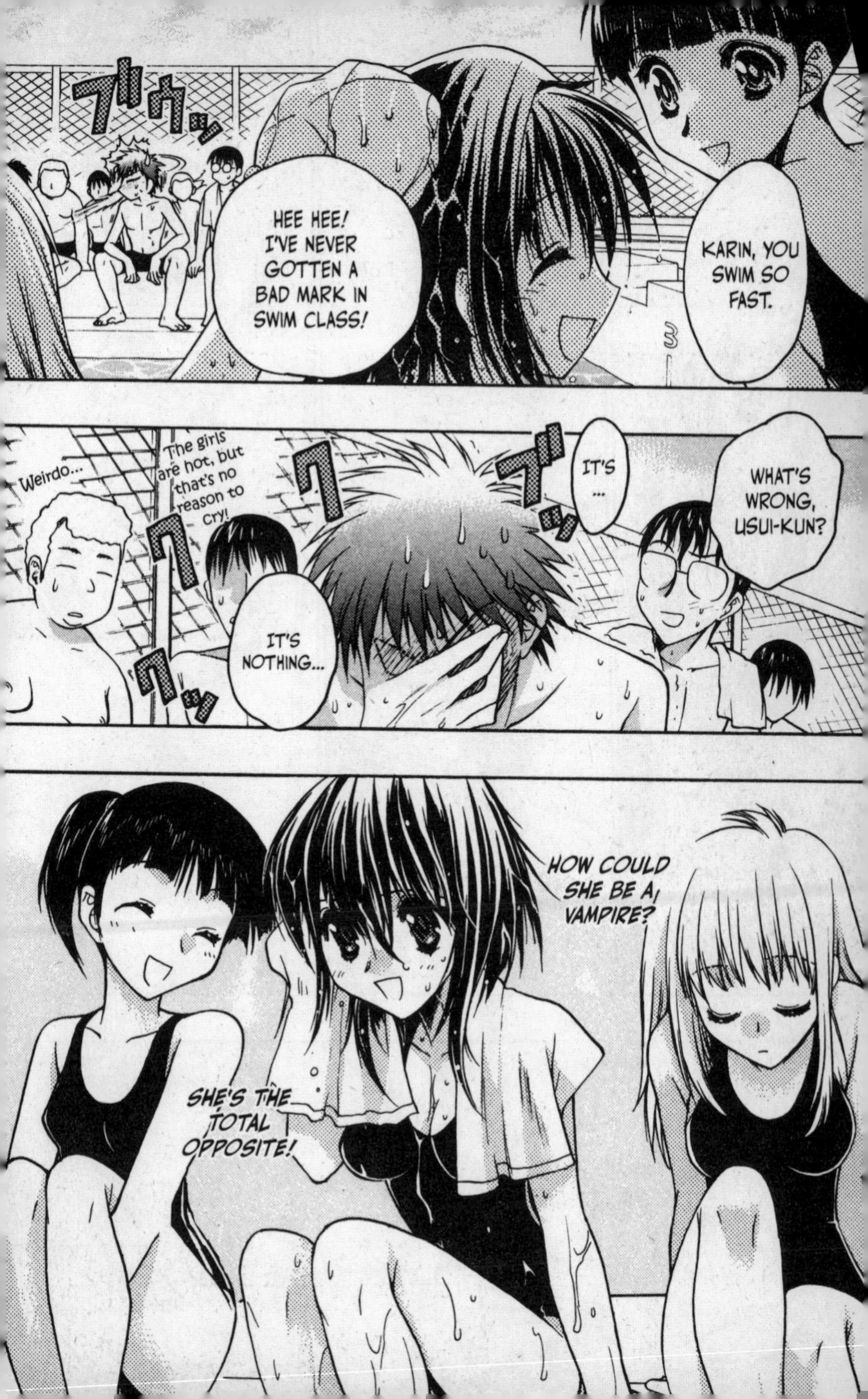
KARIN, YOU SWIM SO FAST.
HEE HEE! I'VE NEVER GOTTEN A BAD MARK IN SWIM CLASS!
WHAT'S WRONG, USUI-KUN?
IT'S ...
IT'S NOTHING...
The girls are hot, but that's no reason to cry!
Weirdo...
HOW COULD SHE BE A VAMPIRE?
SHE'S THE TOTAL OPPOSITE!

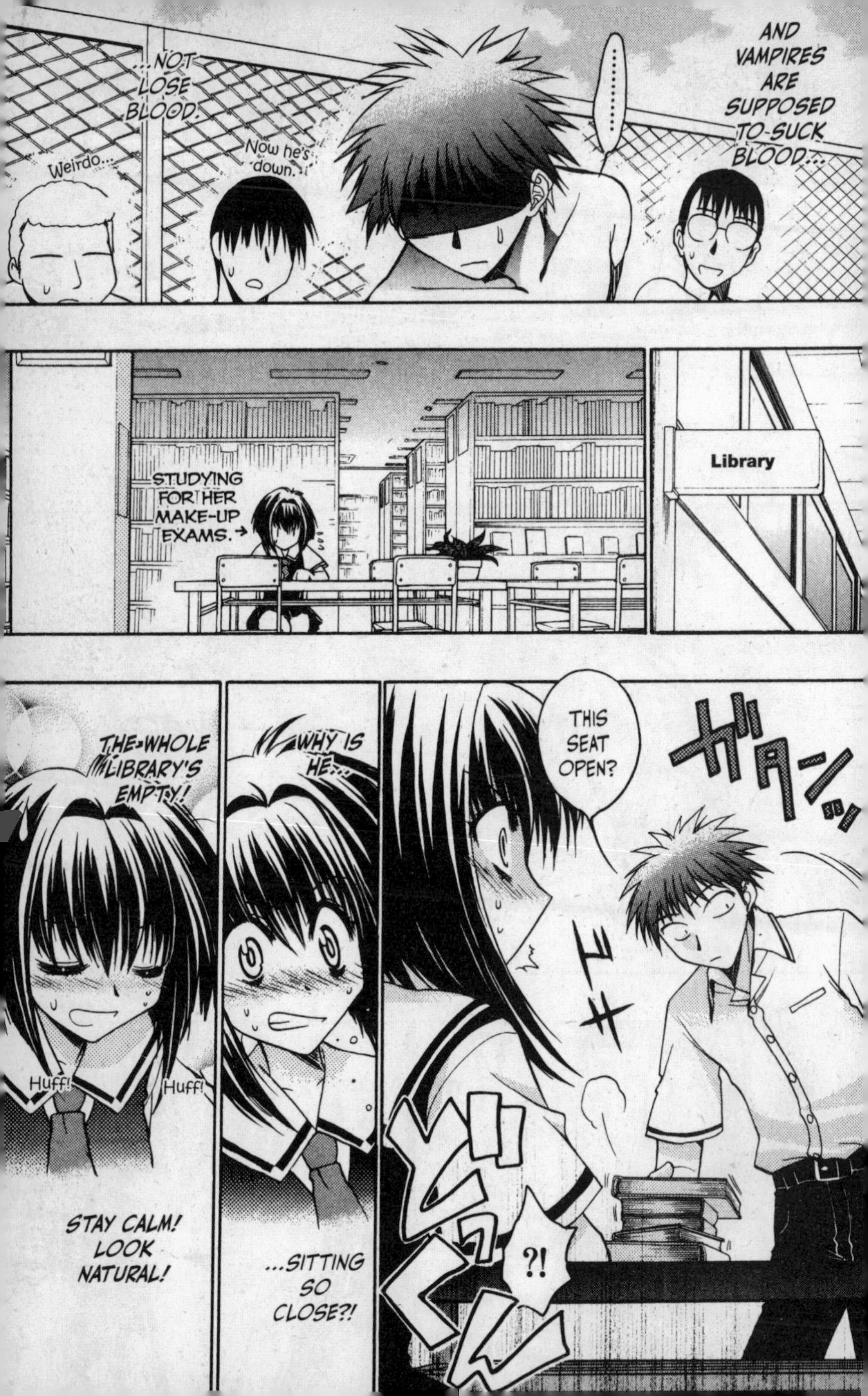
AND VAMPIRES ARE SUPPOSED TO SUCK BLOOD...
......
...NOT LOSE BLOOD.
Now he's down.
Weirdo...
Library
STUDYING FOR HER MAKE-UP EXAMS.
THIS SEAT OPEN?
?!
WHY IS HE...
...SITTING SO CLOSE?!
THE WHOLE LIBRARY'S EMPTY!
Huff! Huff!
STAY CALM! LOOK NATURAL!

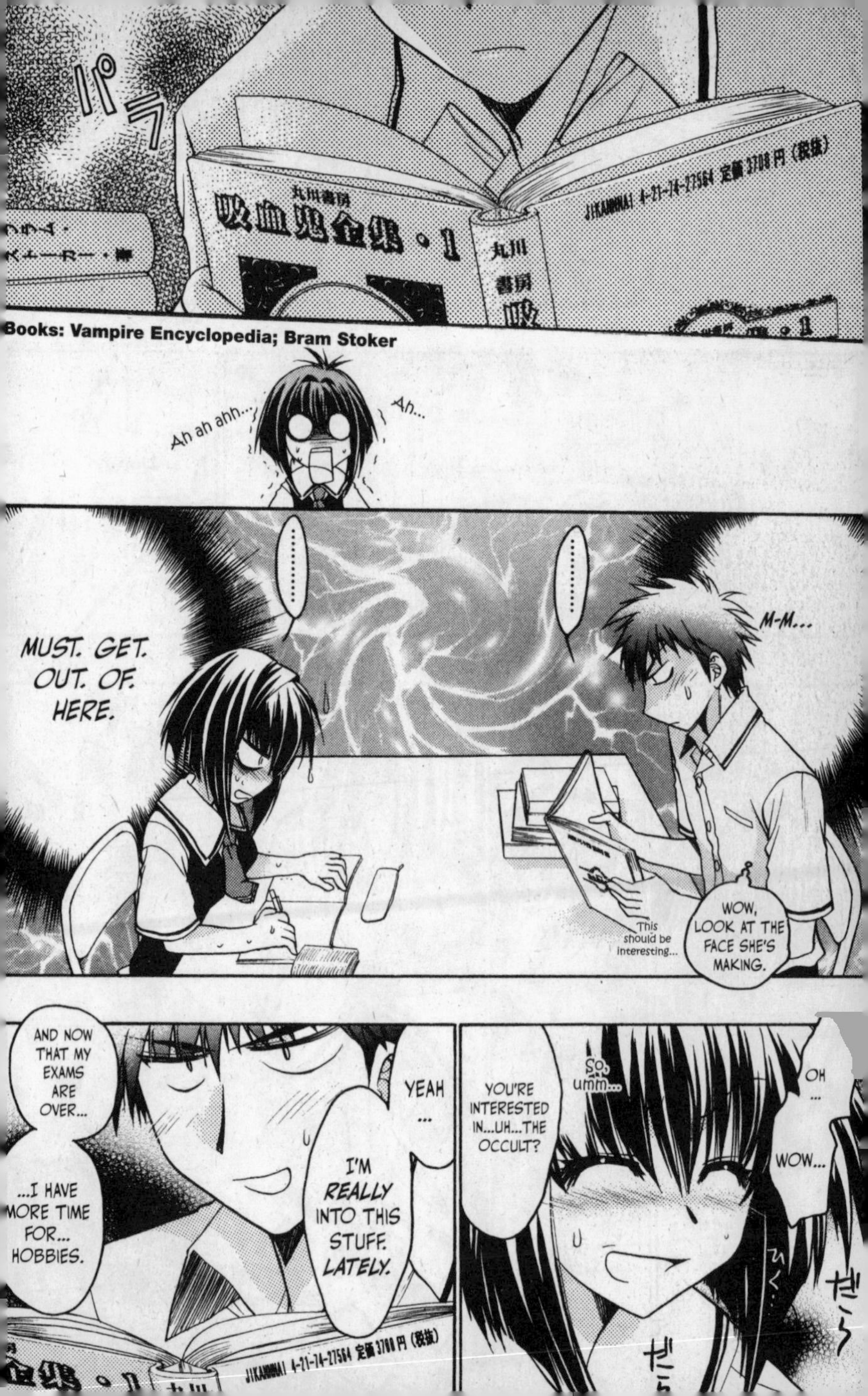
パラ
丸川書房
吸血鬼全集・1
JIKANNAI 4-21-74-27564 定価3708円（税抜）
Books: Vampire Encyclopedia; Bram Stoker
Ah...
Ah ah ahh...
M-M...
WOW, LOOK AT THE FACE SHE'S MAKING.
This should be interesting...
......
......
MUST. GET. OUT. OF. HERE.
OH ... WOW...
So, umm...
YOU'RE INTERESTED IN...UH...THE OCCULT?
だら だら
YEAH ...
I'M REALLY INTO THIS STUFF. LATELY.
AND NOW THAT MY EXAMS ARE OVER...
...I HAVE MORE TIME FOR... HOBBIES.

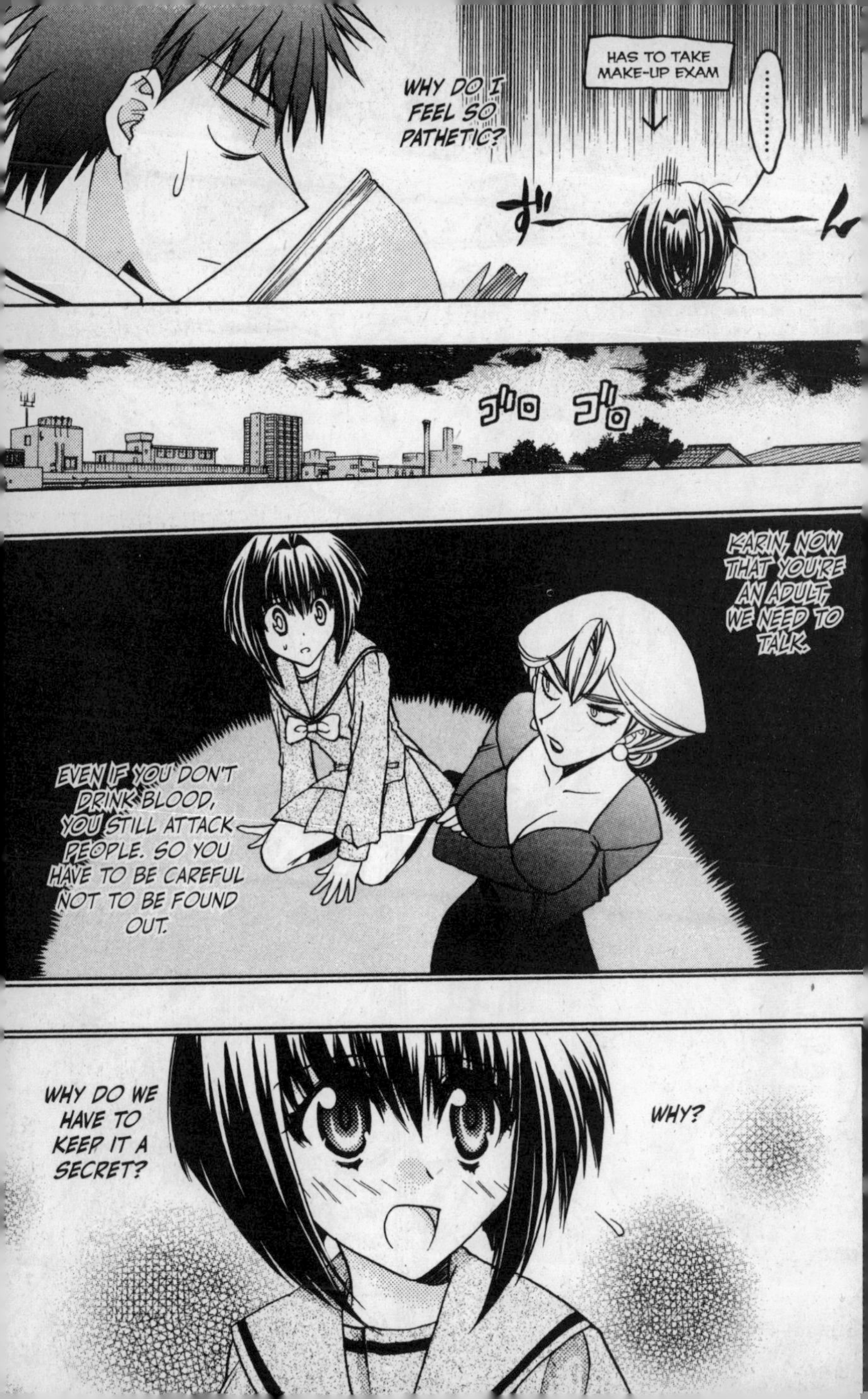

HAS TO TAKE MAKE-UP EXAM
......
ず—ん
WHY DO I FEEL SO PATHETIC?
ゴロ ゴロ
KARIN, NOW THAT YOU'RE AN ADULT, WE NEED TO TALK.
EVEN IF YOU DON'T DRINK BLOOD, YOU STILL ATTACK PEOPLE. SO YOU HAVE TO BE CAREFUL NOT TO BE FOUND OUT.
WHY?
WHY DO WE HAVE TO KEEP IT A SECRET?

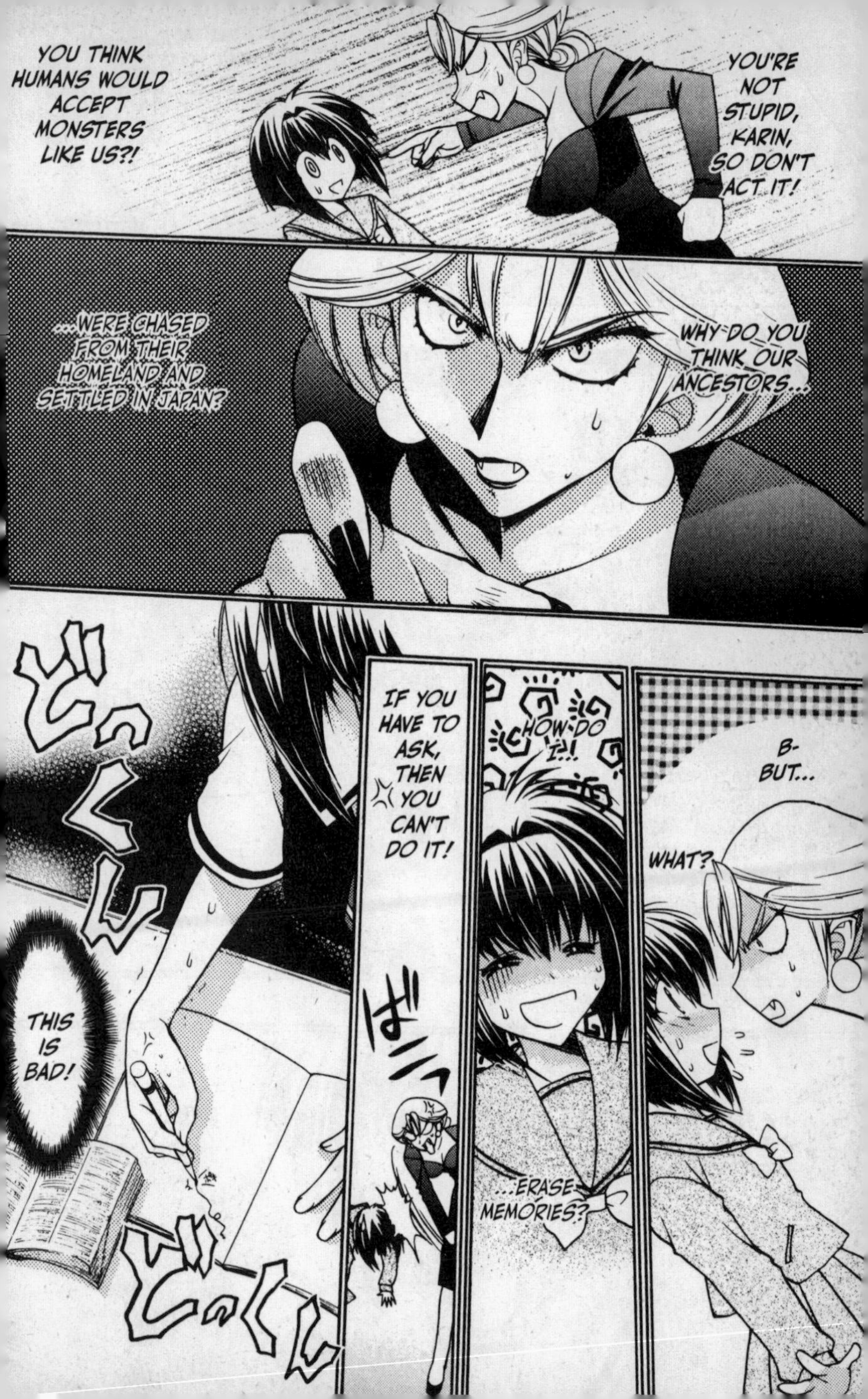
YOU'RE NOT STUPID, KARIN, SO DON'T ACT IT!
YOU THINK HUMANS WOULD ACCEPT MONSTERS LIKE US?!
WHY DO YOU THINK OUR ANCESTORS...
...WERE CHASED FROM THEIR HOMELAND AND SETTLED IN JAPAN?
B-BUT...
WHAT?
...ERASE MEMORIES?
HOW DO I..!
IF YOU HAVE TO ASK, THEN YOU CAN'T DO IT!
どっくん
THIS IS BAD!
どっくん

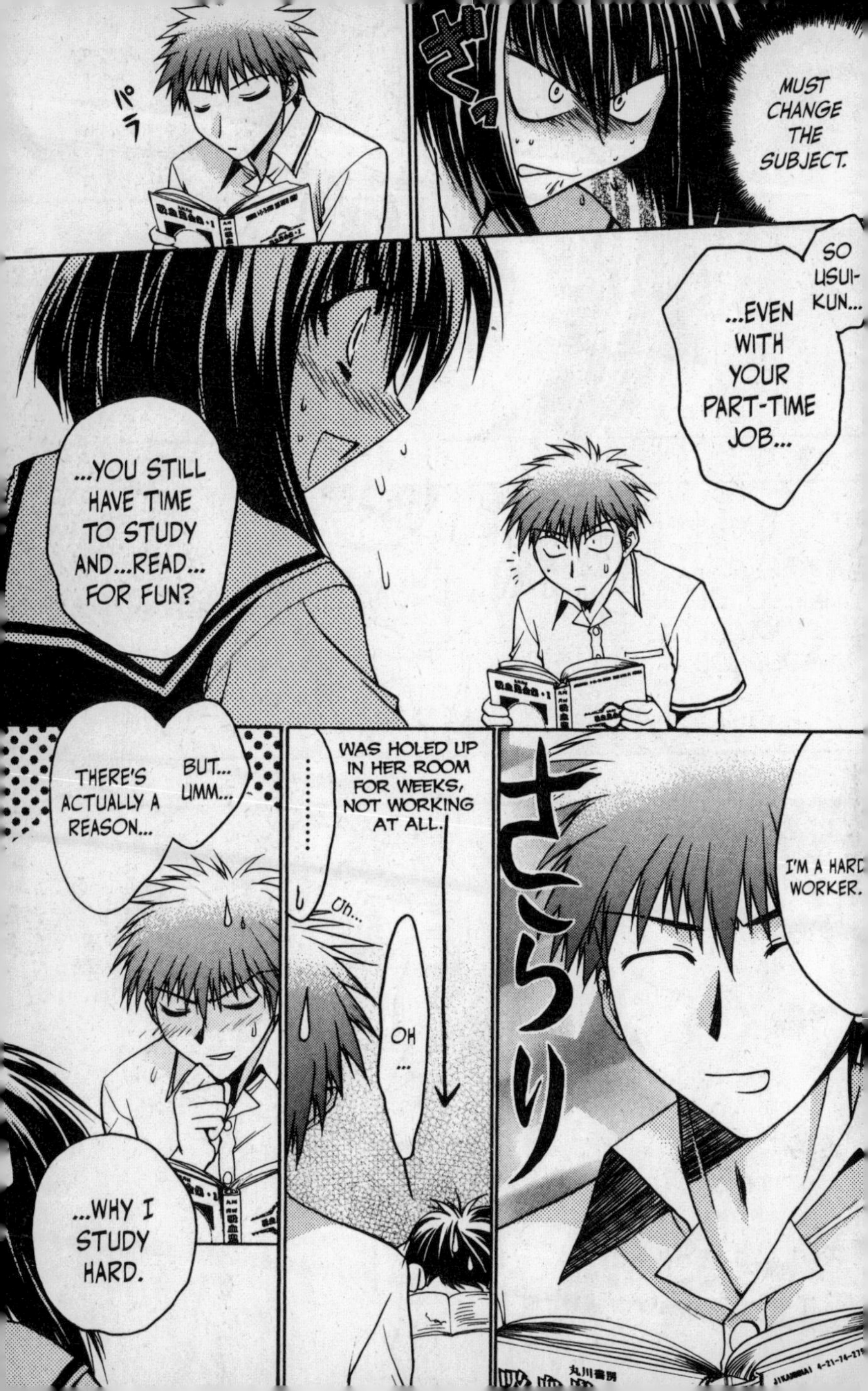
ざっ
MUST CHANGE THE SUBJECT.
パラ
SO USUI-KUN...
...EVEN WITH YOUR PART-TIME JOB...
...YOU STILL HAVE TIME TO STUDY AND...READ... FOR FUN?
I'M A HARD WORKER.
さらり
WAS HOLED UP IN HER ROOM FOR WEEKS, NOT WORKING AT ALL.
....
Oh...
OH ...
BUT... UMM...
THERE'S ACTUALLY A REASON...
...WHY I STUDY HARD.

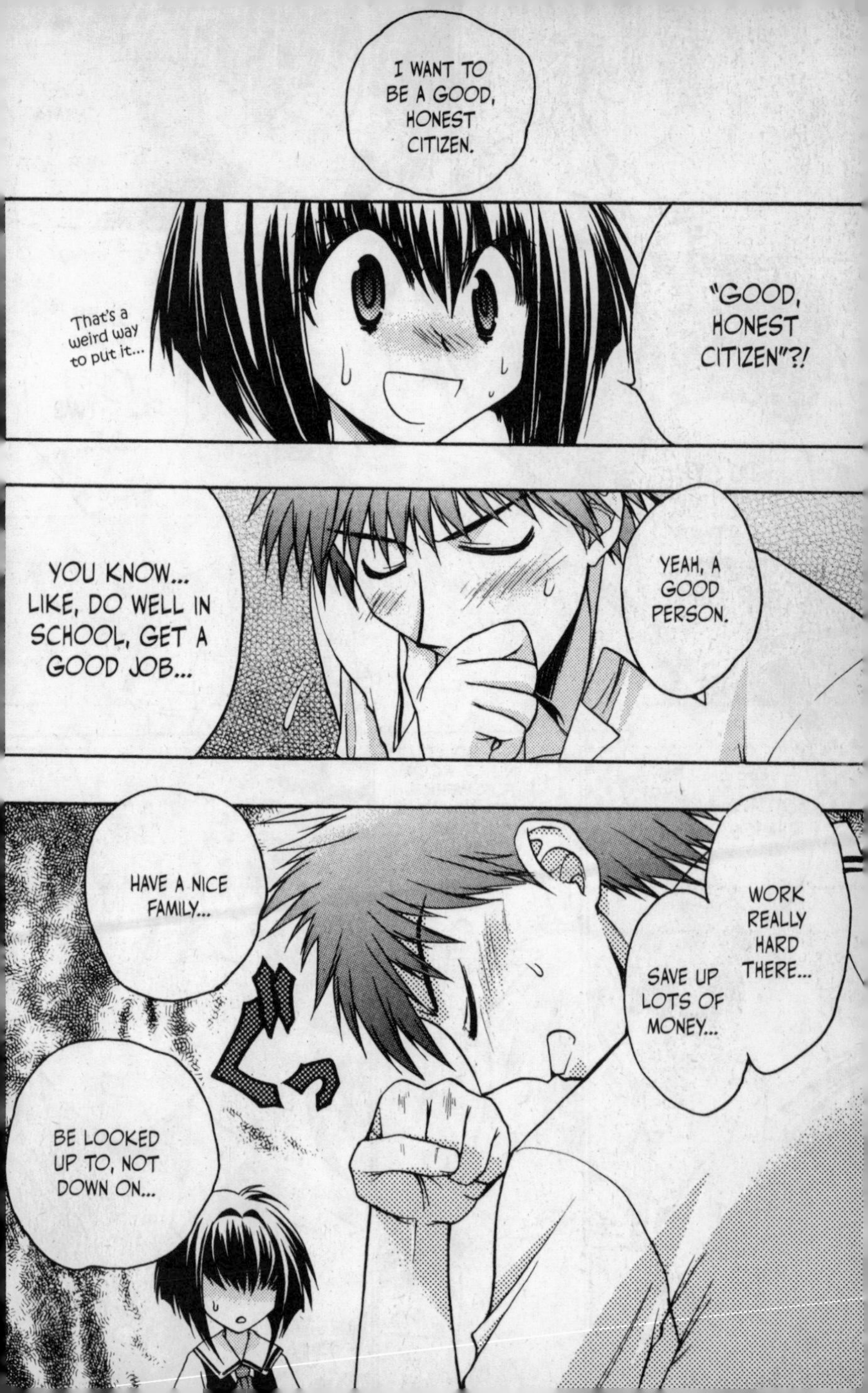
I WANT TO BE A GOOD, HONEST CITIZEN.
"GOOD, HONEST CITIZEN"?!
That's a weird way to put it...
YEAH, A GOOD PERSON.
YOU KNOW... LIKE, DO WELL IN SCHOOL, GET A GOOD JOB...
WORK REALLY HARD THERE...
SAVE UP LOTS OF MONEY...
HAVE A NICE FAMILY...
BE LOOKED UP TO, NOT DOWN ON...

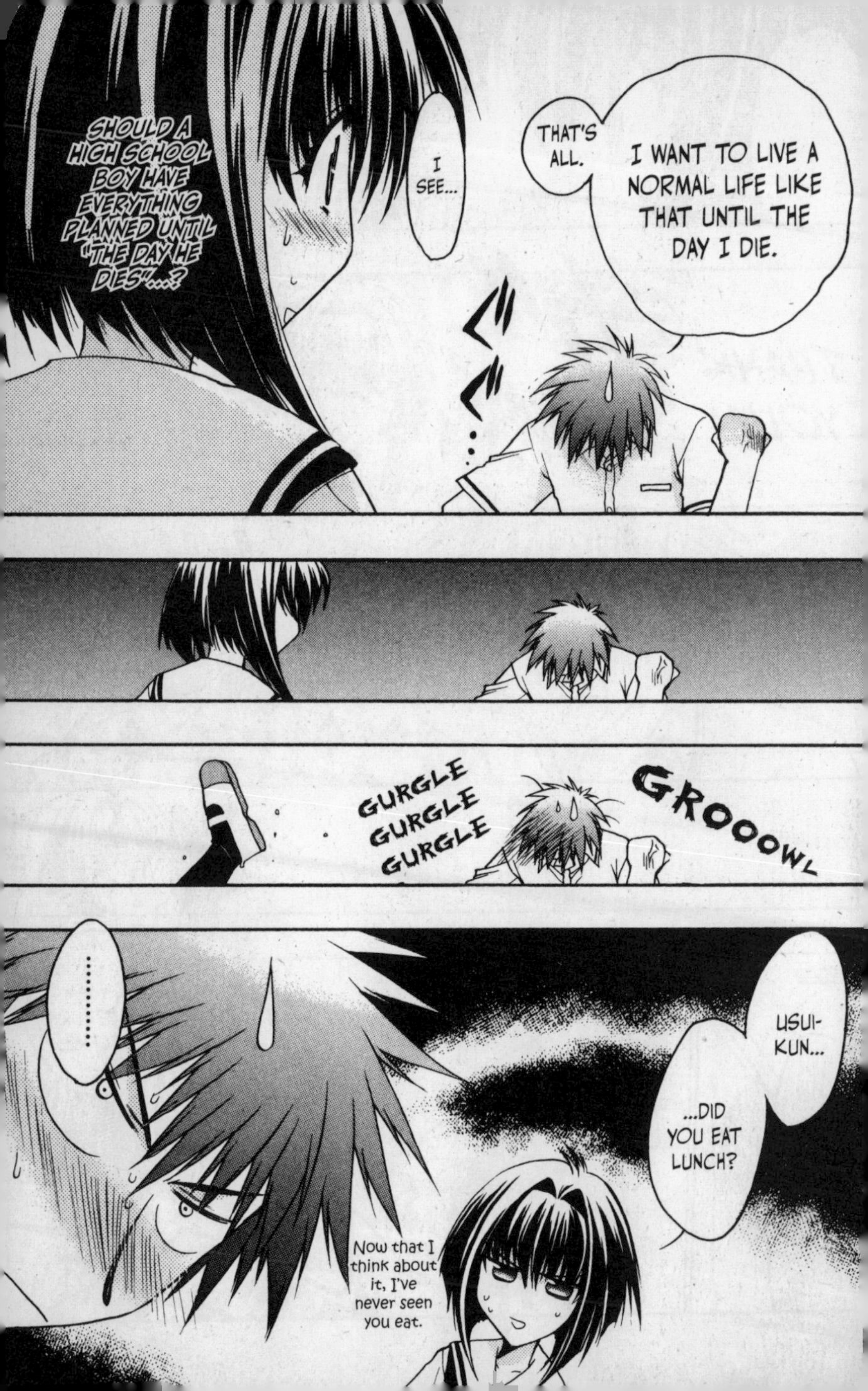
I WANT TO LIVE A NORMAL LIFE LIKE THAT UNTIL THE DAY I DIE.
THAT'S ALL.
I SEE...
SHOULD A HIGH SCHOOL BOY HAVE EVERYTHING PLANNED UNTIL "THE DAY HE DIES"...?
GROOOWL
GURGLE GURGLE GURGLE
USUI-KUN...
...DID YOU EAT LUNCH?
Now that I think about it, I've never seen you eat.
....

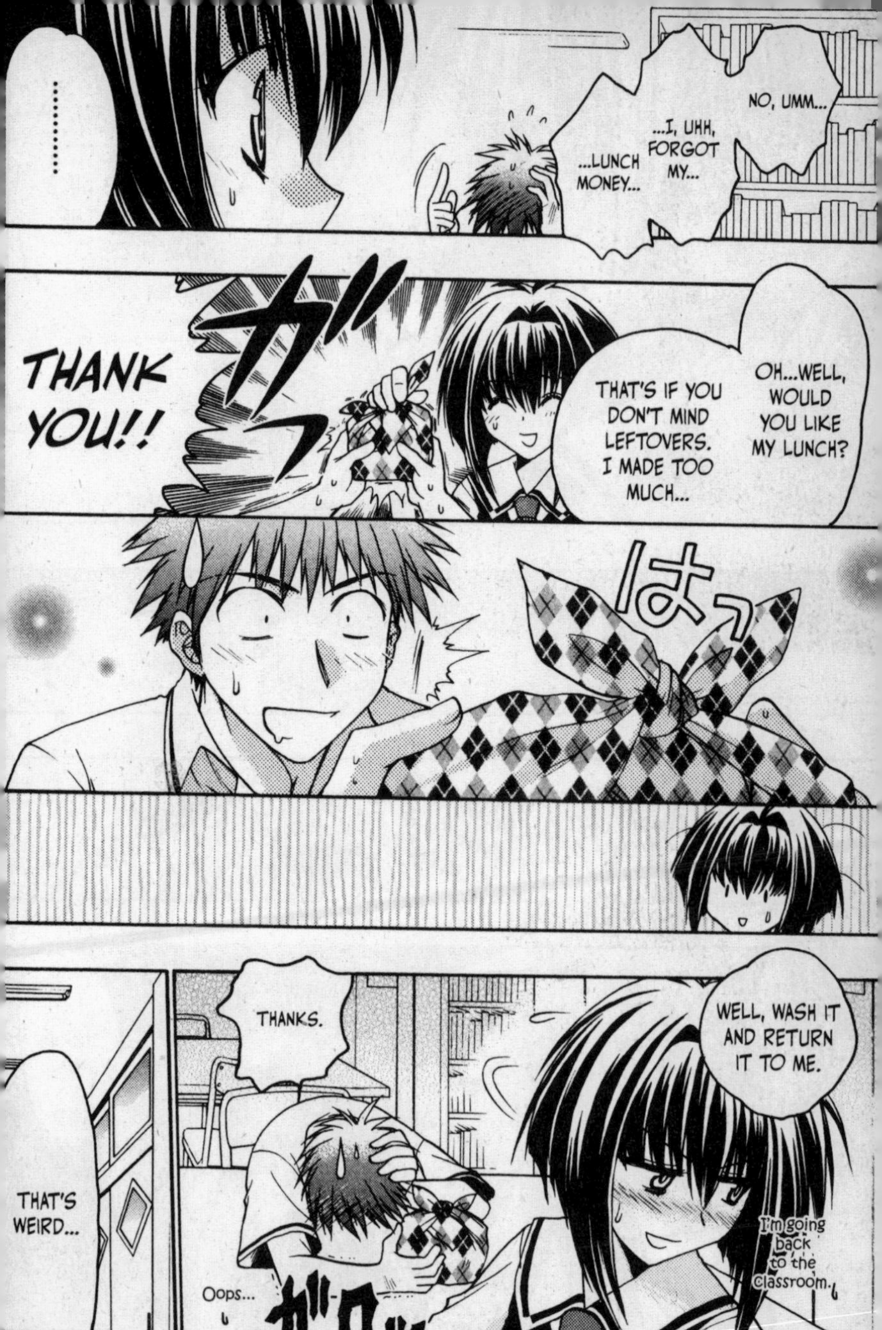
NO, UMM...
...I, UHH, FORGOT MY...
...LUNCH MONEY...
....
OH...WELL, WOULD YOU LIKE MY LUNCH?
THAT'S IF YOU DON'T MIND LEFTOVERS. I MADE TOO MUCH...
ガッ
THANK YOU!!
はっ
WELL, WASH IT AND RETURN IT TO ME.
I'm going back to the classroom.
THANKS.
Oops...
ガクーッ
THAT'S WEIRD...

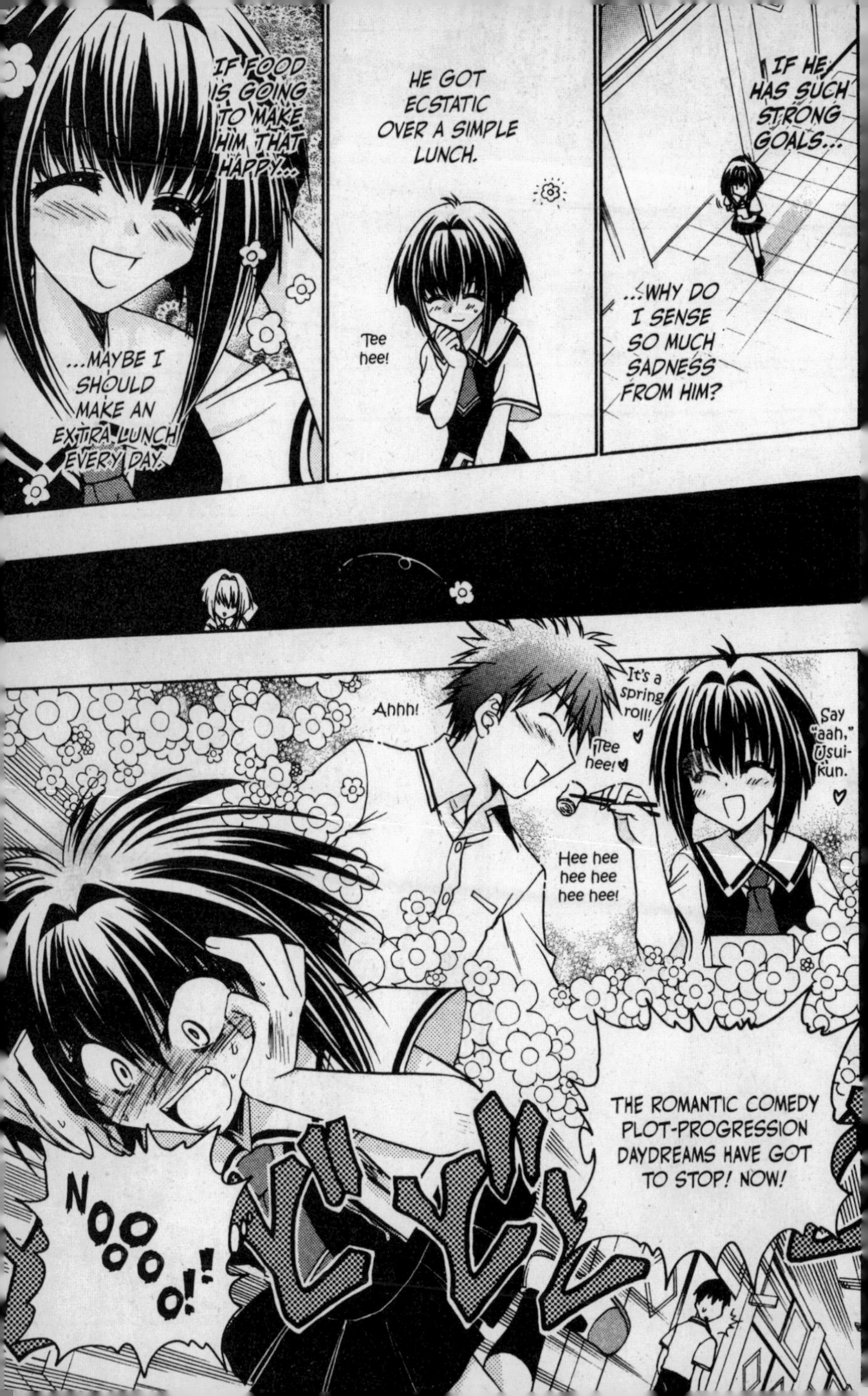
IF HE HAS SUCH STRONG GOALS...
...WHY DO I SENSE SO MUCH SADNESS FROM HIM?
HE GOT ECSTATIC OVER A SIMPLE LUNCH.
Tee hee!
IF FOOD IS GOING TO MAKE HIM THAT HAPPY...
...MAYBE I SHOULD MAKE AN EXTRA LUNCH EVERY DAY.
Say "aah," Usui-kun. ♥
It's a spring roll! ♥
Tee hee! ♥
Ahhh!
Hee hee hee hee hee hee!
THE ROMANTIC COMEDY PLOT-PROGRESSION DAYDREAMS HAVE GOT TO STOP! NOW!
NOOOOO!!

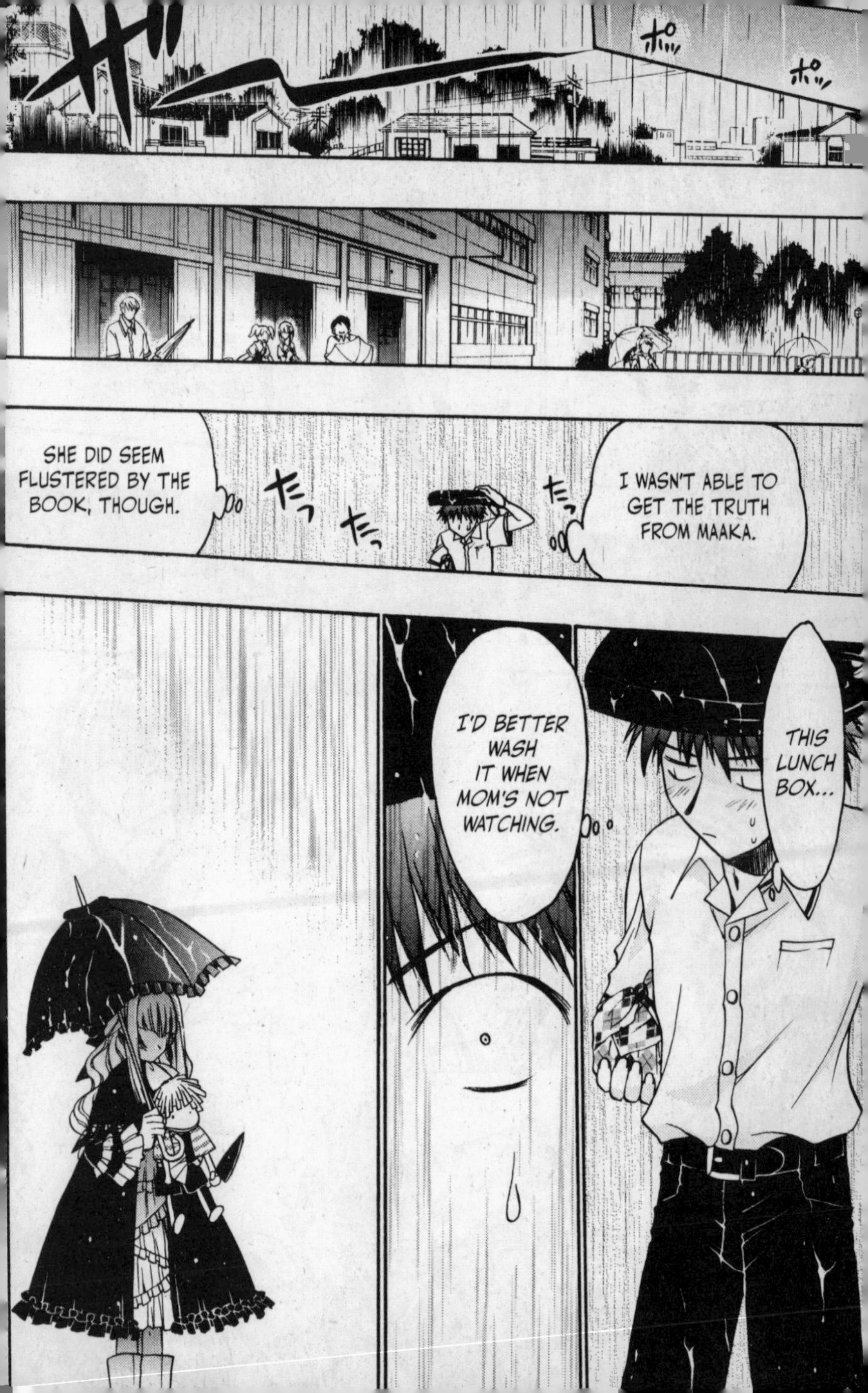
ポッ
ポッ
I WASN'T ABLE TO GET THE TRUTH FROM MAAKA.
たっ
たっ
たっ
SHE DID SEEM FLUSTERED BY THE BOOK, THOUGH.
THIS LUNCH BOX...
I'D BETTER WASH IT WHEN MOM'S NOT WATCHING.

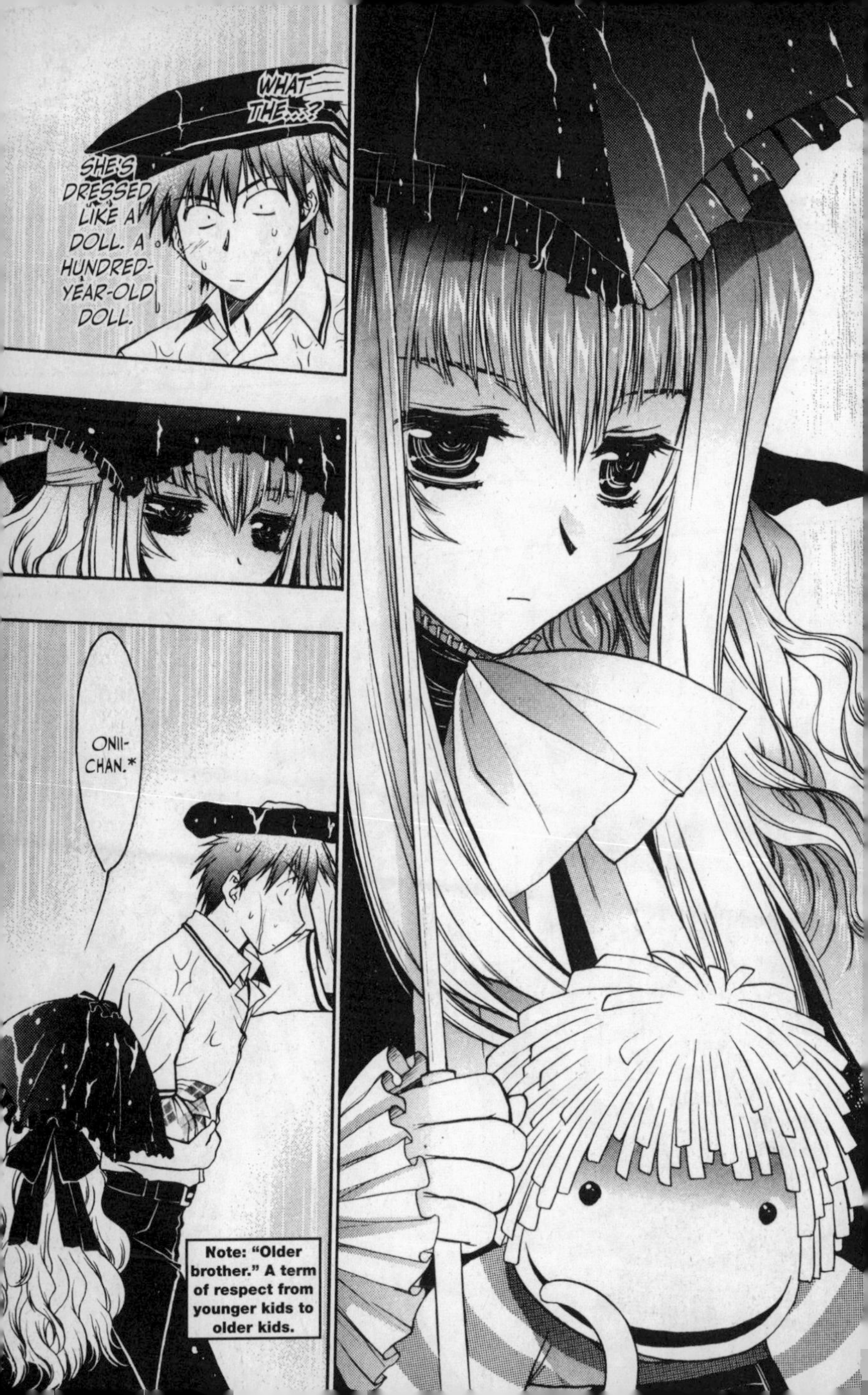
WHAT THE...?
SHE'S DRESSED LIKE A DOLL. A HUNDRED-YEAR-OLD DOLL.
ONII-CHAN.*
Note: "Older brother." A term of respect from younger kids to older kids.

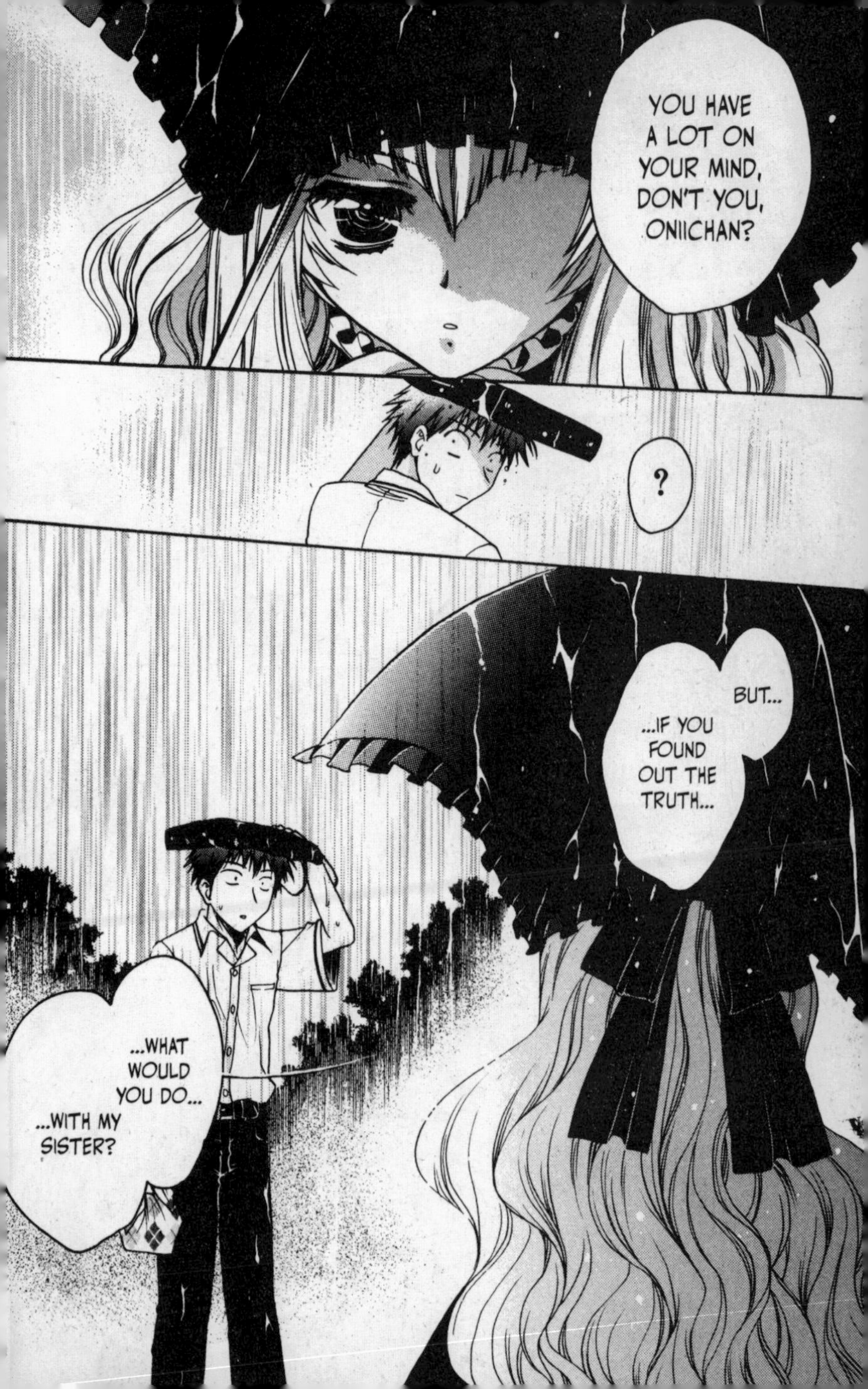
YOU HAVE A LOT ON YOUR MIND, DON'T YOU, ONIICHAN?
?
BUT...
...IF YOU FOUND OUT THE TRUTH...
...WHAT WOULD YOU DO...
...WITH MY SISTER?

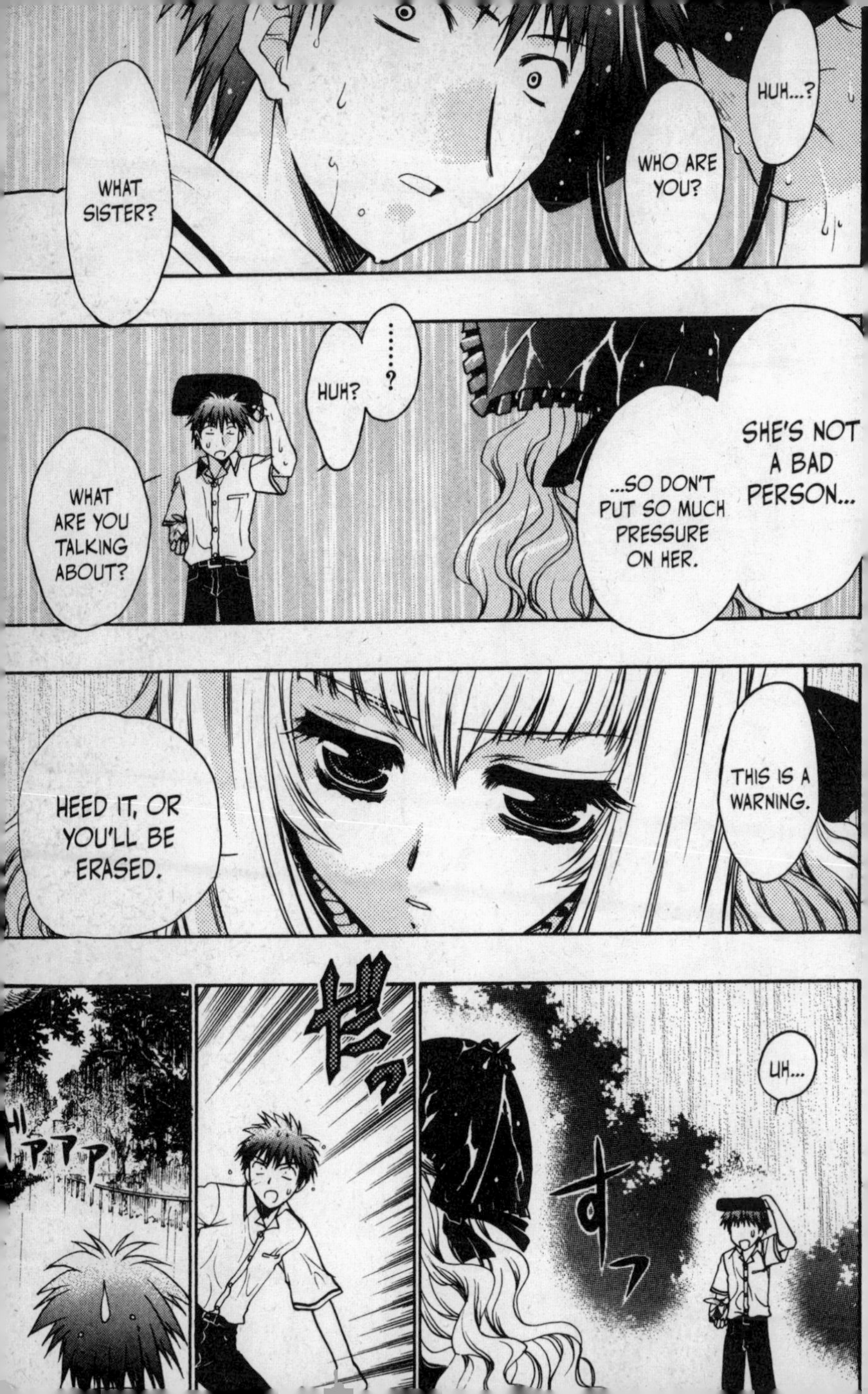
HUH...?
WHO ARE YOU?
WHAT SISTER?
SHE'S NOT A BAD PERSON...
...SO DON'T PUT SO MUCH PRESSURE ON HER.
......?
HUH?
WHAT ARE YOU TALKING ABOUT?
THIS IS A WARNING.
HEED IT, OR YOU'LL BE ERASED.
UH...
すっ
ゼッ

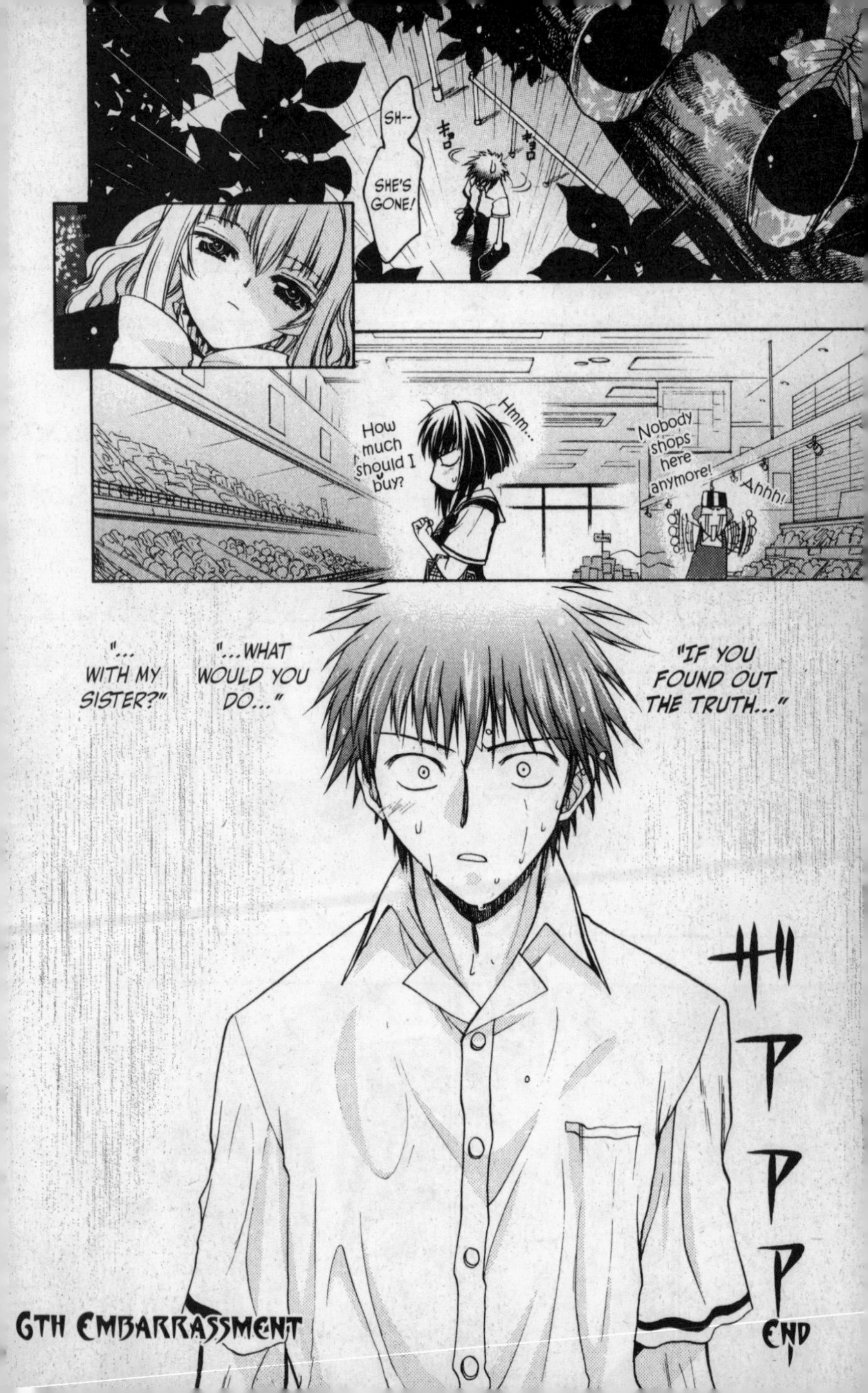
SH--
SHE'S GONE!
Nobody shops here anymore!
Ahhh!
Hmm...
How much should I buy?
"IF YOU FOUND OUT THE TRUTH..."
"...WHAT WOULD YOU DO..."
"... WITH MY SISTER?"
6TH EMBARRASSMENT END

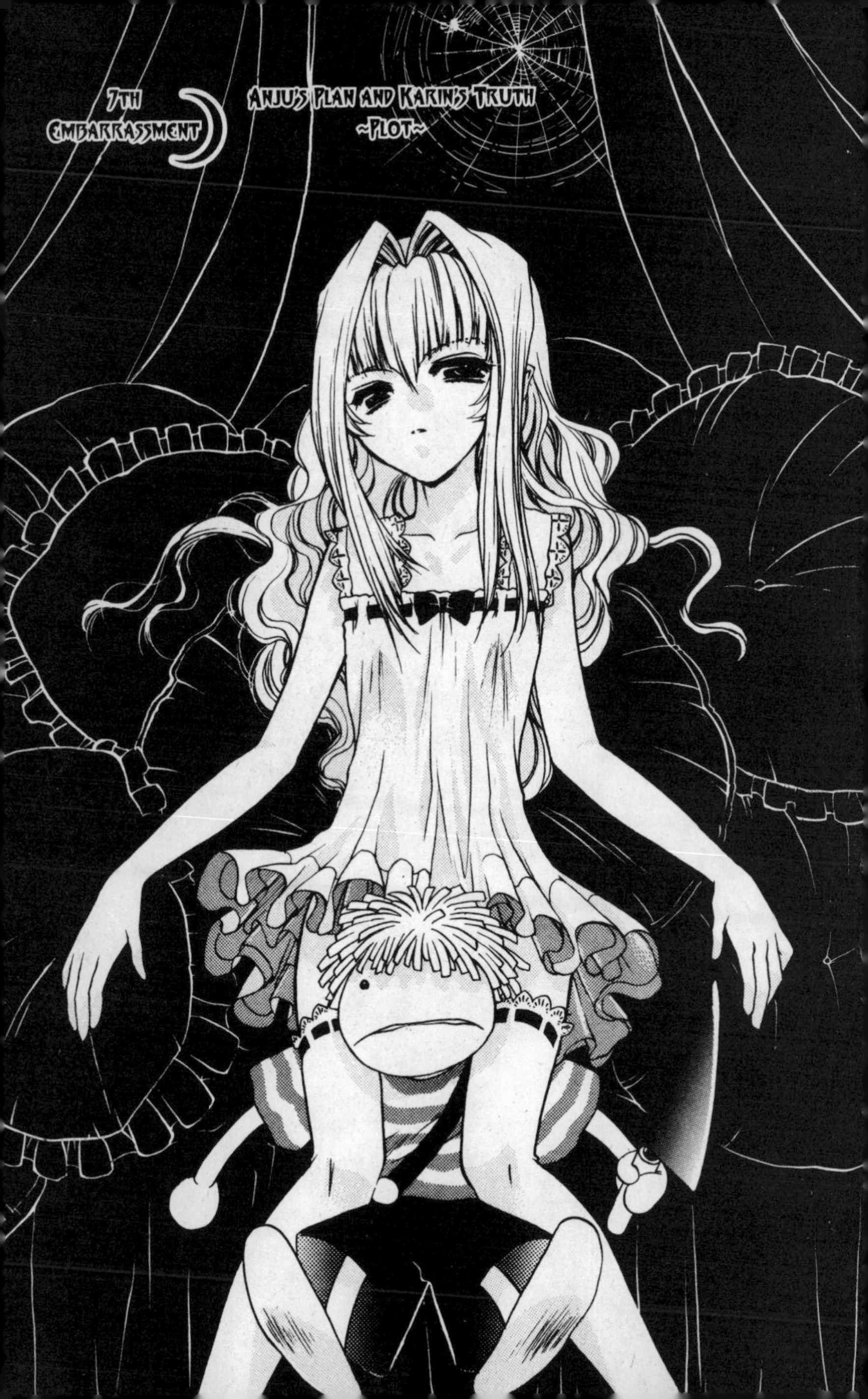
7th Embarrassment
Anju's Plan and Karin's Truth
~Plot~

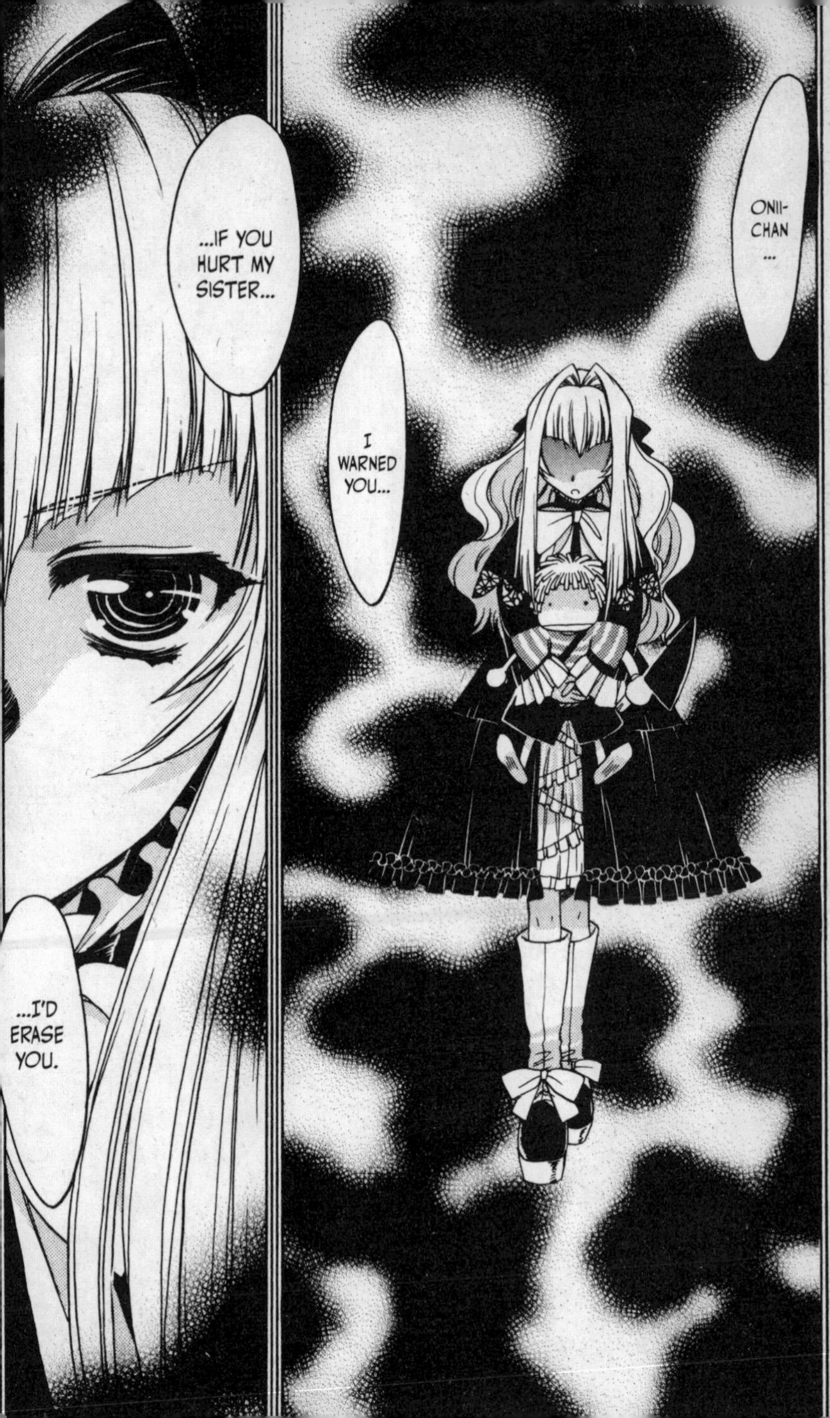
ONII-CHAN ...
I WARNED YOU...
...IF YOU HURT MY SISTER...
...I'D ERASE YOU.

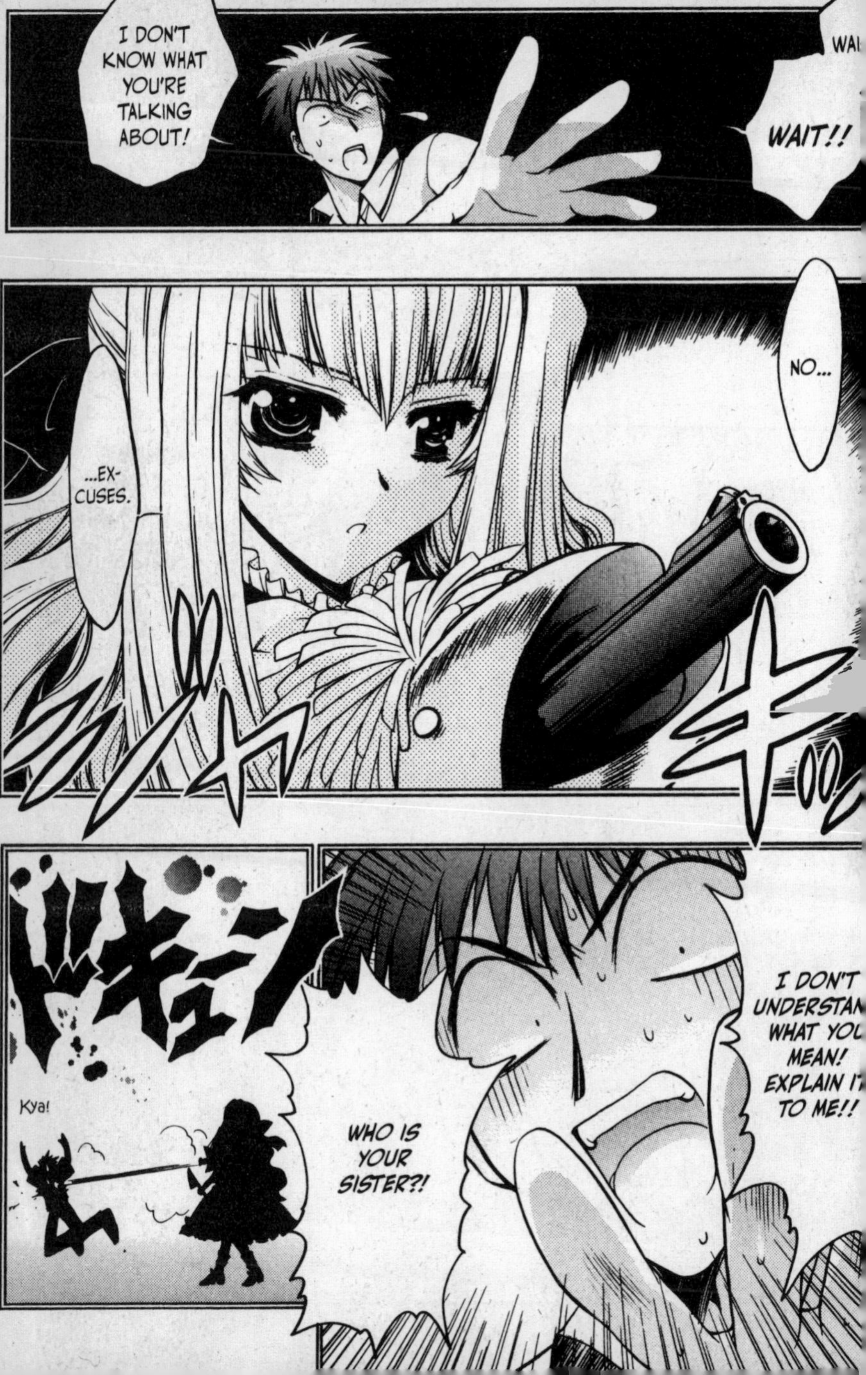
WAI
WAIT!!
I DON'T KNOW WHAT YOU'RE TALKING ABOUT!
NO...
...EX-CUSES.
I DON'T UNDERSTAN WHAT YOU MEAN! EXPLAIN IT TO ME!!
WHO IS YOUR SISTER?!
Kya!

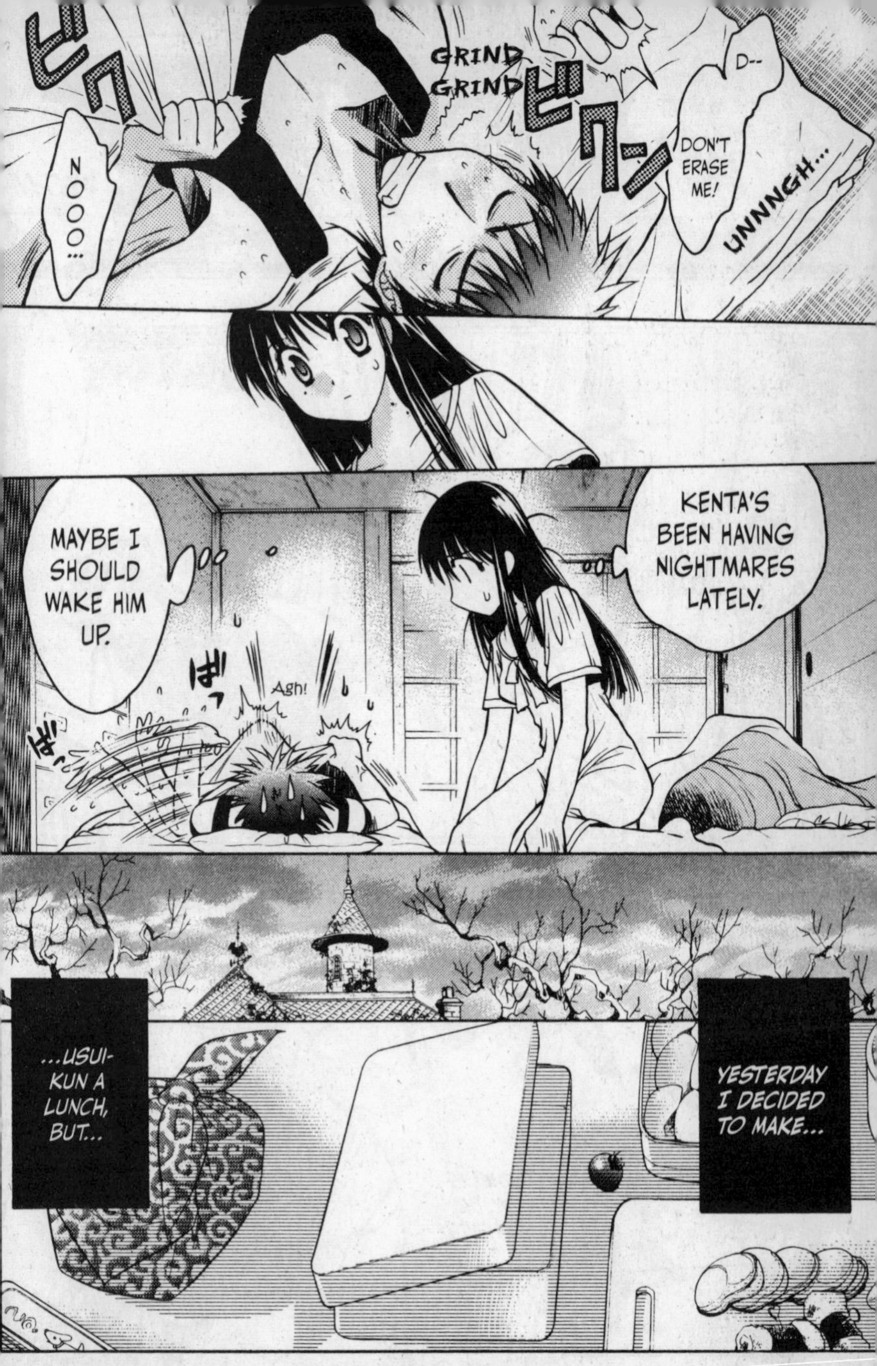
D--
DON'T ERASE ME!
UNNNGH...
ビクン
GRIND GRIND
ビクッ
NOOOO...
KENTA'S BEEN HAVING NIGHTMARES LATELY.
MAYBE I SHOULD WAKE HIM UP.
Agh!
YESTERDAY I DECIDED TO MAKE...
...USUI-KUN A LUNCH, BUT...

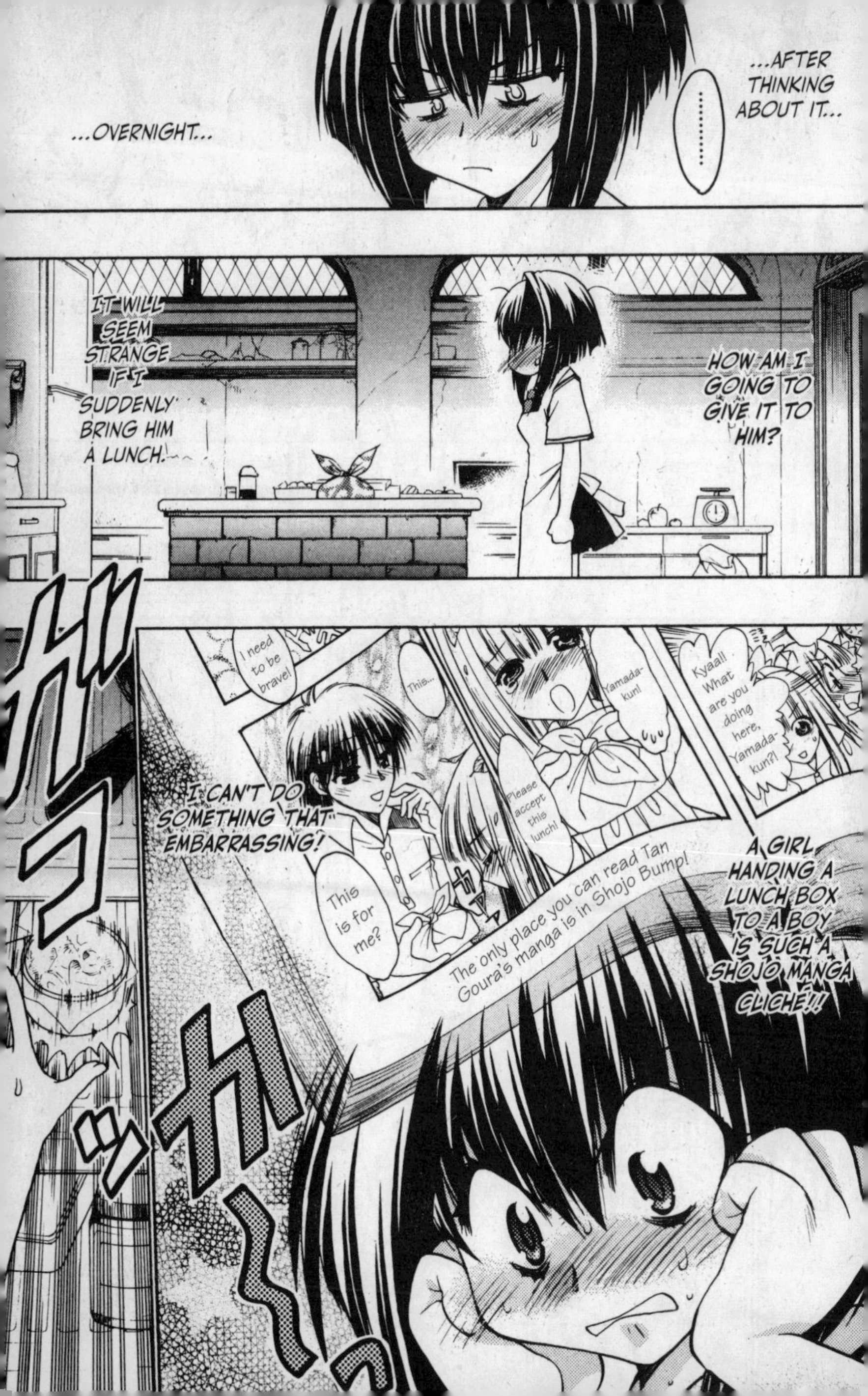
...AFTER THINKING ABOUT IT...
......
...OVERNIGHT...
HOW AM I GOING TO GIVE IT TO HIM?
IT WILL SEEM STRANGE IF I SUDDENLY BRING HIM A LUNCH.
A GIRL HANDING A LUNCH BOX TO A BOY IS SUCH A SHOJO MANGA CLICHÉ!!
Kyaa!! What are you doing here, Yamada-kun?!
I need to be brave!
This...
Yamada-kun!
Please accept this lunch!
This is for me?
The only place you can read Tan Goura's manga is in Shojo Bump!
I CAN'T DO SOMETHING THAT EMBARRASSING!

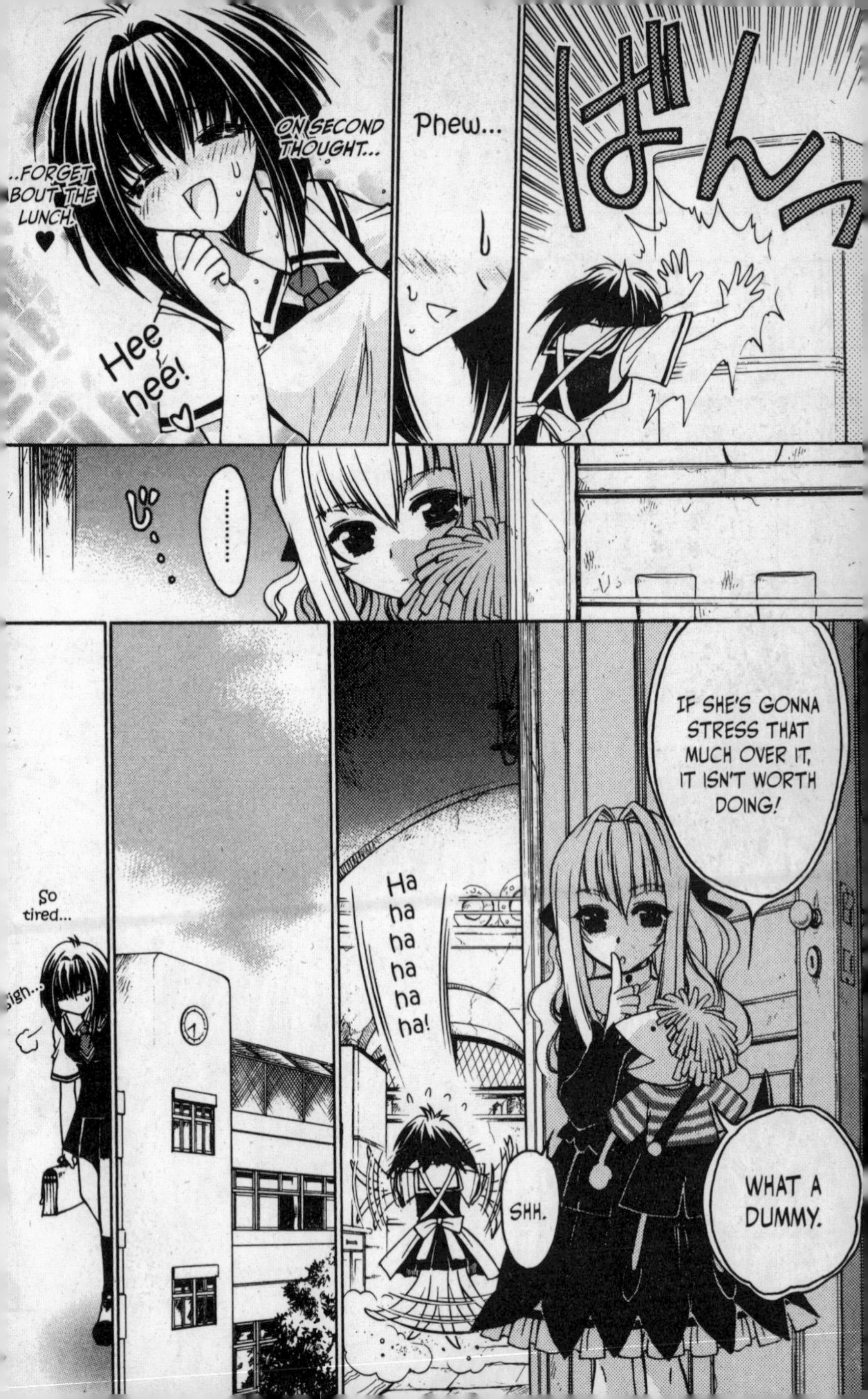
ばんっ
Phew...
ON SECOND THOUGHT...
..FORGET BOUT THE LUNCH! ♥
Hee hee! ♥
じ
......
IF SHE'S GONNA STRESS THAT MUCH OVER IT, IT ISN'T WORTH DOING!
WHAT A DUMMY.
SHH.
Ha ha ha ha ha ha!
So tired...
Sigh...

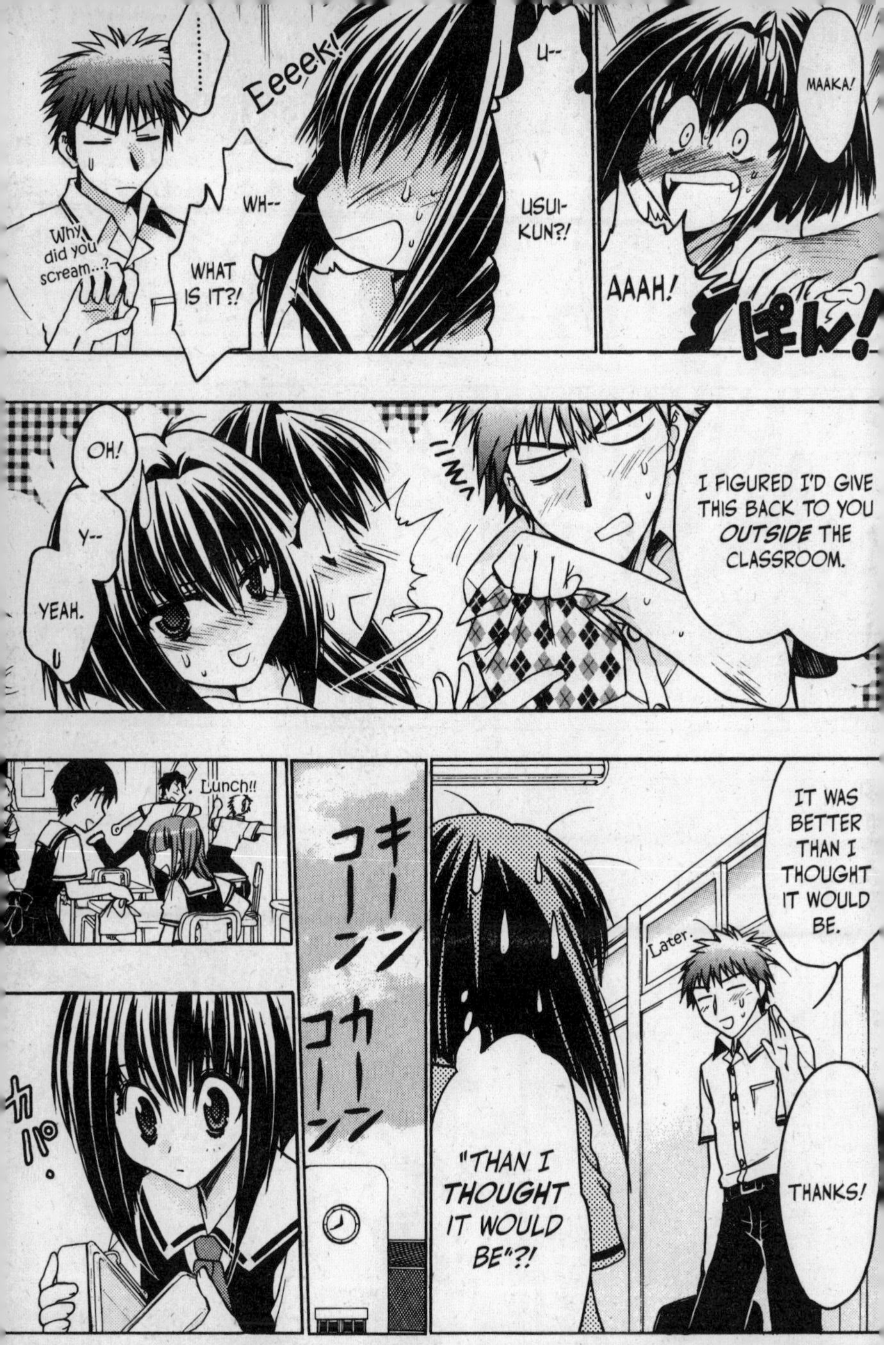
MAAKA!
AAAH!
ぱん!
U--
USUI-KUN?!
Eeeek!
WH--
WHAT IS IT?!
......
Why did you scream...?
I FIGURED I'D GIVE THIS BACK TO YOU *OUTSIDE* THE CLASSROOM.
OH!
Y--
YEAH.
IT WAS BETTER THAN I THOUGHT IT WOULD BE.
Later.
THANKS!
"THAN I *THOUGHT* IT WOULD BE"?!
キーンコーン
カーンコーン
Lunch!!
カパ。

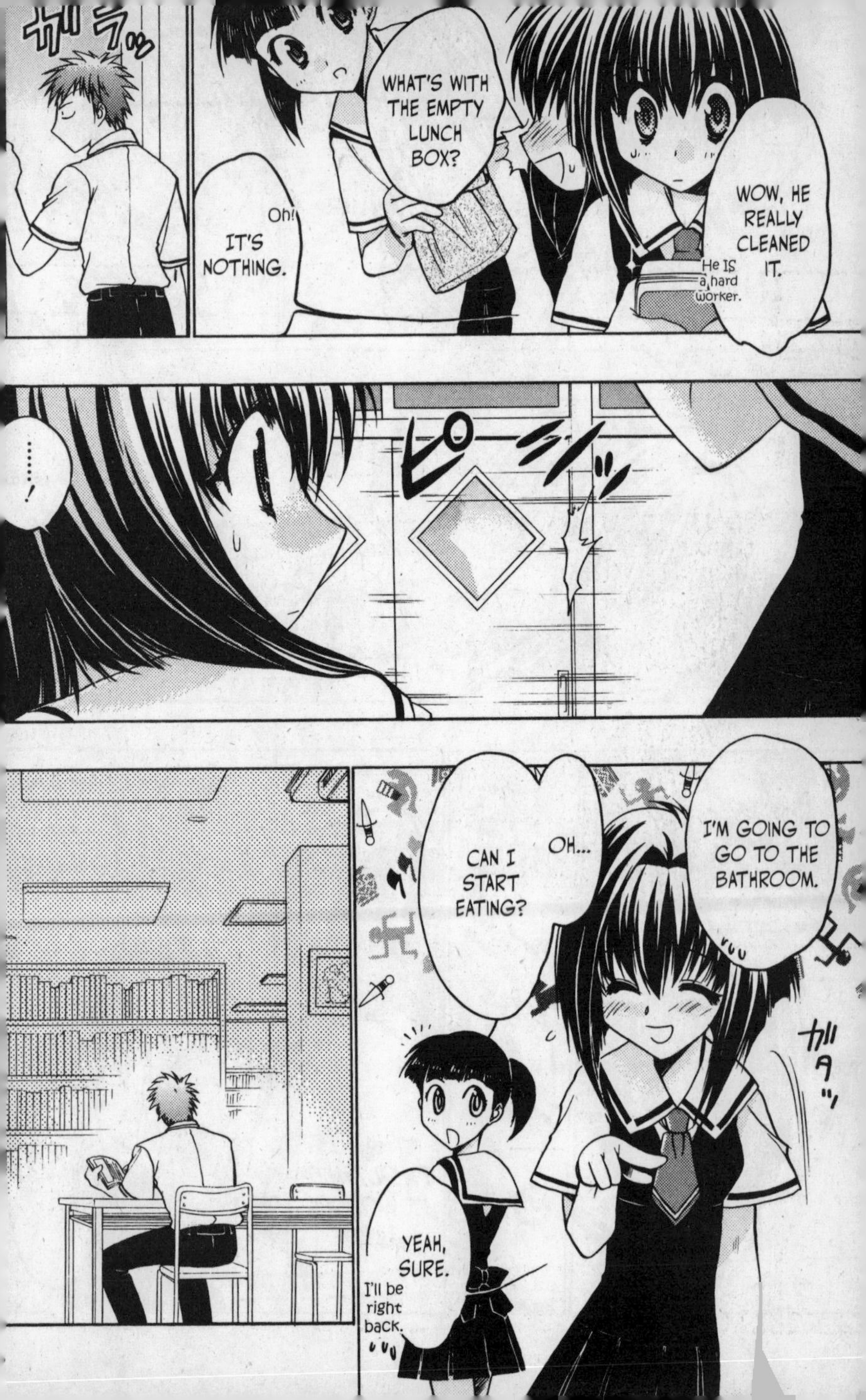
WOW, HE REALLY CLEANED IT.
He IS a hard worker.
WHAT'S WITH THE EMPTY LUNCH BOX?
Oh!
IT'S NOTHING.
ガラッ
ピシッ
......!
I'M GOING TO GO TO THE BATHROOM.
OH...
CAN I START EATING?
ガタッ
YEAH, SURE.
I'll be right back.

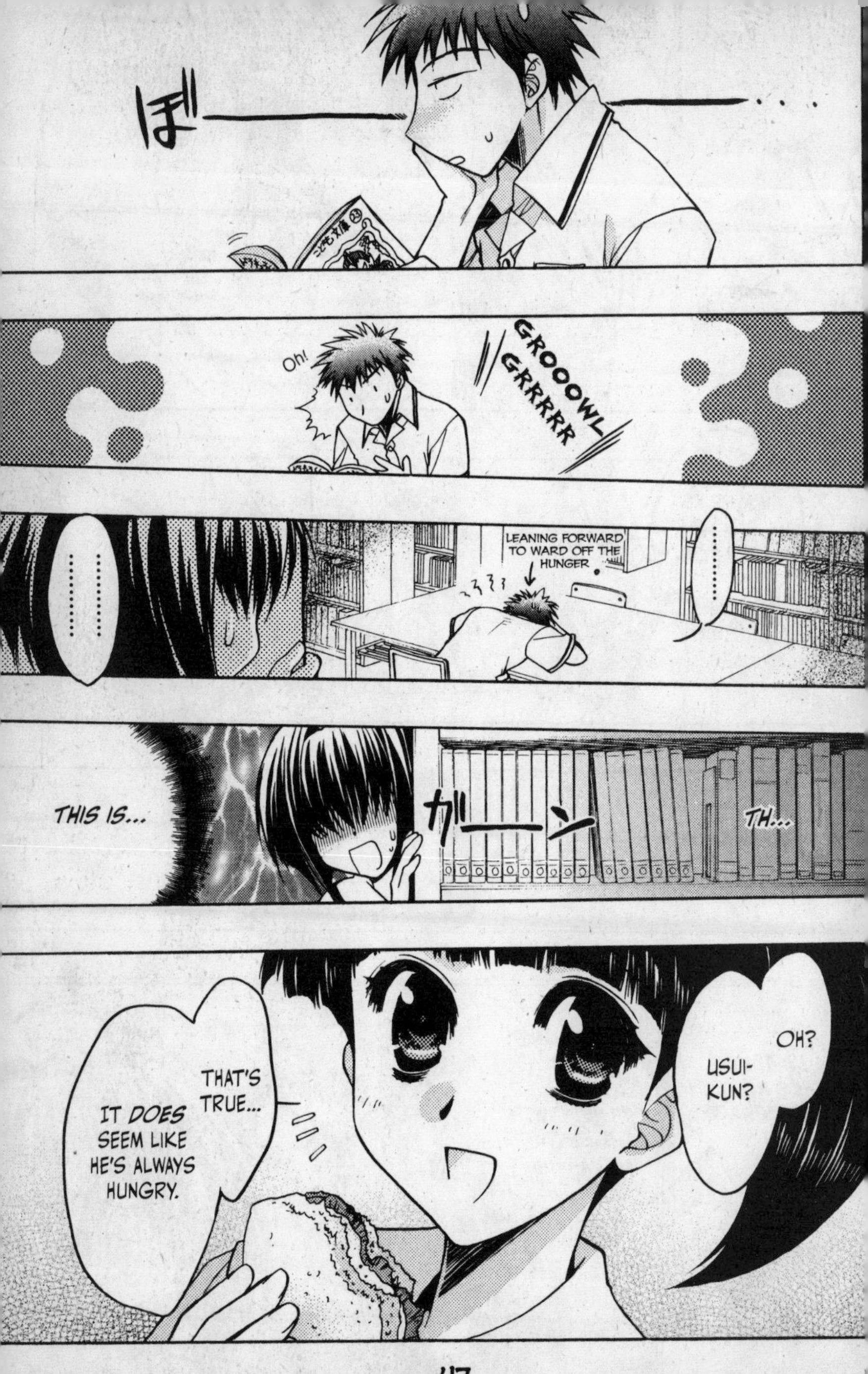
ぼ——————……
GROOOWL GRRRRR
Oh!
……
LEANING FORWARD TO WARD OFF THE HUNGER.
……
TH...
ガーン
THIS IS...
OH? USUI-KUN?
THAT'S TRUE...
IT *DOES* SEEM LIKE HE'S ALWAYS HUNGRY.

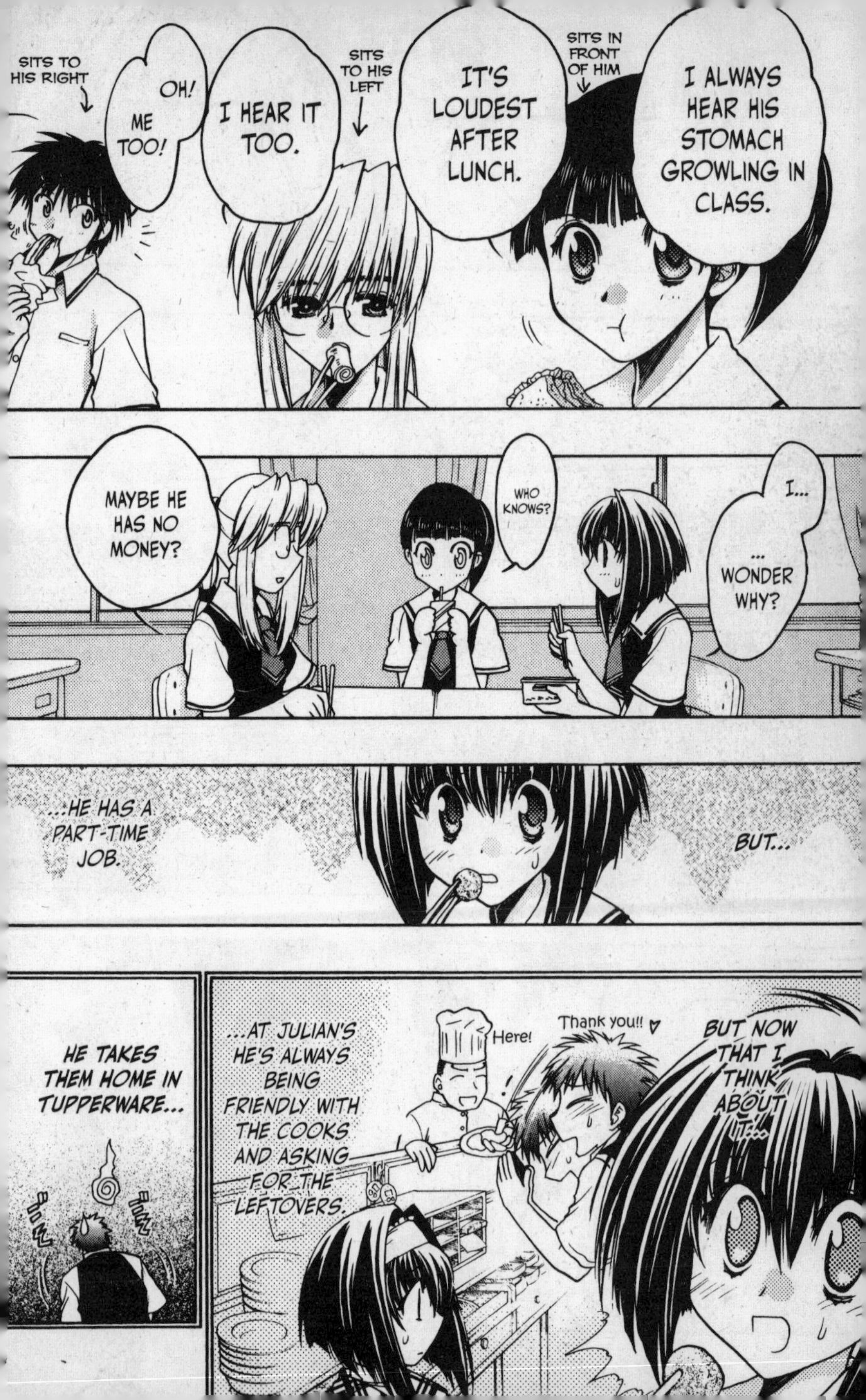
SITS IN FRONT OF HIM
I ALWAYS HEAR HIS STOMACH GROWLING IN CLASS.
IT'S LOUDEST AFTER LUNCH.
SITS TO HIS LEFT
I HEAR IT TOO.
SITS TO HIS RIGHT
OH! ME TOO!
I... ...WONDER WHY?
WHO KNOWS?
MAYBE HE HAS NO MONEY?
BUT...
...HE HAS A PART-TIME JOB.
BUT NOW THAT I THINK ABOUT IT...
Thank you!! ♥
Here!
...AT JULIAN'S HE'S ALWAYS BEING FRIENDLY WITH THE COOKS AND ASKING FOR THE LEFTOVERS.
HE TAKES THEM HOME IN TUPPERWARE...

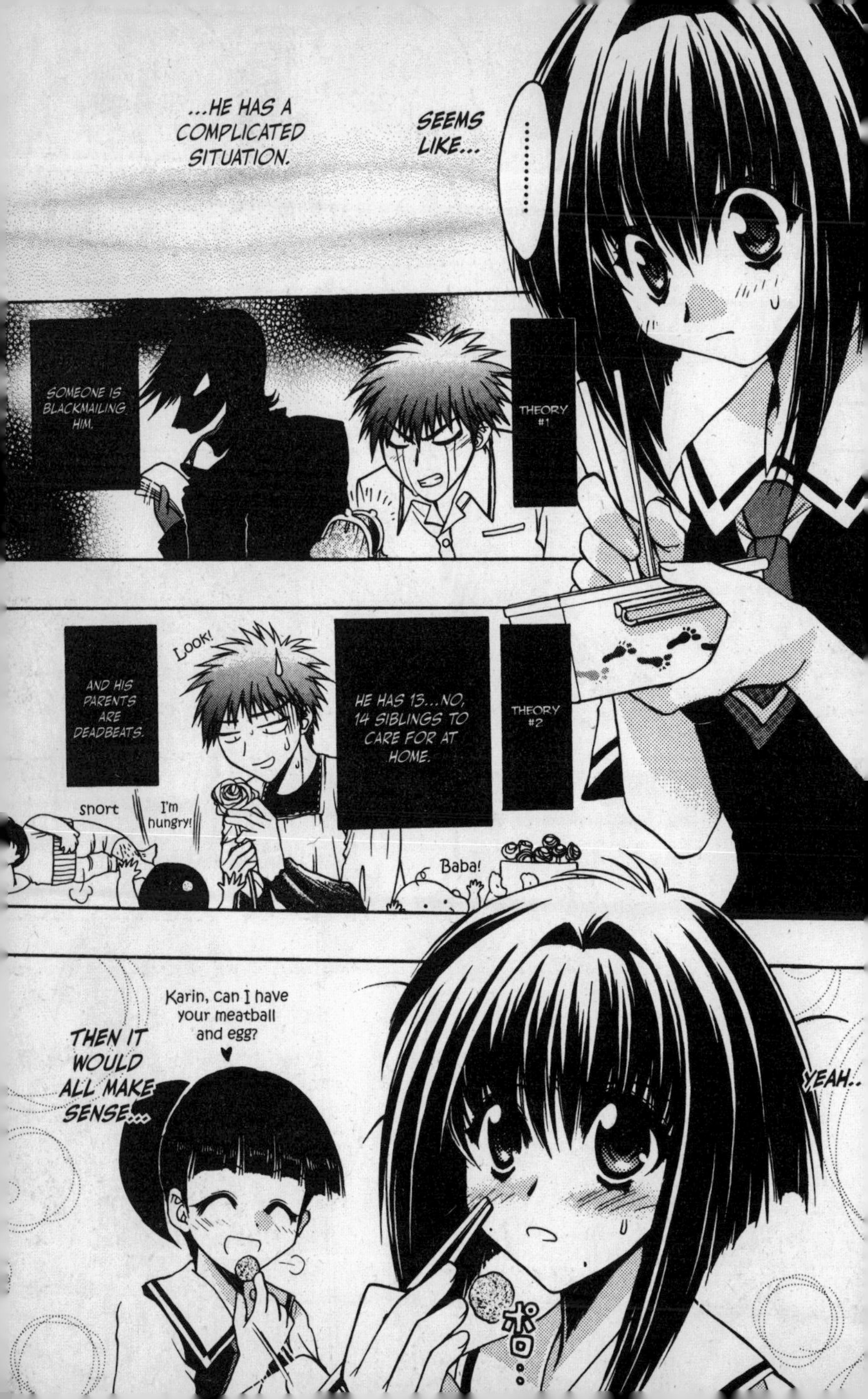
......
SEEMS LIKE...
...HE HAS A COMPLICATED SITUATION.
THEORY #1
SOMEONE IS BLACKMAILING HIM.
THEORY #2
HE HAS 13...NO, 14 SIBLINGS TO CARE FOR AT HOME.
AND HIS PARENTS ARE DEADBEATS.
Look!
Baba!
I'm hungry!
snort
YEAH..
Karin, can I have your meatball and egg?
THEN IT WOULD ALL MAKE SENSE...
ポロ...

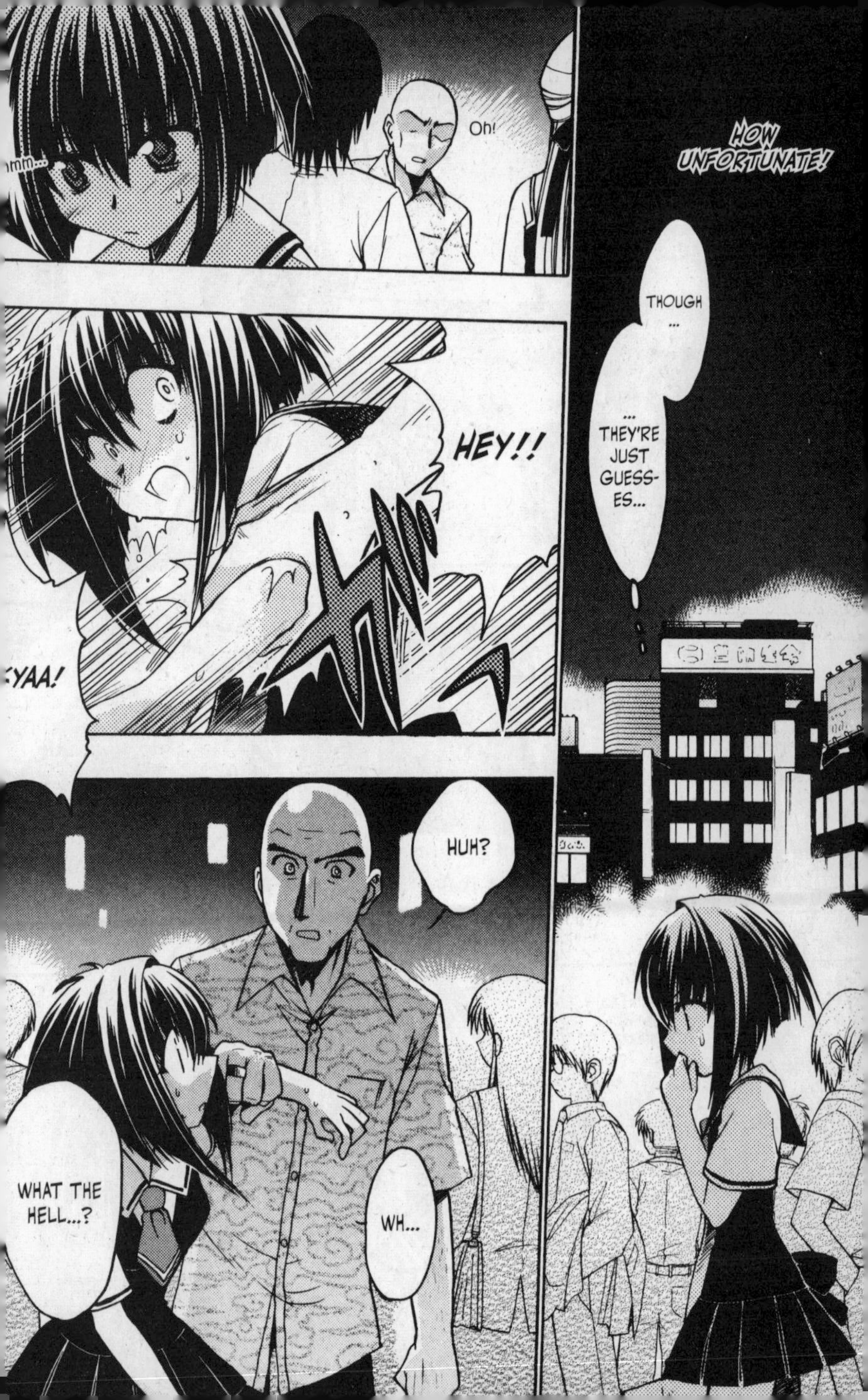
HOW UNFORTUNATE!
THOUGH ...
... THEY'RE JUST GUESS-ES...
Oh!
mmm...
HEY!!
YAA!
HUH?
WH...
WHAT THE HELL...?

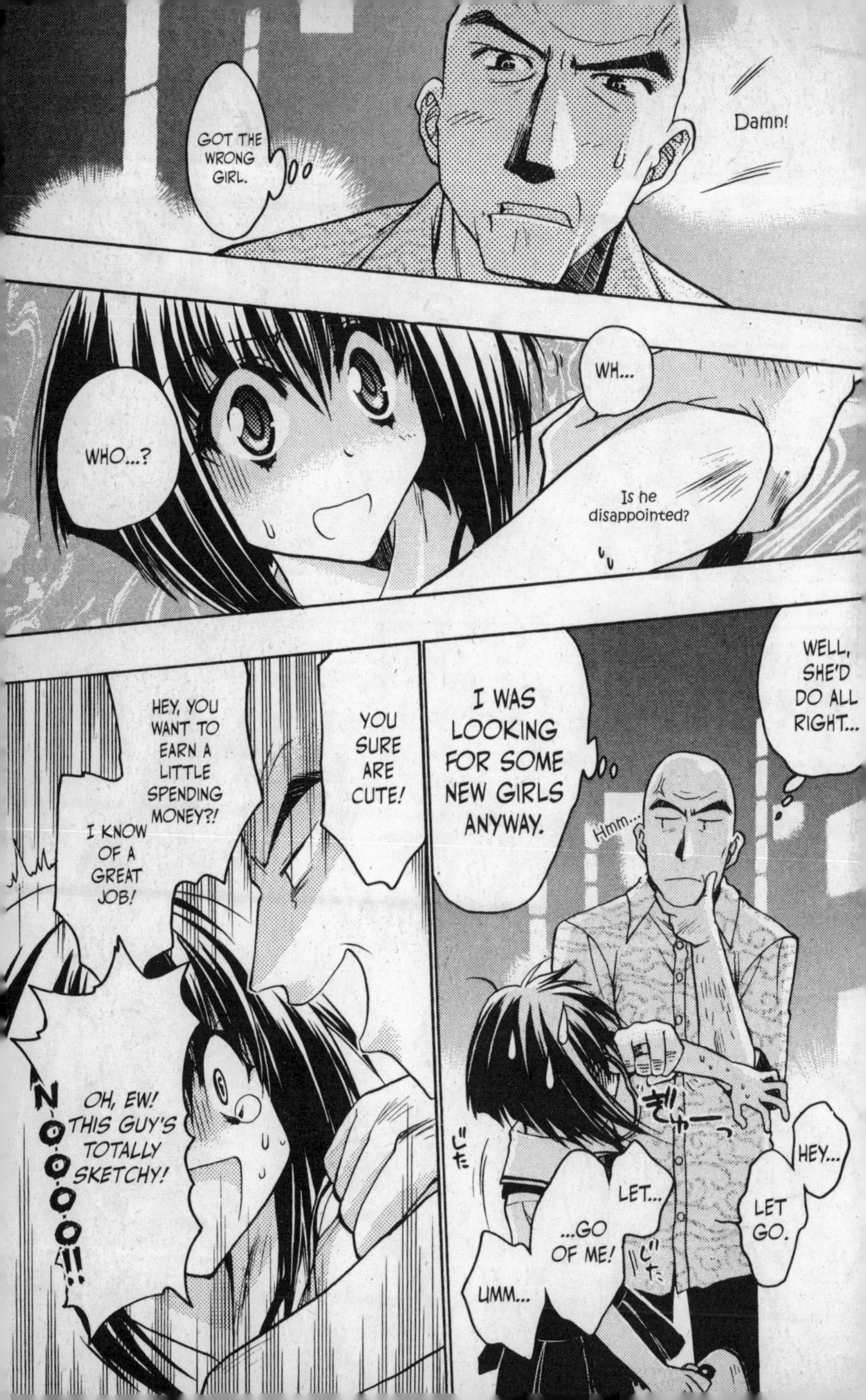
Damn!
GOT THE WRONG GIRL.
WH...
Is he disappointed?
WHO...?
WELL, SHE'D DO ALL RIGHT...
I WAS LOOKING FOR SOME NEW GIRLS ANYWAY.
Hmm...
HEY...
LET GO.
LET...
...GO OF ME!
UMM...
YOU SURE ARE CUTE!
HEY, YOU WANT TO EARN A LITTLE SPENDING MONEY?!
I KNOW OF A GREAT JOB!
OH, EW! THIS GUY'S TOTALLY SKETCHY!
NOOOOOO!!

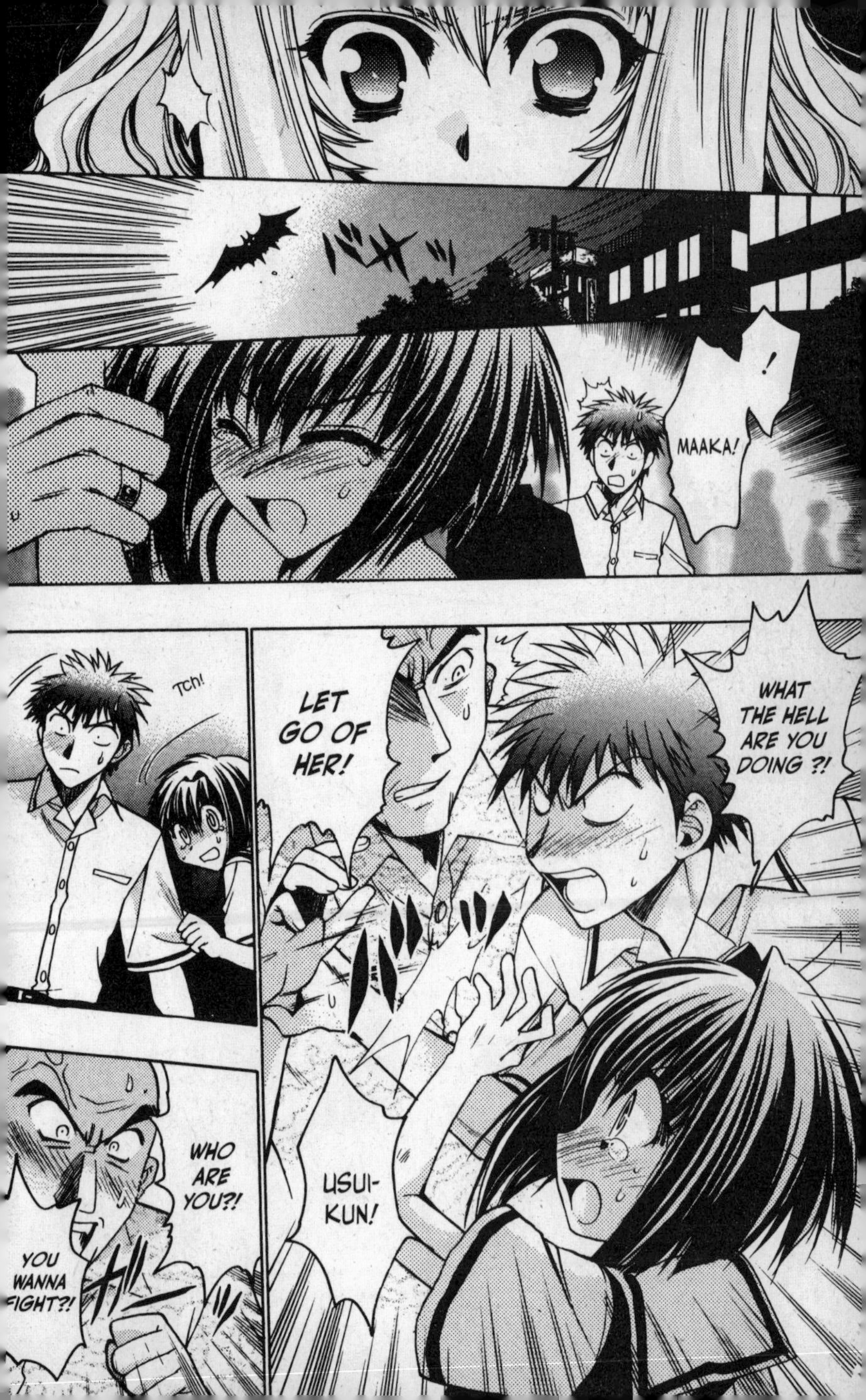
!
MAAKA!
WHAT THE HELL ARE YOU DOING ?!
LET GO OF HER!
USUI-KUN!
Tch!
WHO ARE YOU?!
YOU WANNA FIGHT?!

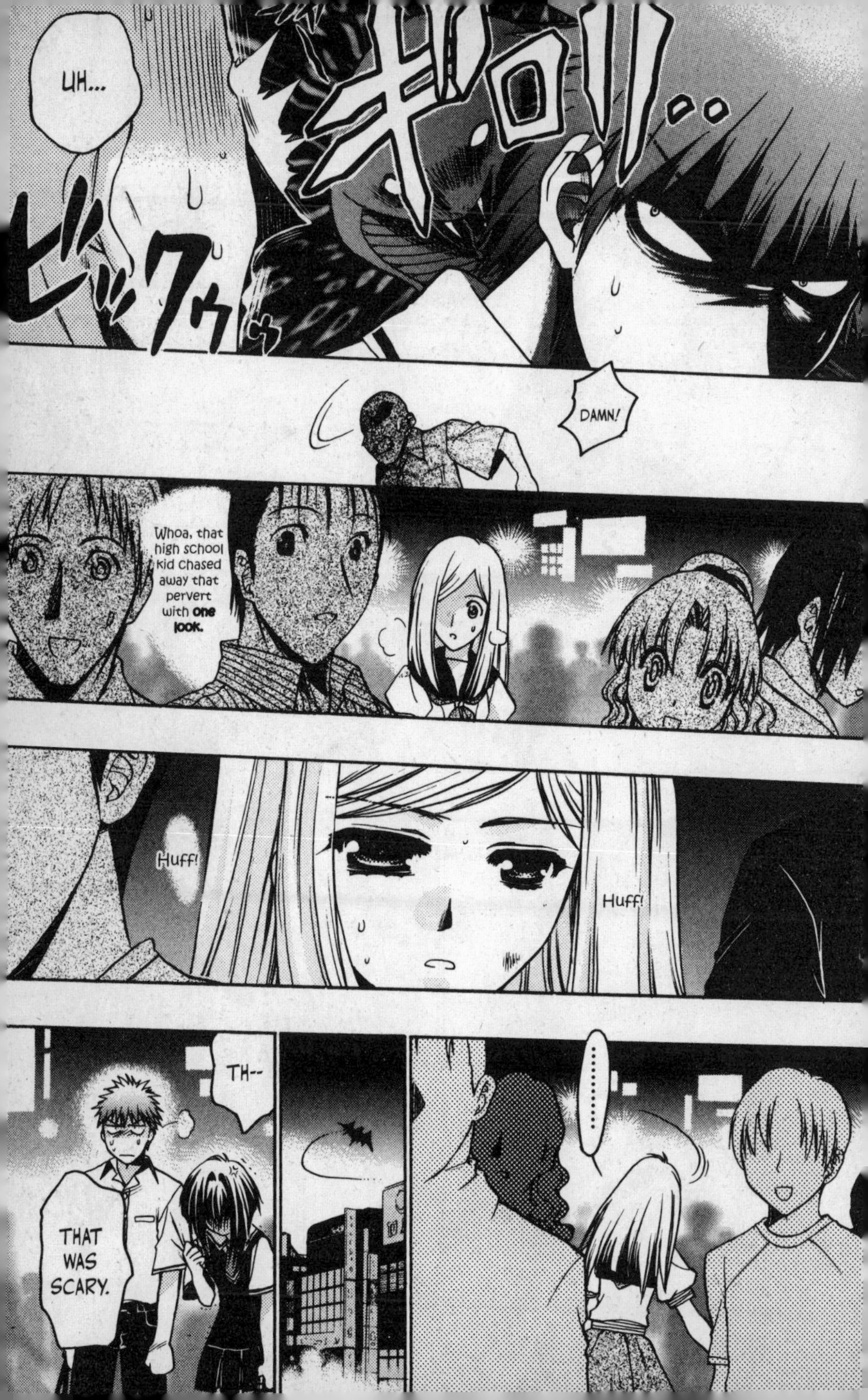
UH...
DAMN!
Whoa, that high school kid chased away that pervert with **one look.**
Huff!
Huff!
......
TH--
THAT WAS SCARY.

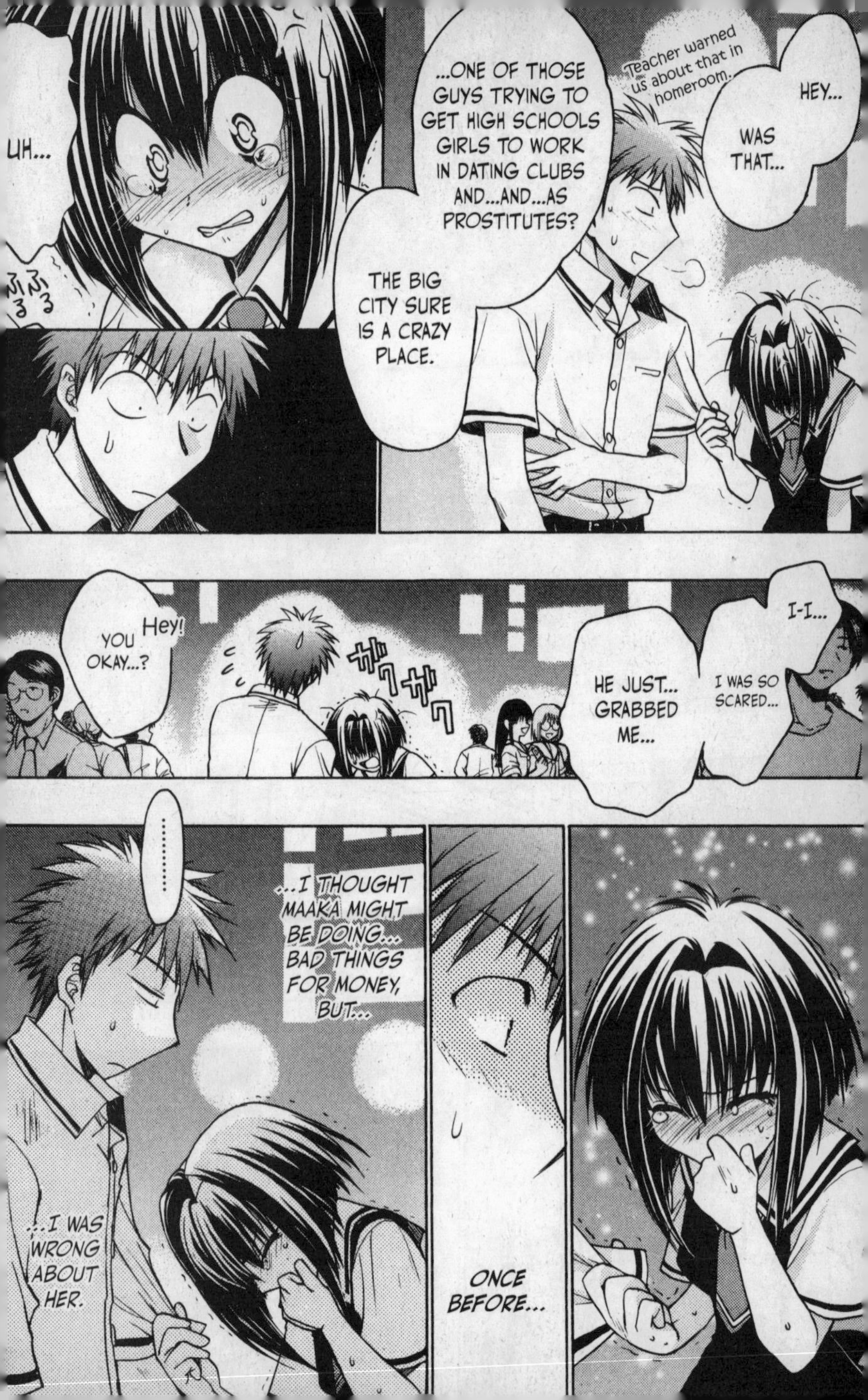
HEY...
WAS THAT...
Teacher warned us about that in homeroom.
...ONE OF THOSE GUYS TRYING TO GET HIGH SCHOOLS GIRLS TO WORK IN DATING CLUBS AND...AND...AS PROSTITUTES?
THE BIG CITY SURE IS A CRAZY PLACE.
UH...
ふるふる
I-I...
I WAS SO SCARED...
HE JUST... GRABBED ME...
ガクガク
Hey!
YOU OKAY...?
ONCE BEFORE...
......
...I THOUGHT MAAKA MIGHT BE DOING... BAD THINGS FOR MONEY, BUT...
...I WAS WRONG ABOUT HER.

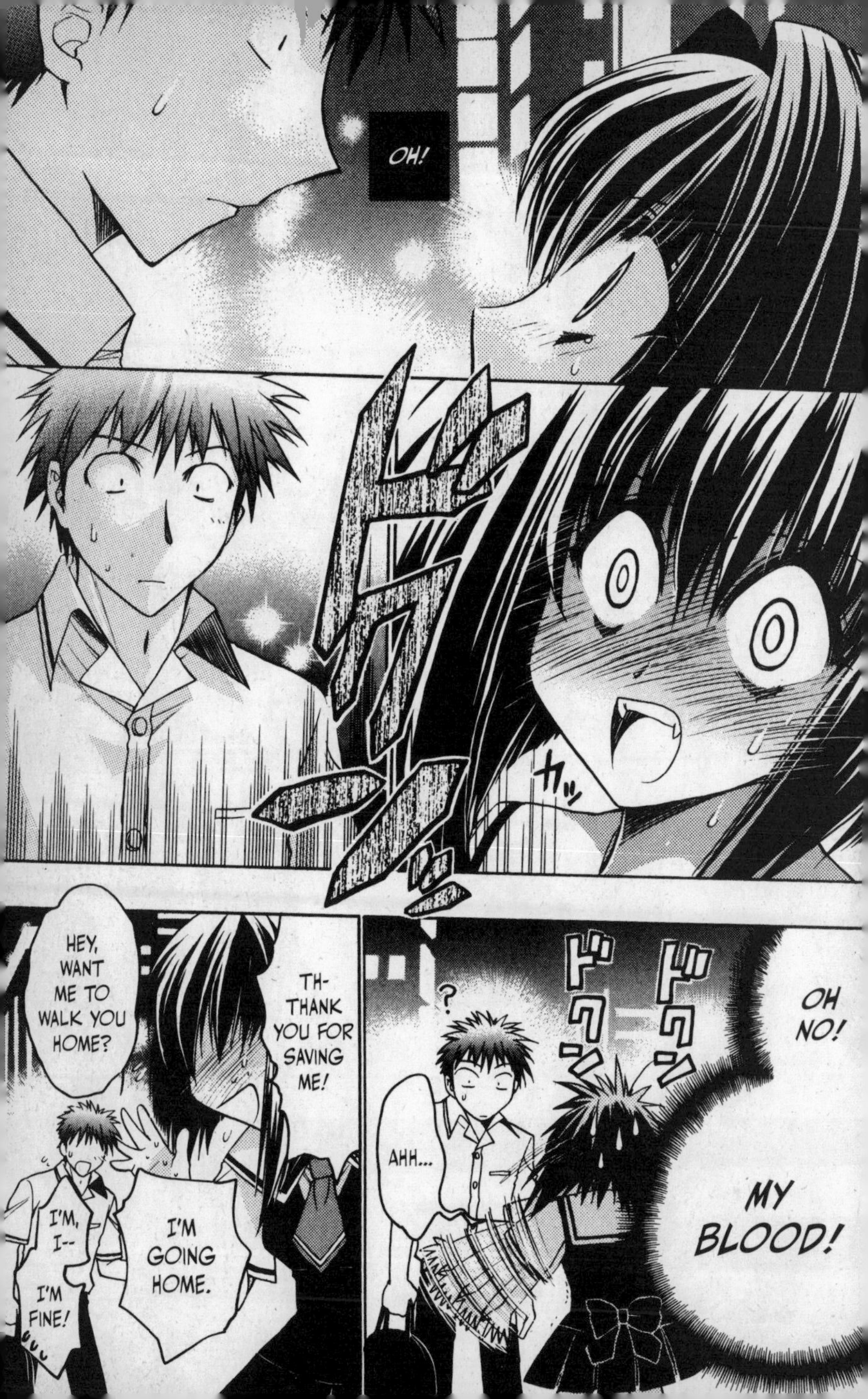
OH!
カッ
OH NO!
ドクン
ドクン
MY BLOOD!
?
AHH...
TH- THANK YOU FOR SAVING ME!
HEY, WANT ME TO WALK YOU HOME?
I'M GOING HOME.
I'M, I--
I'M FINE!

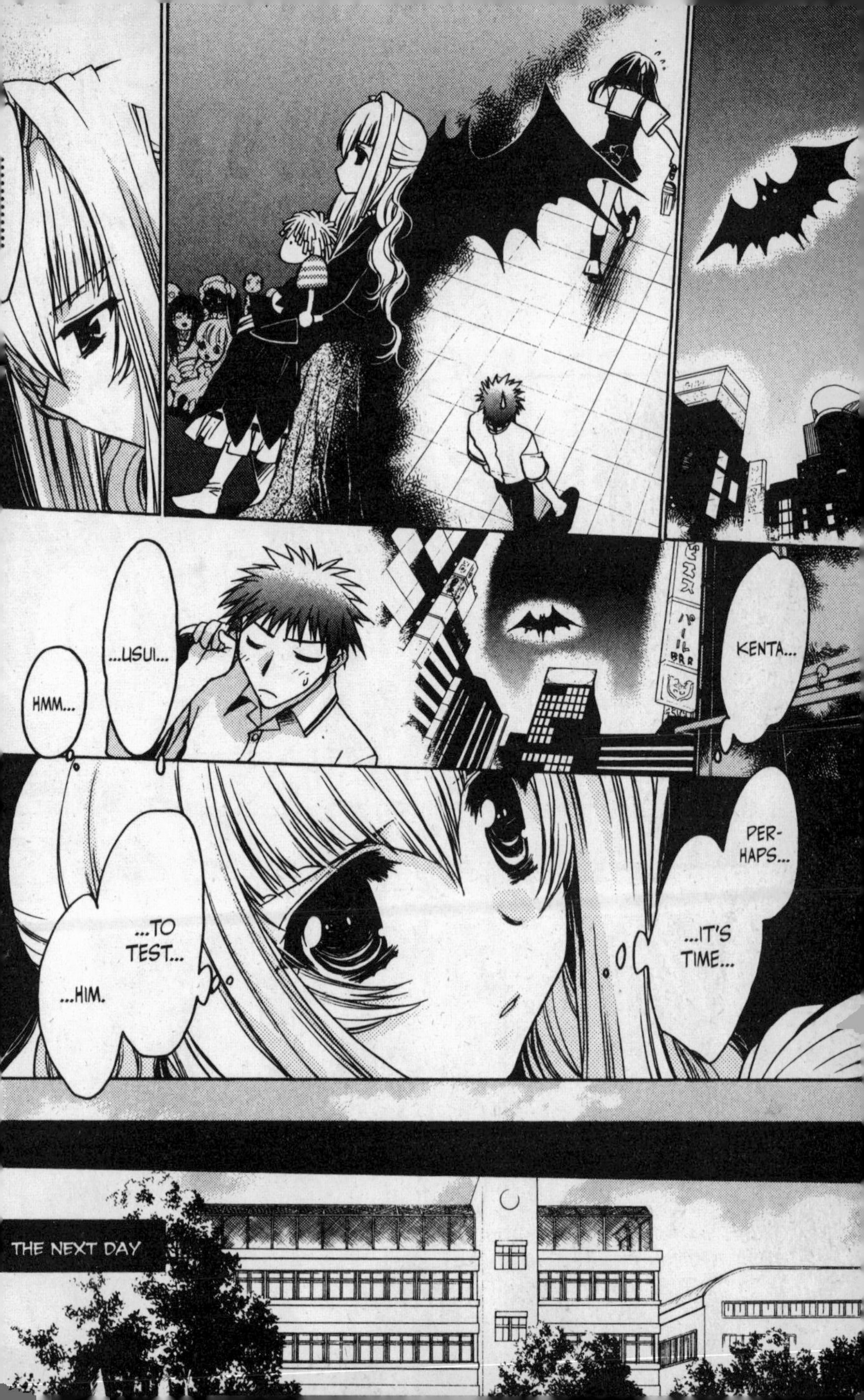
KENTA...
...USUI...
HMM...
PER-HAPS...
...IT'S TIME...
...TO TEST...
...HIM.
THE NEXT DAY

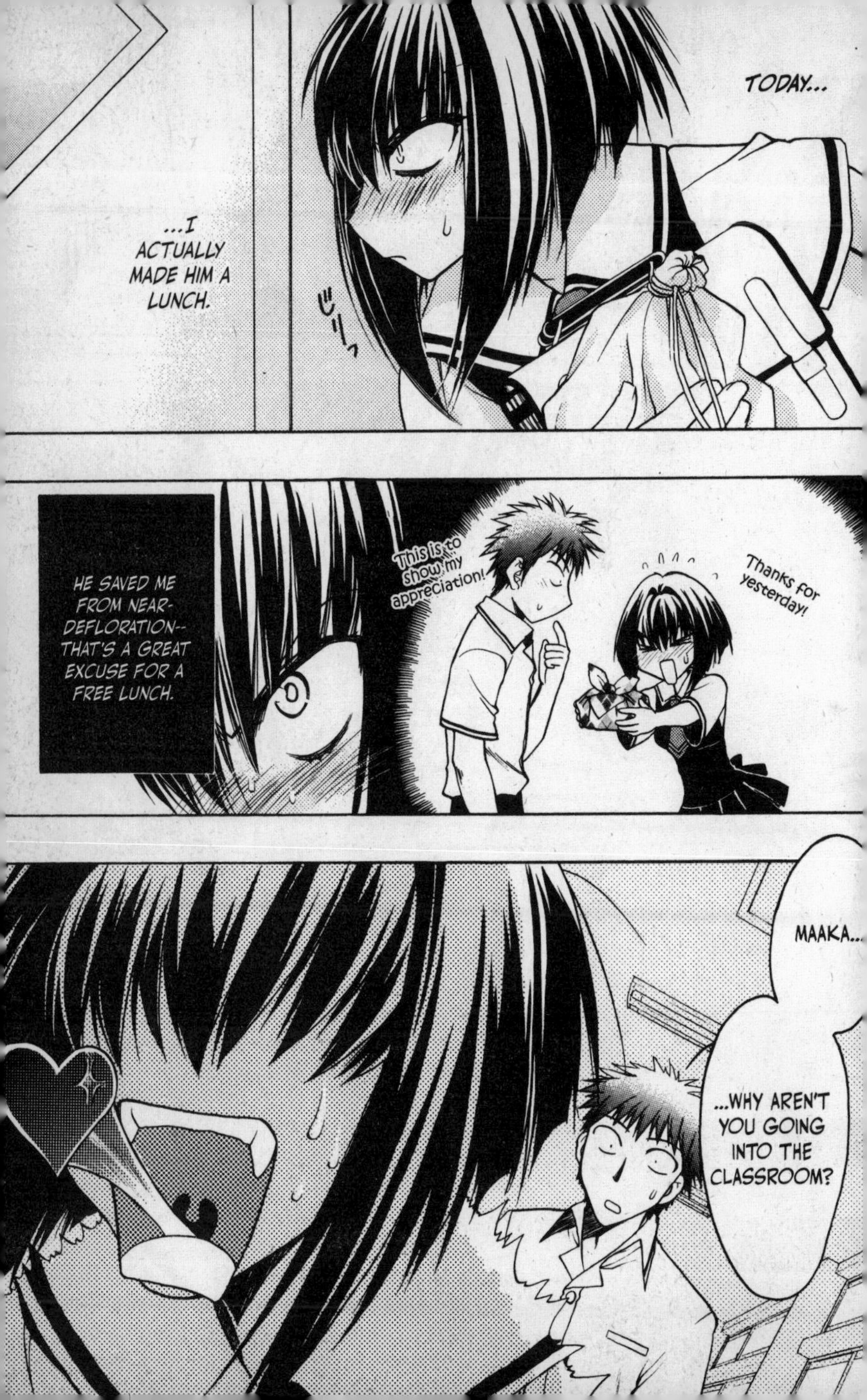
TODAY...
...I ACTUALLY MADE HIM A LUNCH.
Thanks for yesterday!
This is to show my appreciation!
HE SAVED ME FROM NEAR-DEFLORATION-- THAT'S A GREAT EXCUSE FOR A FREE LUNCH.
MAAKA...
...WHY AREN'T YOU GOING INTO THE CLASSROOM?

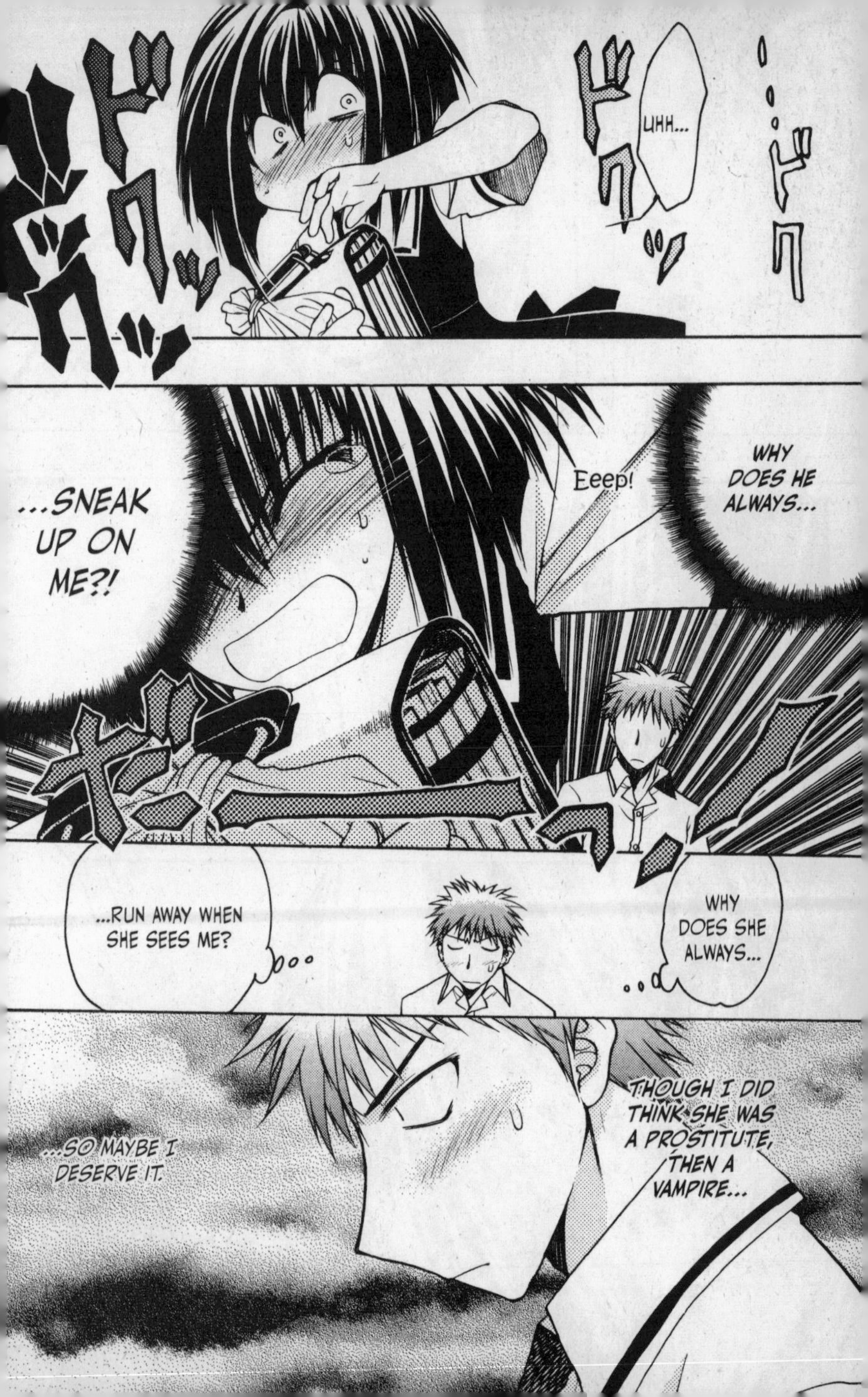
UHH...
WHY DOES HE ALWAYS...
Eeep!
...SNEAK UP ON ME?!
WHY DOES SHE ALWAYS...
...RUN AWAY WHEN SHE SEES ME?
THOUGH I DID THINK SHE WAS A PROSTITUTE, THEN A VAMPIRE...
...SO MAYBE I DESERVE IT.

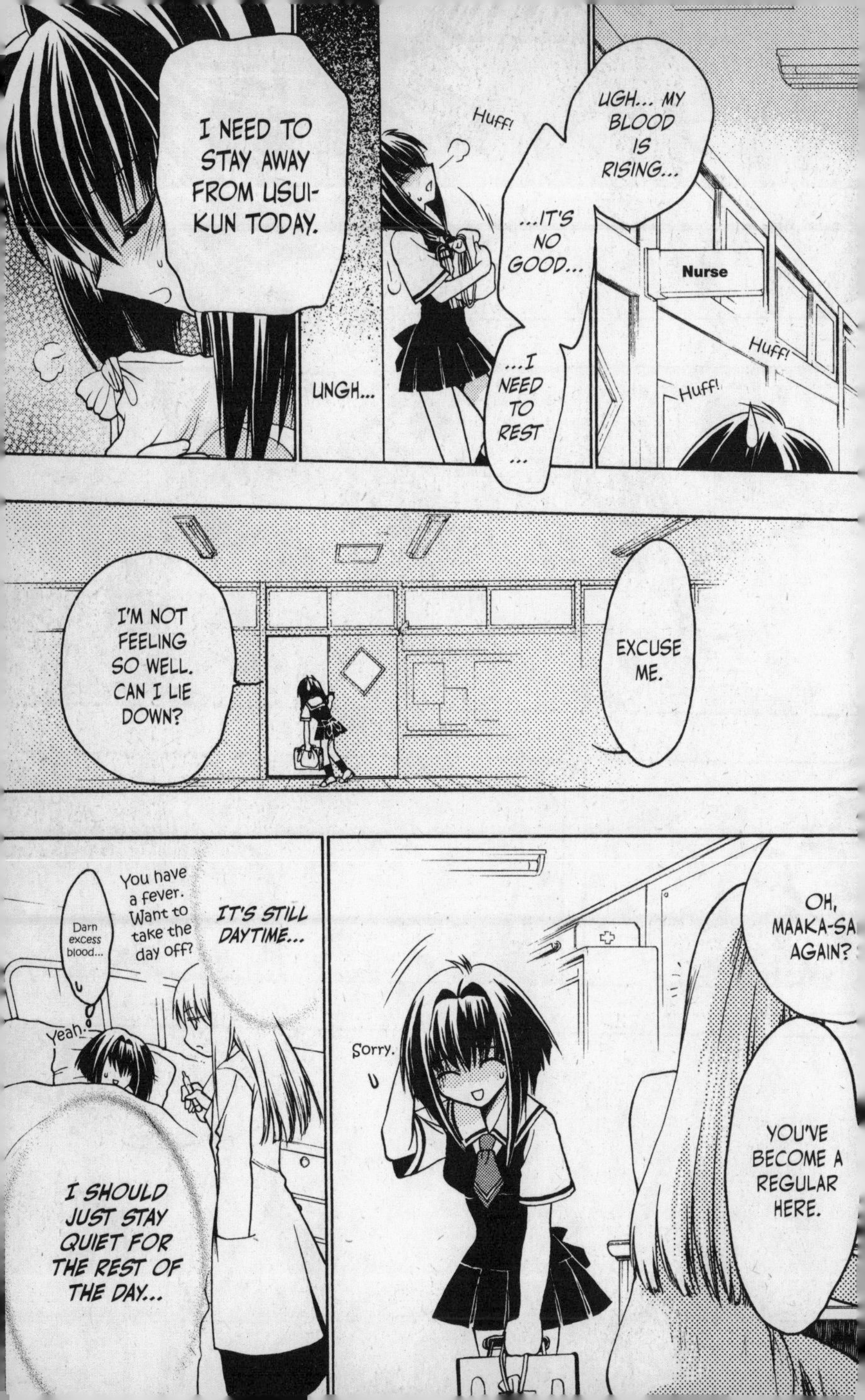
Nurse
Huff!
Huff!
UGH... MY BLOOD IS RISING...
Huff!
...IT'S NO GOOD...
...I NEED TO REST...
UNGH...
I NEED TO STAY AWAY FROM USUI-KUN TODAY.
EXCUSE ME.
I'M NOT FEELING SO WELL. CAN I LIE DOWN?
OH, MAAKA-SA AGAIN?
YOU'VE BECOME A REGULAR HERE.
Sorry.
IT'S STILL DAYTIME...
You have a fever. Want to take the day off?
Darn excess blood...
Yeah.
I SHOULD JUST STAY QUIET FOR THE REST OF THE DAY...

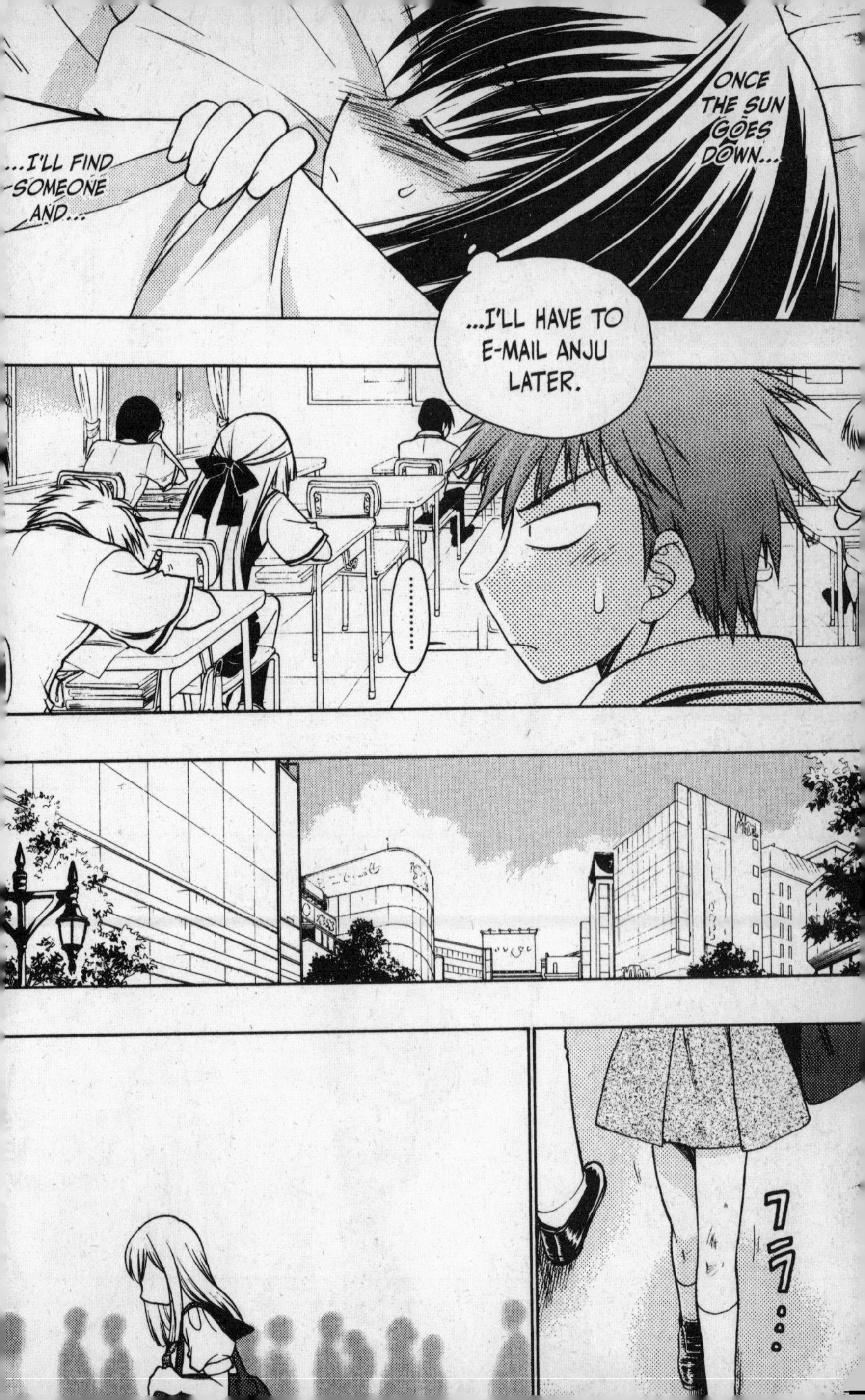
ONCE THE SUN GOES DOWN...
...I'LL FIND SOMEONE AND...
...I'LL HAVE TO E-MAIL ANJU LATER.
......
フラ...

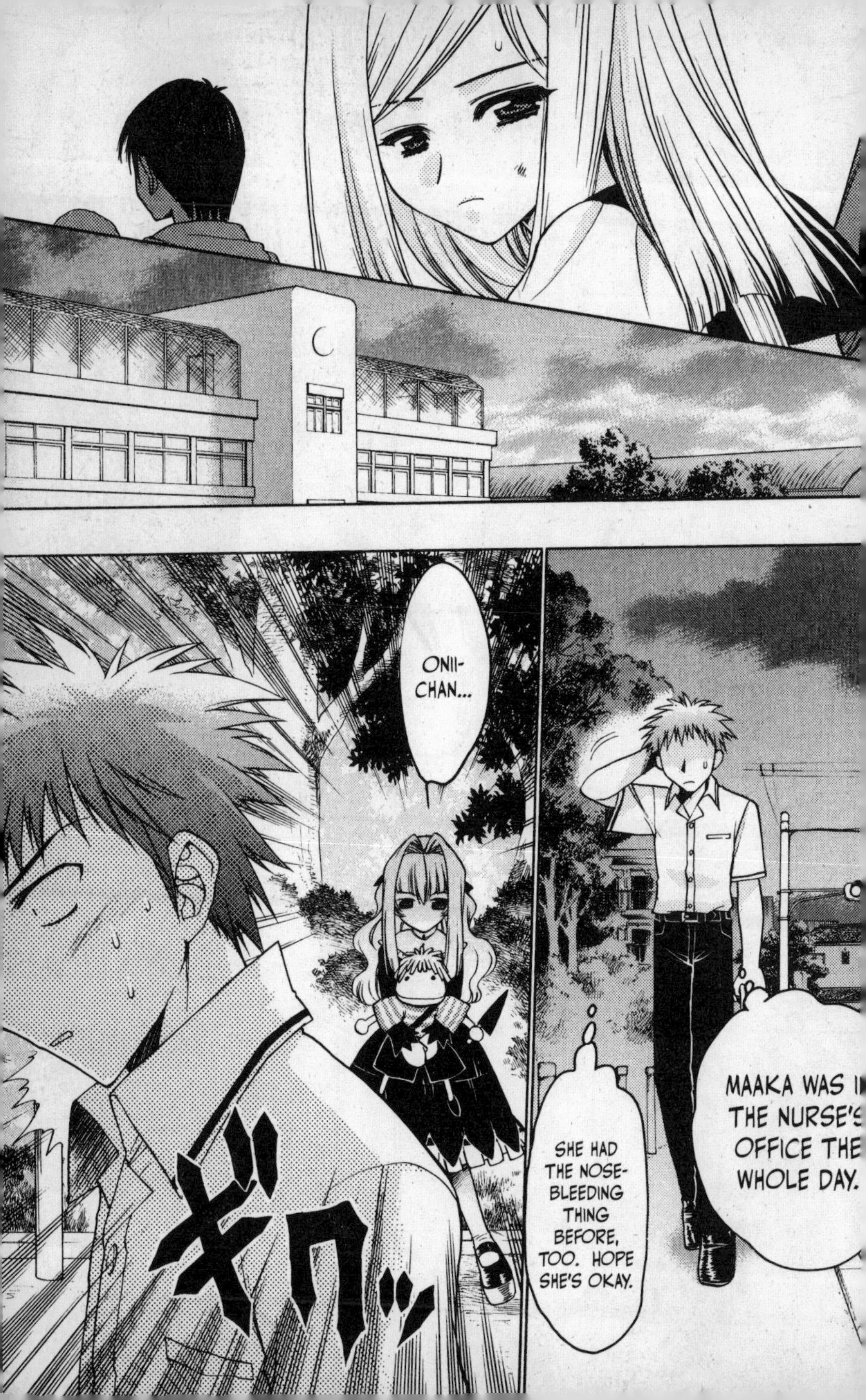

MAAKA WAS I THE NURSE'S OFFICE THE WHOLE DAY.
SHE HAD THE NOSE-BLEEDING THING BEFORE, TOO. HOPE SHE'S OKAY.
ONII-CHAN...
ギクッ

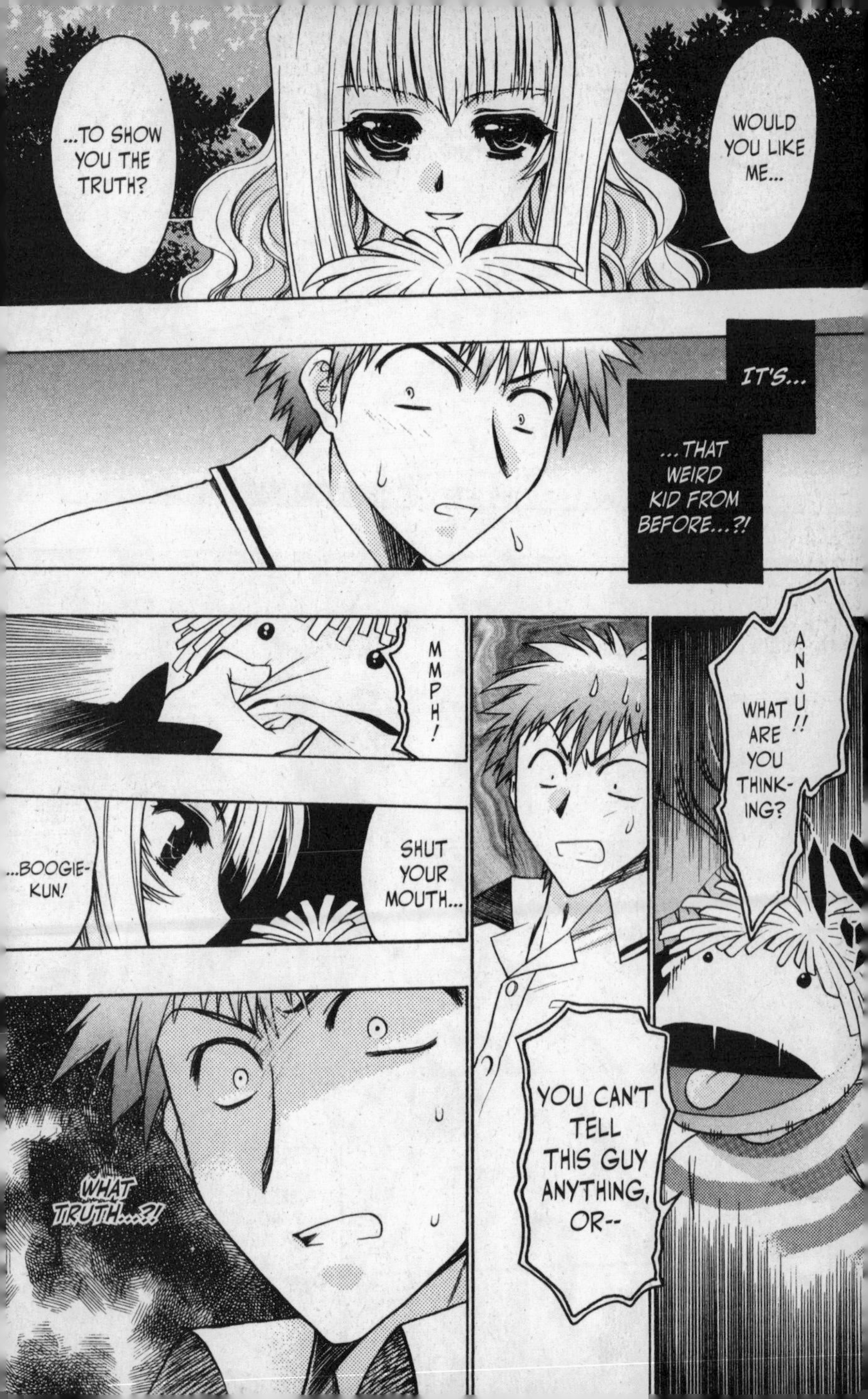
WOULD YOU LIKE ME...
...TO SHOW YOU THE TRUTH?
IT'S...
...THAT WEIRD KID FROM BEFORE...?!
ANJU!! WHAT ARE YOU THINKING?
YOU CAN'T TELL THIS GUY ANYTHING, OR--
MMPH!
SHUT YOUR MOUTH...
...BOOGIE-KUN!
WHAT TRUTH...?!

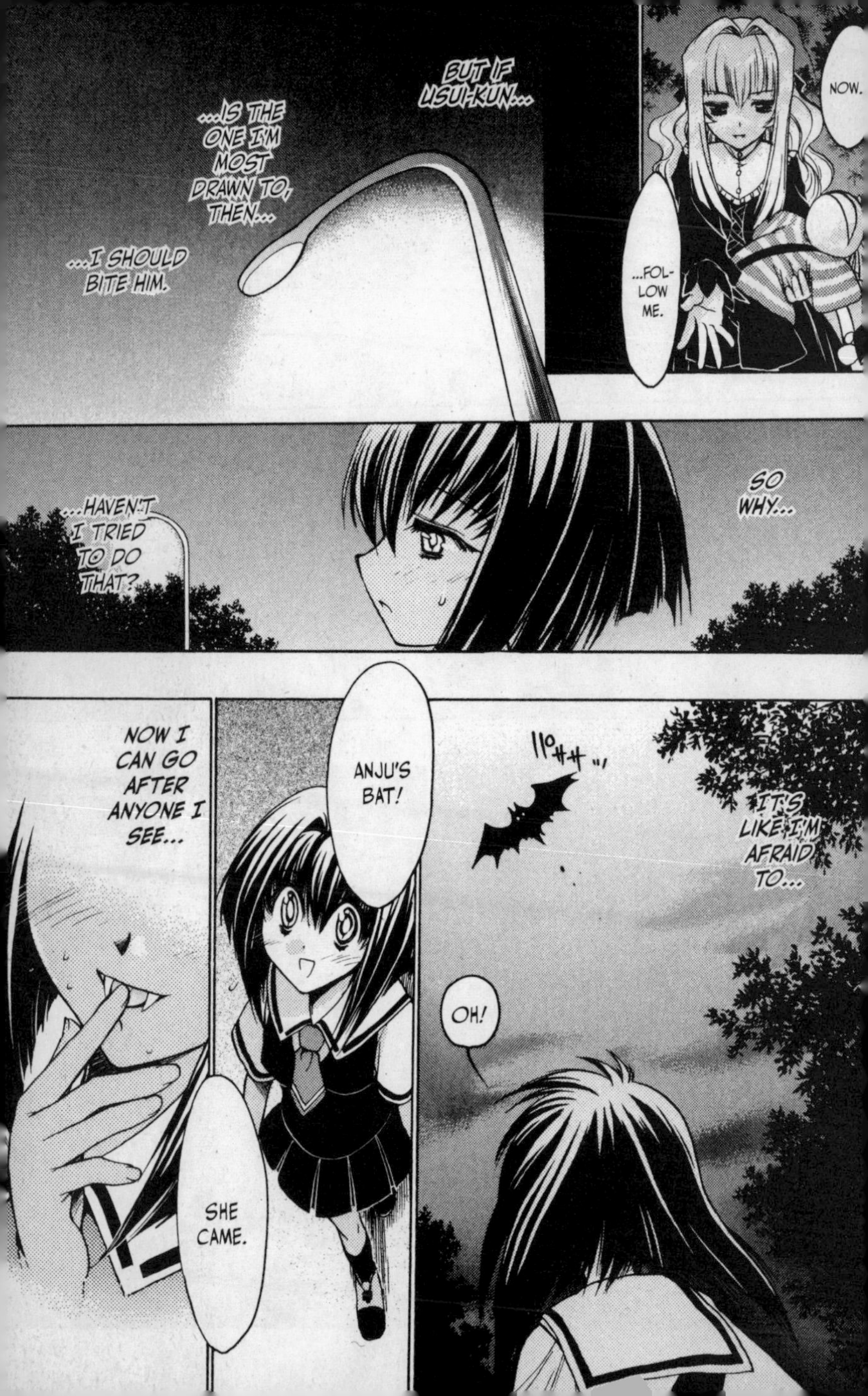
NOW.
...FOL-LOW ME.
BUT IF USUI-KUN...
...IS THE ONE I'M MOST DRAWN TO, THEN...
...I SHOULD BITE HIM.
SO WHY...
...HAVEN'T I TRIED TO DO THAT?
IT'S LIKE I'M AFRAID TO...
OH!
ANJU'S BAT!
SHE CAME.
NOW I CAN GO AFTER ANYONE I SEE...

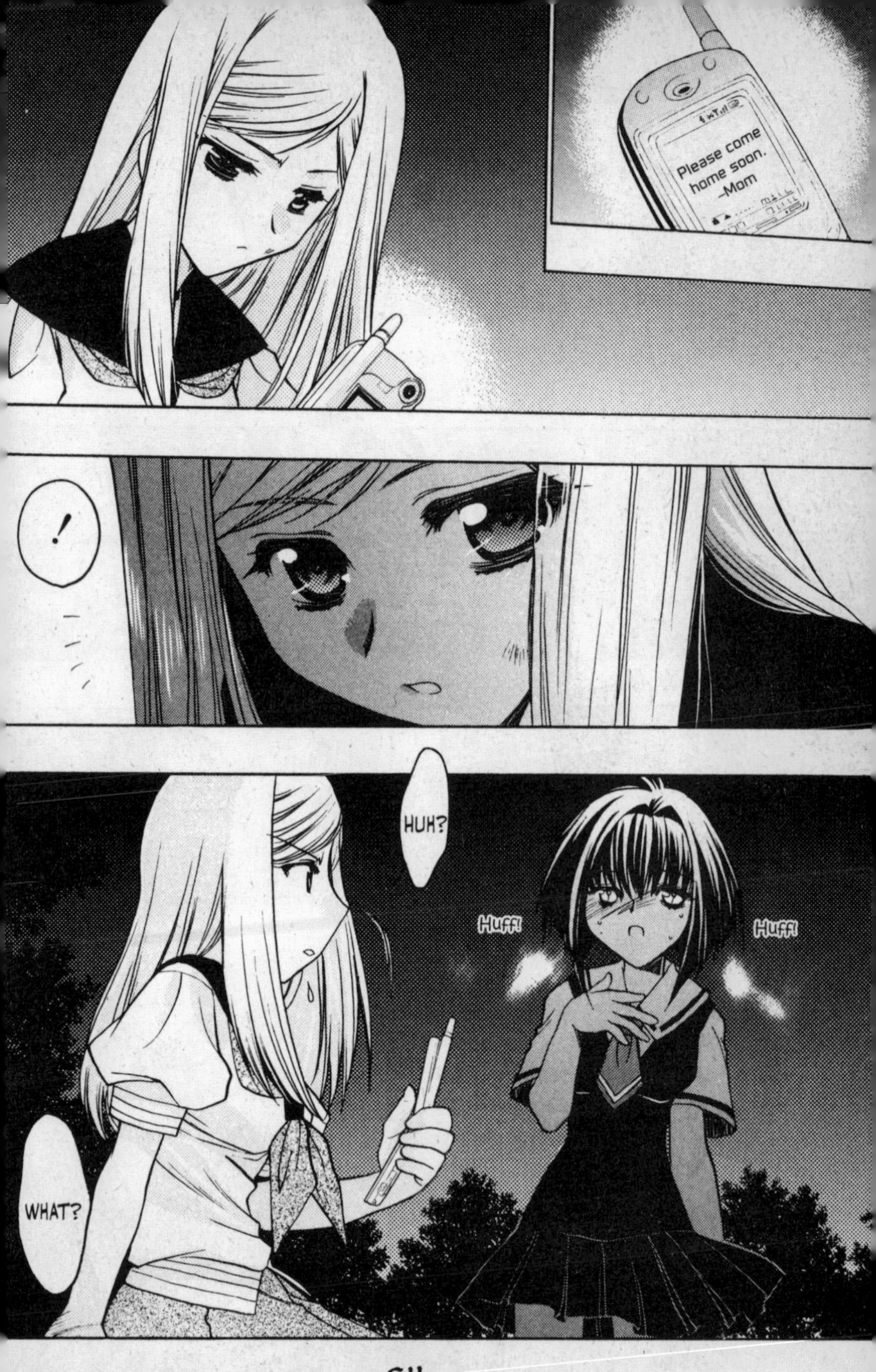
Please come home soon. -Mom
!
HUH?
Huff!
Huff!
WHAT?

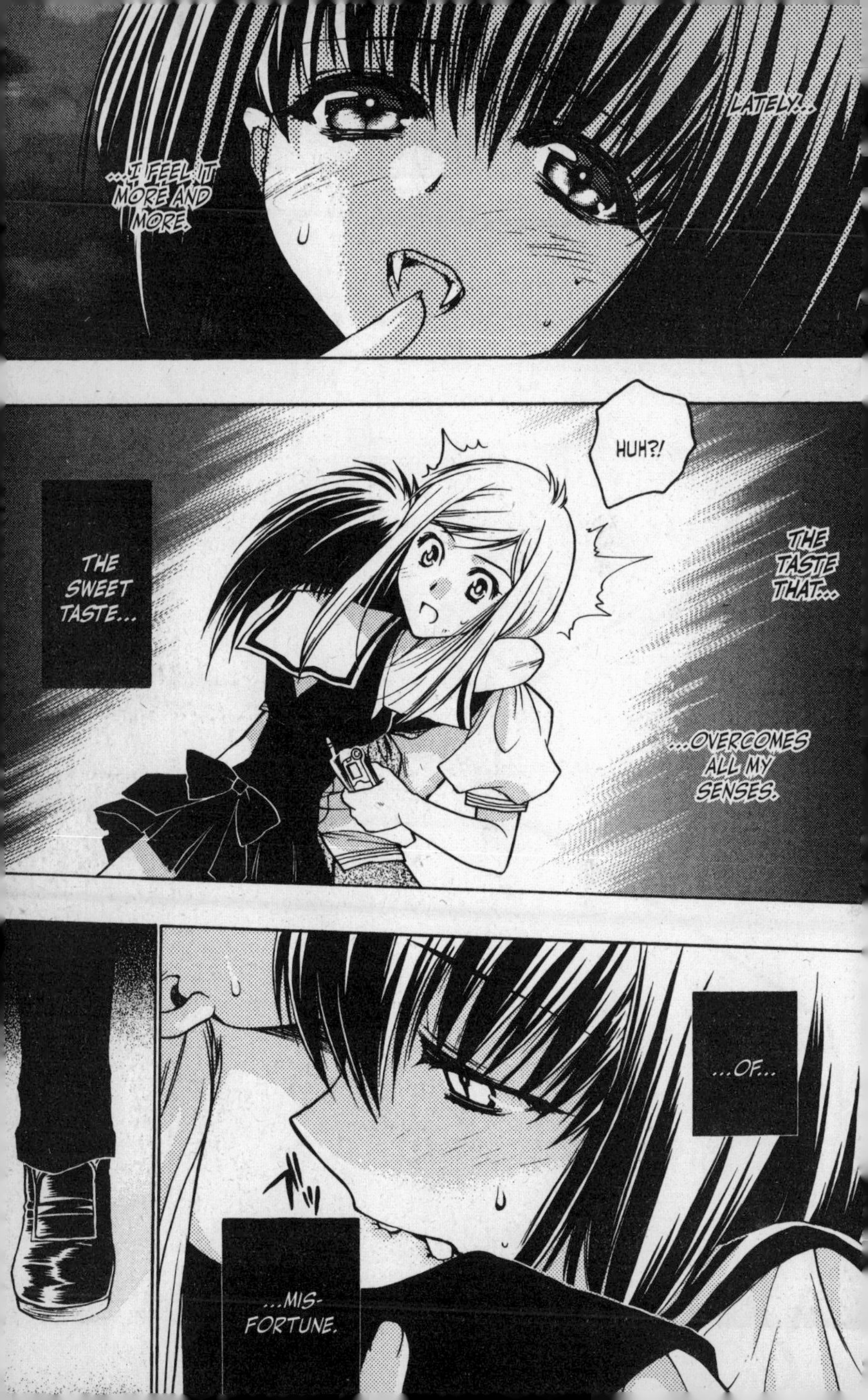
LATELY...
...I FEEL IT MORE AND MORE.
HUH?!
THE TASTE THAT...
...OVERCOMES ALL MY SENSES.
THE SWEET TASTE...
...OF...
...MIS- FORTUNE.

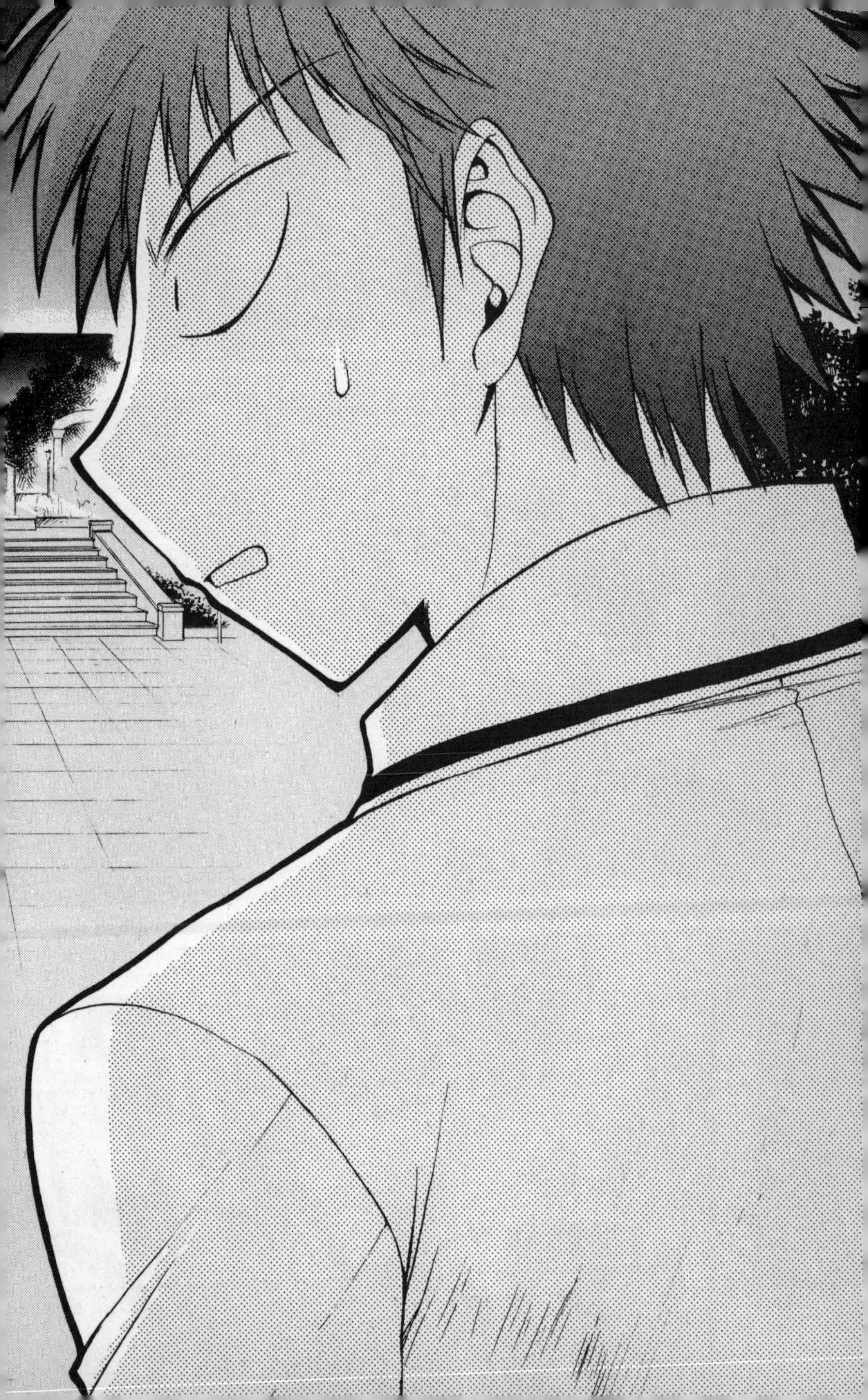

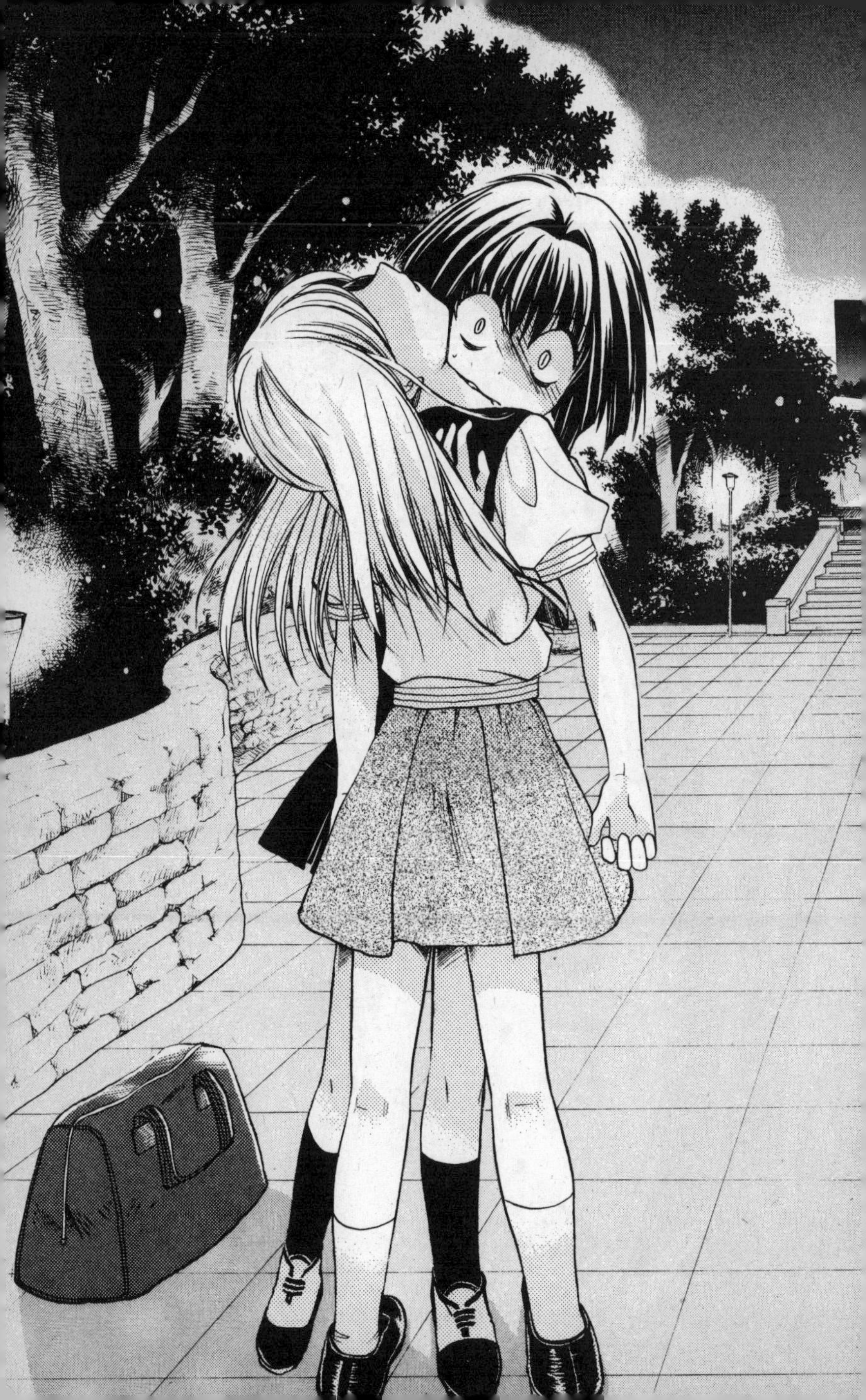

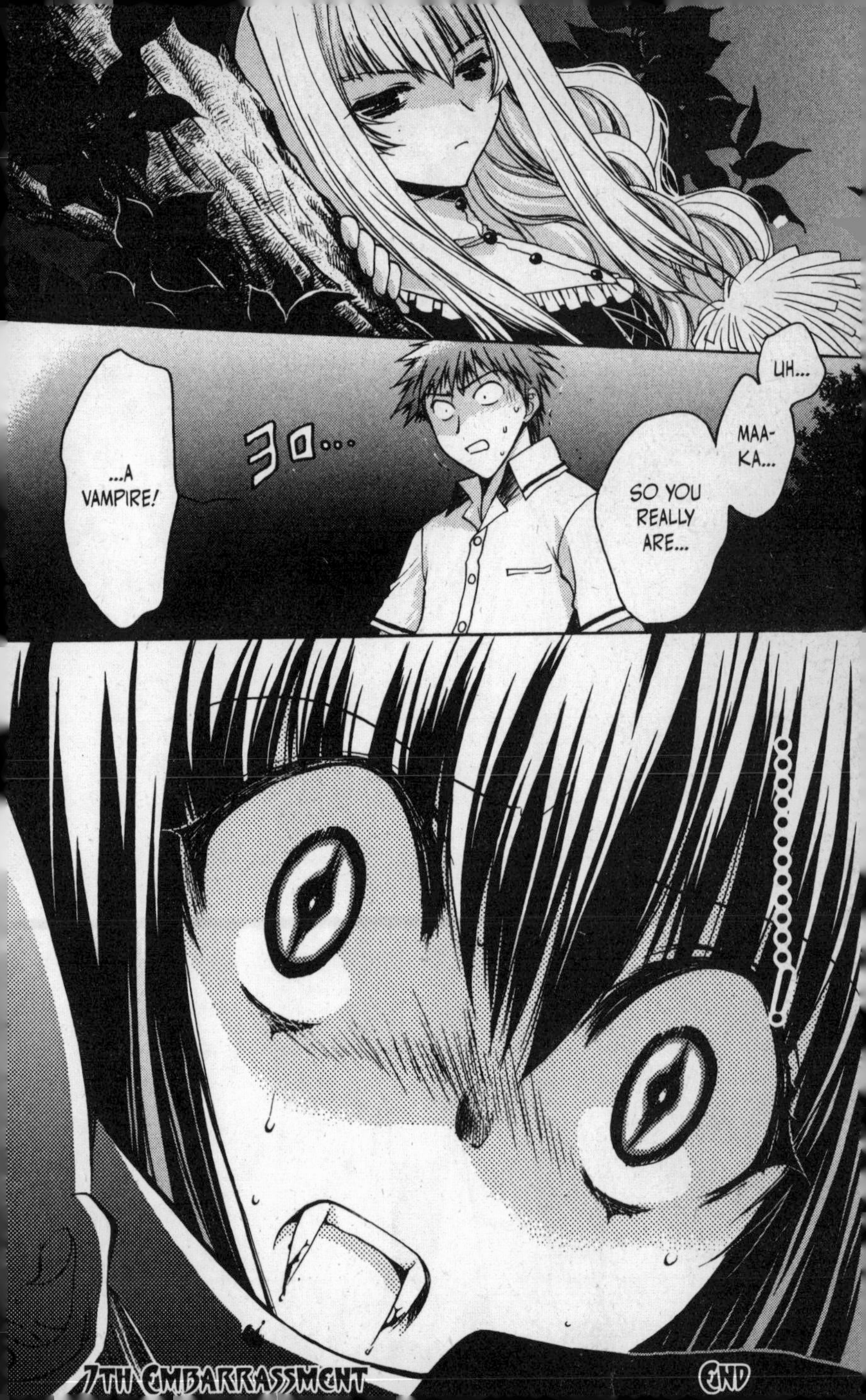
UH...
MAA-KA...
SO YOU REALLY ARE...
...A VAMPIRE!
7TH EMBARRASSMENT
END

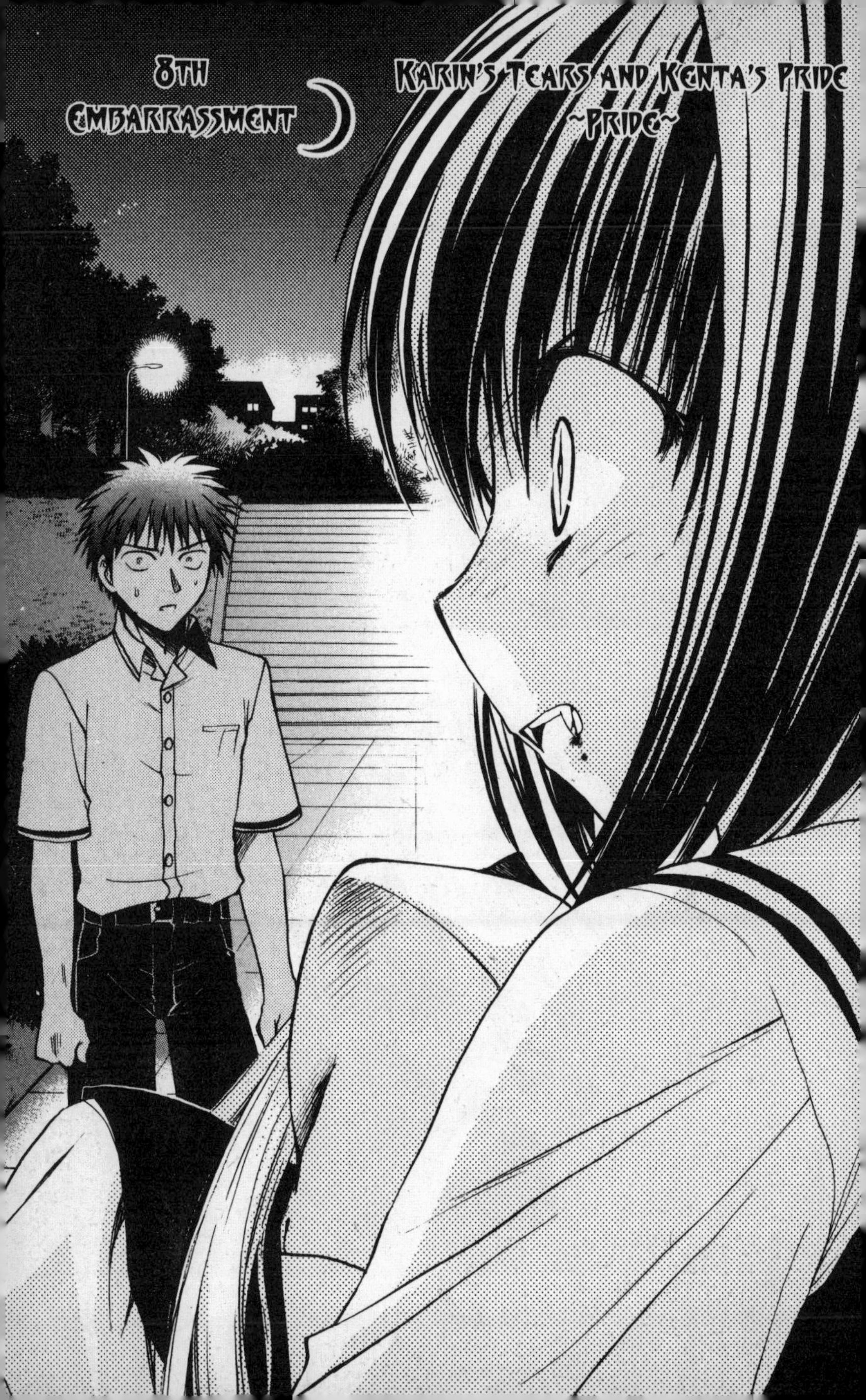

Karin's Tears and Kenta's Pride
~Pride~
8th
Embarrassment

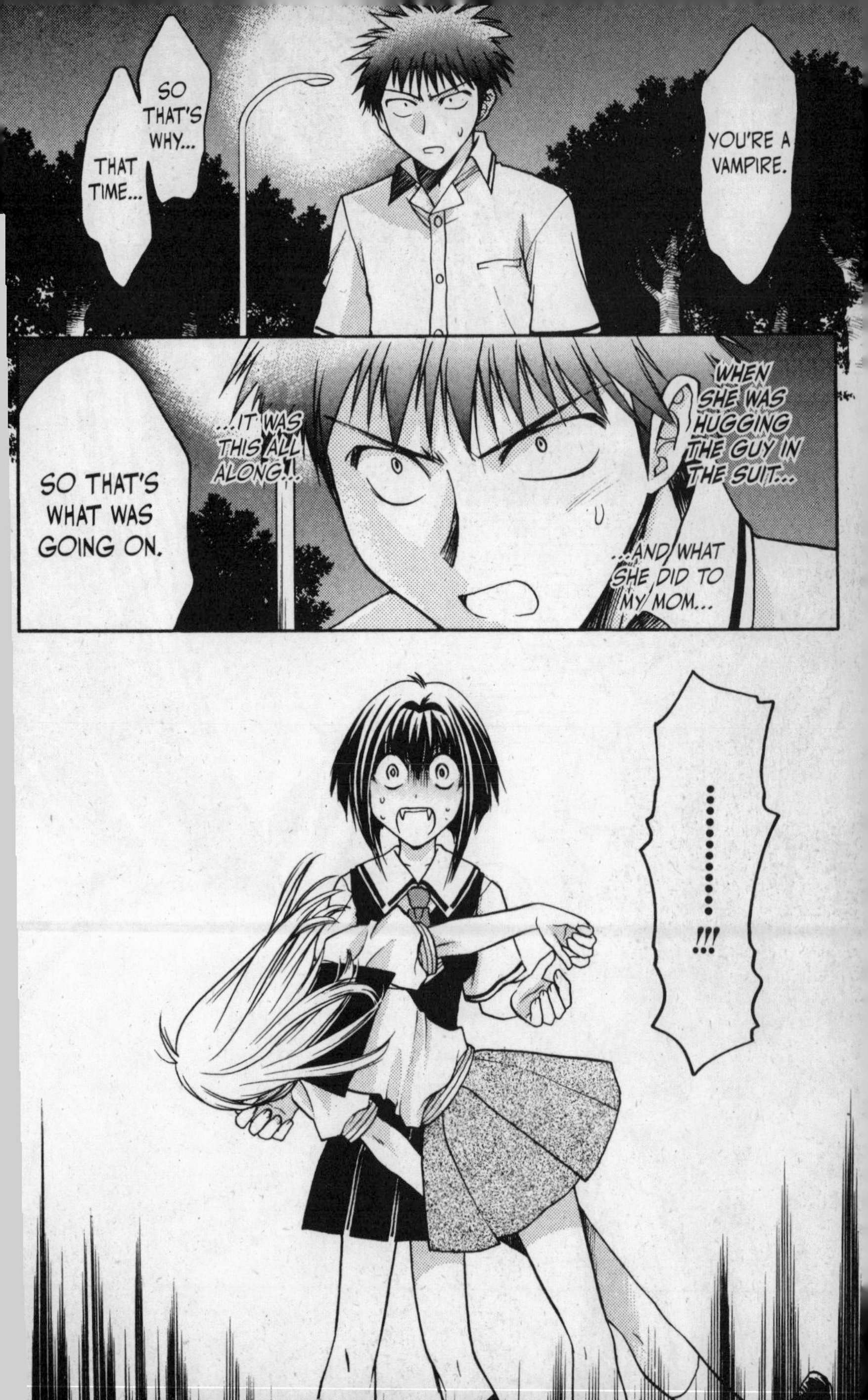
YOU'RE A VAMPIRE.
SO THAT'S WHY...
THAT TIME...
WHEN SHE WAS HUGGING THE GUY IN THE SUIT...
...AND WHAT SHE DID TO MY MOM...
...IT WAS THIS ALL ALONG!!
SO THAT'S WHAT WAS GOING ON.
..............!!!

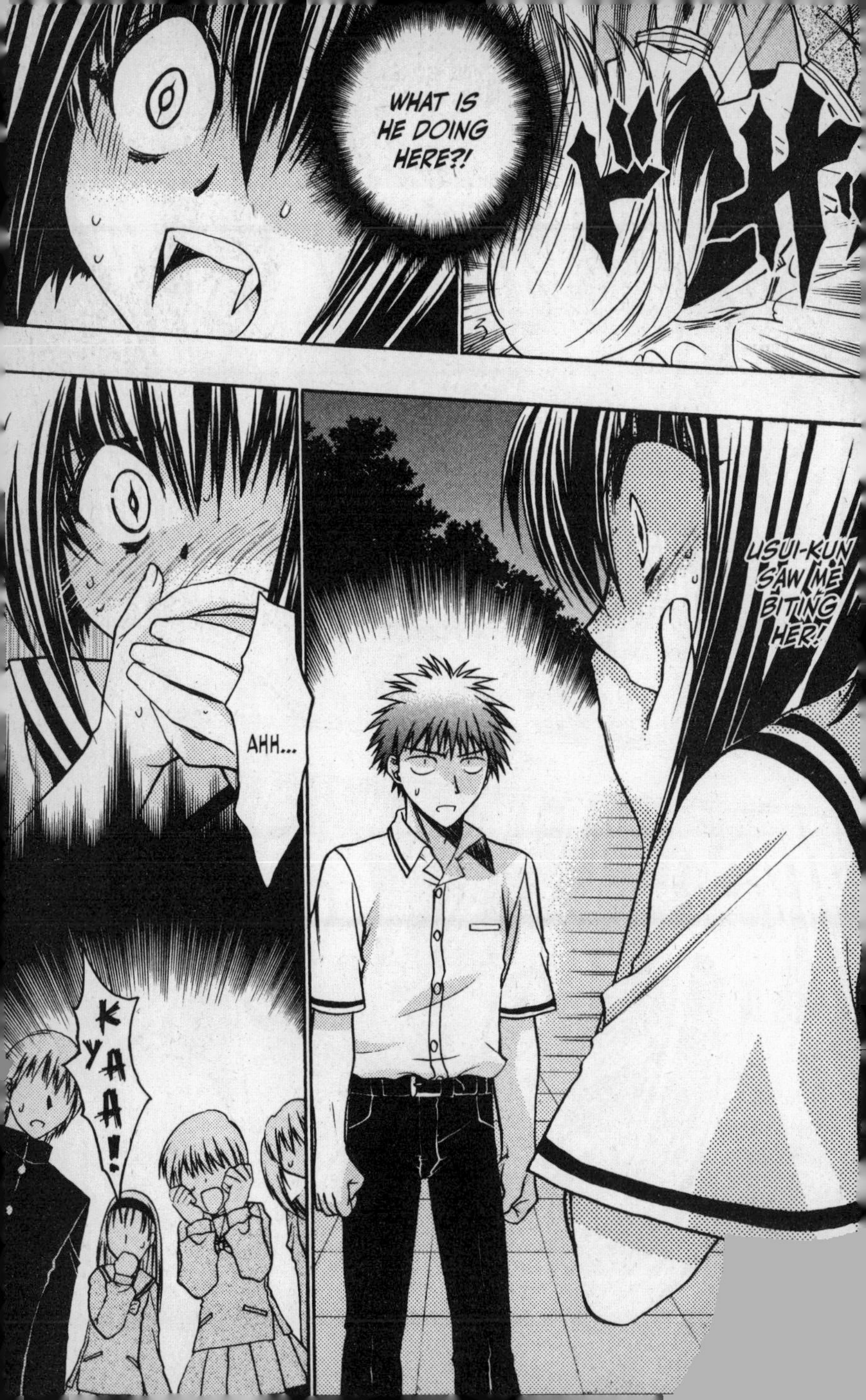
WHAT IS HE DOING HERE?!
USUI-KUN SAW ME BITING HER!
AHH...
KYAA!!

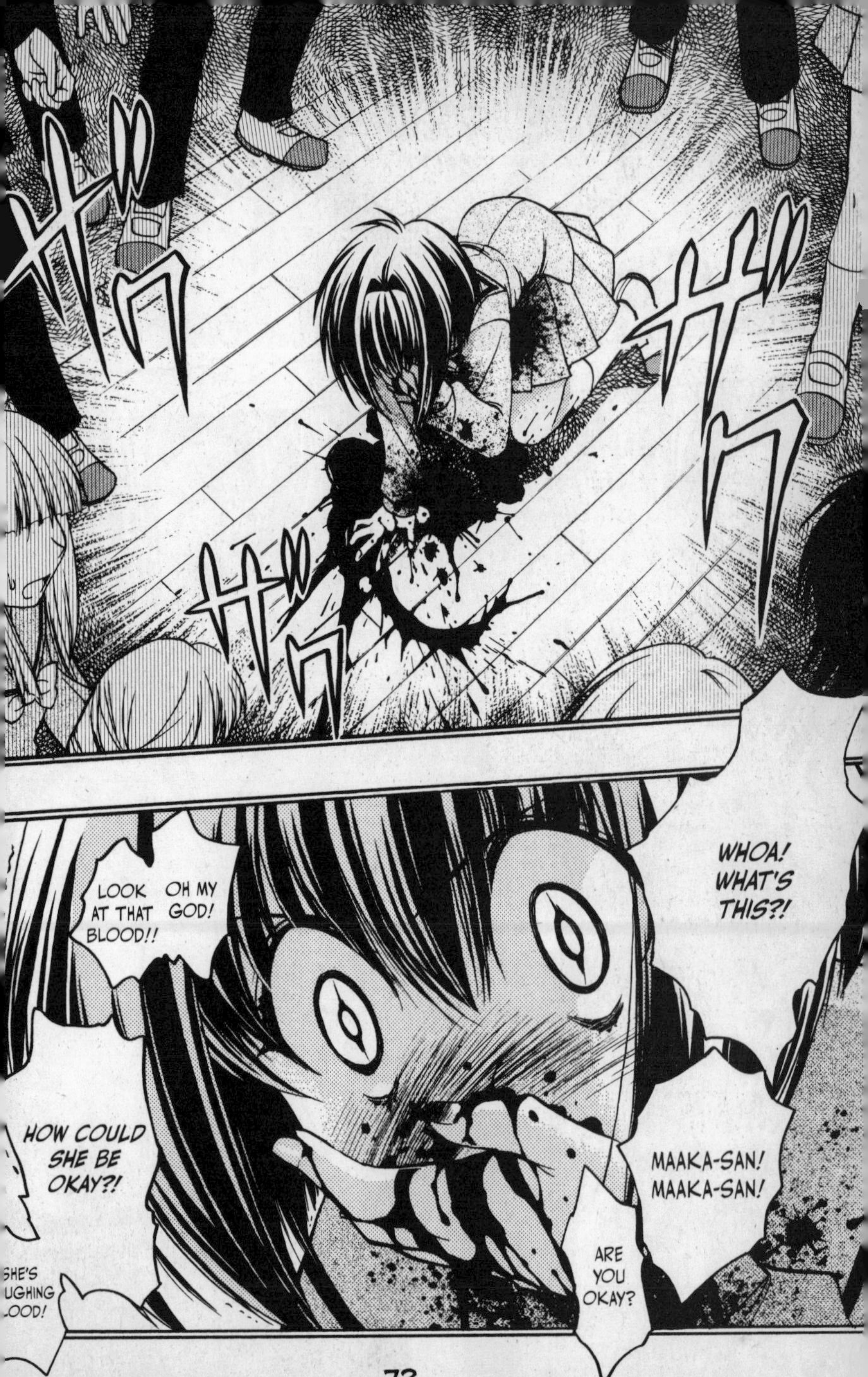
WHOA! WHAT'S THIS?!
OH MY GOD!
LOOK AT THAT BLOOD!!
MAAKA-SAN! MAAKA-SAN!
ARE YOU OKAY?
HOW COULD SHE BE OKAY?!

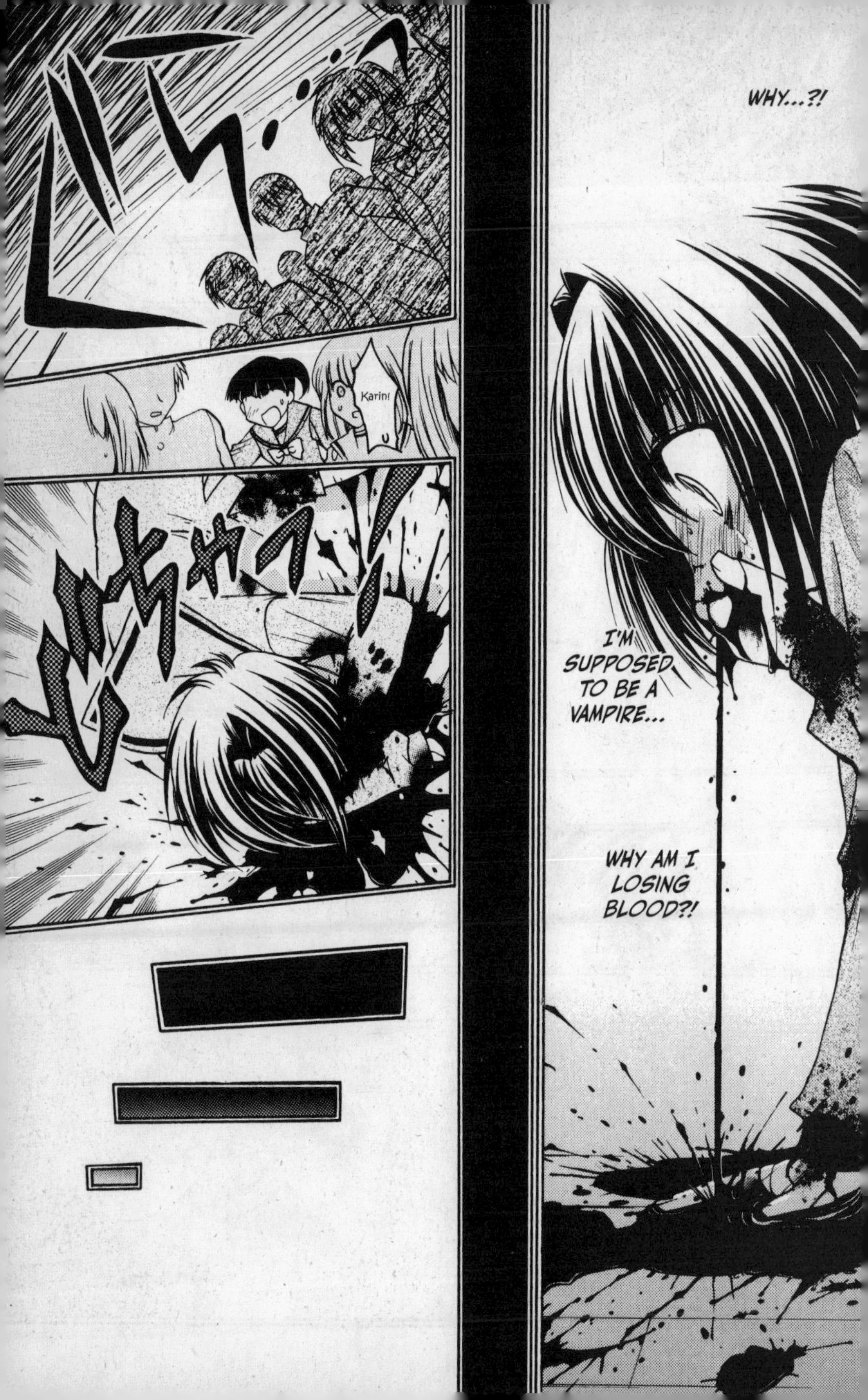
WHY...?!
I'M SUPPOSED TO BE A VAMPIRE...
WHY AM I LOSING BLOOD?!
Karin!

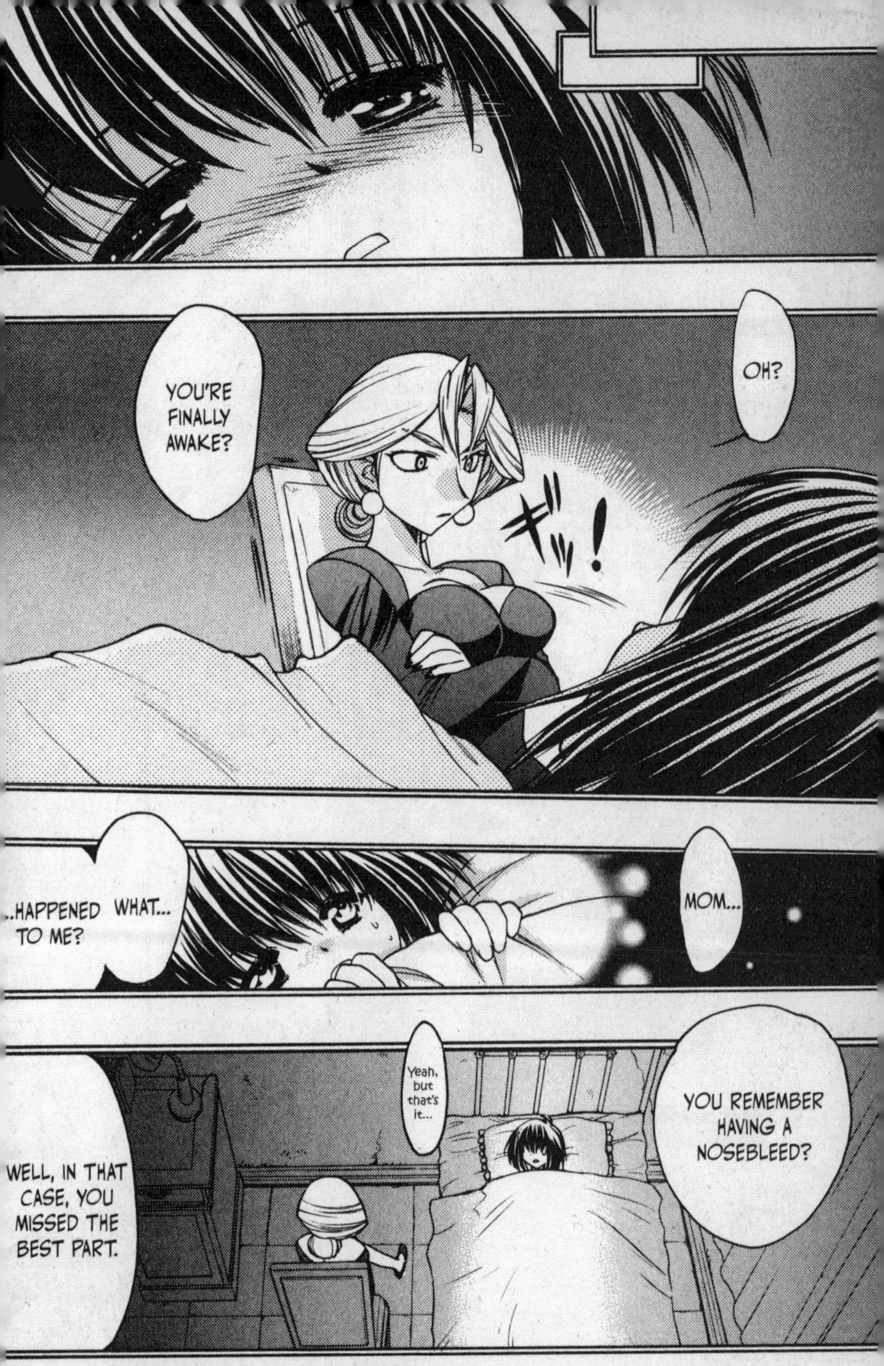
OH?
YOU'RE FINALLY AWAKE?
ギッ!
MOM...
WHAT...
..HAPPENED TO ME?
YOU REMEMBER HAVING A NOSEBLEED?
Yeah, but that's it...
WELL, IN THAT CASE, YOU MISSED THE BEST PART.

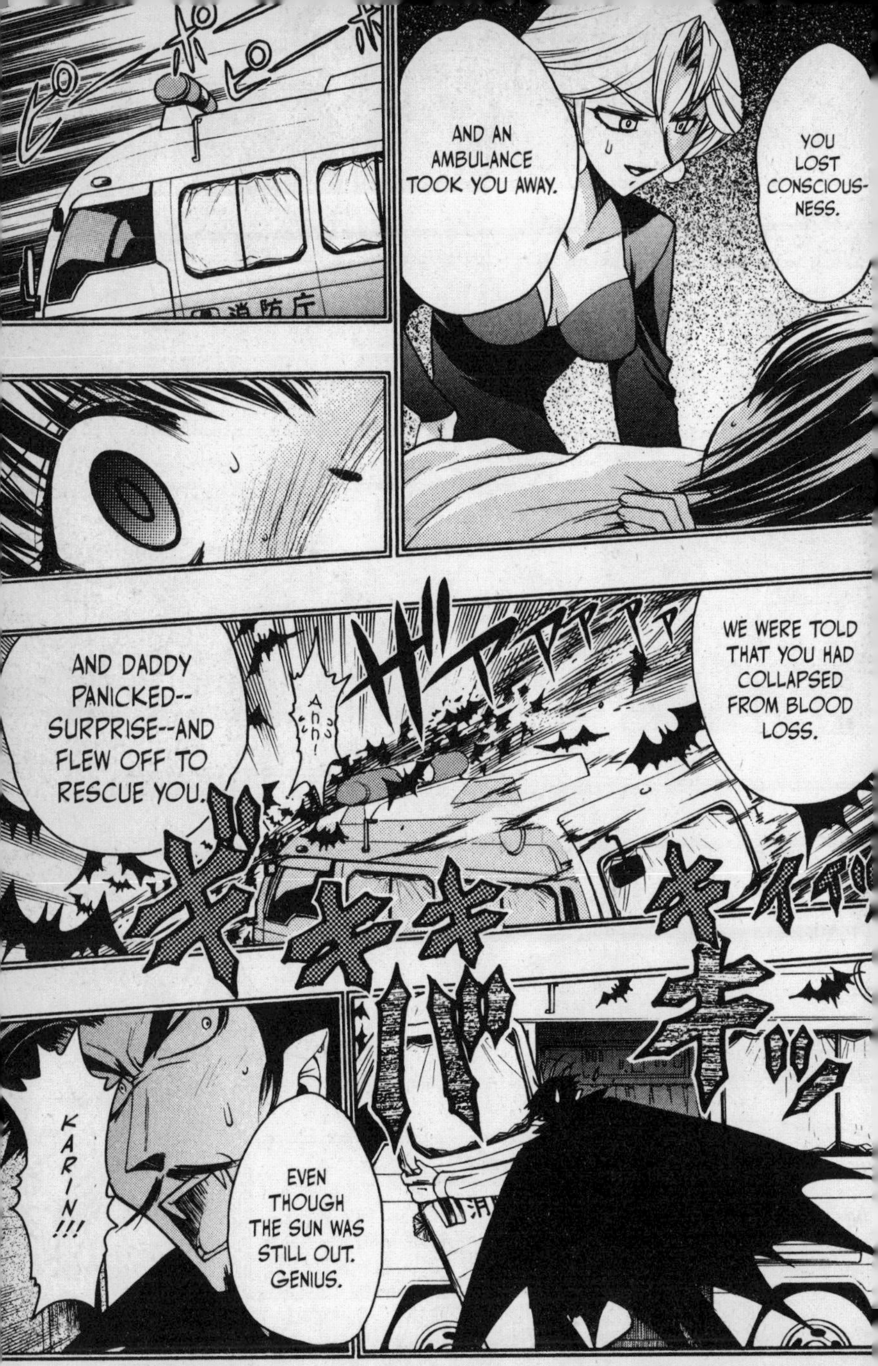
YOU LOST CONSCIOUSNESS.
AND AN AMBULANCE TOOK YOU AWAY.
WE WERE TOLD THAT YOU HAD COLLAPSED FROM BLOOD LOSS.
AND DADDY PANICKED--SURPRISE--AND FLEW OFF TO RESCUE YOU.
Ahh!
EVEN THOUGH THE SUN WAS STILL OUT. GENIUS.
KARIN!!!

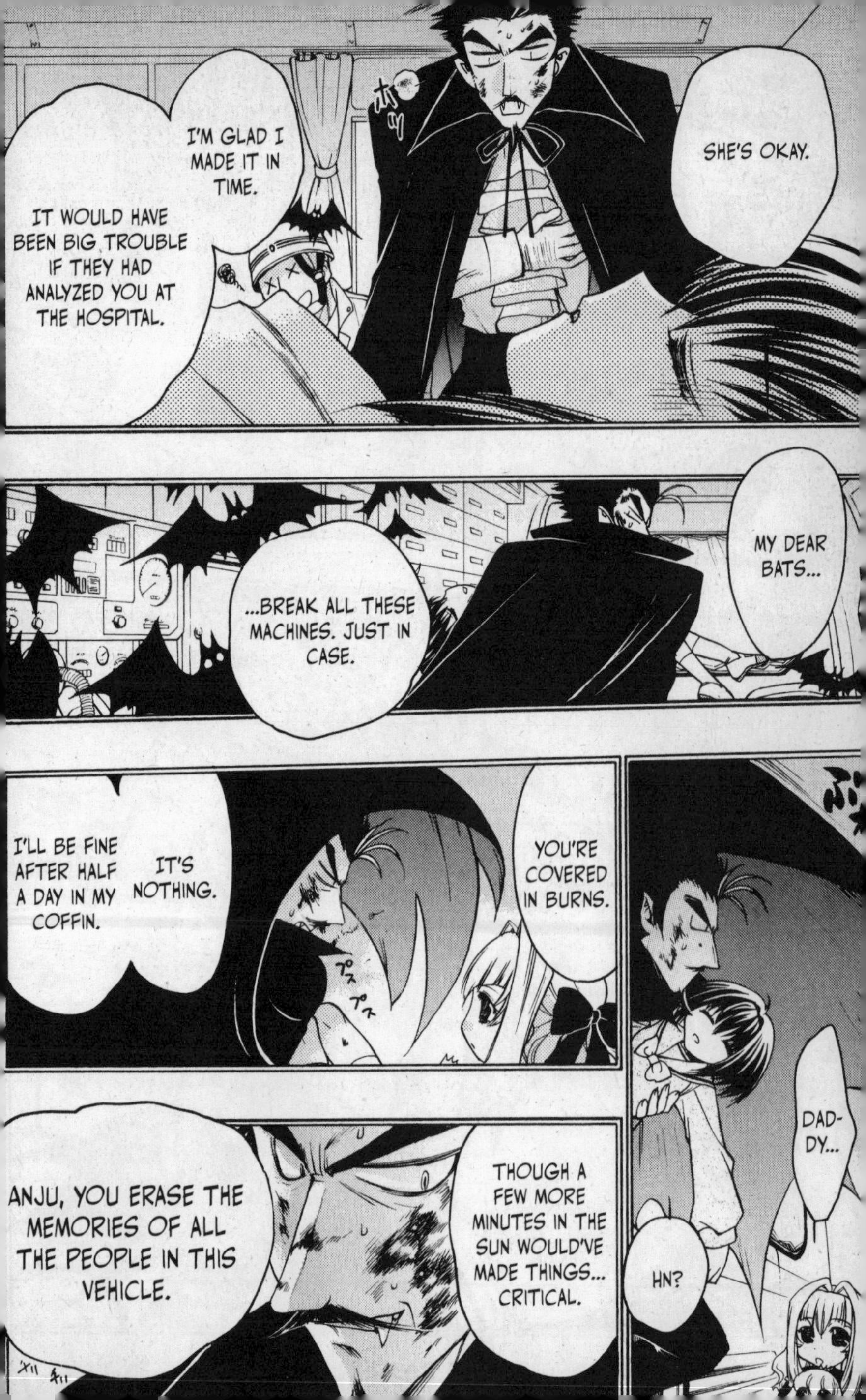
SHE'S OKAY.
I'M GLAD I MADE IT IN TIME.
IT WOULD HAVE BEEN BIG TROUBLE IF THEY HAD ANALYZED YOU AT THE HOSPITAL.
MY DEAR BATS...
...BREAK ALL THESE MACHINES. JUST IN CASE.
DAD-DY...
HN?
YOU'RE COVERED IN BURNS.
IT'S NOTHING.
I'LL BE FINE AFTER HALF A DAY IN MY COFFIN.
THOUGH A FEW MORE MINUTES IN THE SUN WOULD'VE MADE THINGS... CRITICAL.
ANJU, YOU ERASE THE MEMORIES OF ALL THE PEOPLE IN THIS VEHICLE.

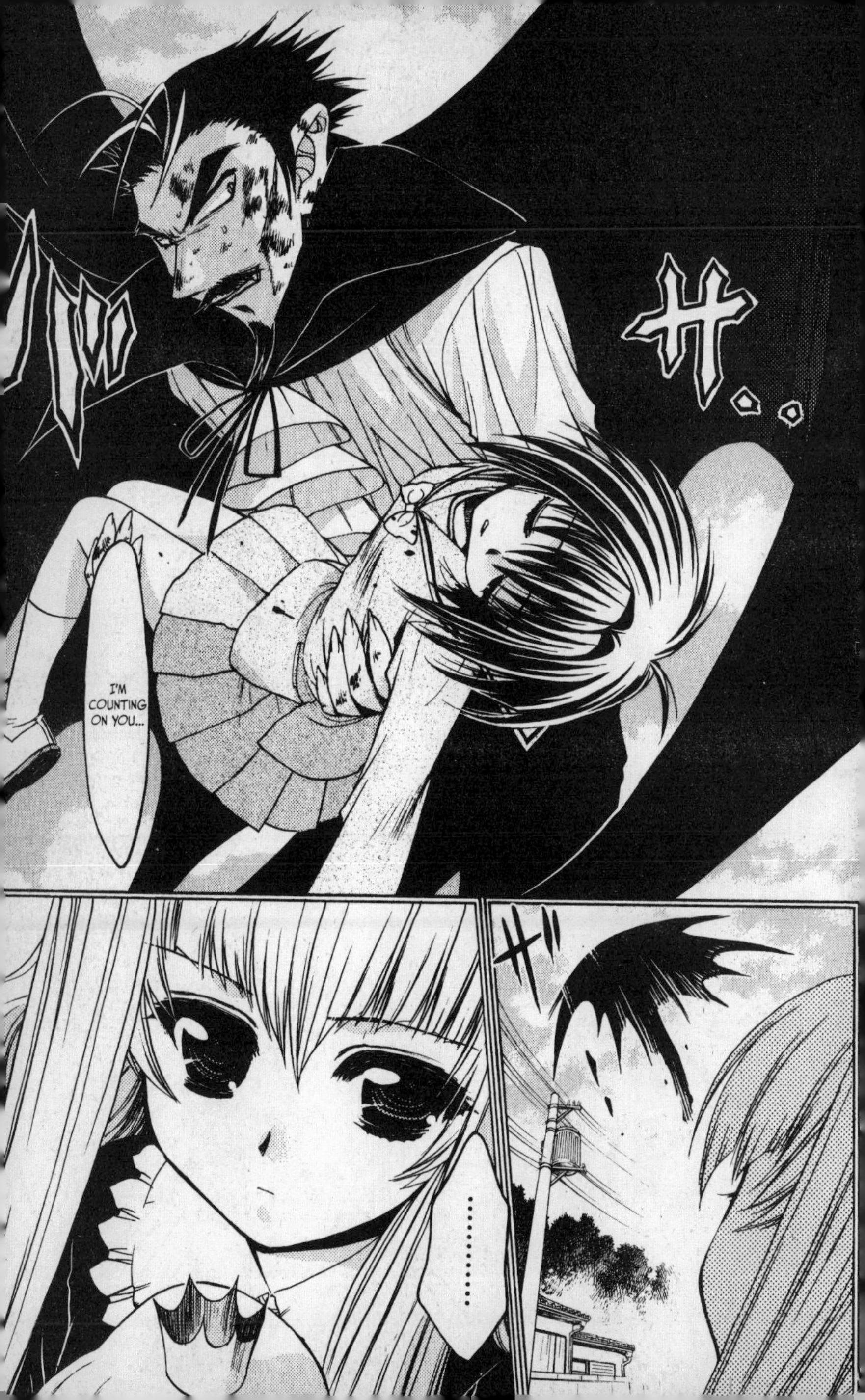
I'M COUNTING ON YOU...
......

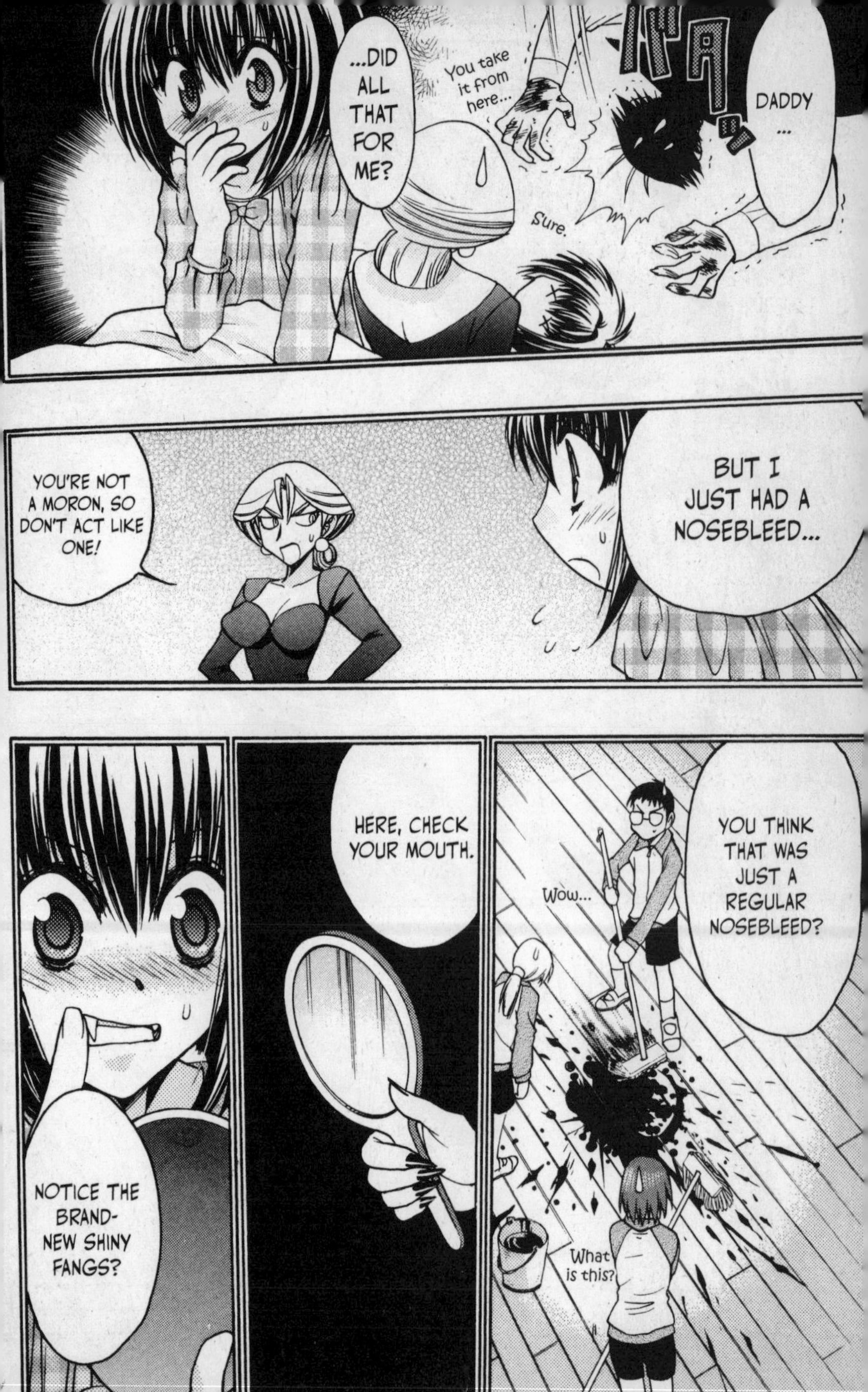
DADDY ...
You take it from here...
...DID ALL THAT FOR ME?
Sure.
BUT I JUST HAD A NOSEBLEED...
YOU'RE NOT A MORON, SO DON'T ACT LIKE ONE!
YOU THINK THAT WAS JUST A REGULAR NOSEBLEED?
Wow...
What is this?
HERE, CHECK YOUR MOUTH.
NOTICE THE BRAND-NEW SHINY FANGS?

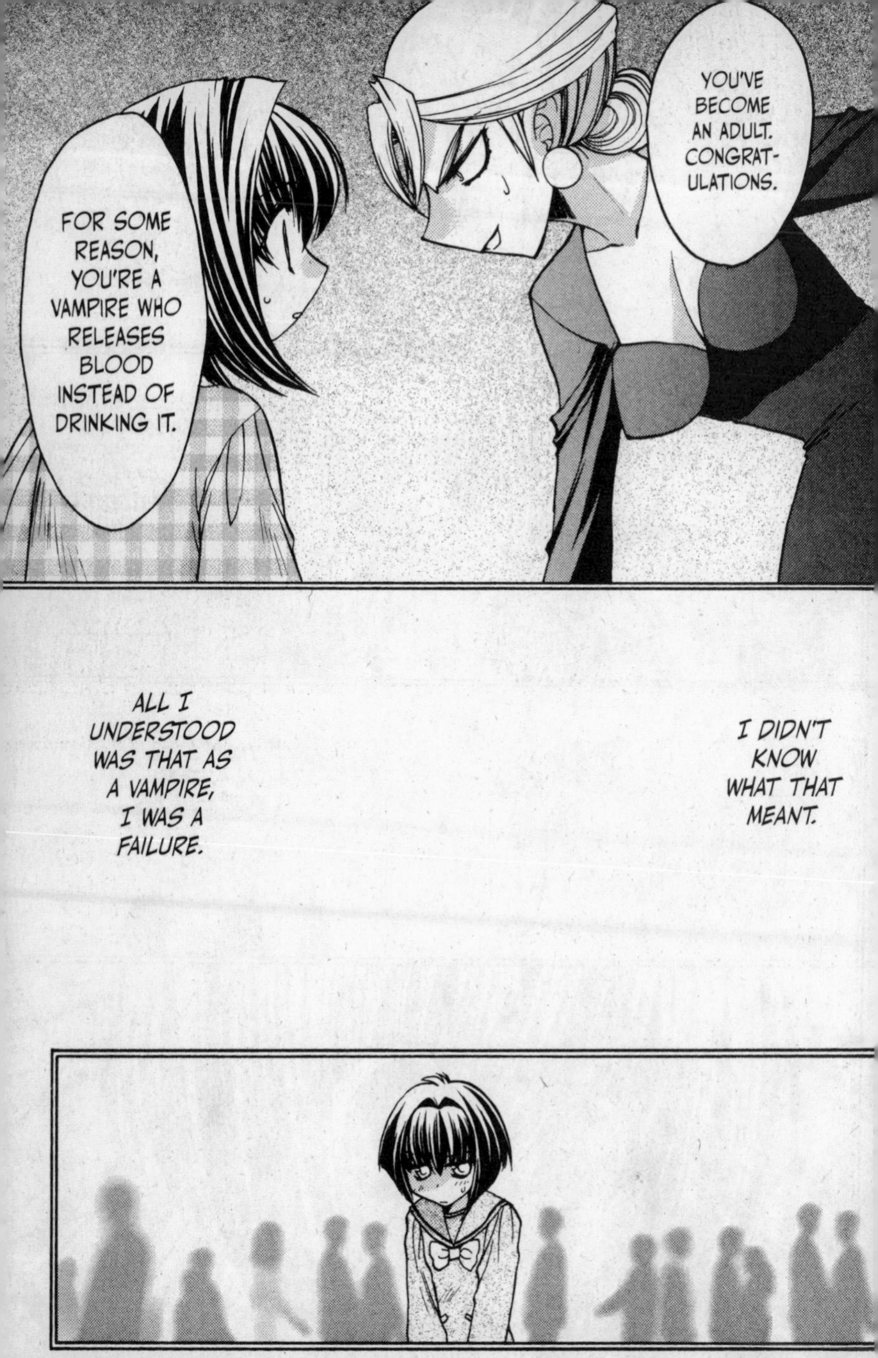
YOU'VE BECOME AN ADULT. CONGRAT-ULATIONS.
FOR SOME REASON, YOU'RE A VAMPIRE WHO RELEASES BLOOD INSTEAD OF DRINKING IT.
I DIDN'T KNOW WHAT THAT MEANT.
ALL I UNDERSTOOD WAS THAT AS A VAMPIRE, I WAS A FAILURE.

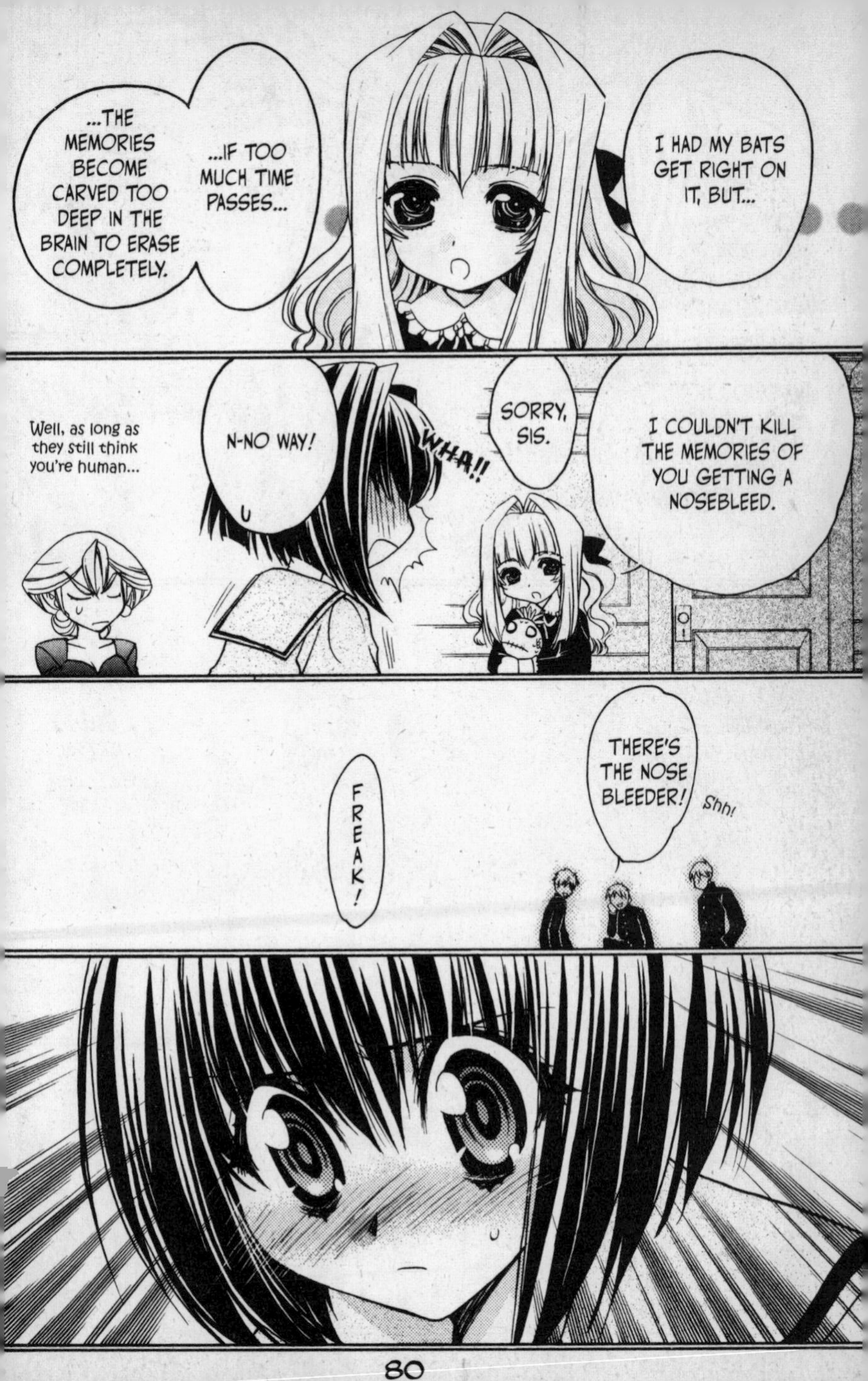
I HAD MY BATS GET RIGHT ON IT, BUT...
...IF TOO MUCH TIME PASSES...
...THE MEMORIES BECOME CARVED TOO DEEP IN THE BRAIN TO ERASE COMPLETELY.
I COULDN'T KILL THE MEMORIES OF YOU GETTING A NOSEBLEED.
SORRY, SIS.
WHA!!
N-NO WAY!
Well, as long as they still think you're human...
THERE'S THE NOSE BLEEDER!
Shh!
FREAK!

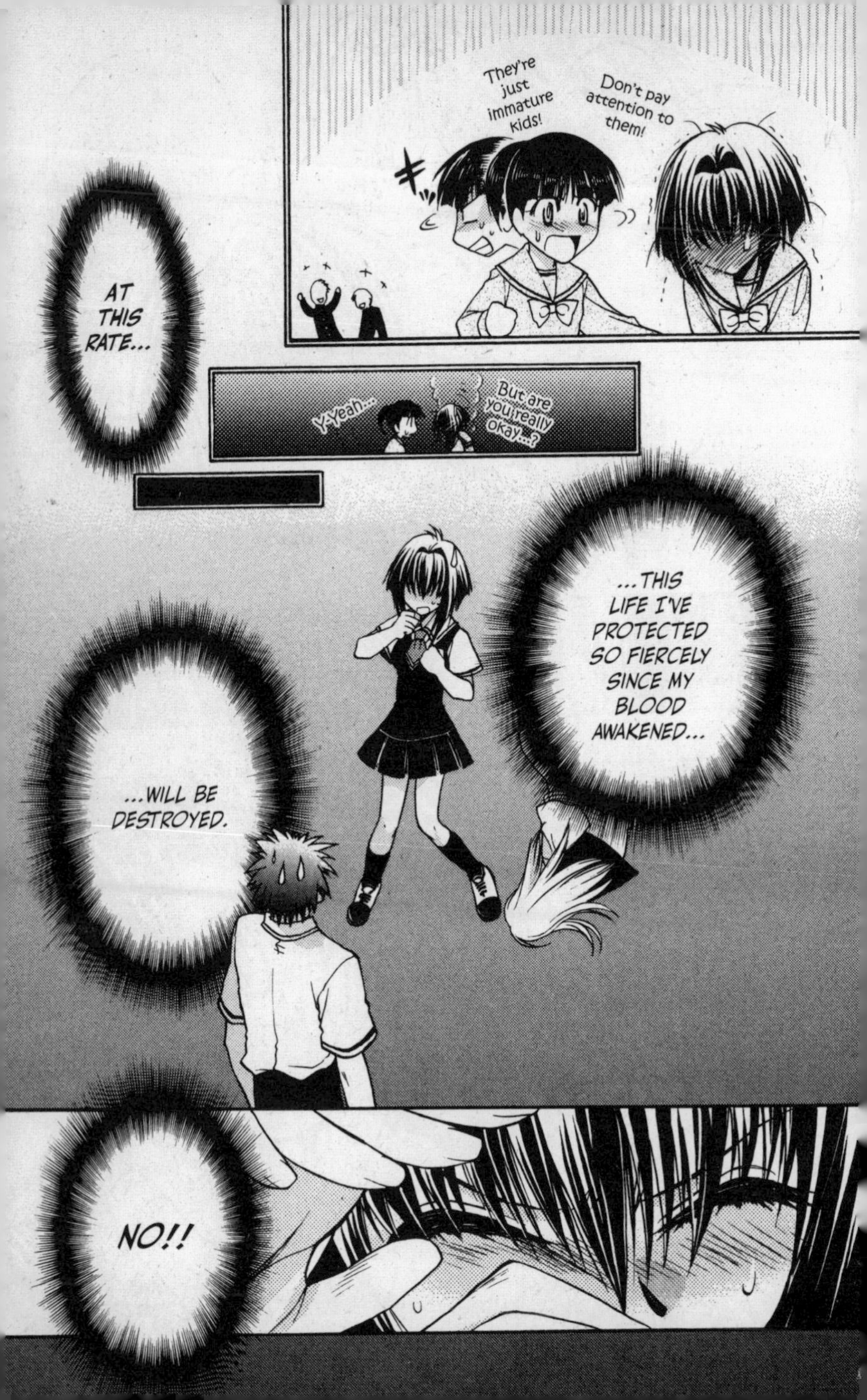
Don't pay attention to them!
They're just immature kids!
AT THIS RATE...
But are you really okay...?
Y-Yeah...
...THIS LIFE I'VE PROTECTED SO FIERCELY SINCE MY BLOOD AWAKENED...
...WILL BE DESTROYED.
NO!!

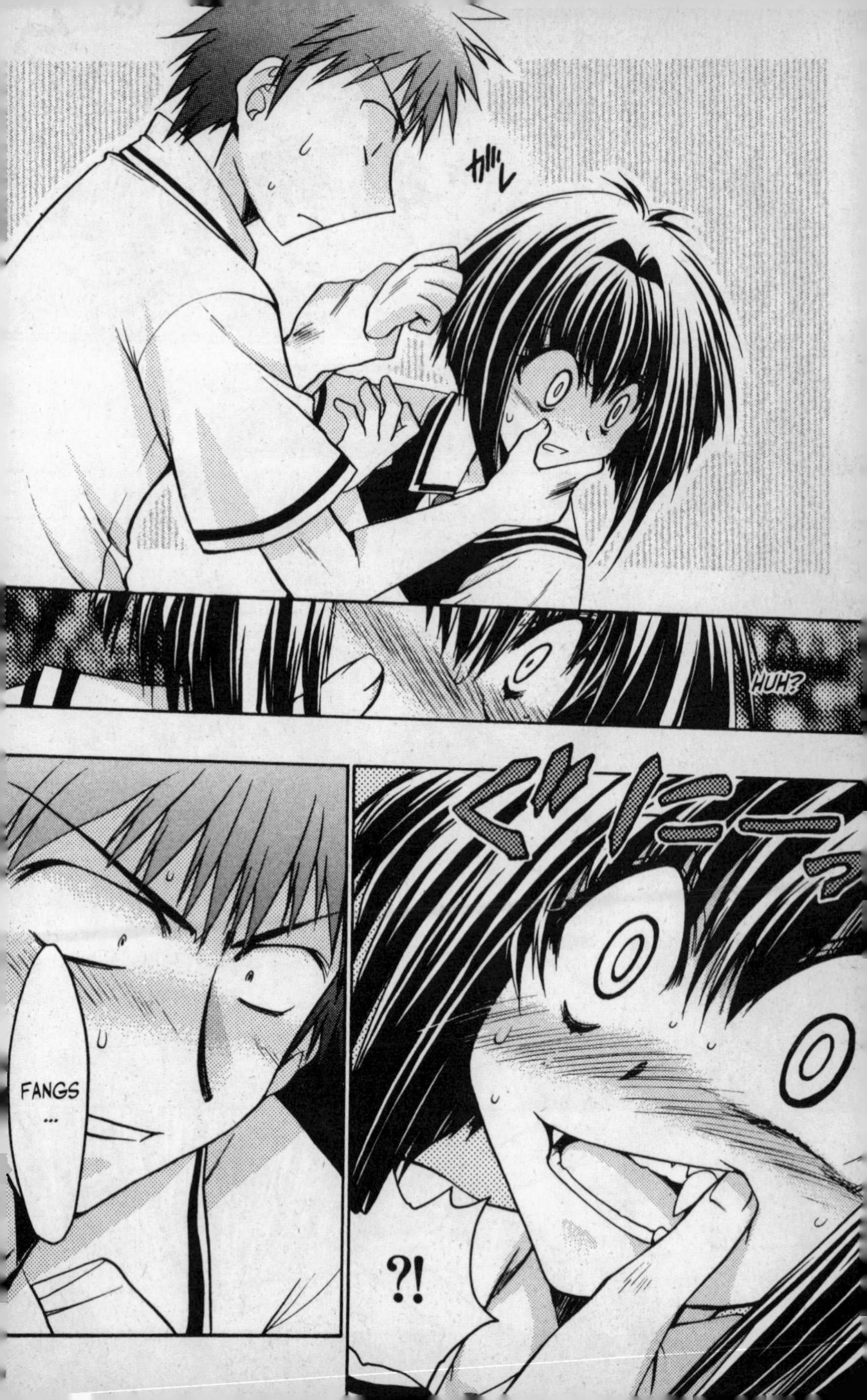
HUH?
?!
FANGS ...

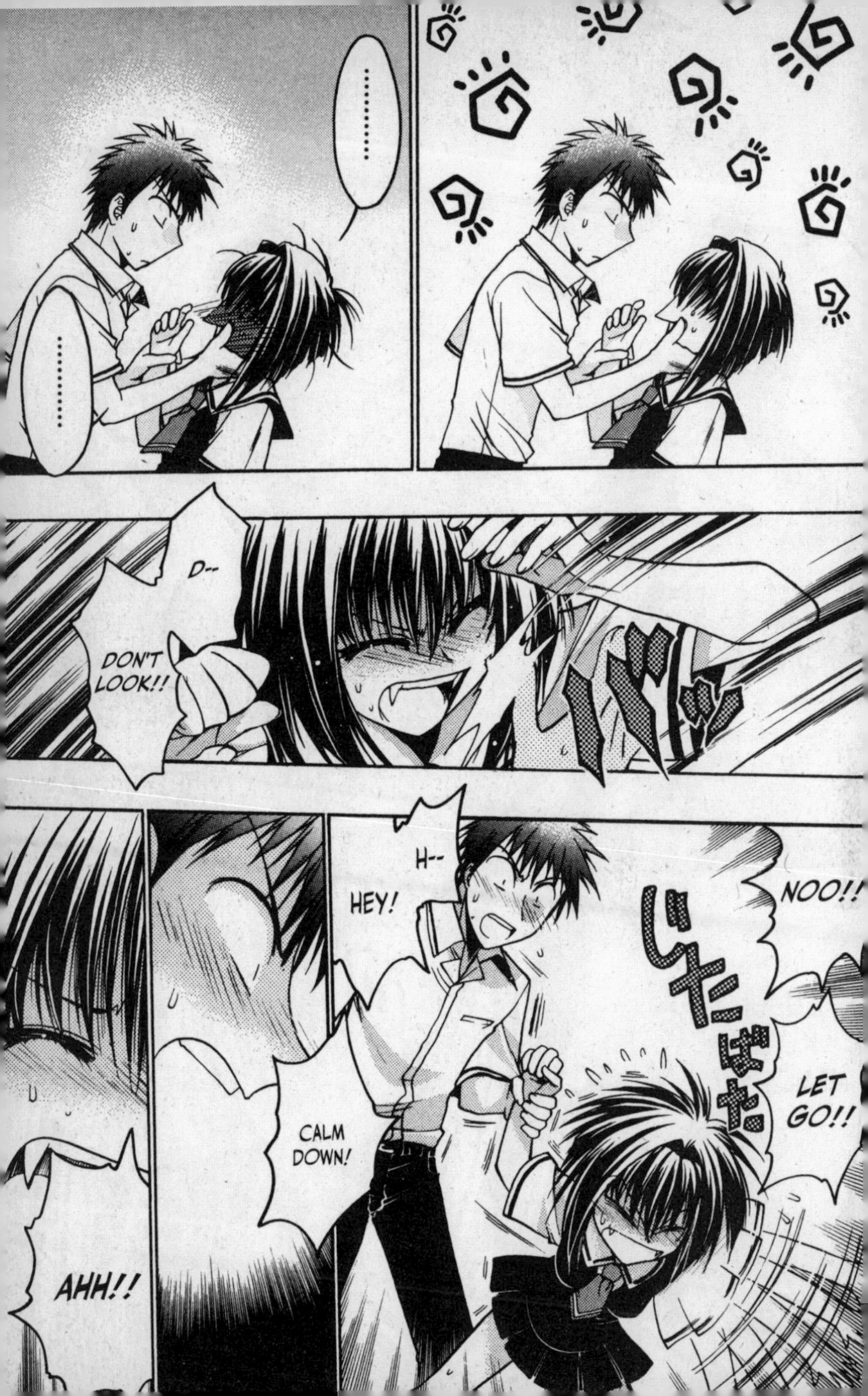
......
......
D--
DON'T LOOK!!
バッ
NOO!!
じたばた
LET GO!!
H--
HEY!
CALM DOWN!
AHH!!

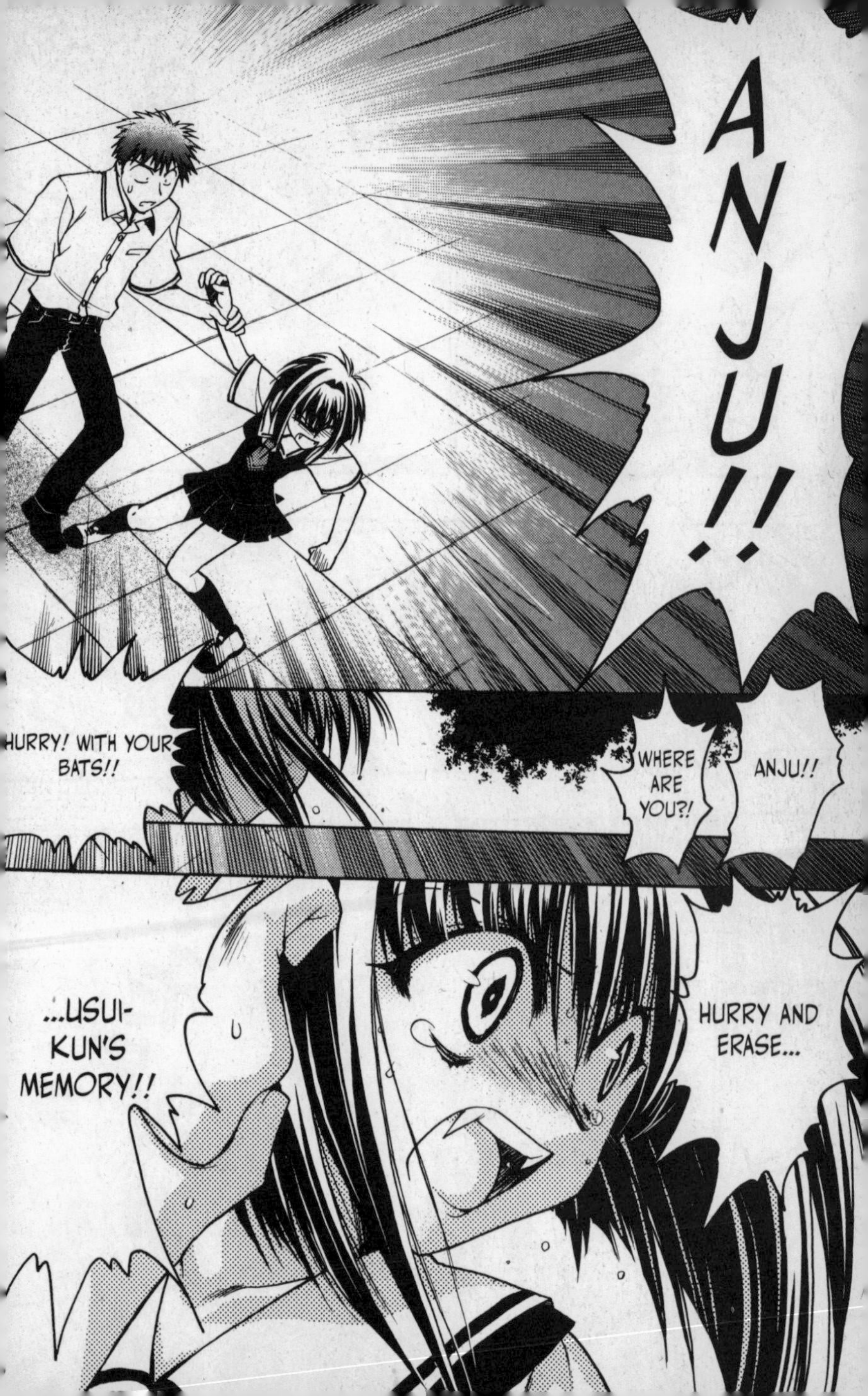
ANJU!!
ANJU!!
WHERE ARE YOU?!
HURRY! WITH YOUR BATS!!
HURRY AND ERASE...
...USUI-KUN'S MEMORY!!

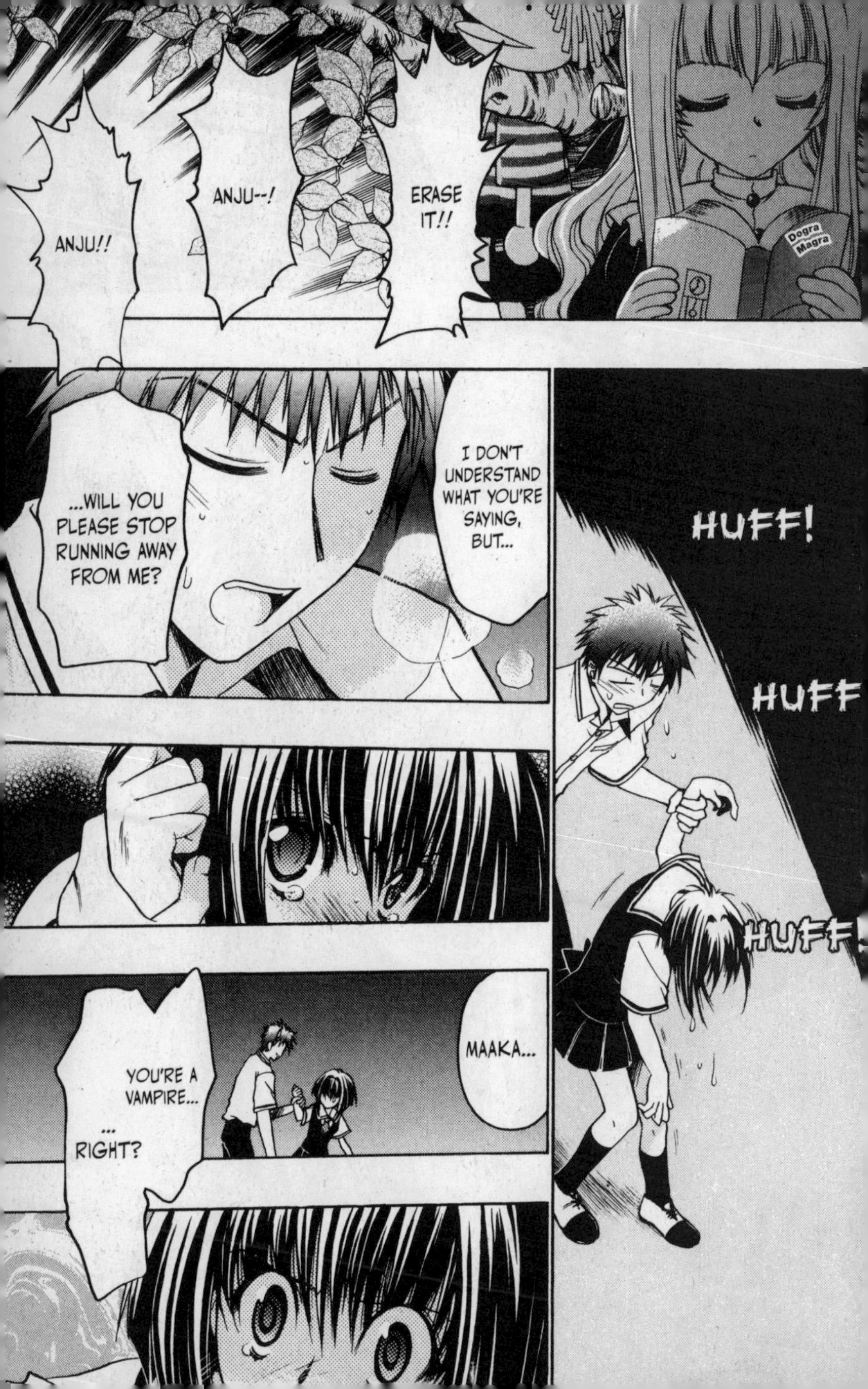
Dogra Magra
ERASE IT!!
ANJU--!
ANJU!!
HUFF!
HUFF
HUFF!
I DON'T UNDERSTAND WHAT YOU'RE SAYING, BUT...
...WILL YOU PLEASE STOP RUNNING AWAY FROM ME?
MAAKA...
YOU'RE A VAMPIRE... ...RIGHT?

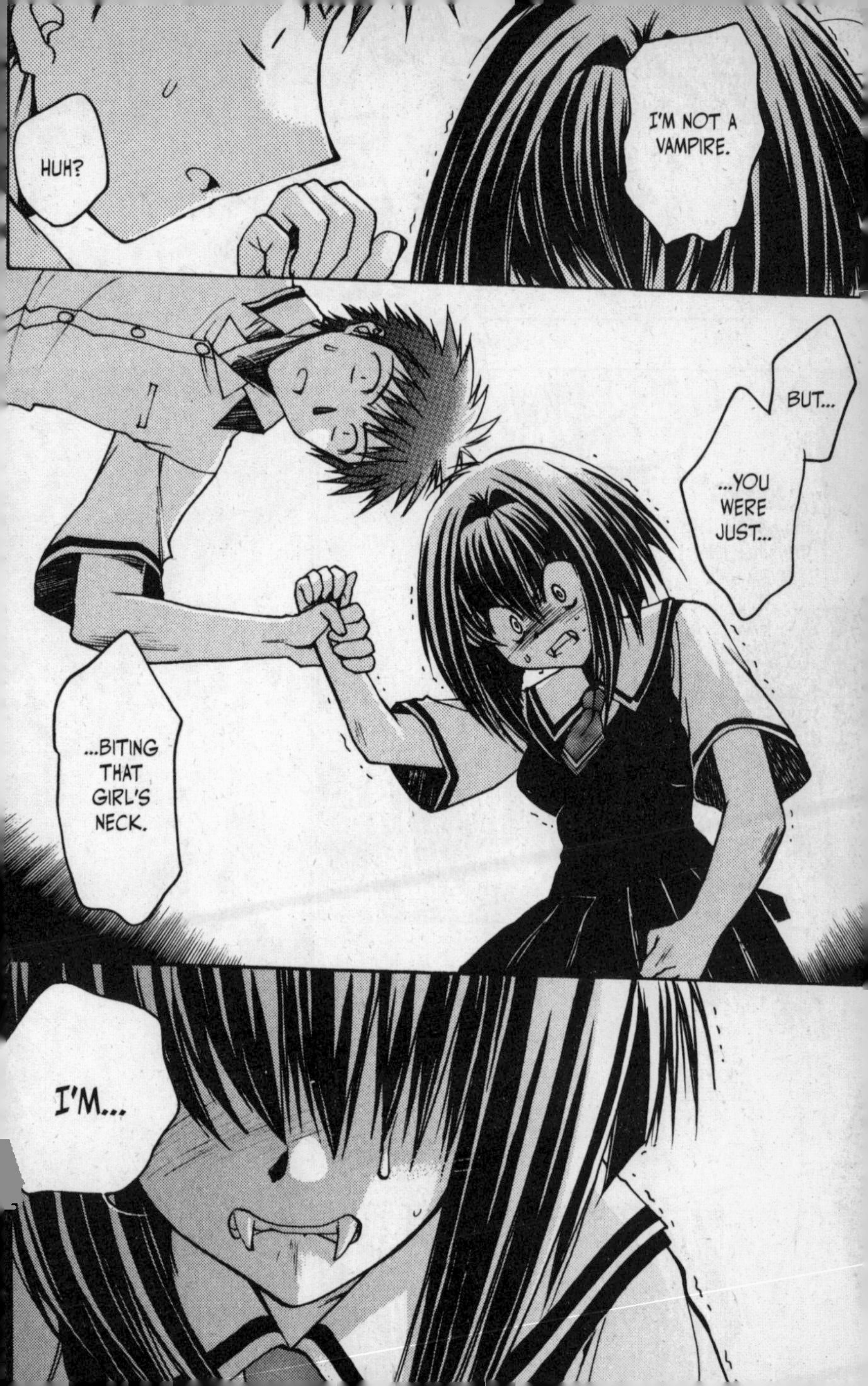
I'M NOT A VAMPIRE.
HUH?
BUT...
...YOU WERE JUST...
...BITING THAT GIRL'S NECK.
I'M...

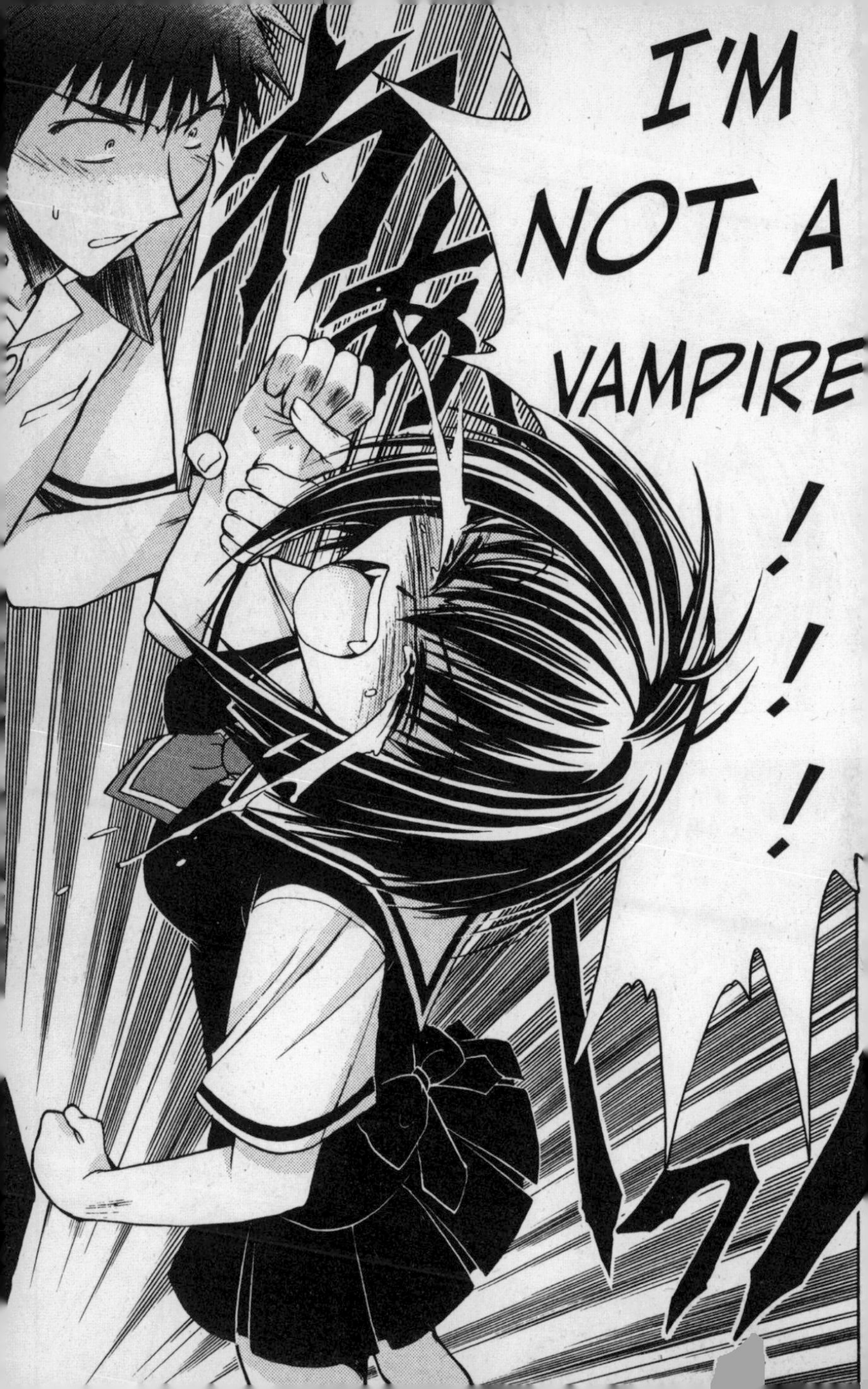
I'M NOT A VAMPIRE!!!

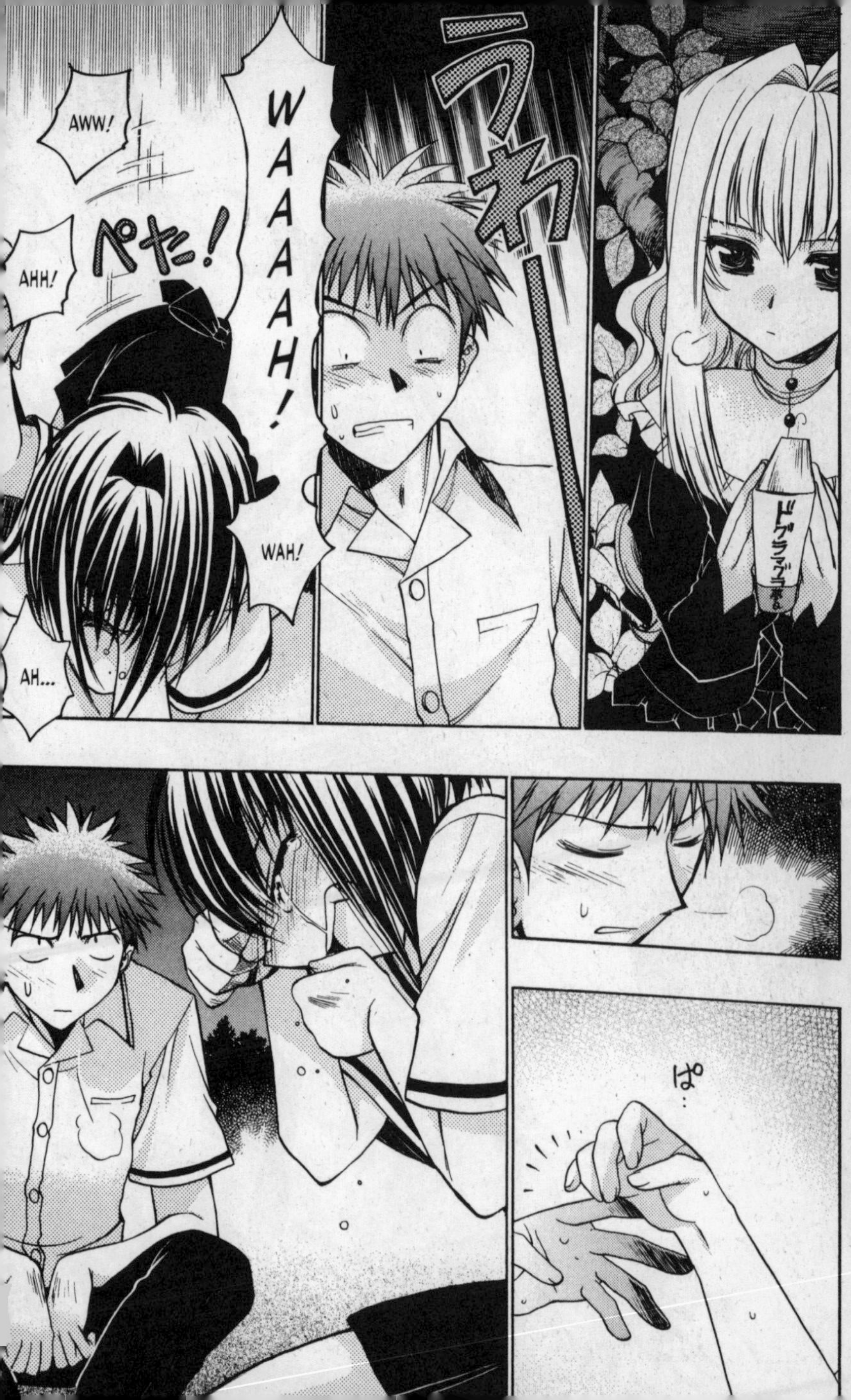
ドグラマグラ
うわ
WAAAAAH!
WAH!
AWW!
ぺた!
AHH!
AH...
ぱ..

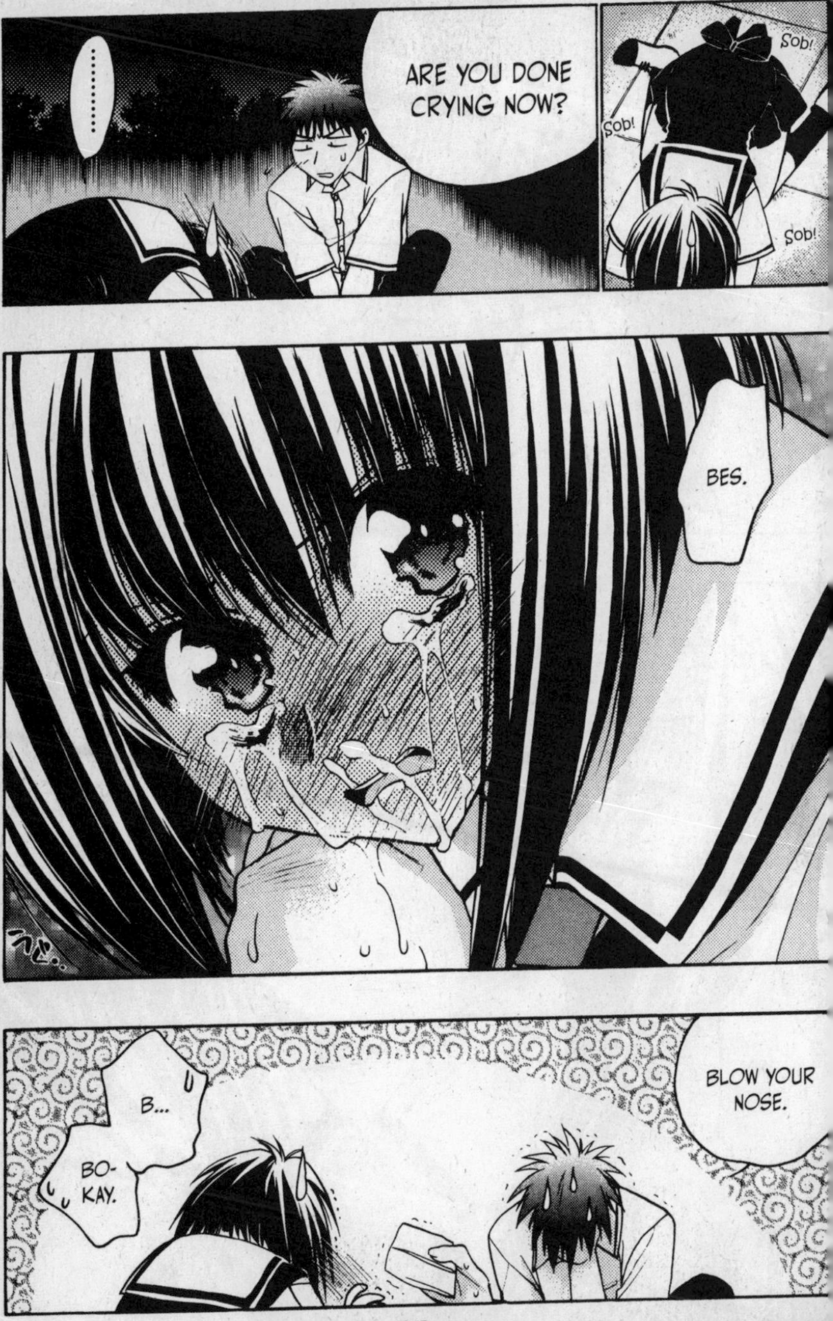
Sob!
Sob!
Sob!
ARE YOU DONE CRYING NOW?
......
BES.
うぐ..
BLOW YOUR NOSE.
B...
BO-KAY.

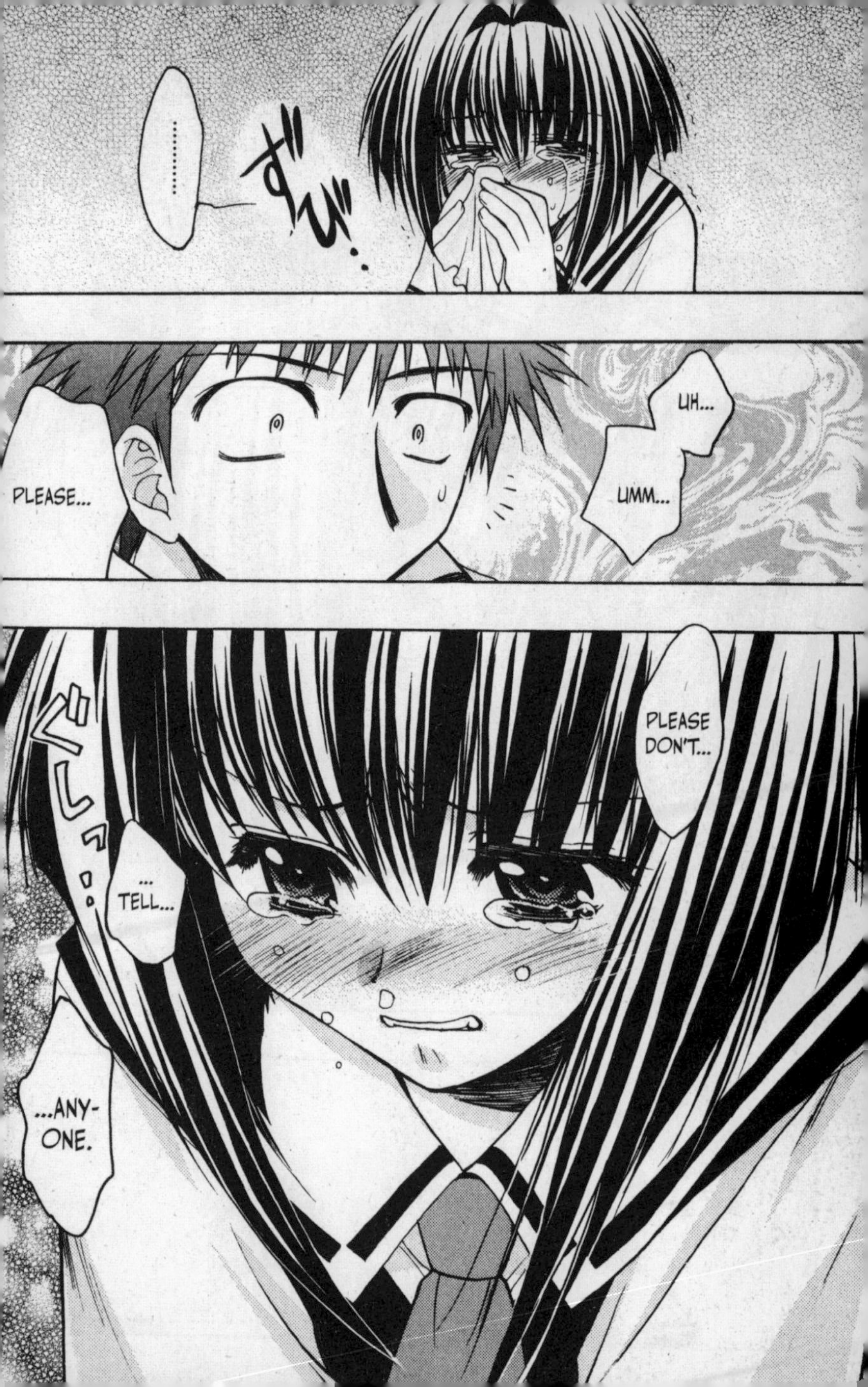
......
UH...
UMM...
PLEASE...
PLEASE DON'T...
... TELL...
...ANY-ONE.

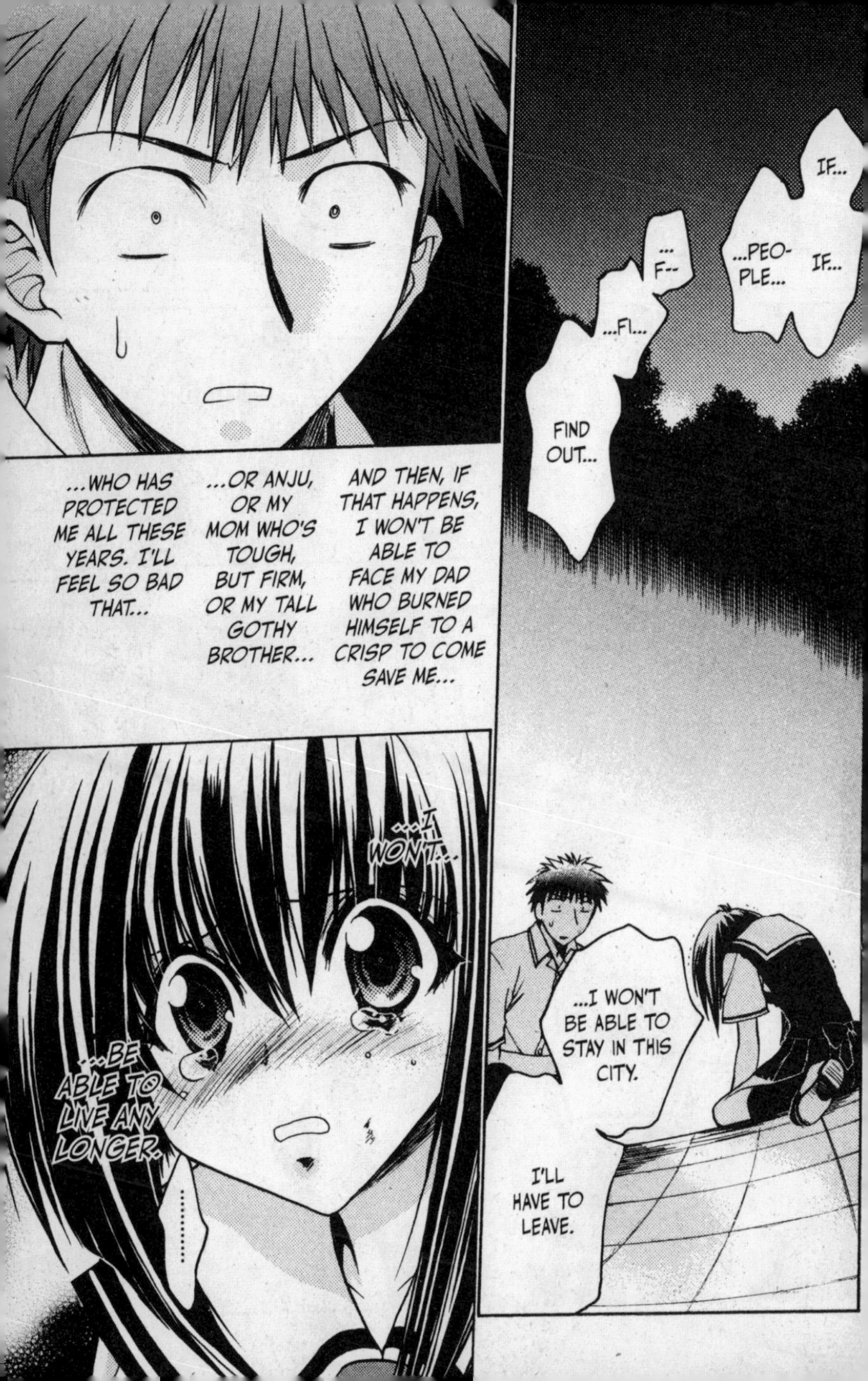
IF...
IF...
...PEO-PLE...
...F--
...FI...
FIND OUT...
...I WON'T BE ABLE TO STAY IN THIS CITY.
I'LL HAVE TO LEAVE.
AND THEN, IF THAT HAPPENS, I WON'T BE ABLE TO FACE MY DAD WHO BURNED HIMSELF TO A CRISP TO COME SAVE ME...
...OR ANJU, OR MY MOM WHO'S TOUGH, BUT FIRM, OR MY TALL GOTHY BROTHER...
...WHO HAS PROTECTED ME ALL THESE YEARS. I'LL FEEL SO BAD THAT...
...I WON'T...
...BE ABLE TO LIVE ANY LONGER.

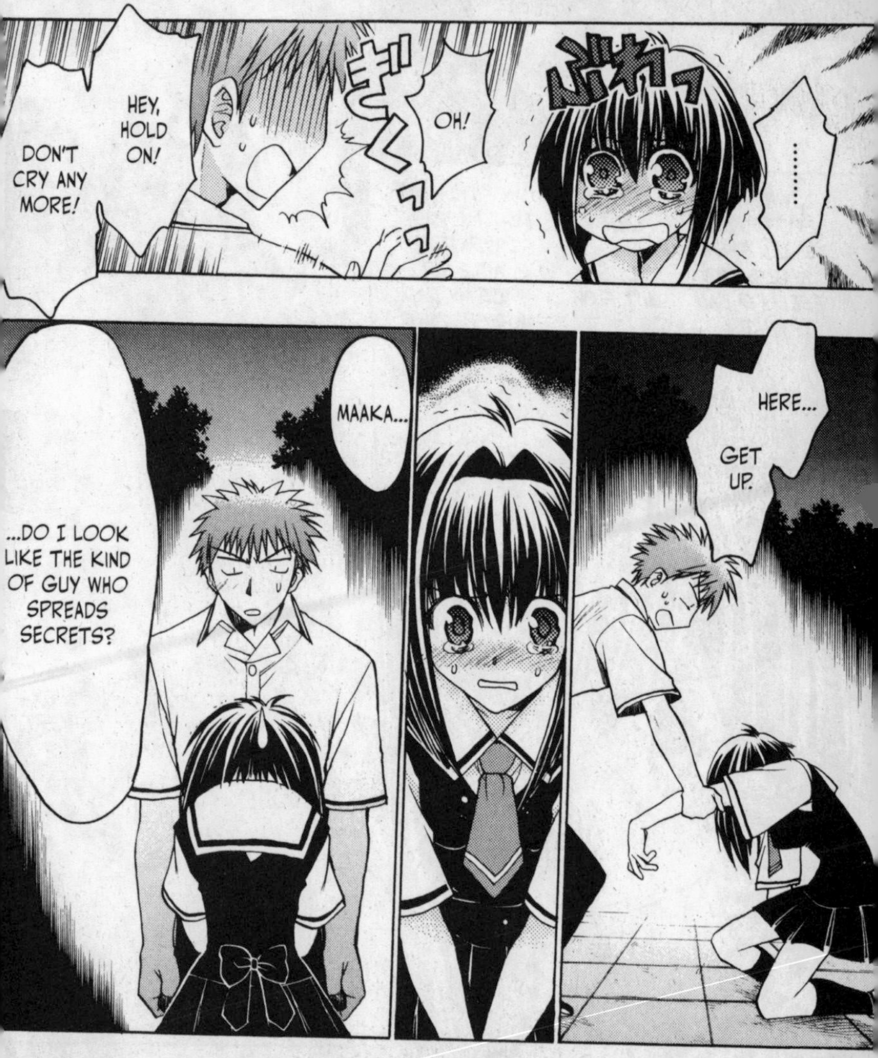
......
ぶわっ
OH!
ぎくっ
HEY, HOLD ON!
DON'T CRY ANY MORE!
HERE...
GET UP.
MAAKA...
...DO I LOOK LIKE THE KIND OF GUY WHO SPREADS SECRETS?

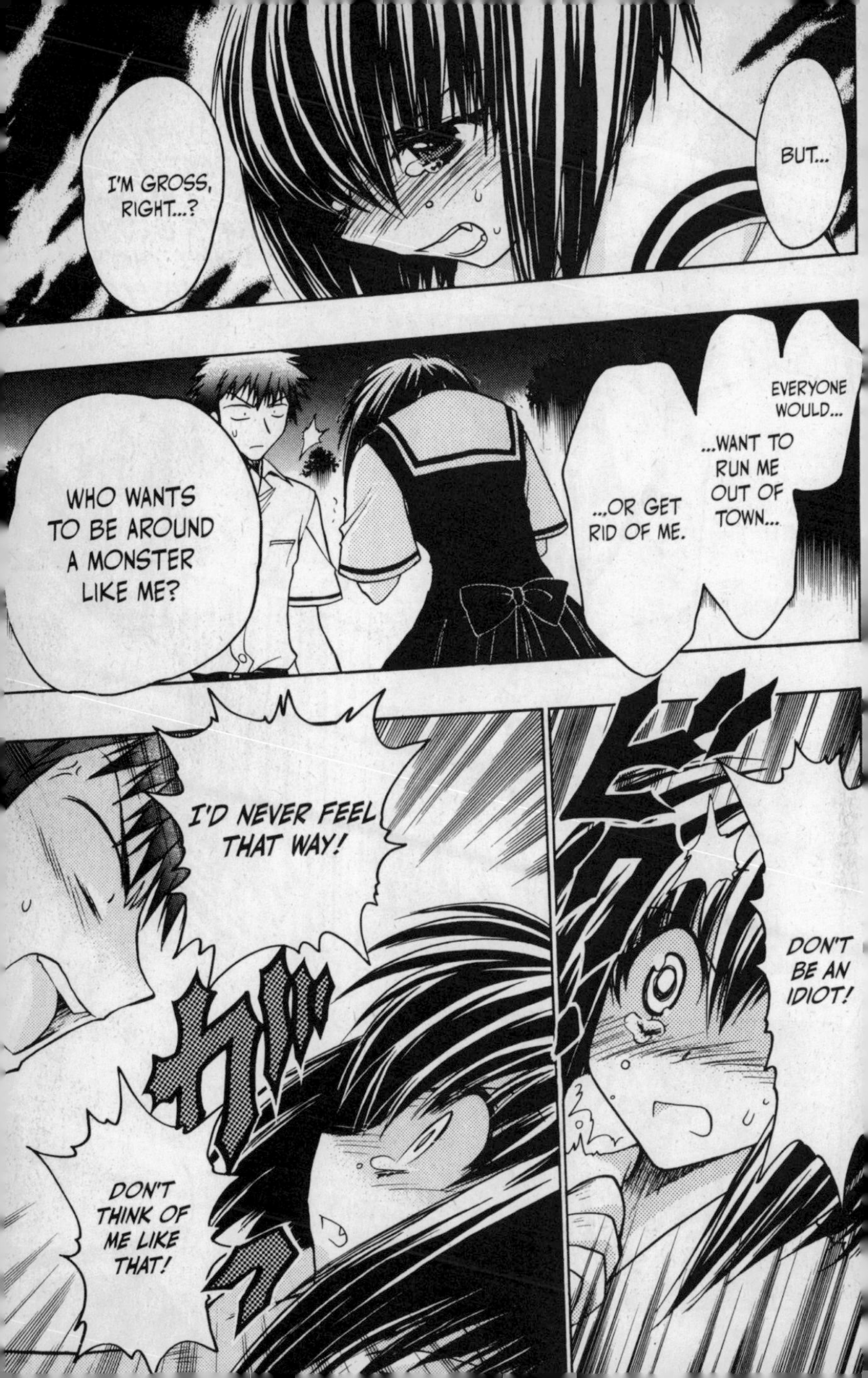
BUT...
I'M GROSS, RIGHT...?
EVERYONE WOULD...
...WANT TO RUN ME OUT OF TOWN...
...OR GET RID OF ME.
WHO WANTS TO BE AROUND A MONSTER LIKE ME?
DON'T BE AN IDIOT!
I'D NEVER FEEL THAT WAY!
DON'T THINK OF ME LIKE THAT!

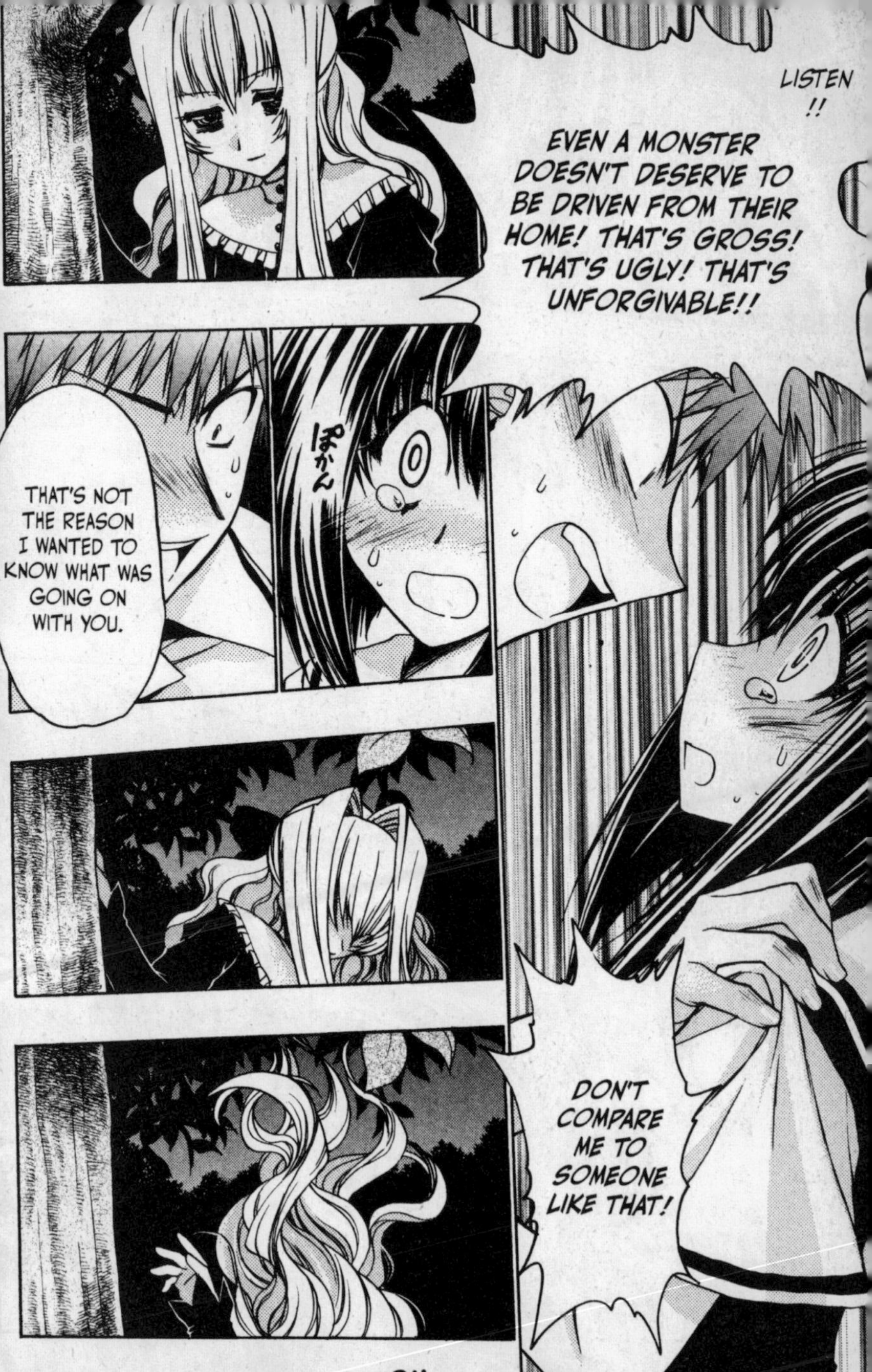
LISTEN !!
EVEN A MONSTER DOESN'T DESERVE TO BE DRIVEN FROM THEIR HOME! THAT'S GROSS! THAT'S UGLY! THAT'S UNFORGIVABLE!!
DON'T COMPARE ME TO SOMEONE LIKE THAT!
ぽかん
THAT'S NOT THE REASON I WANTED TO KNOW WHAT WAS GOING ON WITH YOU.

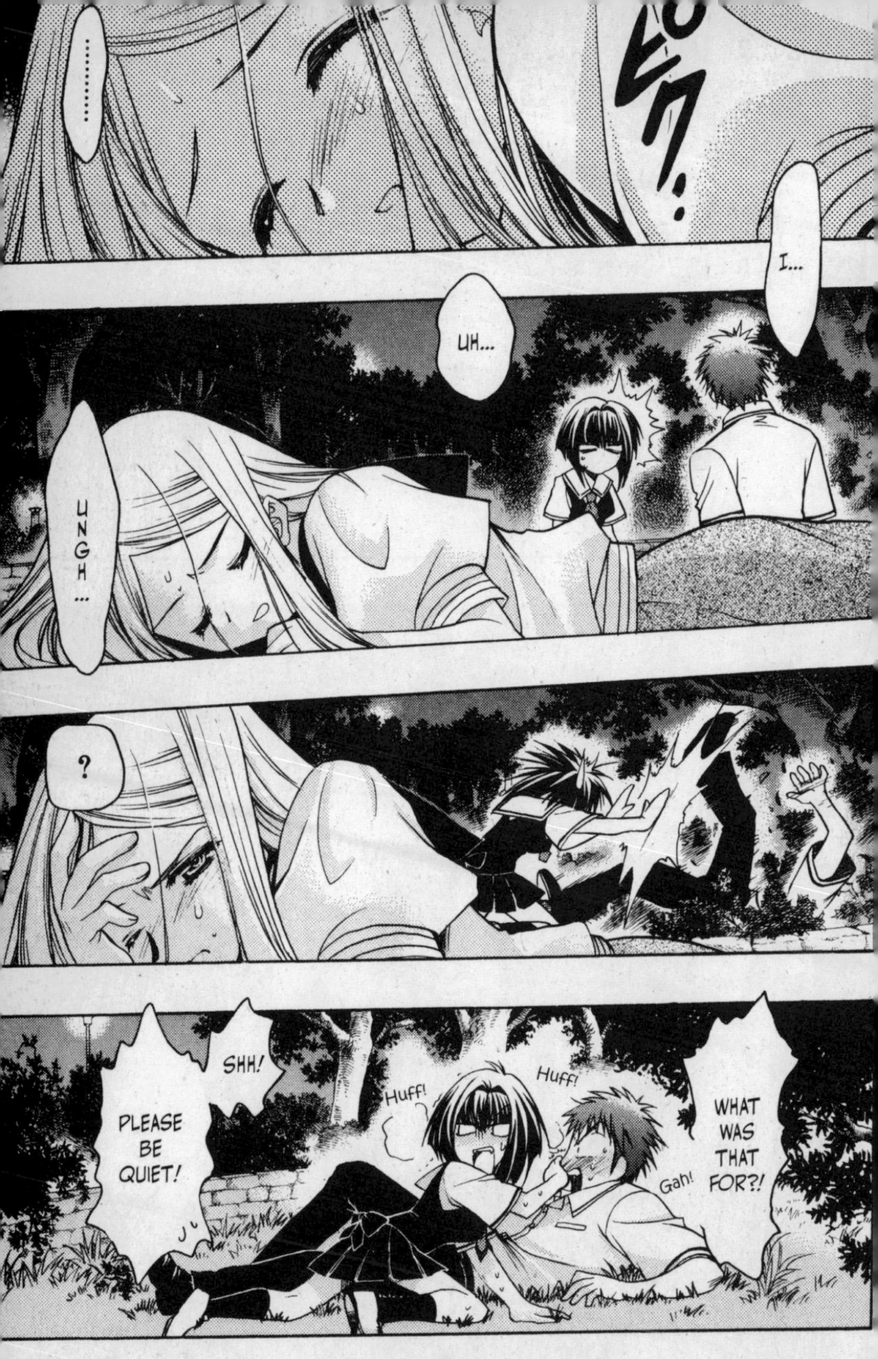
......
I...
UH...
UNGH...
?
WHAT WAS THAT FOR?!
Gah!
Huff!
Huff!
SHH!
PLEASE BE QUIET!

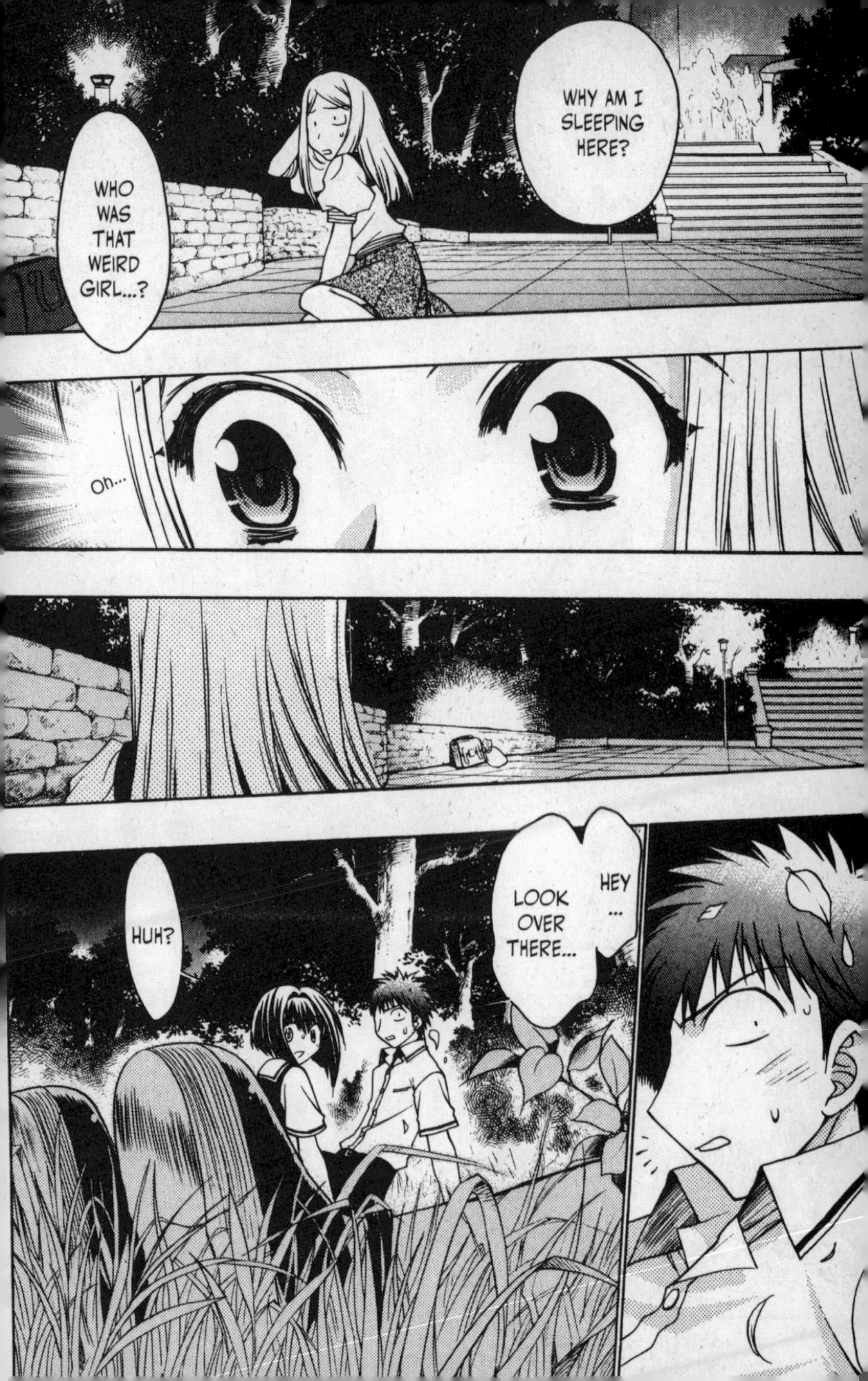
WHY AM I SLEEPING HERE?
WHO WAS THAT WEIRD GIRL...?
Oh...
HEY ... LOOK OVER THERE...
HUH?

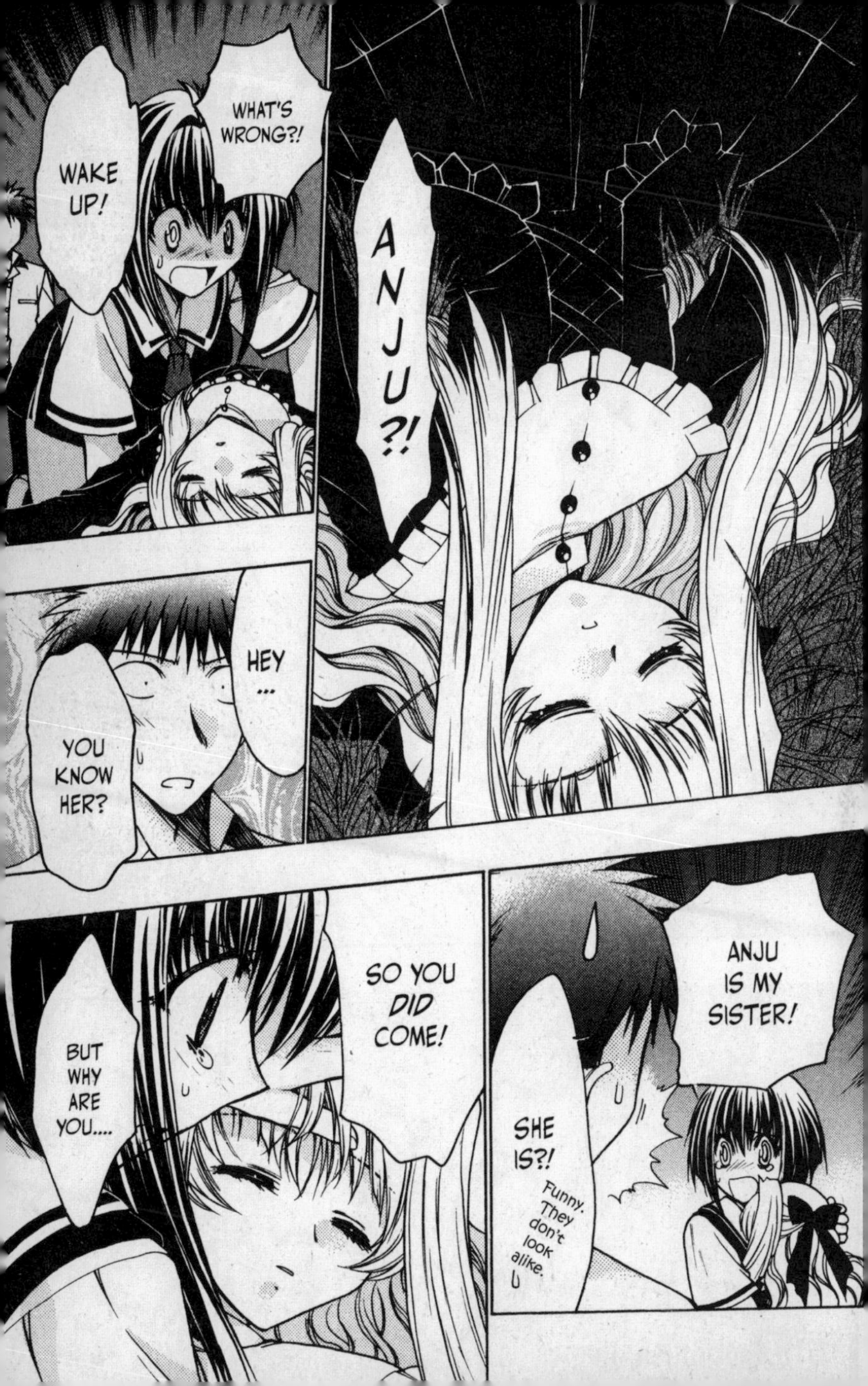
ANJU?!
WHAT'S WRONG?!
WAKE UP!
HEY ...
YOU KNOW HER?
ANJU IS MY SISTER!
SHE IS?!
Funny. They don't look alike.
SO YOU DID COME!
BUT WHY ARE YOU....

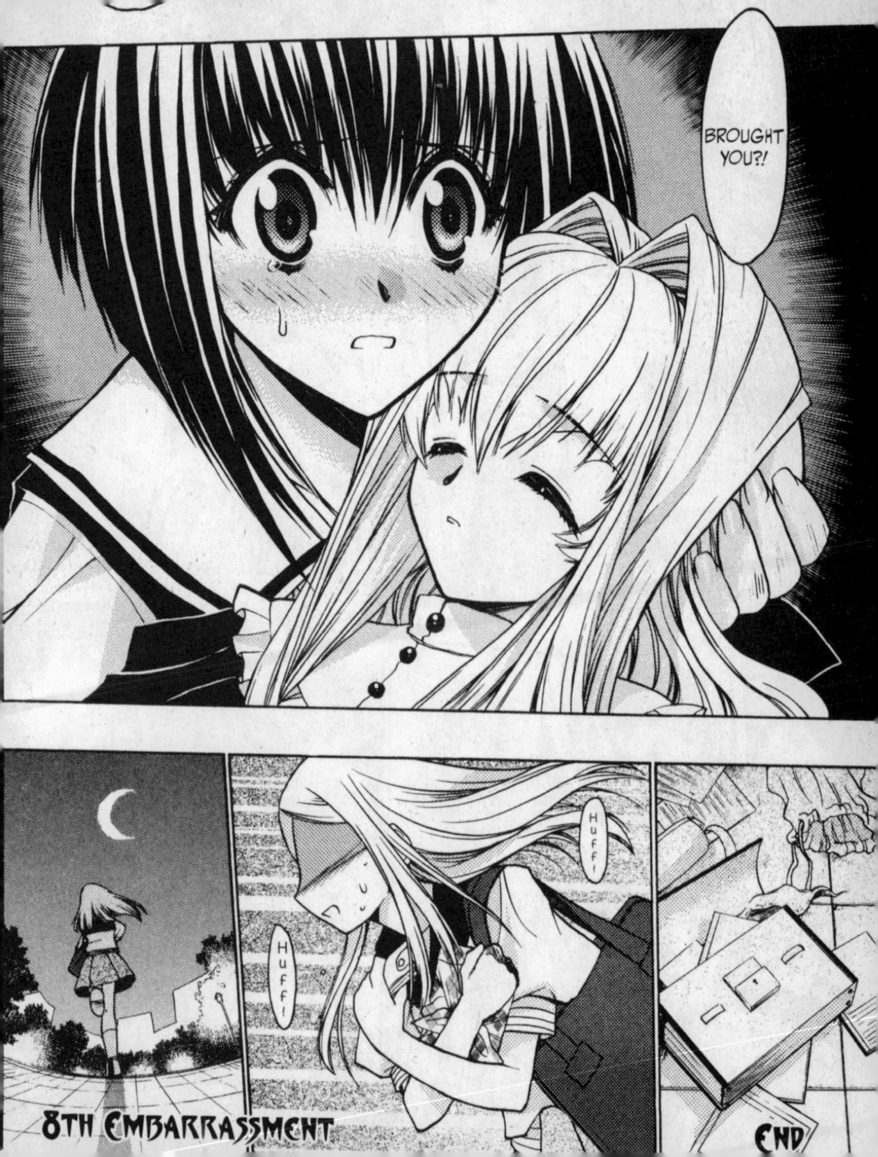
BROUGHT YOU?!
Huff!
Huff!
8TH EMBARRASSMENT
END

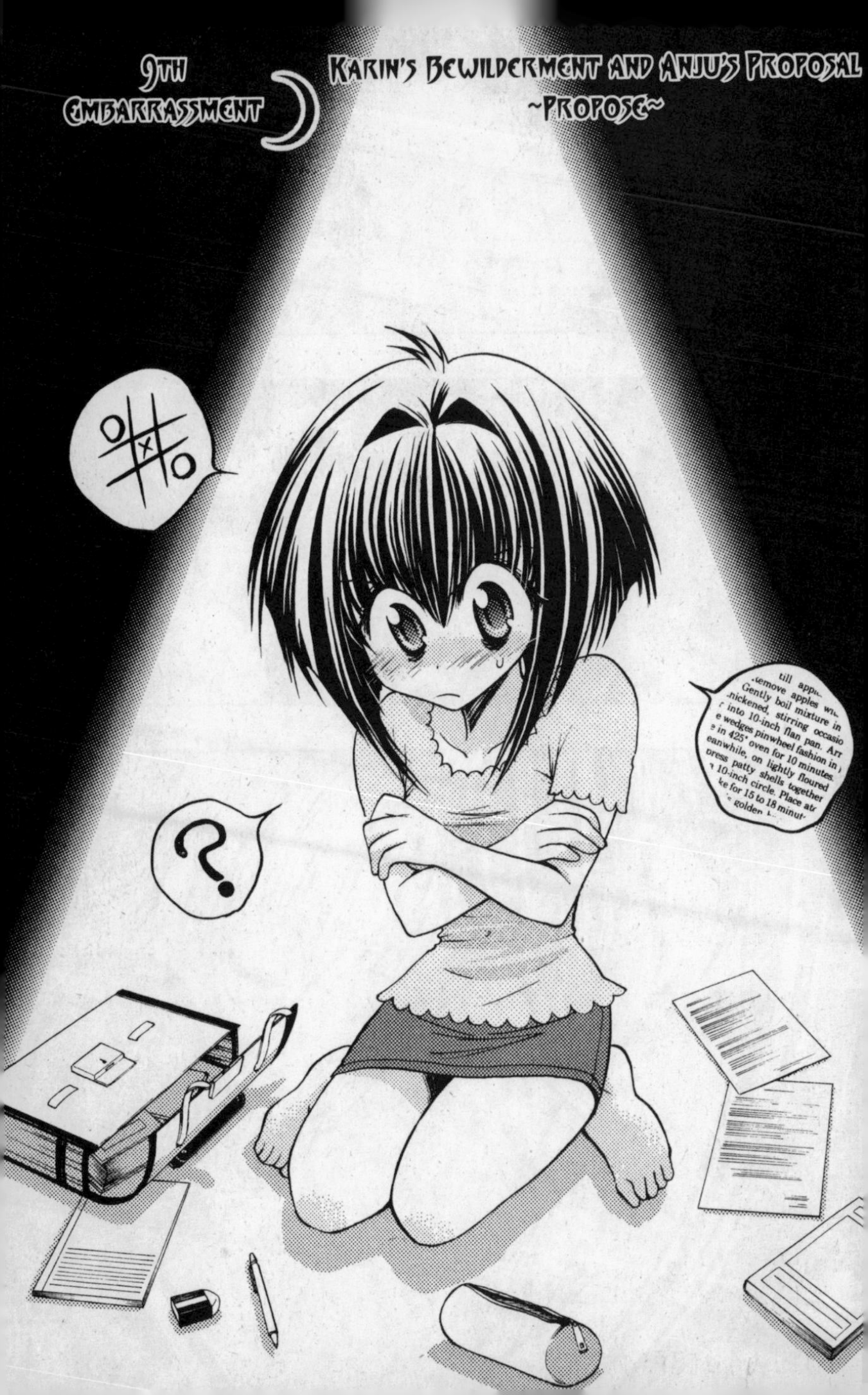
9th Embarrassment
Karin's Bewilderment and Anju's Proposal
~Propose~
O X O
?
till appl
emove apples wi
Gently boil mixture in
hickened, stirring occasio
into 10-inch flan pan. Arr
e wedges pinwheel fashion in
e in 425° oven for 10 minutes.
eanwhile, on lightly floured
press patty shells together
10-inch circle. Place at
ke for 15 to 18 minut
golden

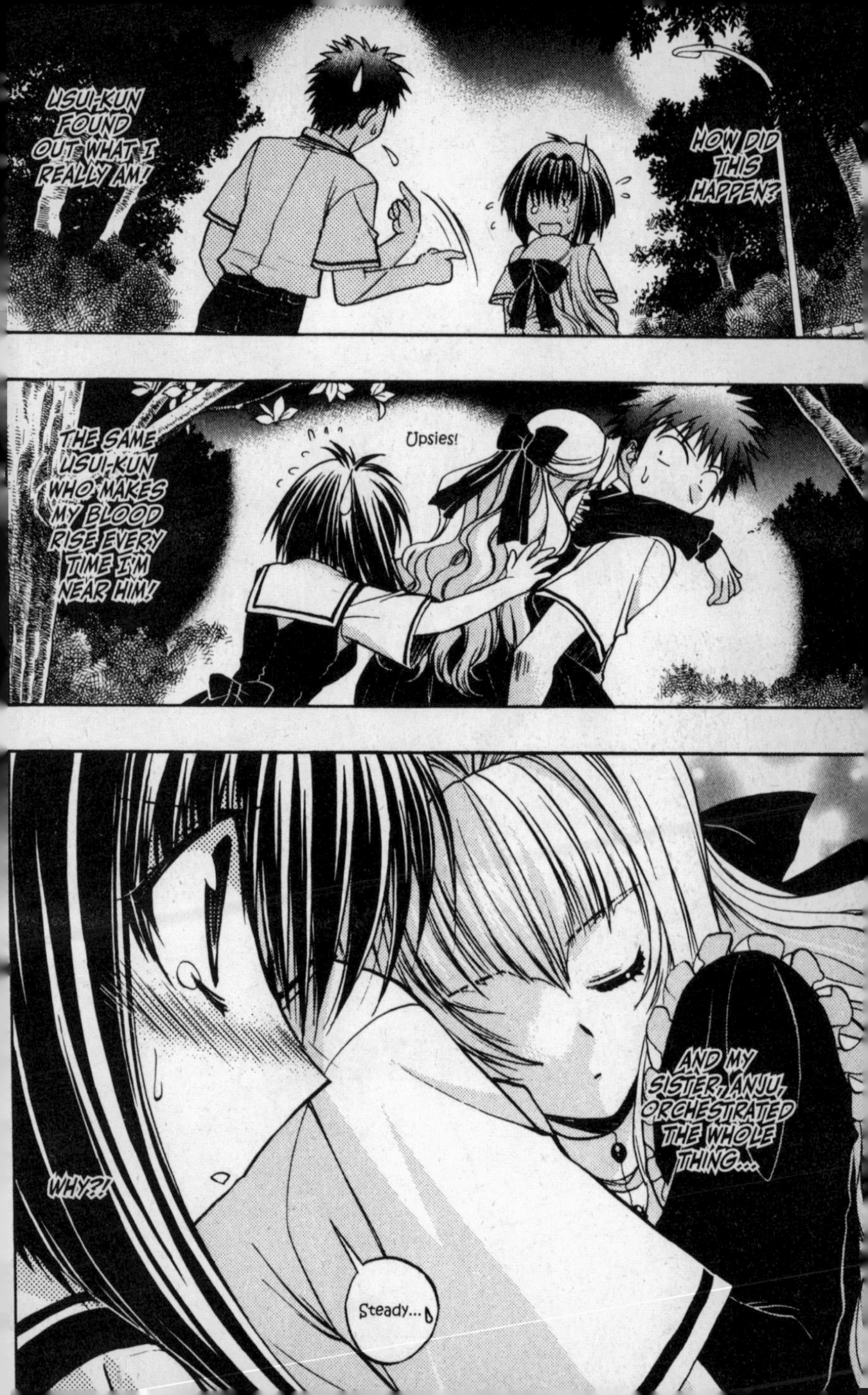
HOW DID THIS HAPPEN?
USUI-KUN FOUND OUT WHAT I REALLY AM!
Upsies!
THE SAME USUI-KUN WHO MAKES MY BLOOD RISE EVERY TIME I'M NEAR HIM!
AND MY SISTER, ANJU, ORCHESTRATED THE WHOLE THING...
WHY?!
Steady...

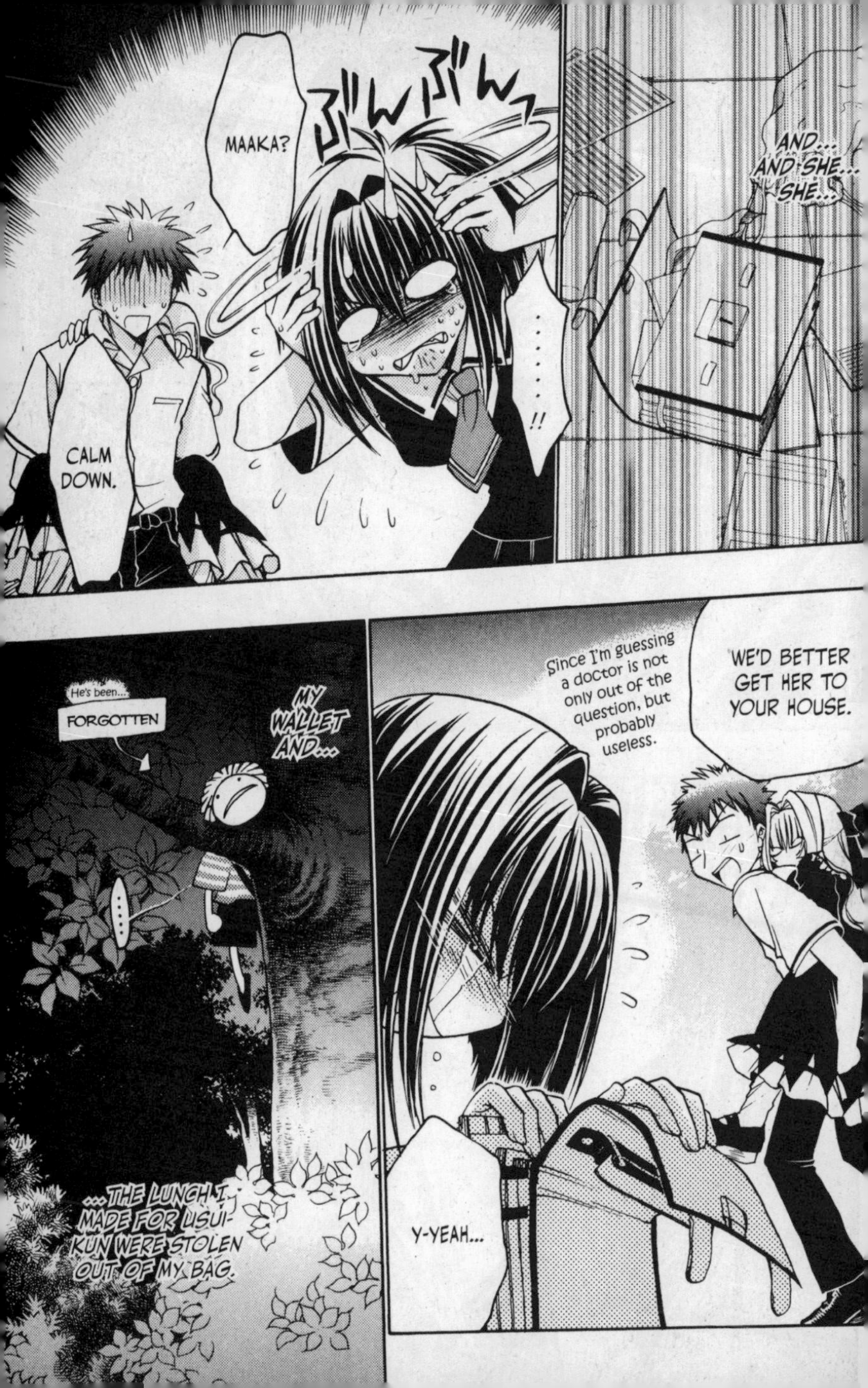
AND... AND SHE... SHE...
ぶんぶん
MAAKA?
......!!
CALM DOWN.
WE'D BETTER GET HER TO YOUR HOUSE.
Since I'm guessing a doctor is not only out of the question, but probably useless.
Y-YEAH...
MY WALLET AND...
...THE LUNCH I MADE FOR USUI-KUN WERE STOLEN OUT OF MY BAG.
He's been...
FORGOTTEN
....

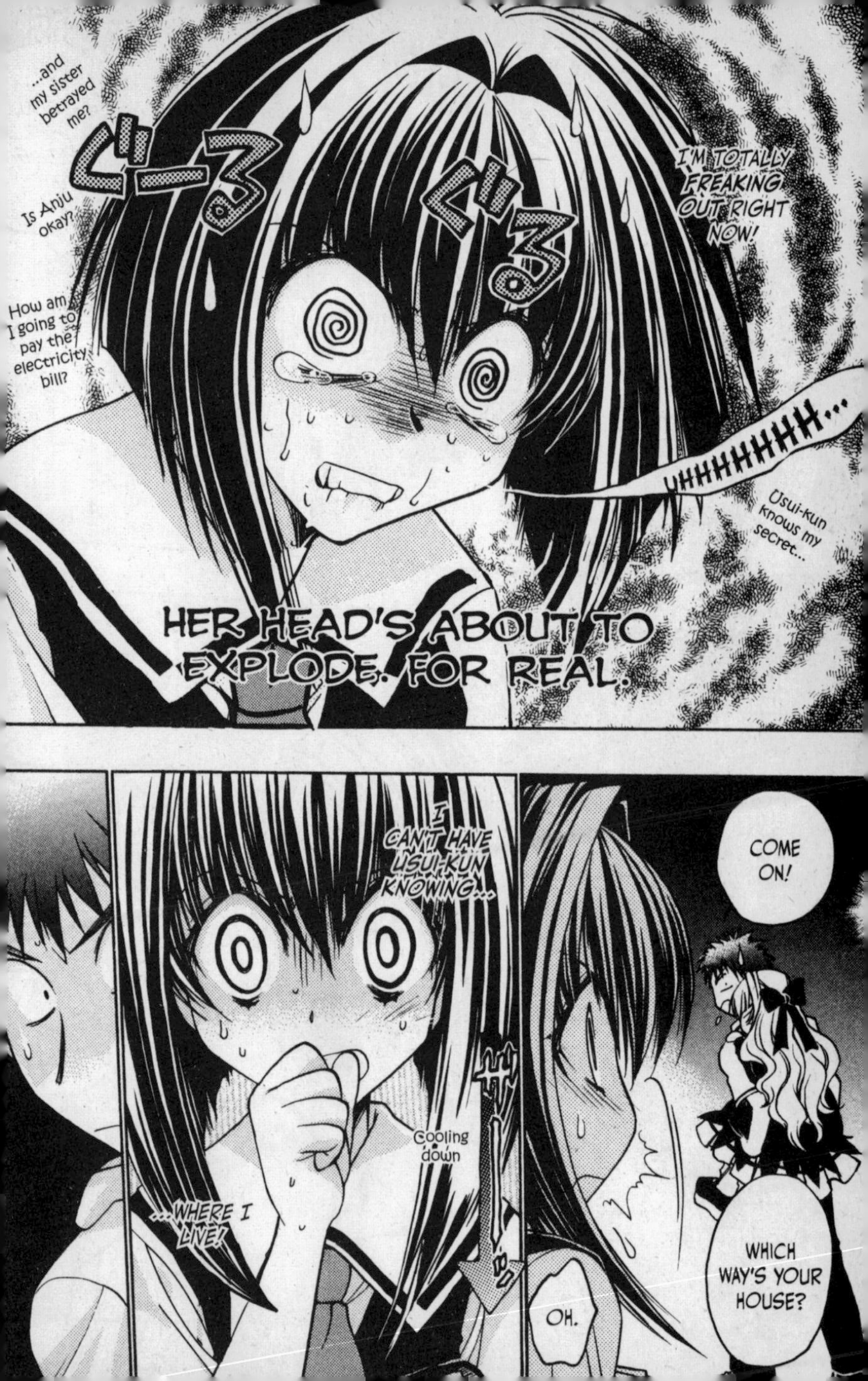
I'M TOTALLY FREAKING OUT RIGHT NOW!
ぐる
ぐーる
UHHHHHHHH...
Usui-kun knows my secret...
...and my sister betrayed me?
Is Anju okay?
How am I going to pay the electricity bill?
HER HEAD'S ABOUT TO EXPLODE. FOR REAL.
COME ON!
WHICH WAY'S YOUR HOUSE?
OH.
I CAN'T HAVE USUI-KUN KNOWING...
Cooling down
...WHERE I LIVE!

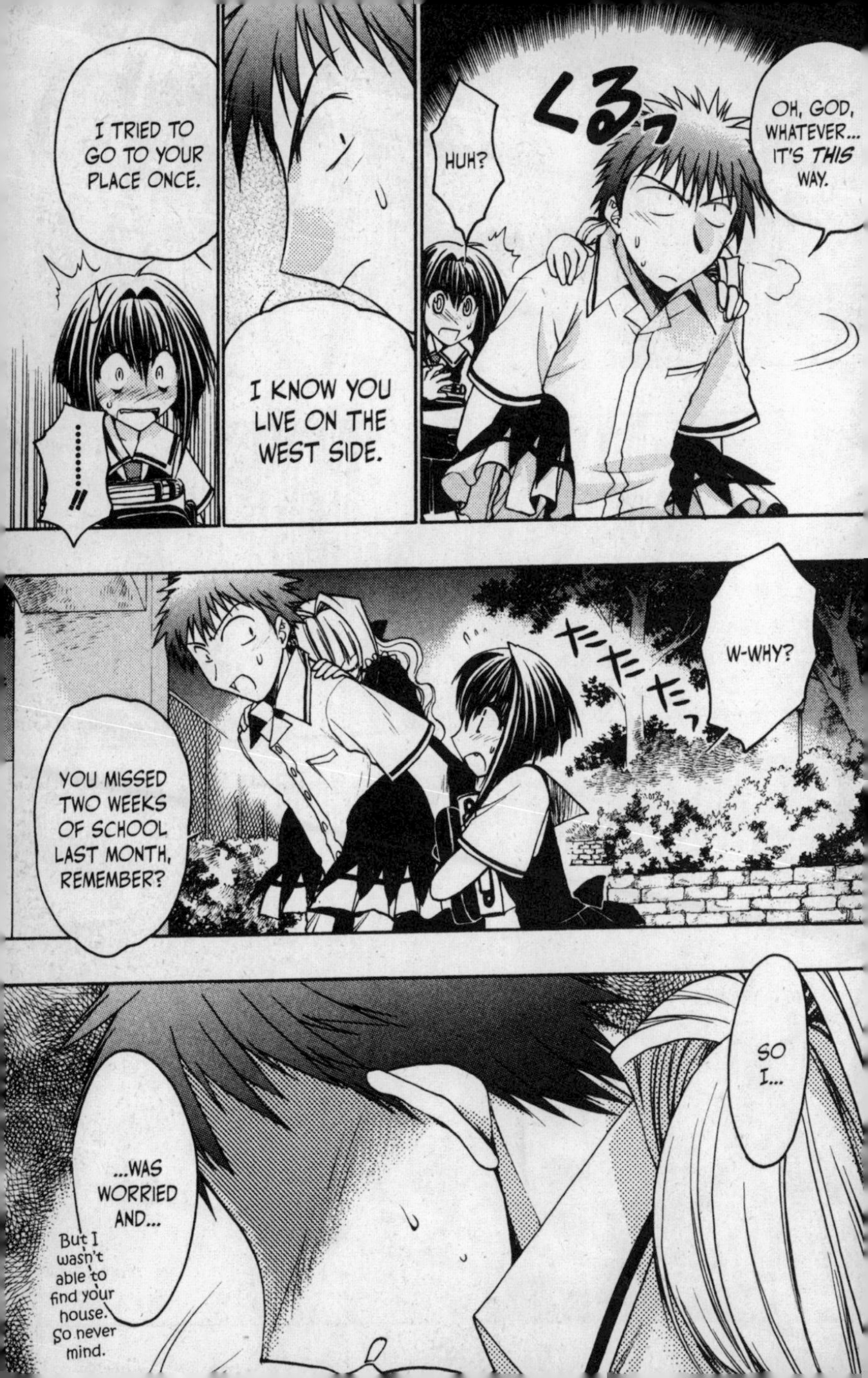
OH, GOD, WHATEVER... IT'S *THIS* WAY.
くるっ
HUH?
I KNOW YOU LIVE ON THE WEST SIDE.
I TRIED TO GO TO YOUR PLACE ONCE.
......!!
W-WHY?
たたたっ
YOU MISSED TWO WEEKS OF SCHOOL LAST MONTH, REMEMBER?
SO I...
...WAS WORRIED AND...
But I wasn't able to find your house. So never mind.

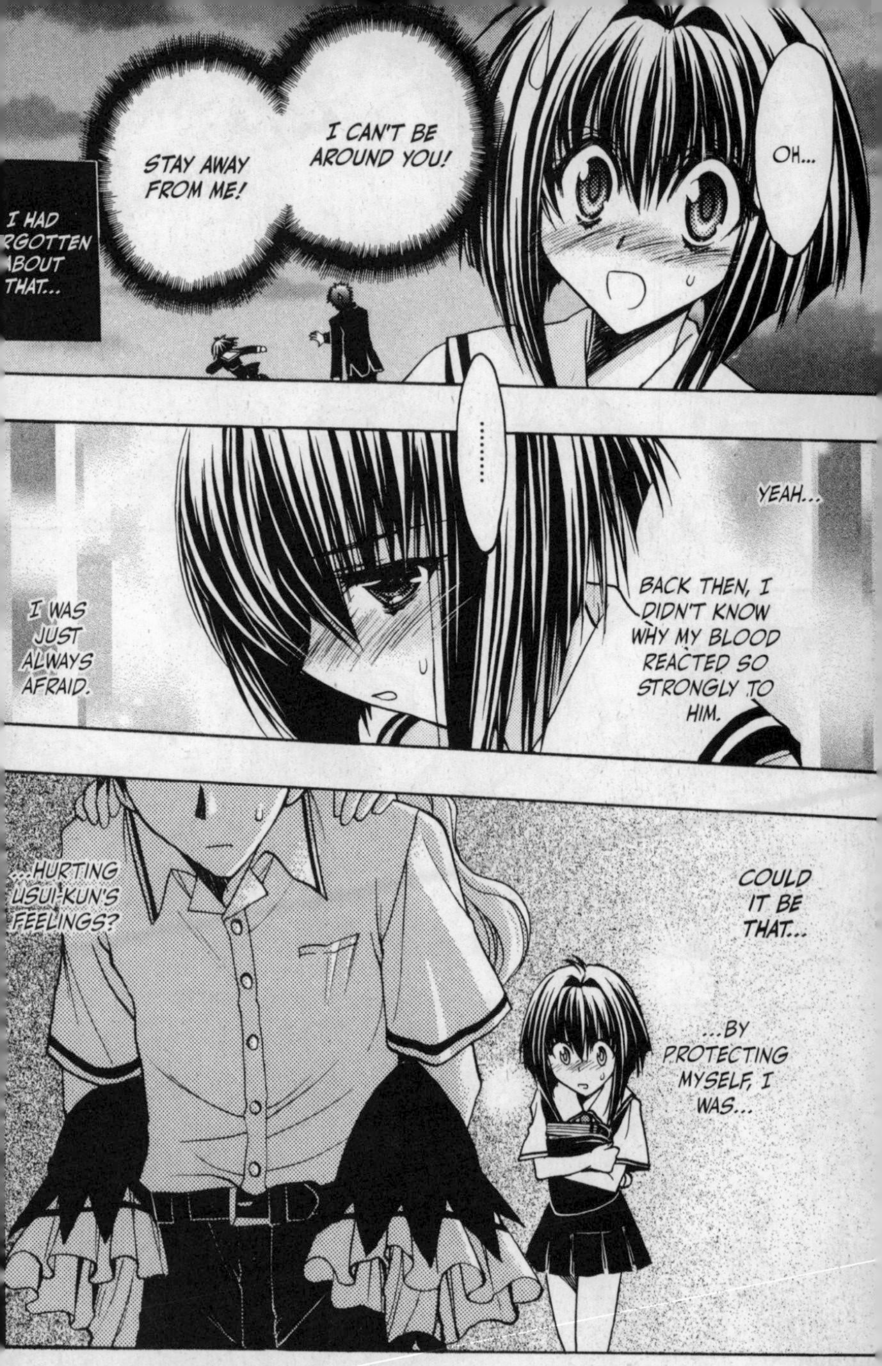
OH...
I CAN'T BE AROUND YOU!
STAY AWAY FROM ME!
I HAD RGOTTEN ABOUT THAT...
......
YEAH...
BACK THEN, I DIDN'T KNOW WHY MY BLOOD REACTED SO STRONGLY TO HIM.
I WAS JUST ALWAYS AFRAID.
COULD IT BE THAT...
...BY PROTECTING MYSELF, I WAS...
...HURTING USUI-KUN'S FEELINGS?

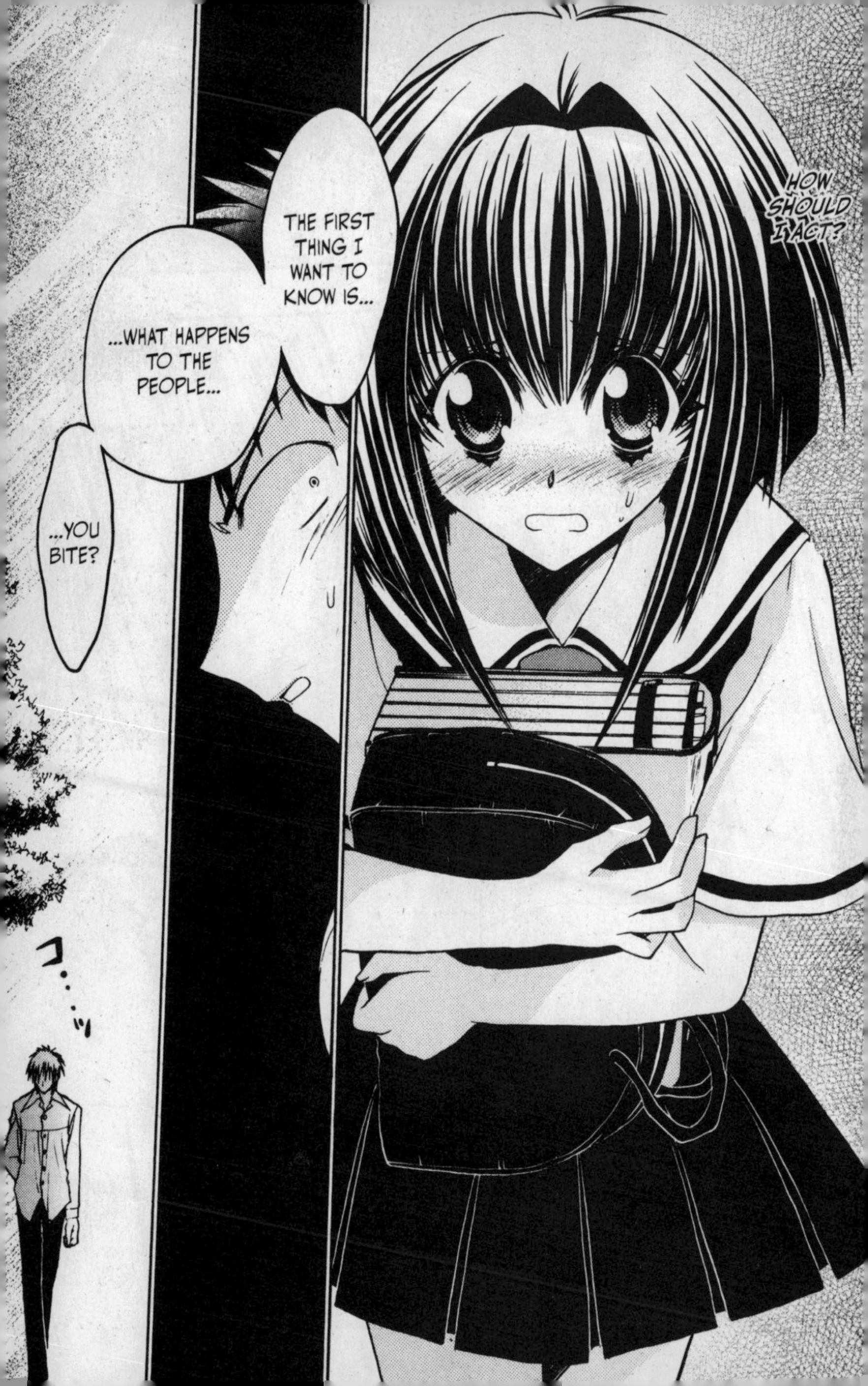
HOW SHOULD I ACT?
THE FIRST THING I WANT TO KNOW IS...
...WHAT HAPPENS TO THE PEOPLE...
...YOU BITE?

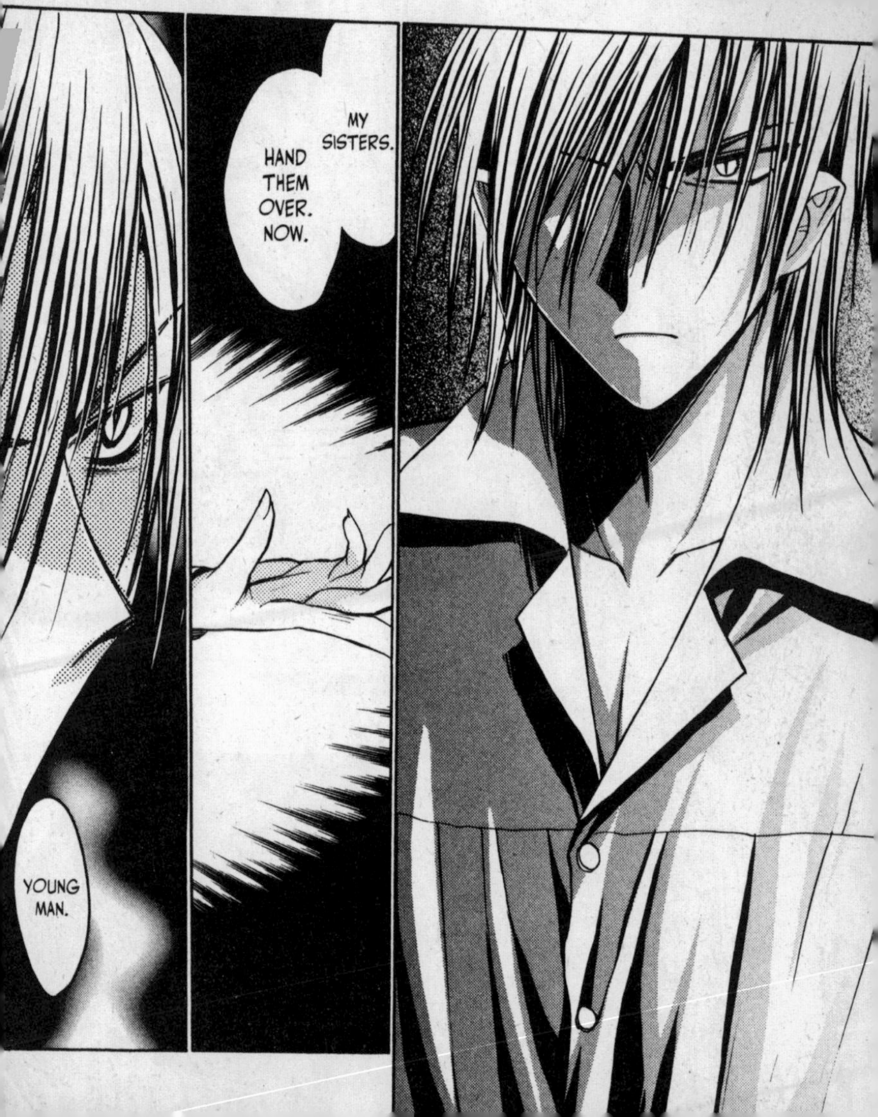
MY SISTERS.
HAND THEM OVER. NOW.
YOUNG MAN.

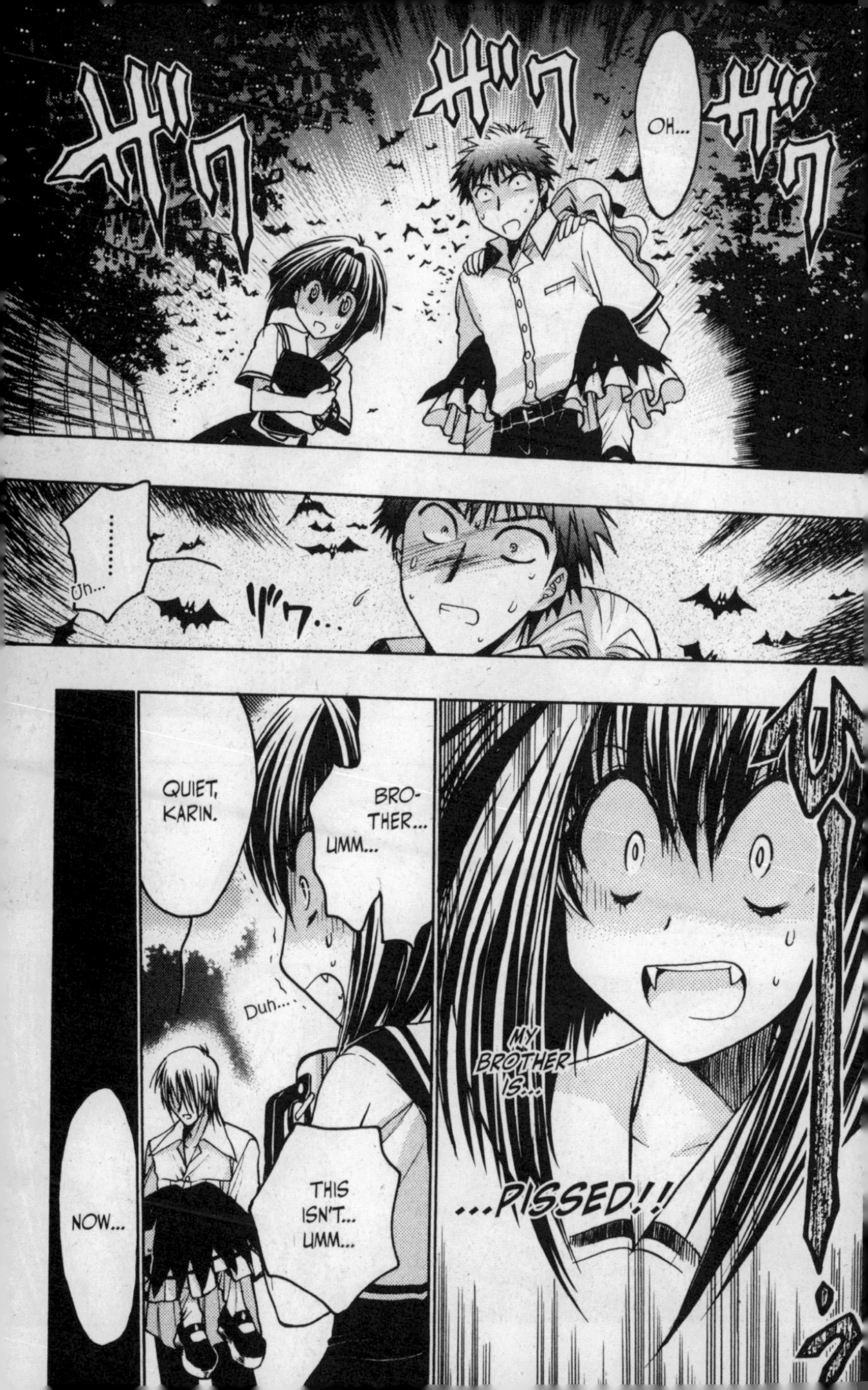
ザワ
OH...
ザワ
ザワ
......
Uh...
ゾワ...
MY BROTHER IS...
...PISSED!!
BRO- THER... UMM...
QUIET, KARIN.
Duh...
THIS ISN'T... UMM...
NOW...

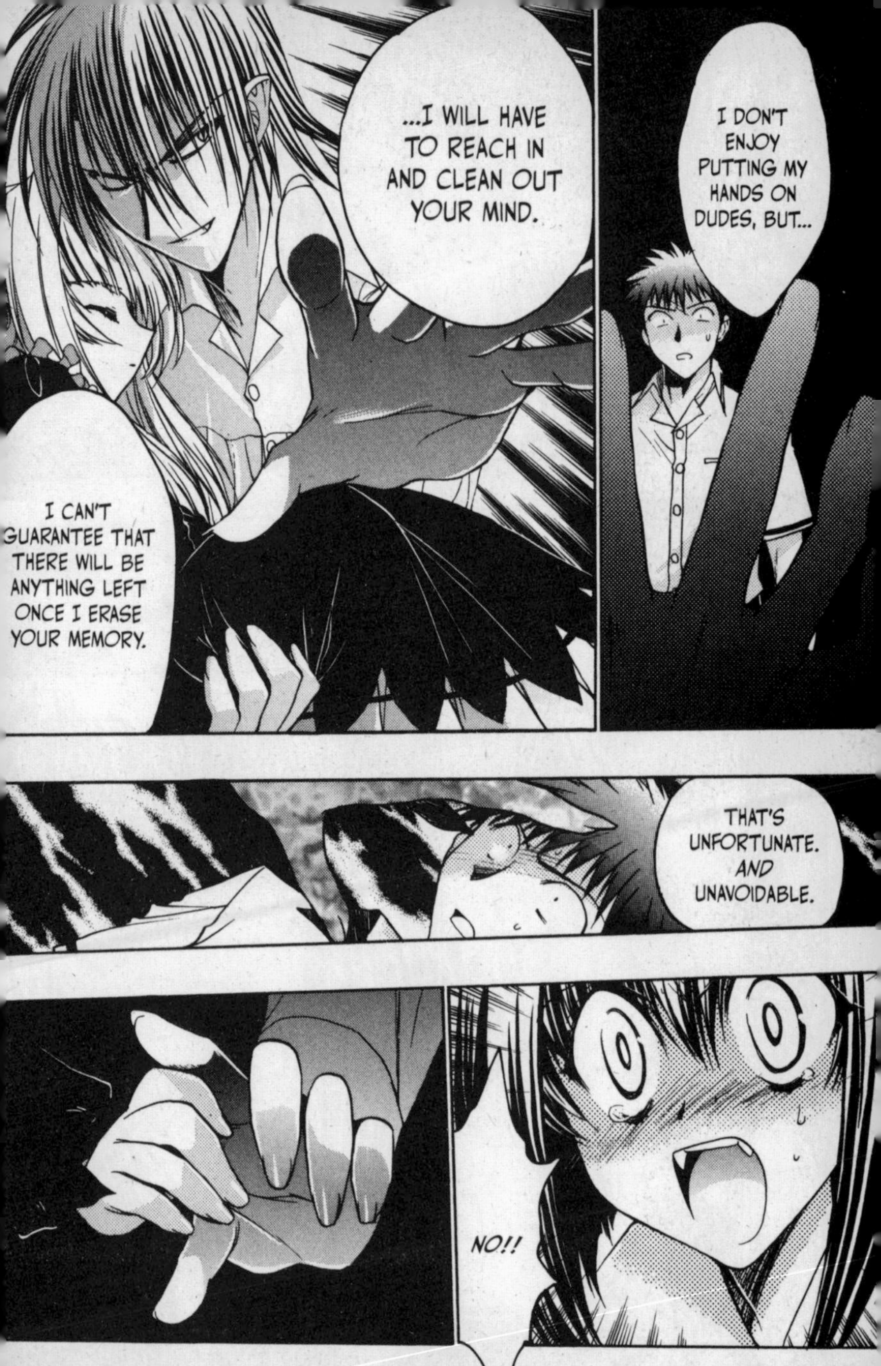
I DON'T ENJOY PUTTING MY HANDS ON DUDES, BUT...
...I WILL HAVE TO REACH IN AND CLEAN OUT YOUR MIND.
I CAN'T GUARANTEE THAT THERE WILL BE ANYTHING LEFT ONCE I ERASE YOUR MEMORY.
THAT'S UNFORTUNATE. AND UNAVOIDABLE.
NO!!

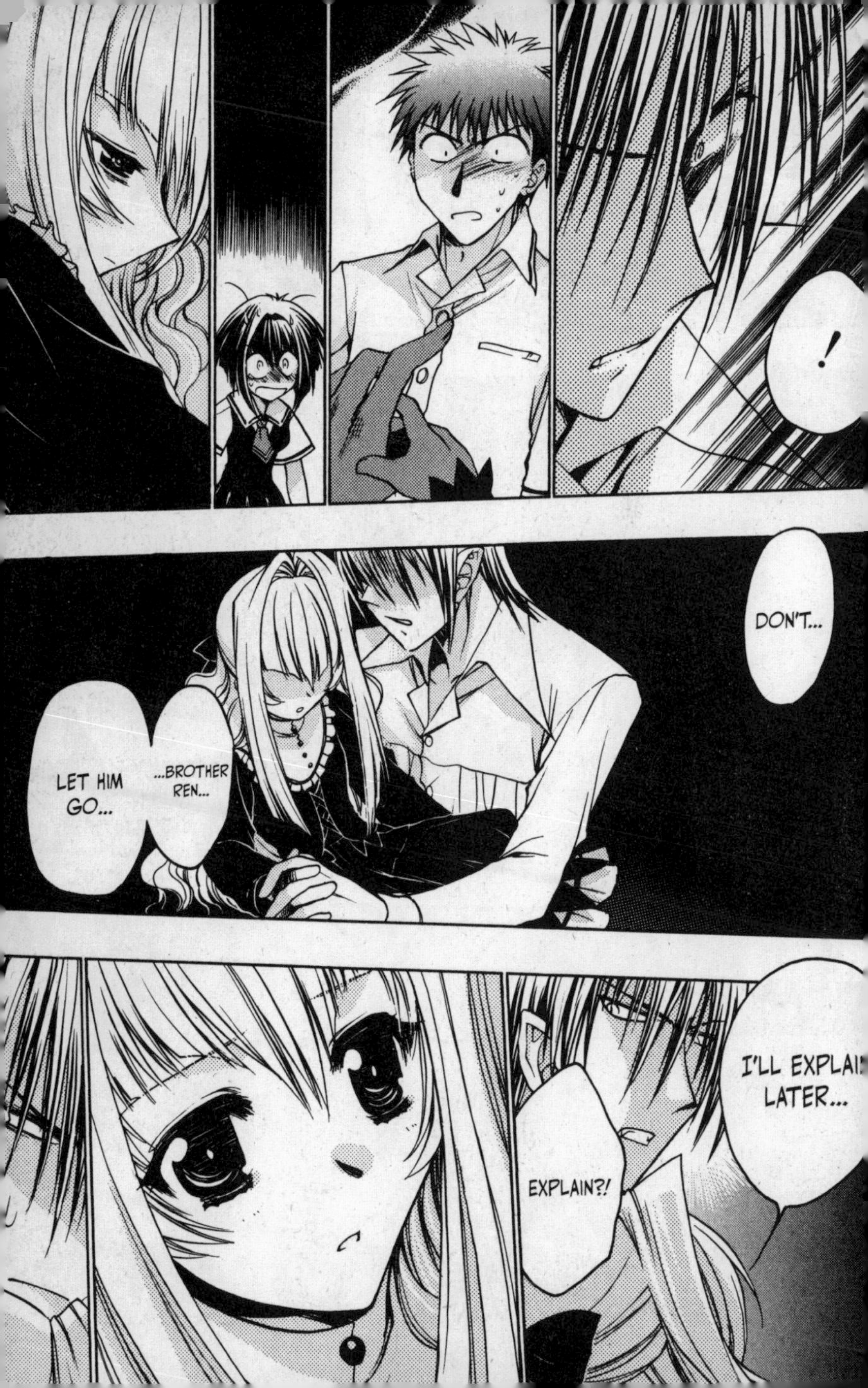
!
DON'T...
...BROTHER REN...
LET HIM GO...
I'LL EXPLAIN LATER...
EXPLAIN?!

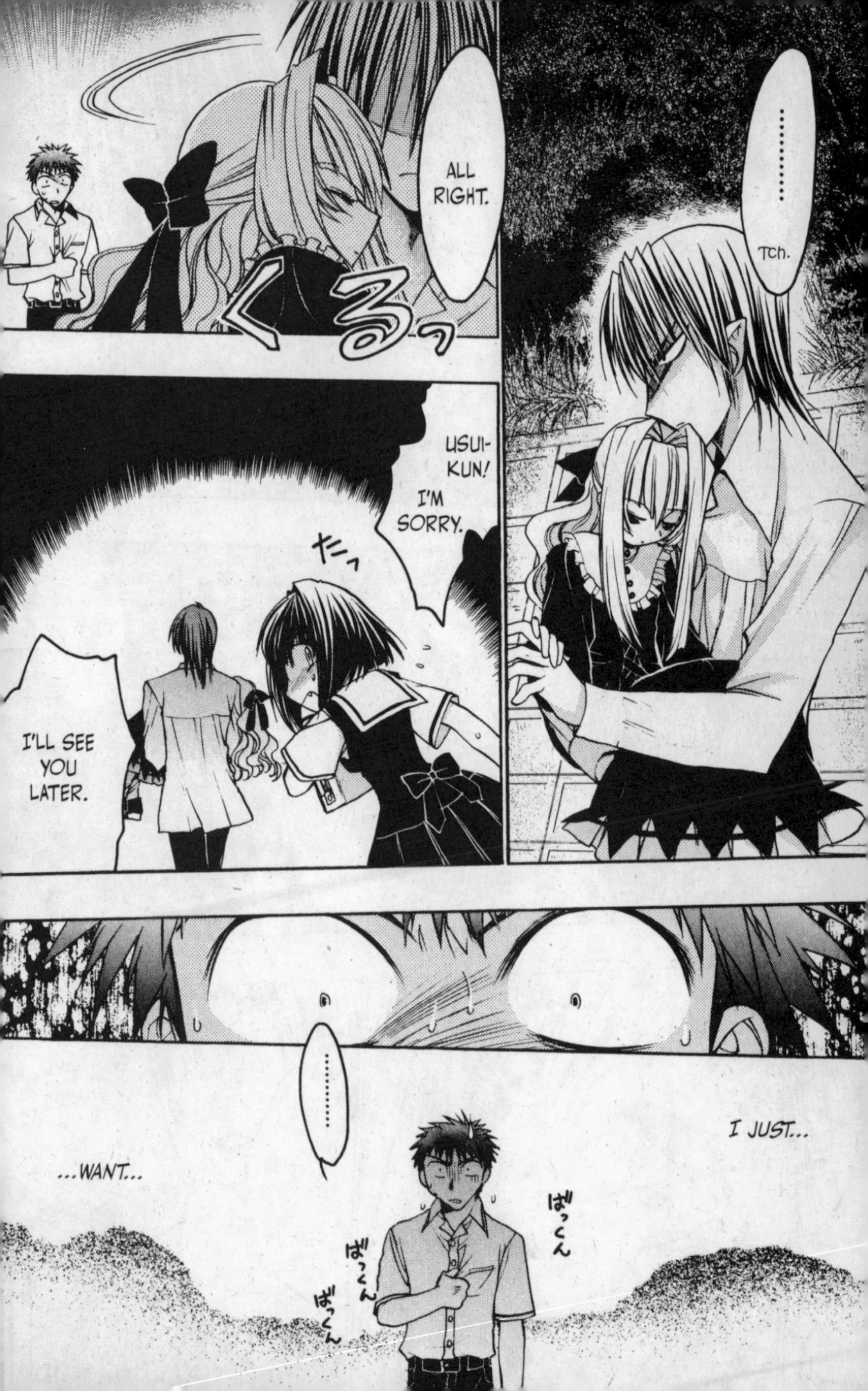
......
Tch.
ALL RIGHT.
くるっ
USUI-KUN! I'M SORRY.
たっ
I'LL SEE YOU LATER.
......
I JUST...
...WANT...
ばっくん
ばっくん
ばっくん

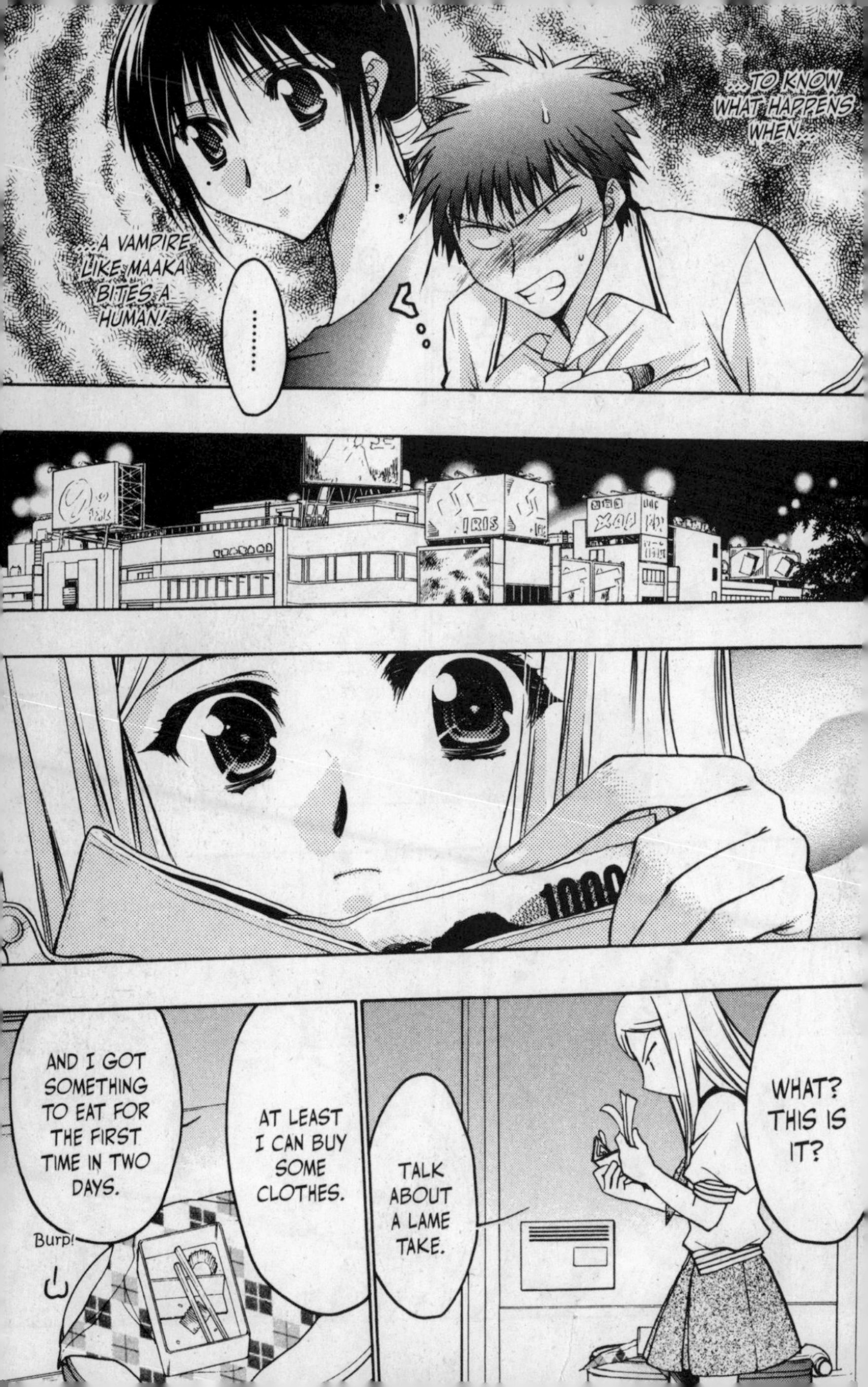
...TO KNOW WHAT HAPPENS WHEN...
...A VAMPIRE LIKE MAAKA BITES A HUMAN!
......
IRIS
1000
WHAT? THIS IS IT?
TALK ABOUT A LAME TAKE.
AT LEAST I CAN BUY SOME CLOTHES.
AND I GOT SOMETHING TO EAT FOR THE FIRST TIME IN TWO DAYS.
Burp!

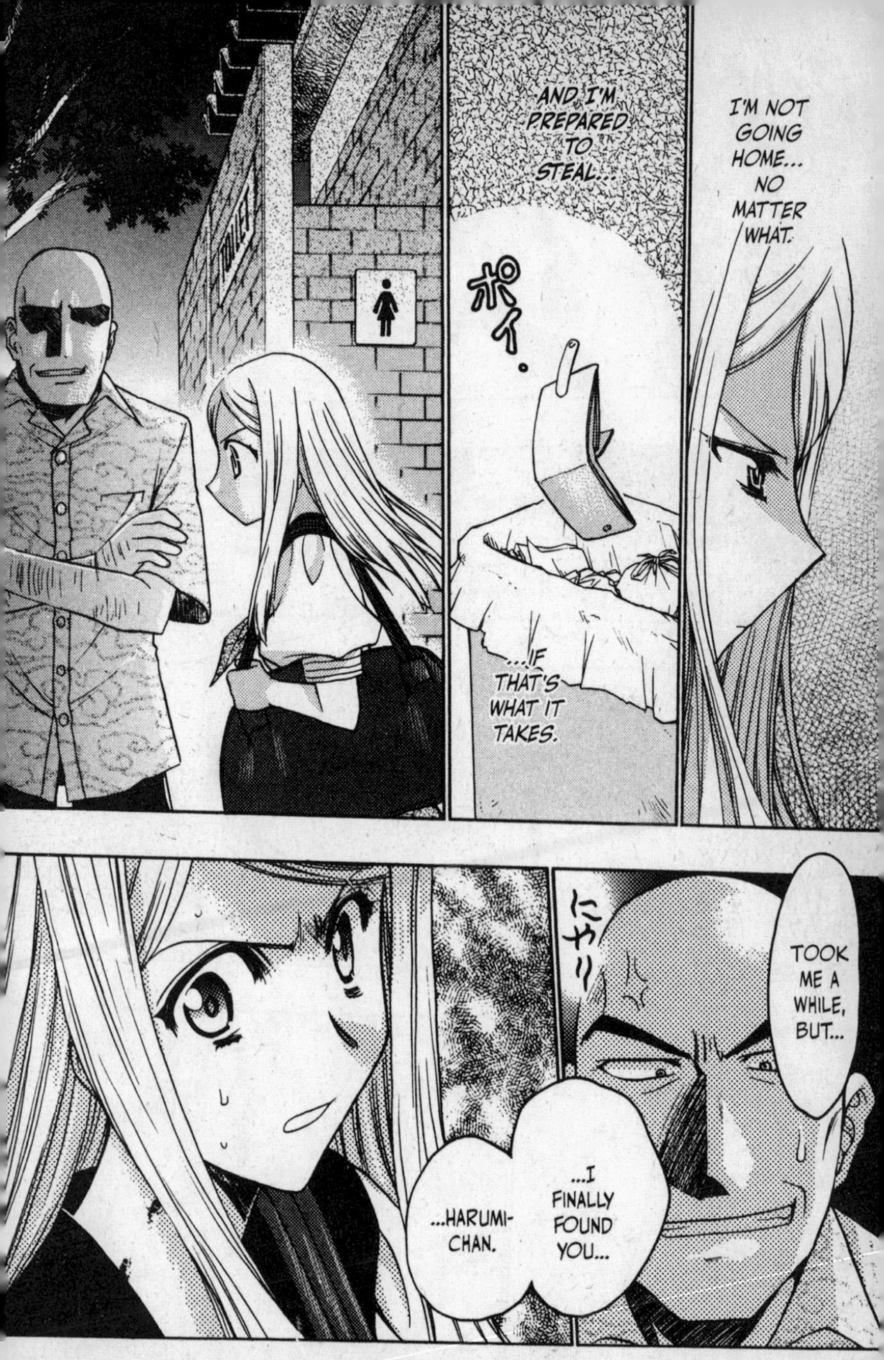
I'M NOT GOING HOME... NO MATTER WHAT.
AND I'M PREPARED TO STEAL...
ポイ。
...IF THAT'S WHAT IT TAKES.
TOILET
にやり
TOOK ME A WHILE, BUT...
...I FINALLY FOUND YOU...
...HARUMI-CHAN.

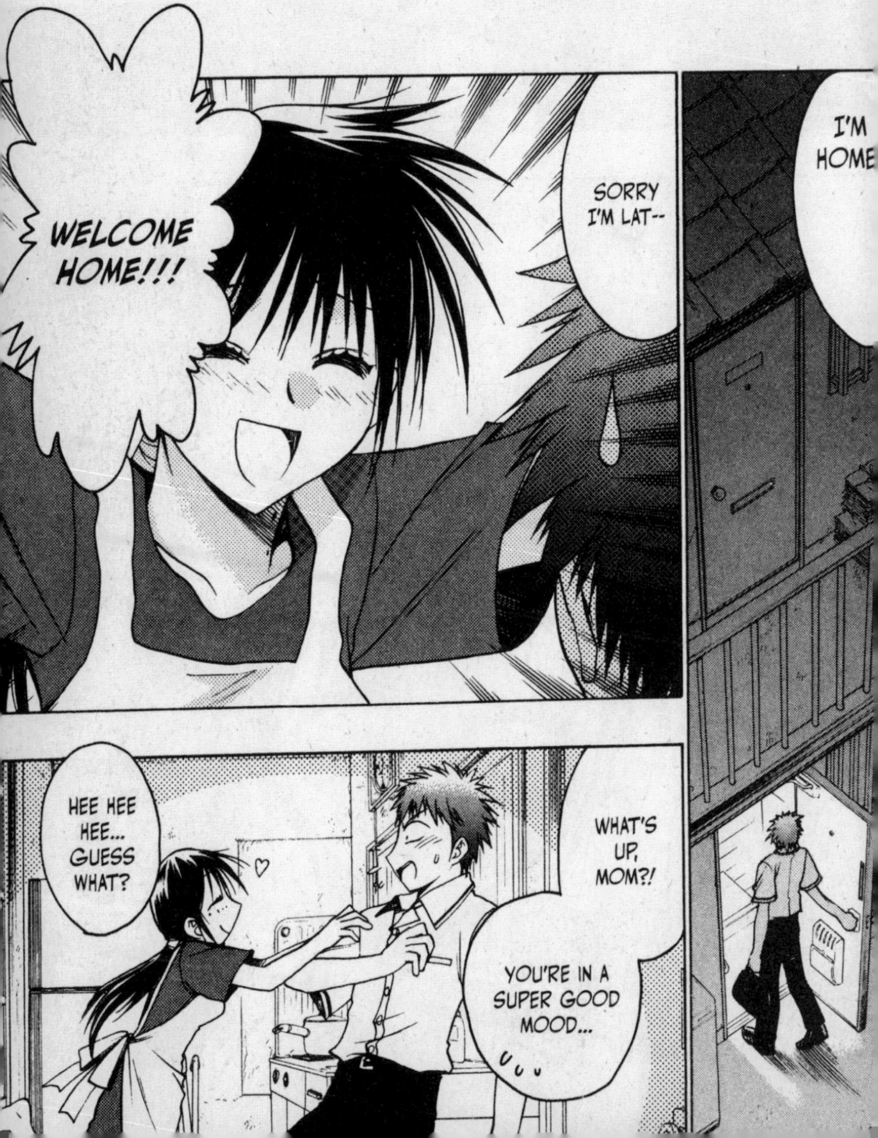
I'M HOME
SORRY I'M LAT--
WELCOME HOME!!!
WHAT'S UP, MOM?!
HEE HEE HEE... GUESS WHAT?
YOU'RE IN A SUPER GOOD MOOD...

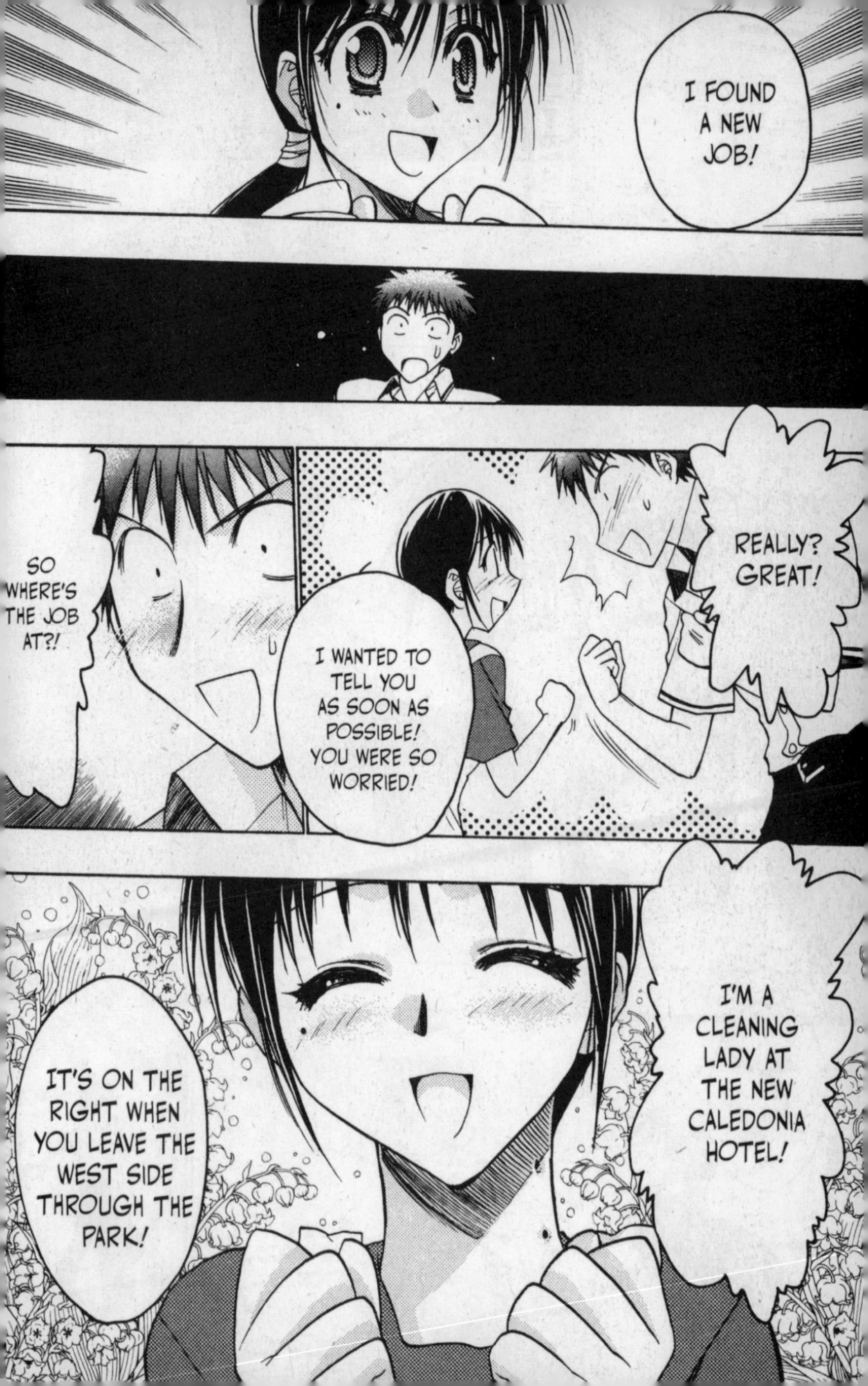
I FOUND A NEW JOB!
REALLY? GREAT!
I WANTED TO TELL YOU AS SOON AS POSSIBLE! YOU WERE SO WORRIED!
SO WHERE'S THE JOB AT?!
I'M A CLEANING LADY AT THE NEW CALEDONIA HOTEL!
IT'S ON THE RIGHT WHEN YOU LEAVE THE WEST SIDE THROUGH THE PARK!

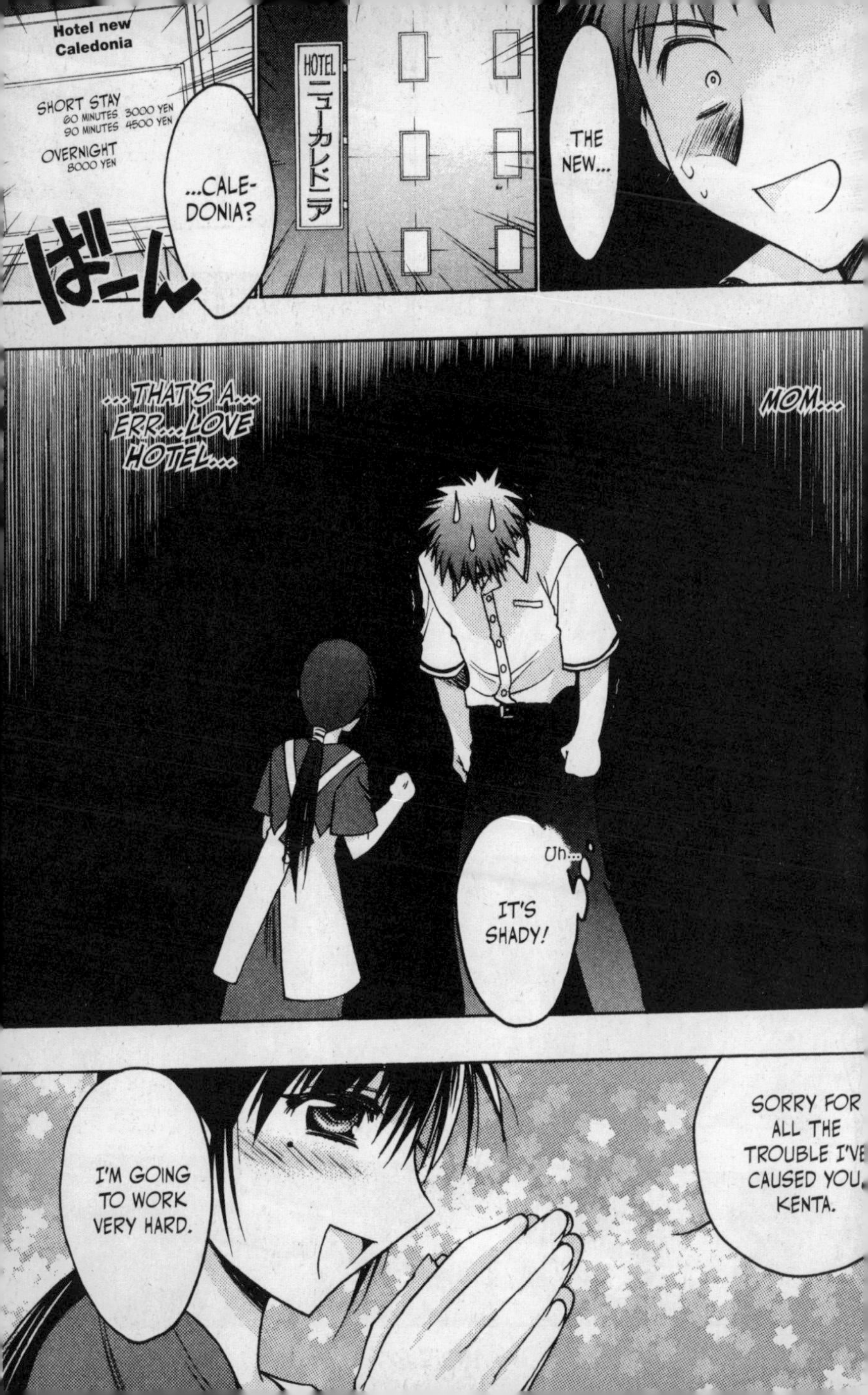
THE NEW...
HOTEL
ニューカレドニア
Hotel new Caledonia
SHORT STAY
60 MINUTES 3000 YEN
90 MINUTES 4500 YEN
OVERNIGHT
8000 YEN
...CALE-DONIA?
ばーん
MOM...
...THAT'S A... ERR...LOVE HOTEL...
Uh...
IT'S SHADY!
SORRY FOR ALL THE TROUBLE I'VE CAUSED YOU, KENTA.
I'M GOING TO WORK VERY HARD.

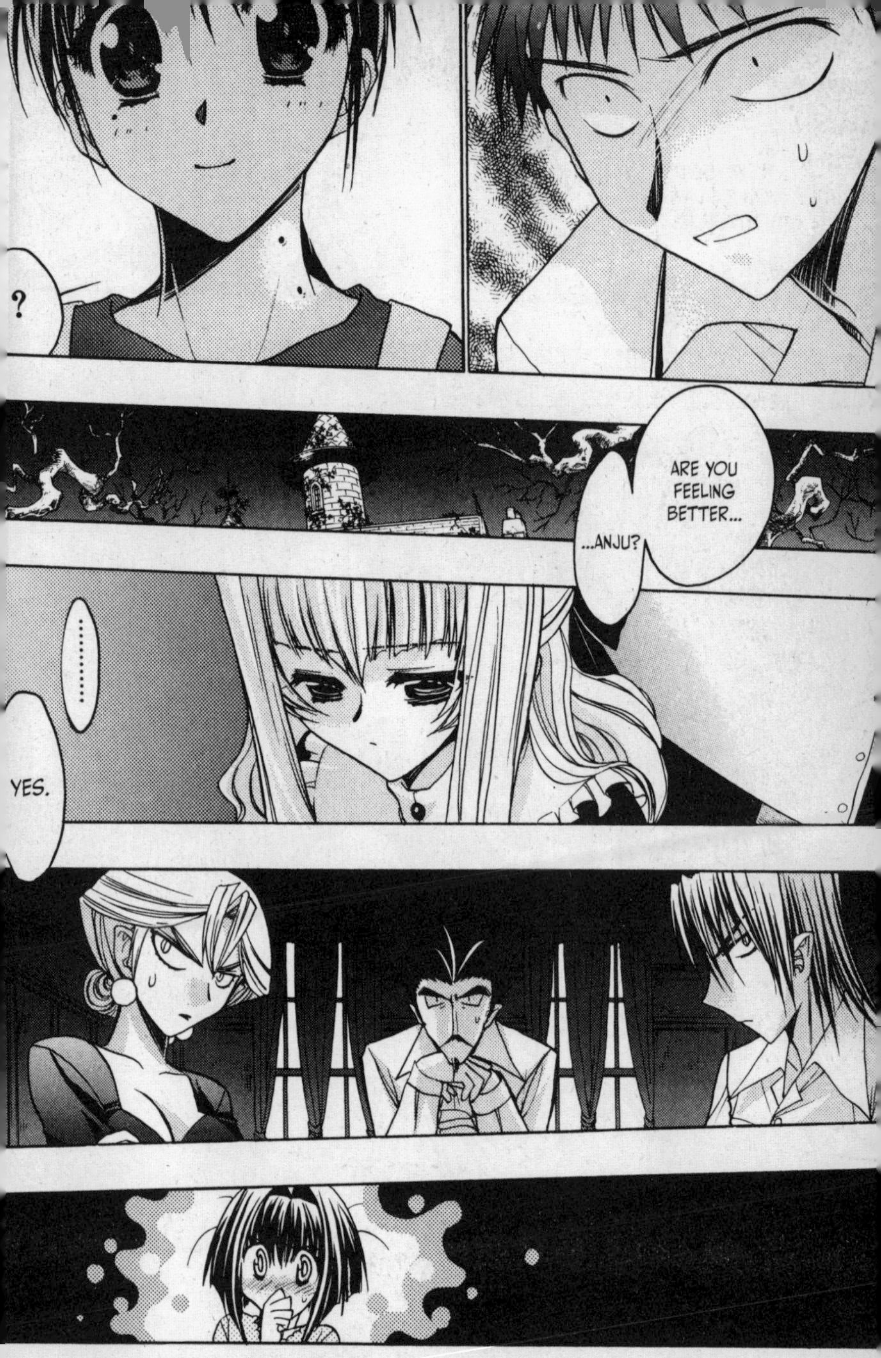
?
ARE YOU FEELING BETTER...
...ANJU?
......
YES.

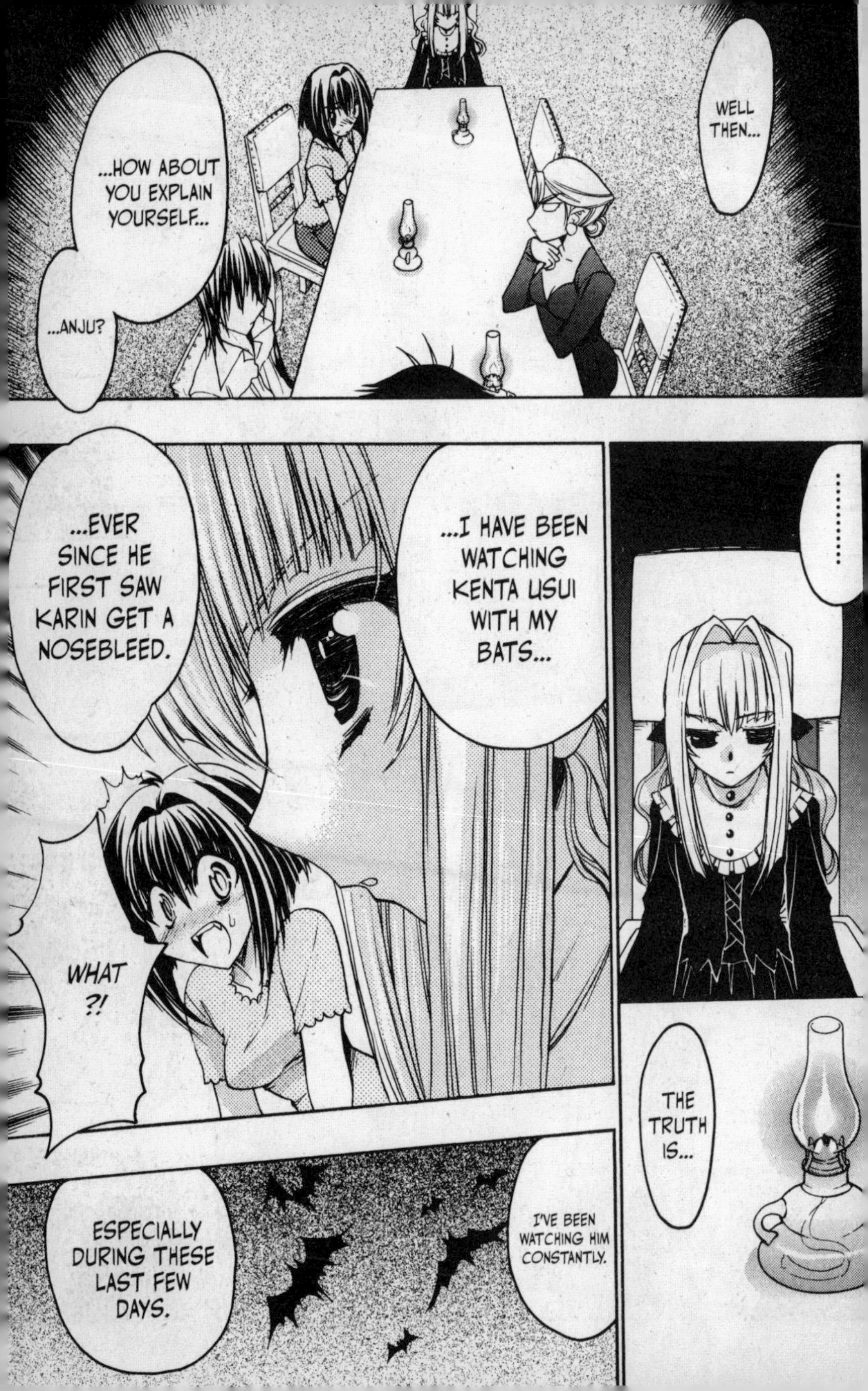
WELL THEN...
...HOW ABOUT YOU EXPLAIN YOURSELF...
...ANJU?
......
THE TRUTH IS...
...I HAVE BEEN WATCHING KENTA USUI WITH MY BATS...
...EVER SINCE HE FIRST SAW KARIN GET A NOSEBLEED.
WHAT ?!
I'VE BEEN WATCHING HIM CONSTANTLY.
ESPECIALLY DURING THESE LAST FEW DAYS.

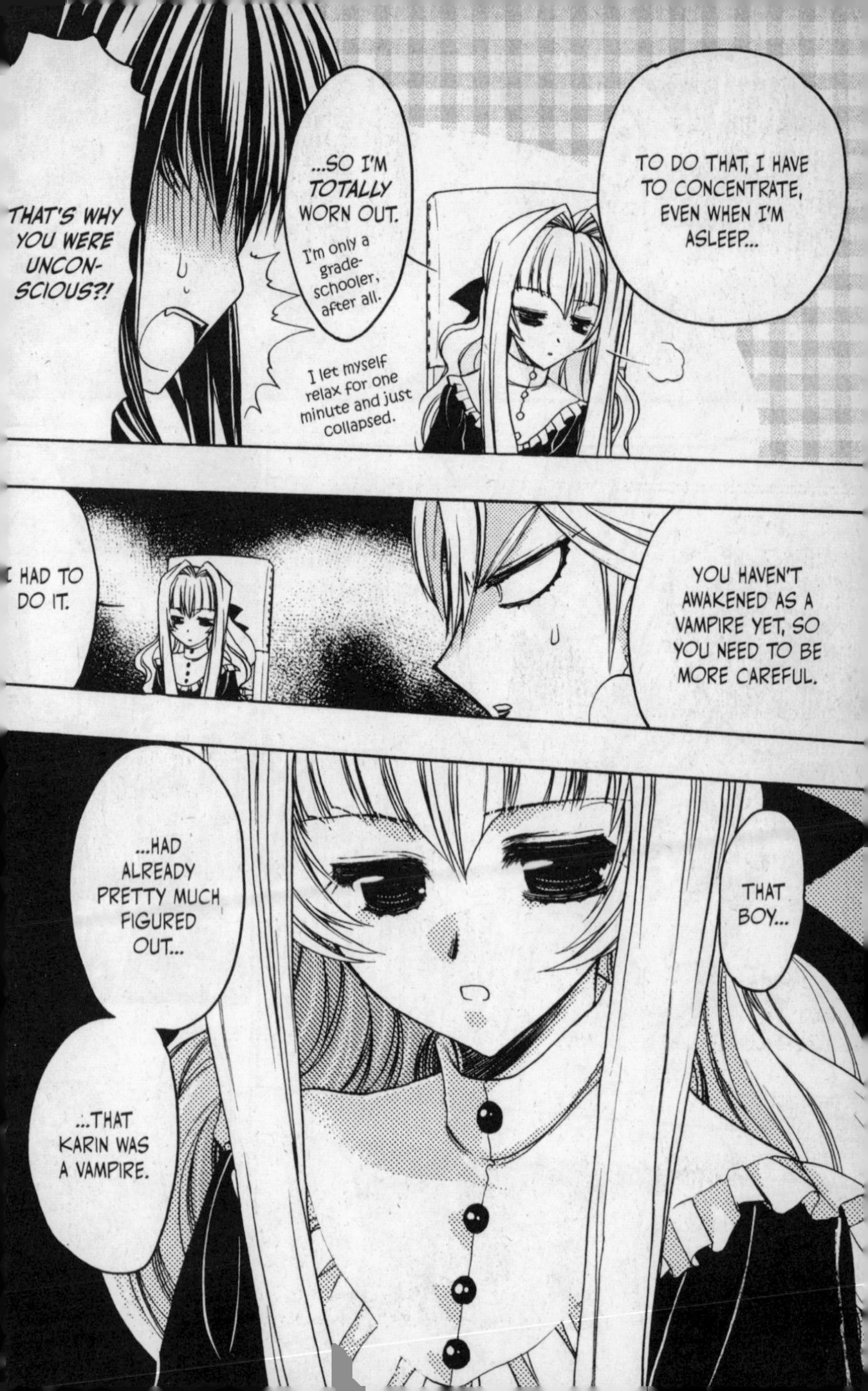
TO DO THAT, I HAVE TO CONCENTRATE, EVEN WHEN I'M ASLEEP...
...SO I'M *TOTALLY* WORN OUT.
I'm only a grade-schooler, after all.
I let myself relax for one minute and just collapsed.
THAT'S WHY YOU WERE UNCON-SCIOUS?!
YOU HAVEN'T AWAKENED AS A VAMPIRE YET, SO YOU NEED TO BE MORE CAREFUL.
I HAD TO DO IT.
THAT BOY...
...HAD ALREADY PRETTY MUCH FIGURED OUT...
...THAT KARIN WAS A VAMPIRE.

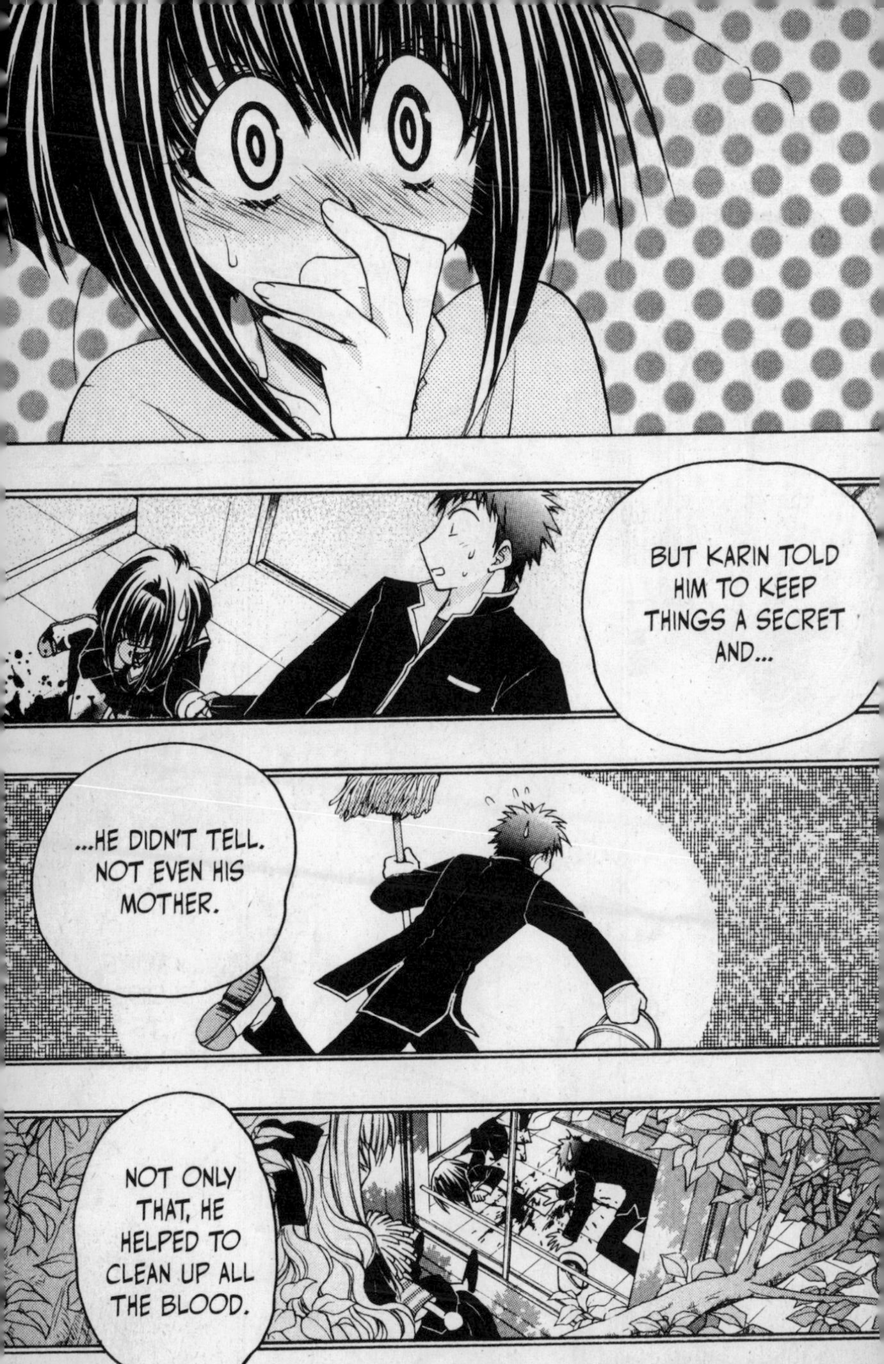

BUT KARIN TOLD HIM TO KEEP THINGS A SECRET AND...
...HE DIDN'T TELL. NOT EVEN HIS MOTHER.
NOT ONLY THAT, HE HELPED TO CLEAN UP ALL THE BLOOD.

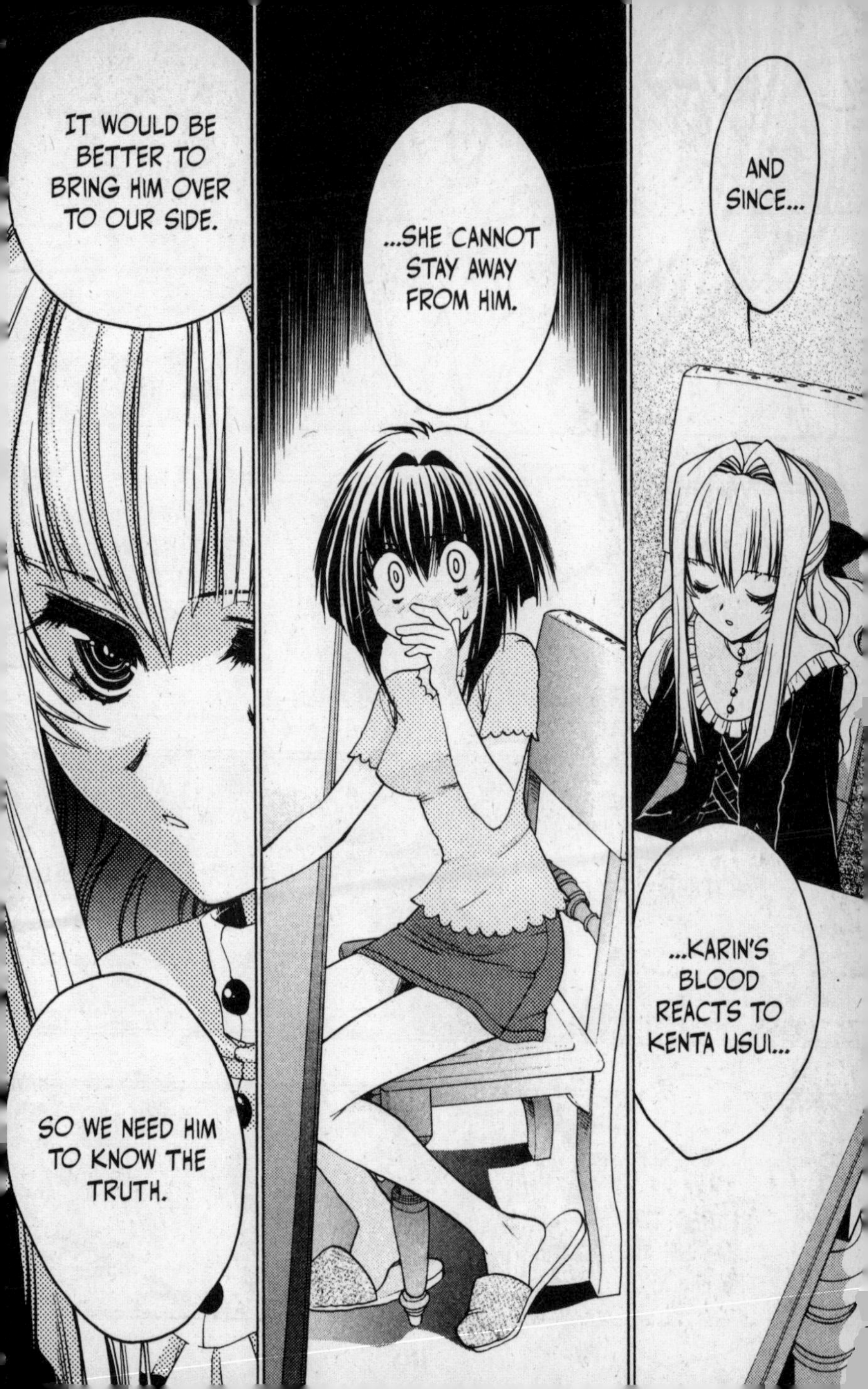
AND SINCE...
...KARIN'S BLOOD REACTS TO KENTA USUI...
...SHE CANNOT STAY AWAY FROM HIM.
IT WOULD BE BETTER TO BRING HIM OVER TO OUR SIDE.
SO WE NEED HIM TO KNOW THE TRUTH.

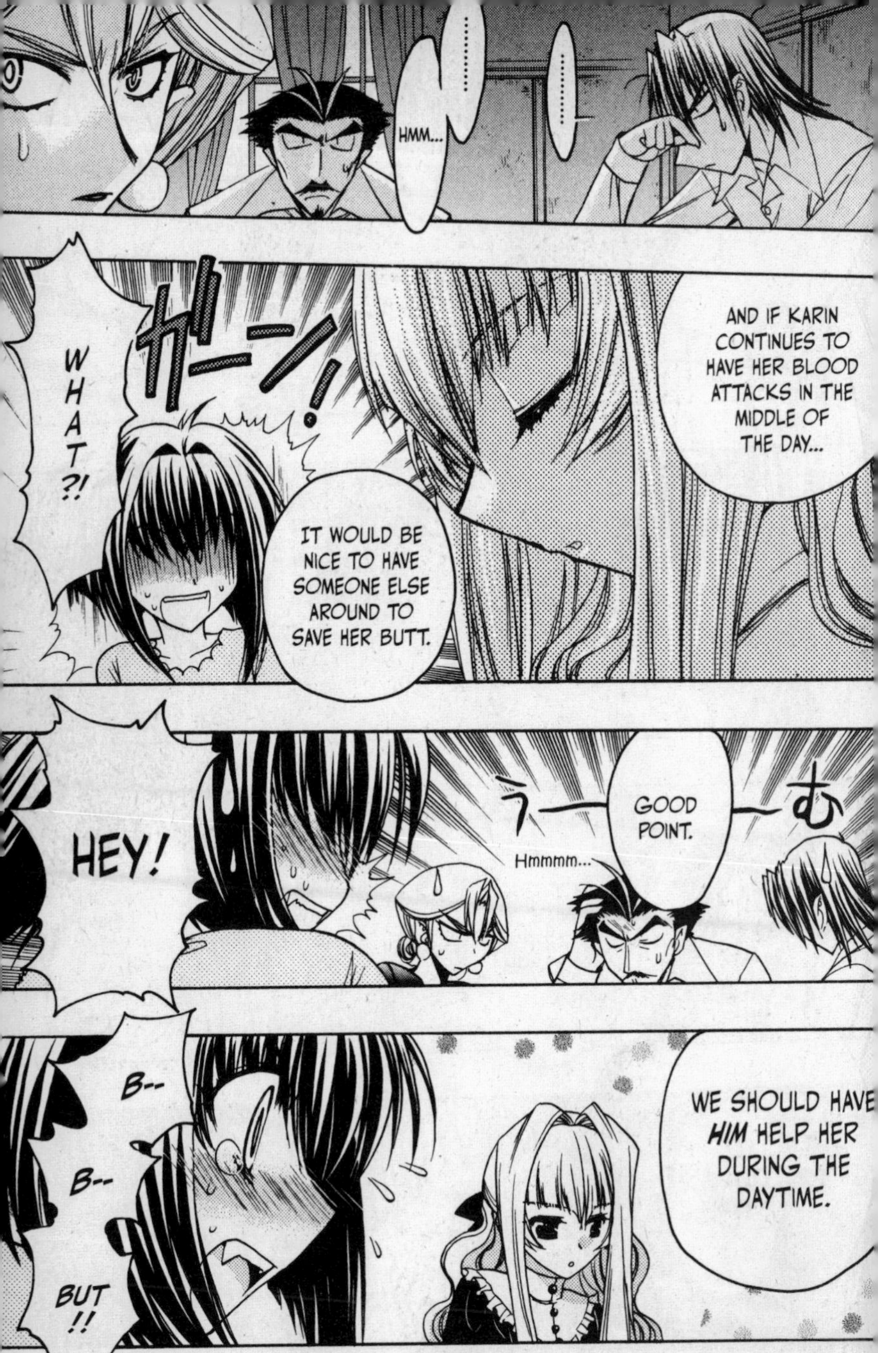
......
......
HMM...
AND IF KARIN CONTINUES TO HAVE HER BLOOD ATTACKS IN THE MIDDLE OF THE DAY...
IT WOULD BE NICE TO HAVE SOMEONE ELSE AROUND TO SAVE HER BUTT.
ガーン!
WHAT?!
GOOD POINT.
うーむ
Hmmmm...
HEY!
WE SHOULD HAVE *HIM* HELP HER DURING THE DAYTIME.
B--
B--
BUT!!

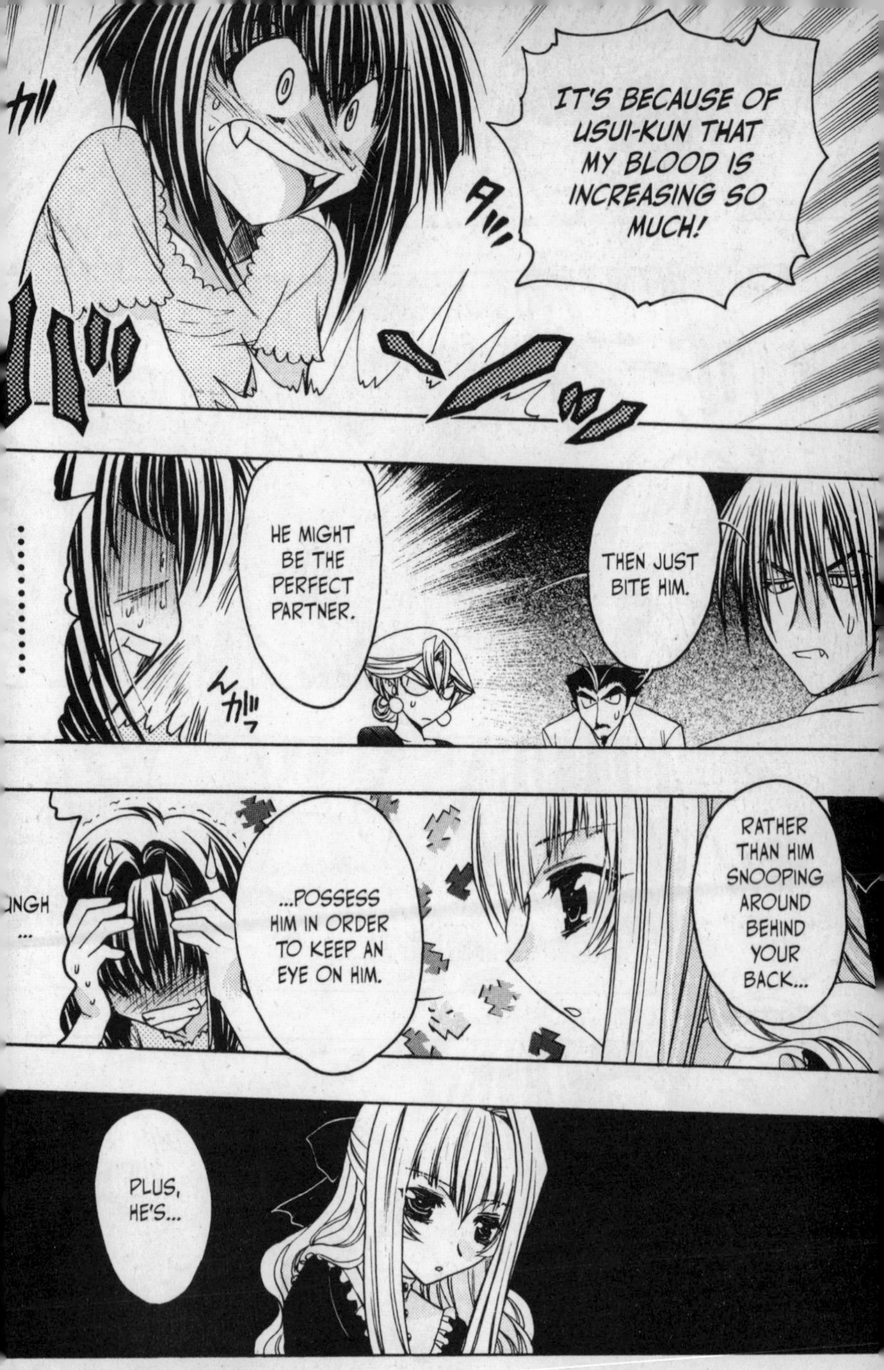
IT'S BECAUSE OF USUI-KUN THAT MY BLOOD IS INCREASING SO MUCH!
THEN JUST BITE HIM.
HE MIGHT BE THE PERFECT PARTNER.
RATHER THAN HIM SNOOPING AROUND BEHIND YOUR BACK...
...POSSESS HIM IN ORDER TO KEEP AN EYE ON HIM.
NGH ...
PLUS, HE'S...

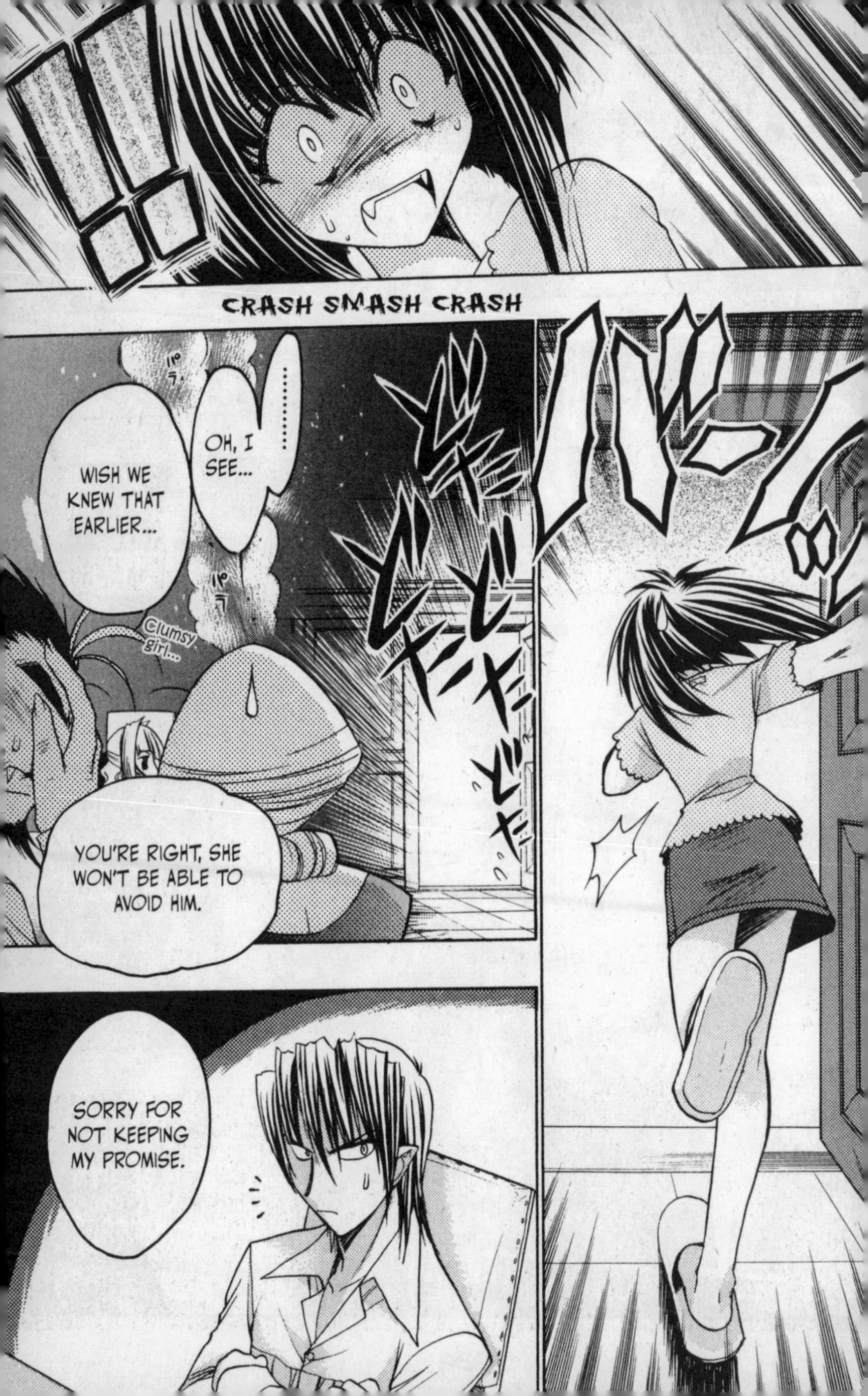
CRASH SMASH CRASH
......
OH, I SEE...
WISH WE KNEW THAT EARLIER...
Clumsy girl...
YOU'RE RIGHT, SHE WON'T BE ABLE TO AVOID HIM.
SORRY FOR NOT KEEPING MY PROMISE.

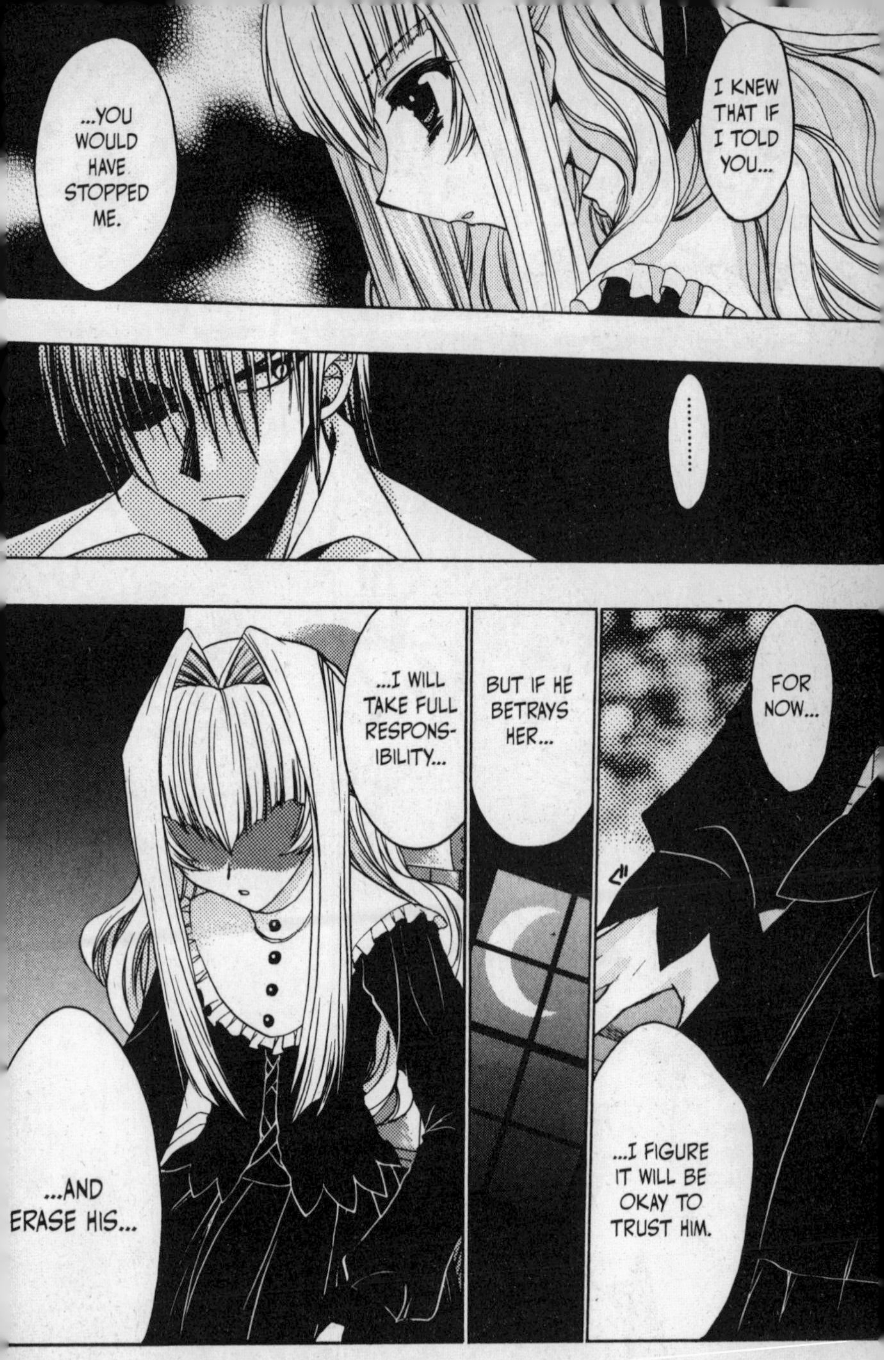
I KNEW THAT IF I TOLD YOU...
...YOU WOULD HAVE STOPPED ME.
....
FOR NOW...
...I FIGURE IT WILL BE OKAY TO TRUST HIM.
BUT IF HE BETRAYS HER...
...I WILL TAKE FULL RESPONSIBILITY...
...AND ERASE HIS...

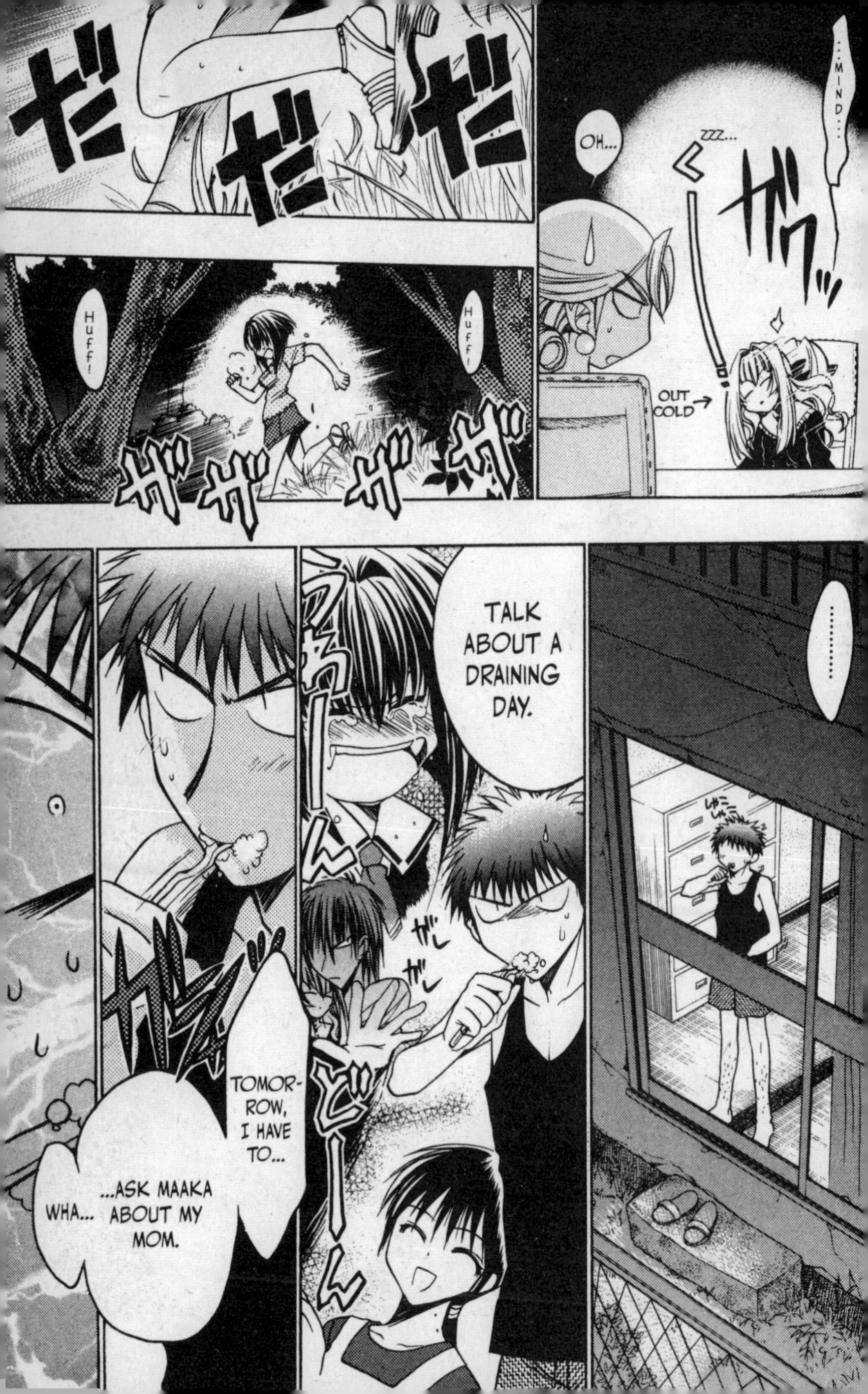
...MIND...
OH...
ZZZ...
OUT COLD
Huff!
Huff!
....
TALK ABOUT A DRAINING DAY.
TOMOR-ROW, I HAVE TO...
...ASK MAAKA ABOUT MY MOM.
WHA...

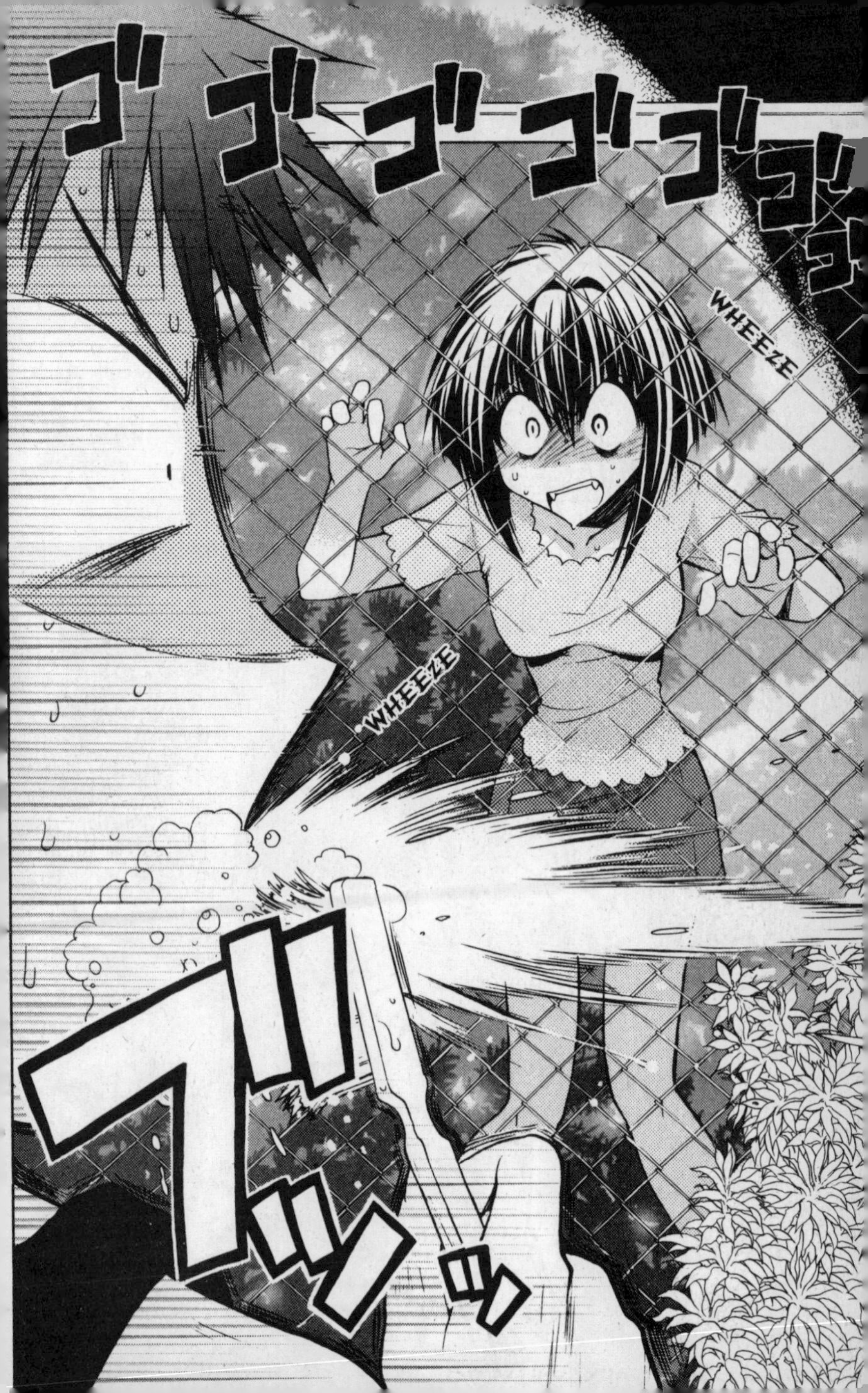
WHEEZE
WHEEZE

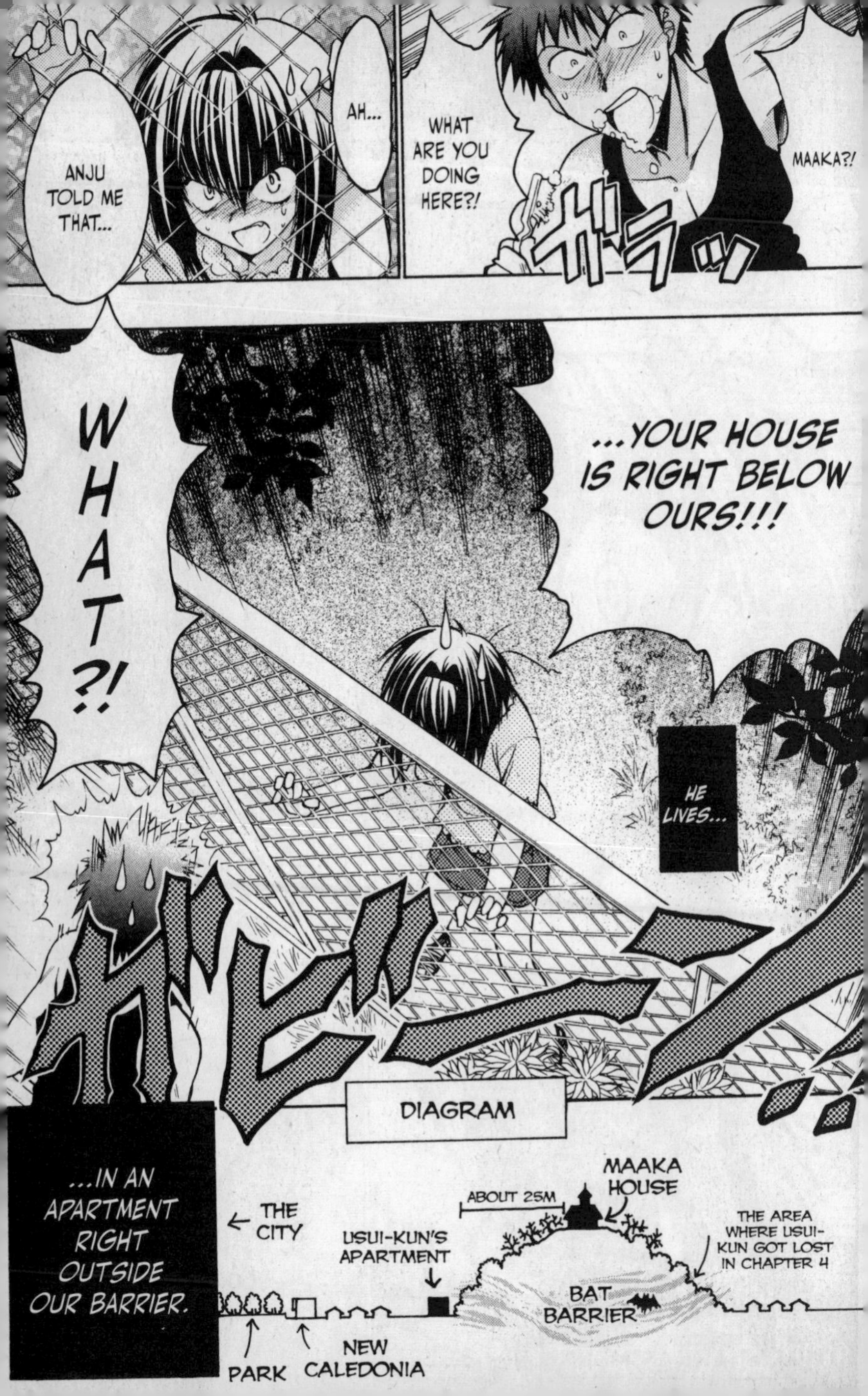
MAAKA?!
ガラッ
WHAT ARE YOU DOING HERE?!
AH...
ANJU TOLD ME THAT...
...YOUR HOUSE IS RIGHT BELOW OURS!!!
WHAT?!
HE LIVES...
ガビーン
...IN AN APARTMENT RIGHT OUTSIDE OUR BARRIER.
DIAGRAM
MAAKA HOUSE
ABOUT 25M
THE AREA WHERE USUI-KUN GOT LOST IN CHAPTER 4
THE CITY
USUI-KUN'S APARTMENT
BAT BARRIER
PARK
NEW CALEDONIA

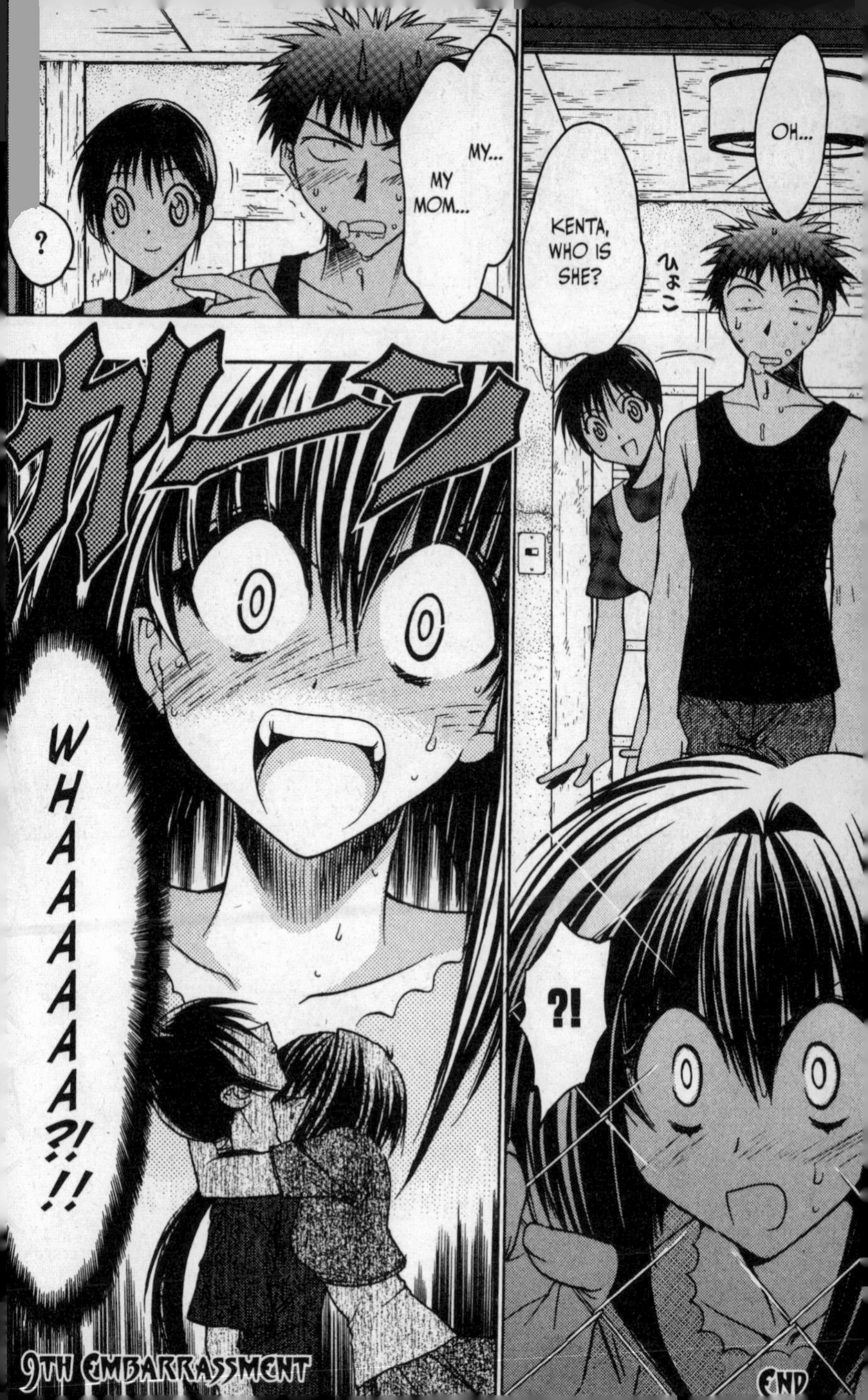
OH...
KENTA, WHO IS SHE?
ひょこ
?!
MY... MY MOM...
?
ガーン
WHAAAAAAAAAA?!!!
9TH EMBARRASSMENT
END

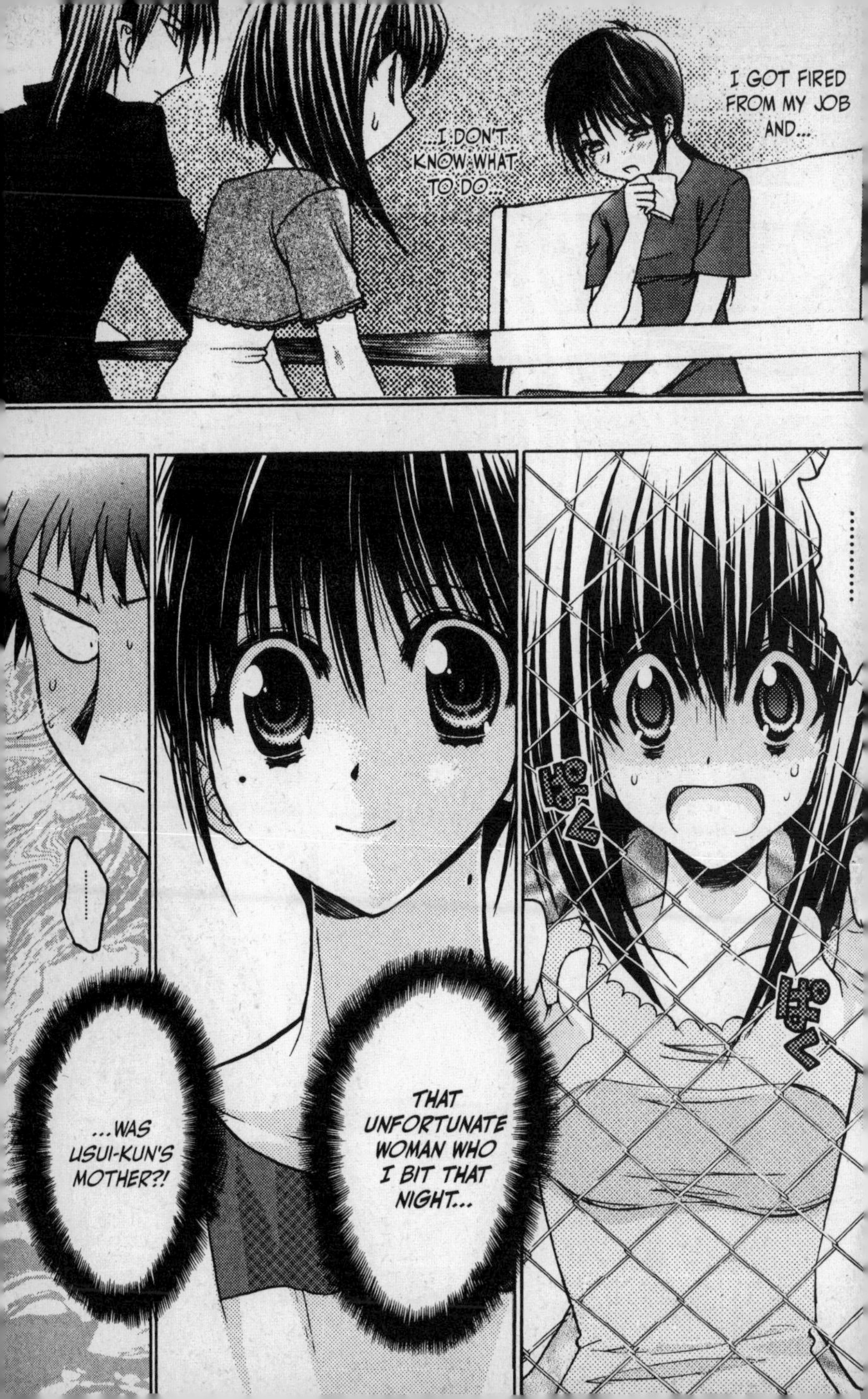
I GOT FIRED FROM MY JOB AND...
...I DON'T KNOW WHAT TO DO...
......
ぽく
ぽく
THAT UNFORTUNATE WOMAN WHO I BIT THAT NIGHT...
...WAS USUI-KUN'S MOTHER?!
......

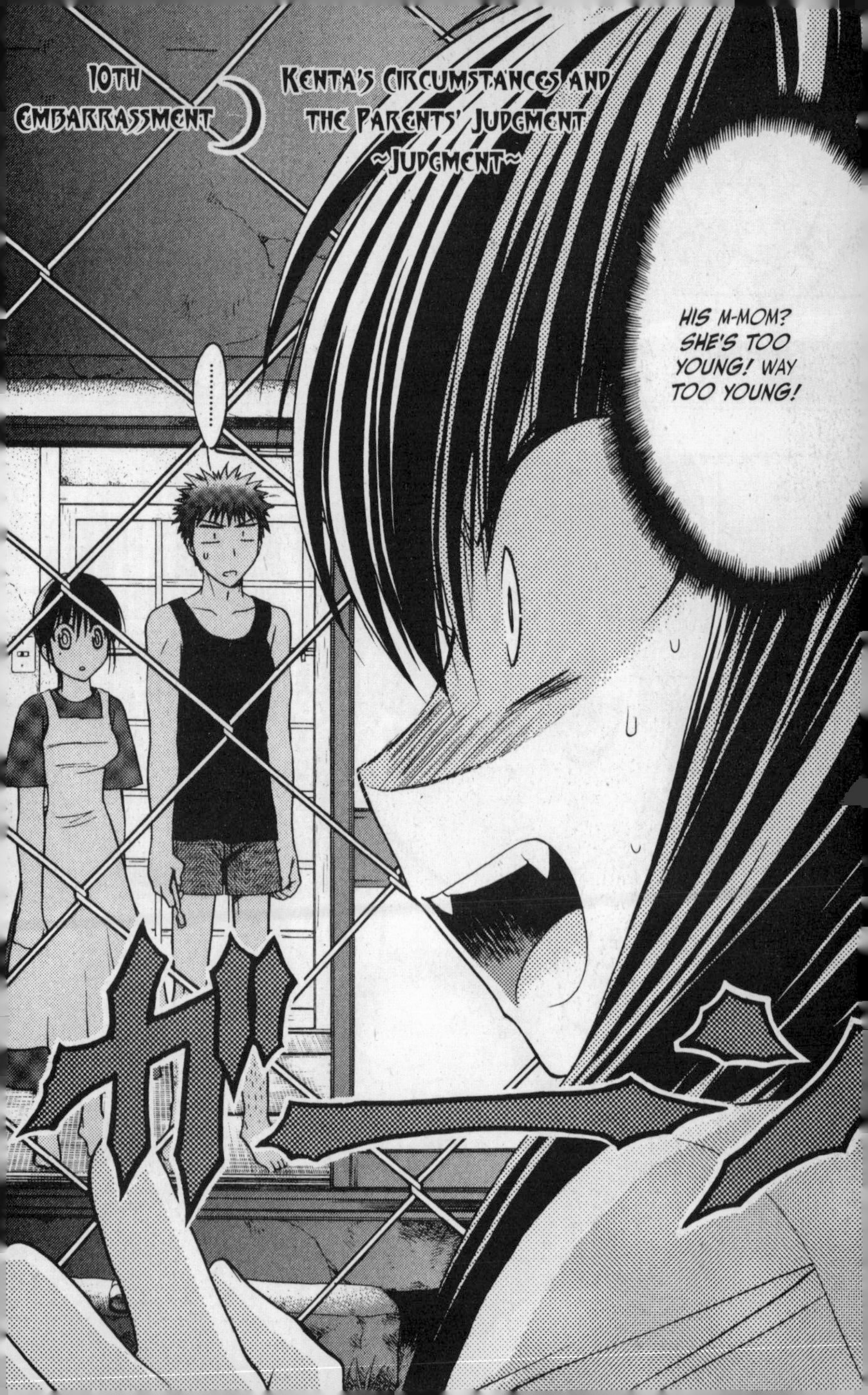
10th Embarrassment
Kenta's Circumstances and the Parents' Judgement ~Judgement~
HIS M-MOM? SHE'S TOO YOUNG! WAY TOO YOUNG!
......!

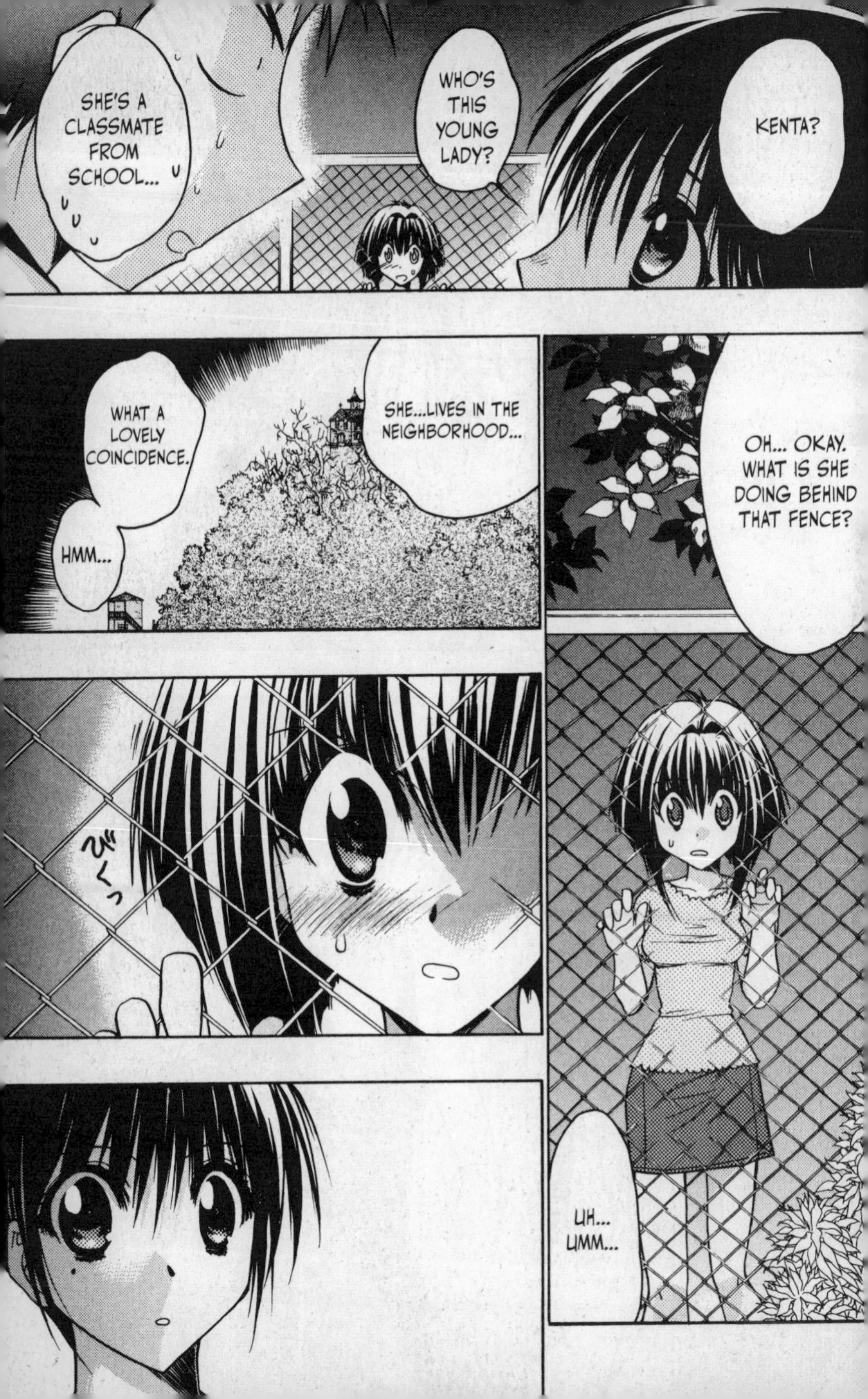
KENTA?
WHO'S THIS YOUNG LADY?
SHE'S A CLASSMATE FROM SCHOOL...
OH... OKAY. WHAT IS SHE DOING BEHIND THAT FENCE?
SHE...LIVES IN THE NEIGHBORHOOD...
WHAT A LOVELY COINCIDENCE.
HMM...
UH... UMM...
びくっ

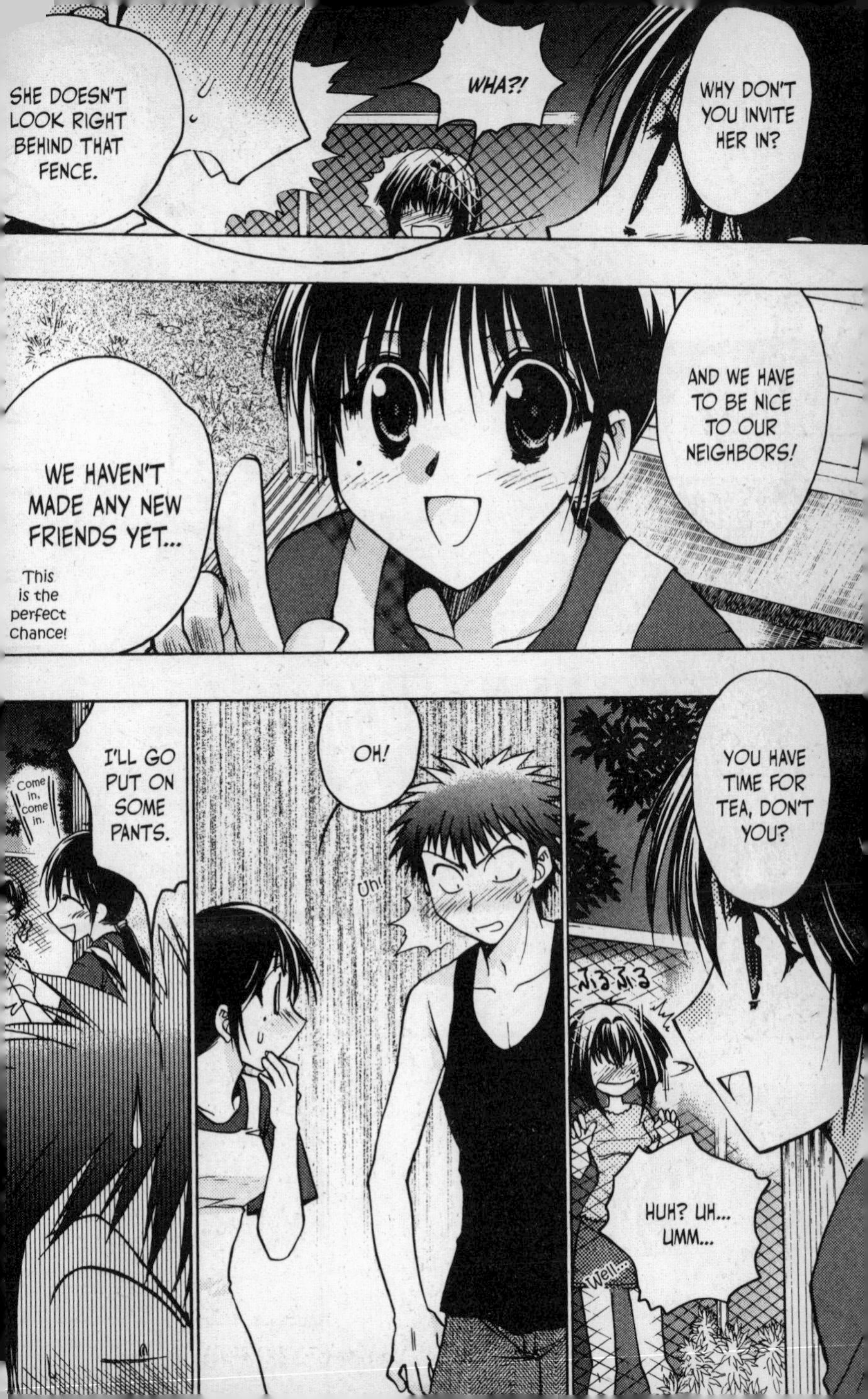
WHY DON'T YOU INVITE HER IN?
WHA?!
SHE DOESN'T LOOK RIGHT BEHIND THAT FENCE.
AND WE HAVE TO BE NICE TO OUR NEIGHBORS!
WE HAVEN'T MADE ANY NEW FRIENDS YET...
This is the perfect chance!
YOU HAVE TIME FOR TEA, DON'T YOU?
ふるふる
HUH? UH... UMM...
Well...
OH!
Uh!
I'LL GO PUT ON SOME PANTS.
Come in, come in.

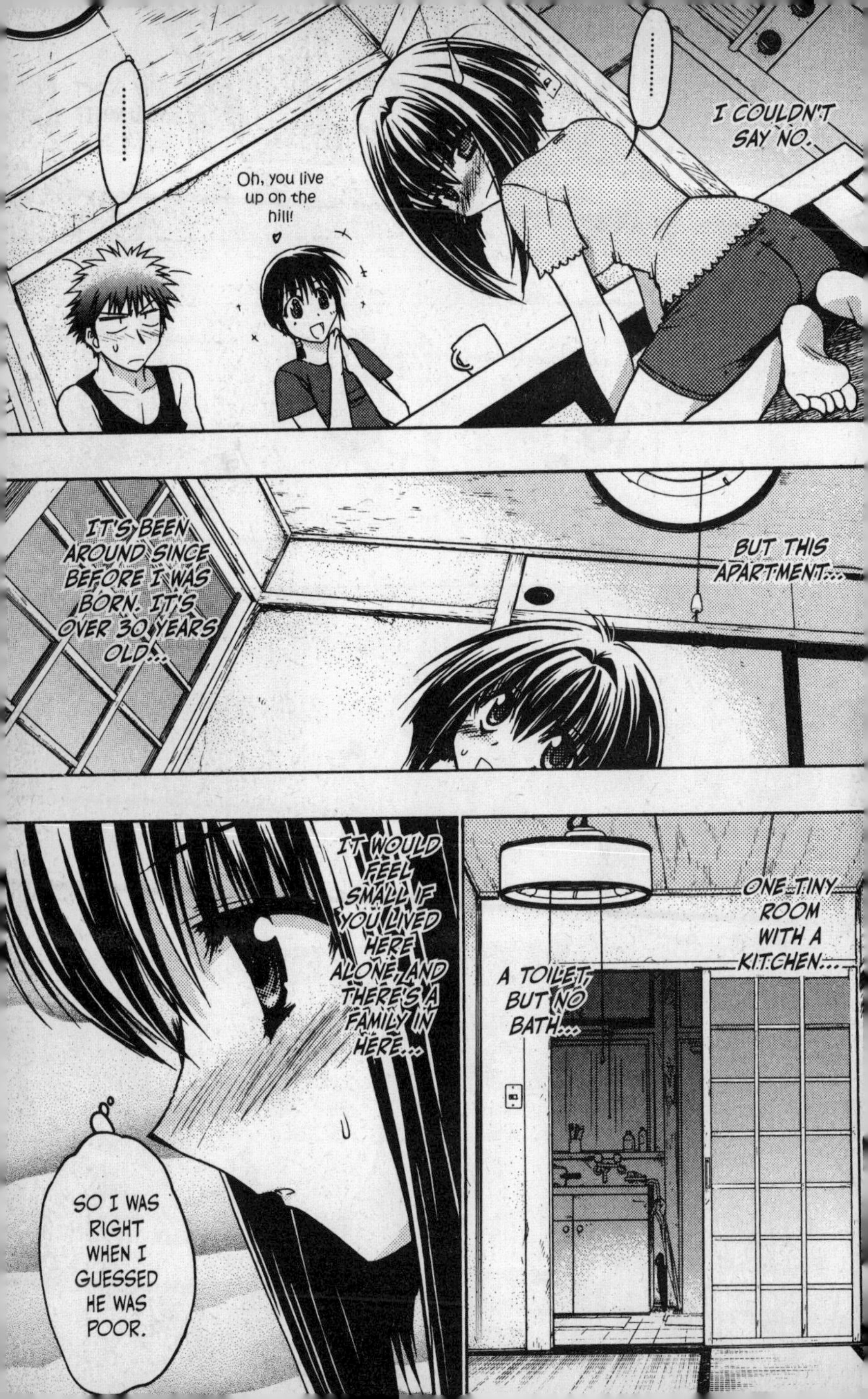
......
I COULDN'T SAY NO.
Oh, you live up on the hill! ♥
......
BUT THIS APARTMENT...
IT'S BEEN AROUND SINCE BEFORE I WAS BORN. IT'S OVER 30 YEARS OLD...
ONE TINY ROOM WITH A KITCHEN...
A TOILET, BUT NO BATH...
IT WOULD FEEL SMALL IF YOU LIVED HERE ALONE, AND THERE'S A FAMILY IN HERE...
SO I WAS RIGHT WHEN I GUESSED HE WAS POOR.

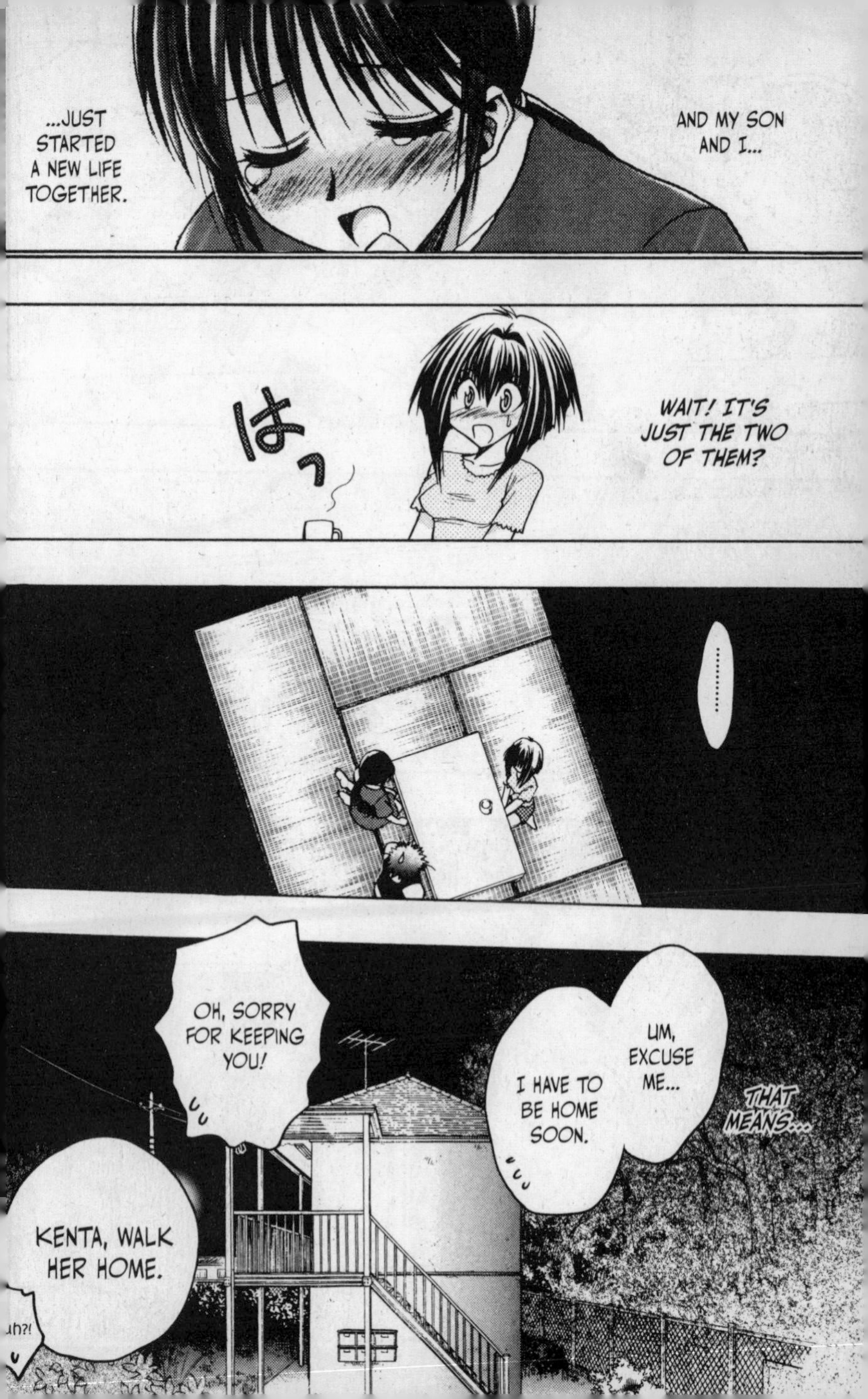

AND MY SON AND I...
...JUST STARTED A NEW LIFE TOGETHER.
WAIT! IT'S JUST THE TWO OF THEM?
はっ
......
THAT MEANS...
UM, EXCUSE ME...
I HAVE TO BE HOME SOON.
OH, SORRY FOR KEEPING YOU!
KENTA, WALK HER HOME.

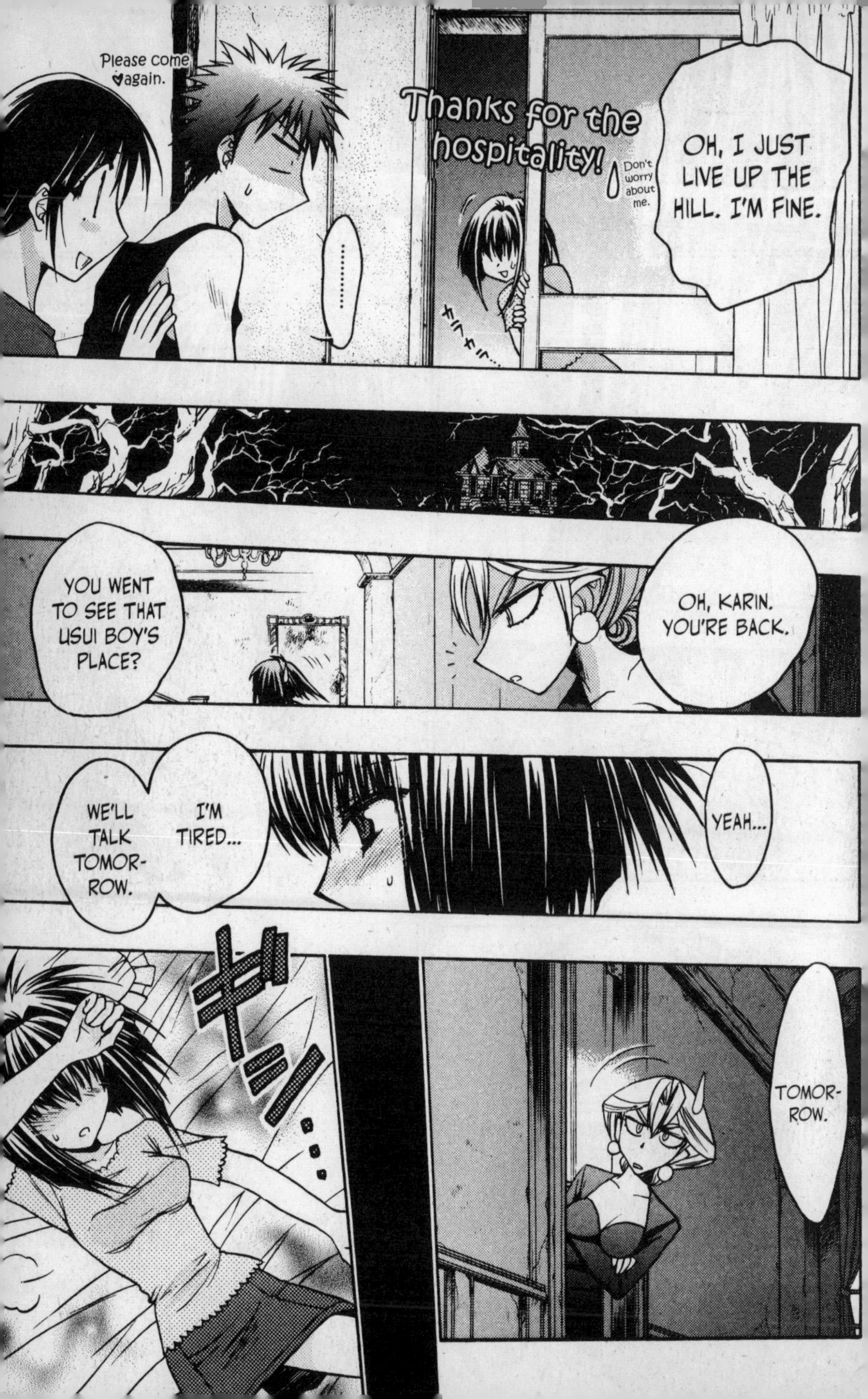
OH, I JUST LIVE UP THE HILL. I'M FINE.
Don't worry about me.
Thanks for the hospitality!
......
Please come again.
OH, KARIN. YOU'RE BACK.
YOU WENT TO SEE THAT USUI BOY'S PLACE?
YEAH...
I'M TIRED...
WE'LL TALK TOMOR-ROW.
TOMOR-ROW.

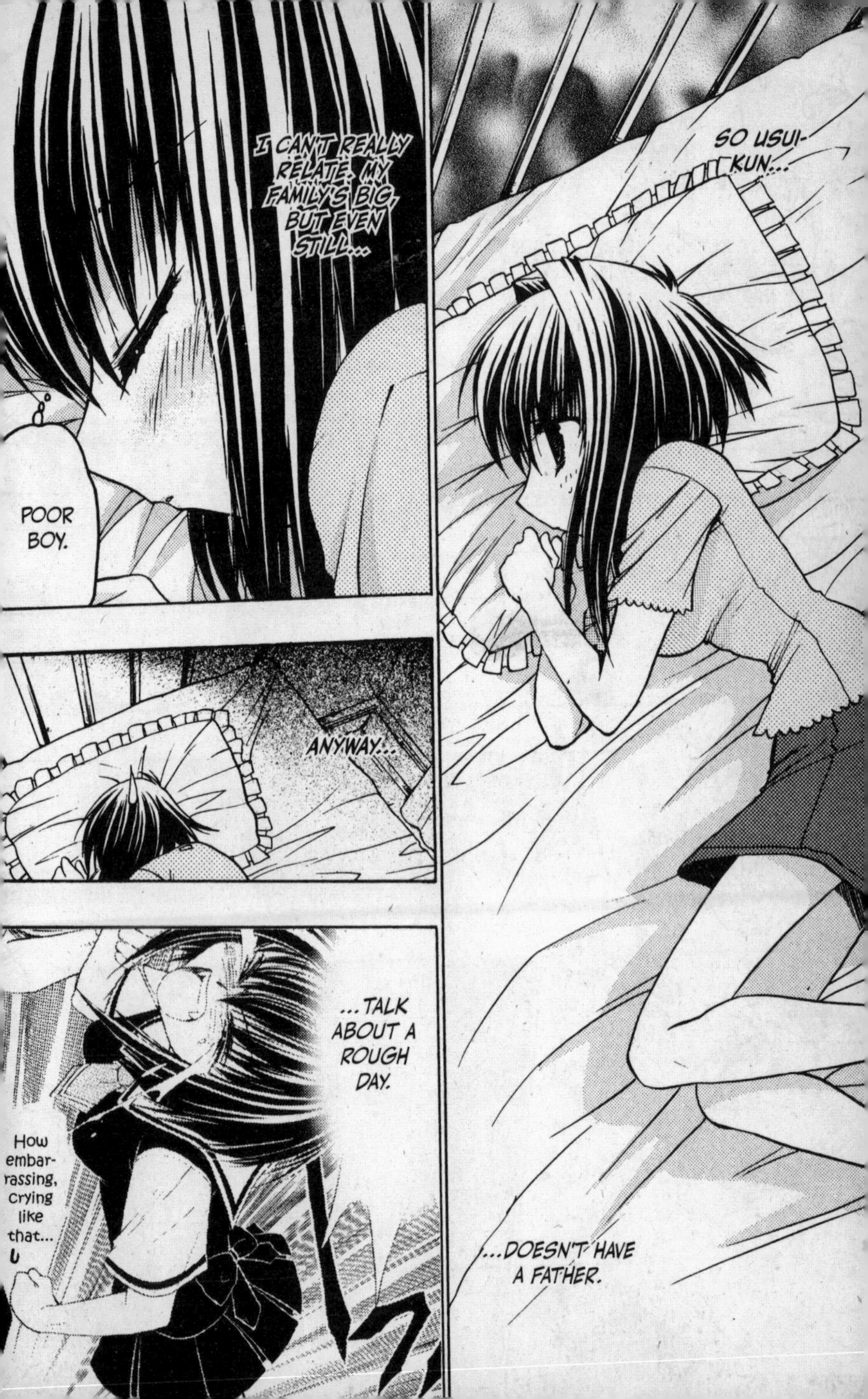
SO USUI-KUN...
...DOESN'T HAVE A FATHER.
I CAN'T REALLY RELATE. MY FAMILY'S BIG, BUT EVEN STILL...
POOR BOY.
ANYWAY...
...TALK ABOUT A ROUGH DAY.
How embarrassing, crying like that...

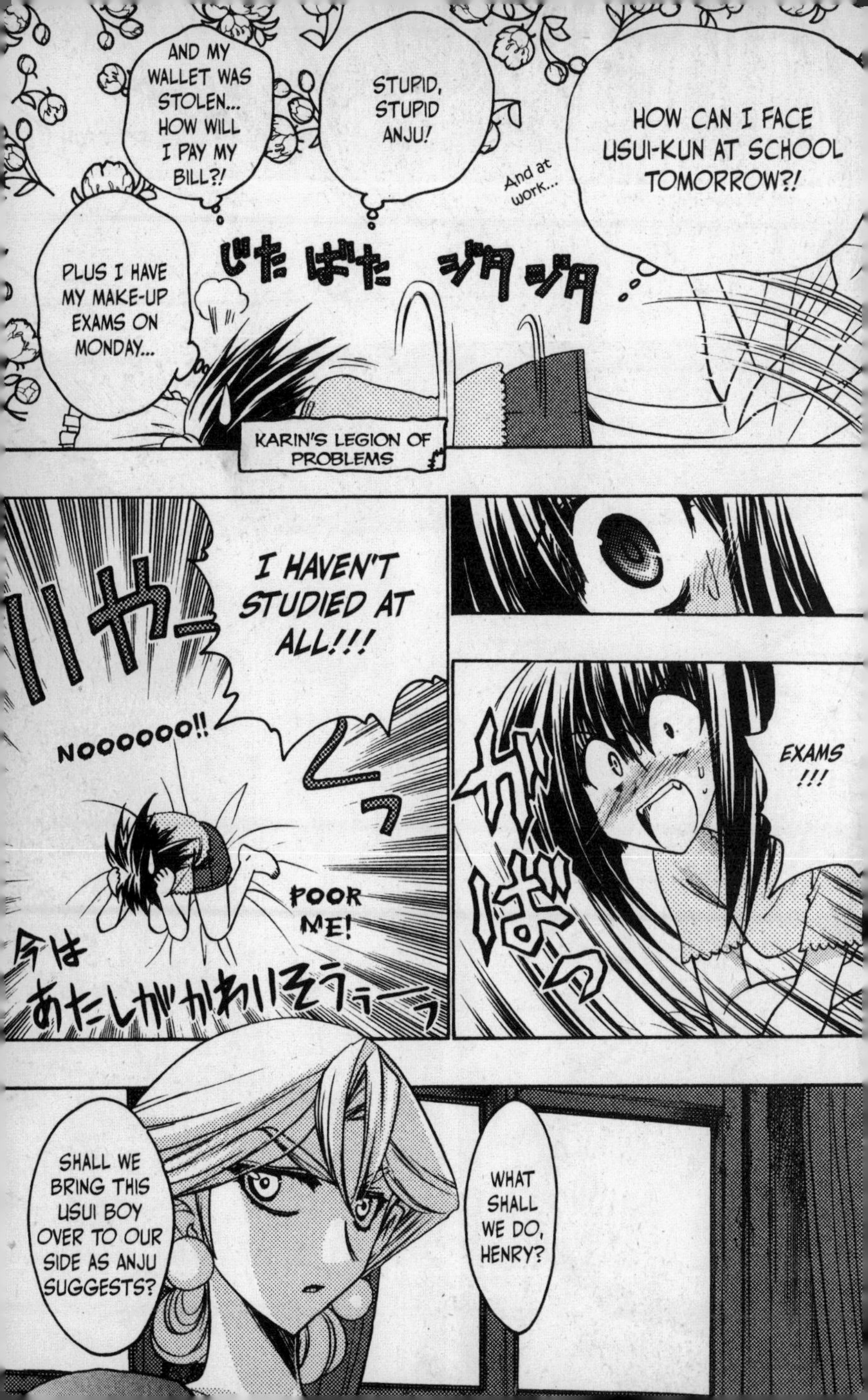
HOW CAN I FACE USUI-KUN AT SCHOOL TOMORROW?!
And at work...
STUPID, STUPID ANJU!
AND MY WALLET WAS STOLEN... HOW WILL I PAY MY BILL?!
PLUS I HAVE MY MAKE-UP EXAMS ON MONDAY...
じたばた ジタジタ
KARIN'S LEGION OF PROBLEMS
がばっ
EXAMS !!!
いやー
I HAVEN'T STUDIED AT ALL!!!
NOOOOOO!!
くっ
POOR ME!
今は あたしがかわいそうぅーっ
WHAT SHALL WE DO, HENRY?
SHALL WE BRING THIS USUI BOY OVER TO OUR SIDE AS ANJU SUGGESTS?

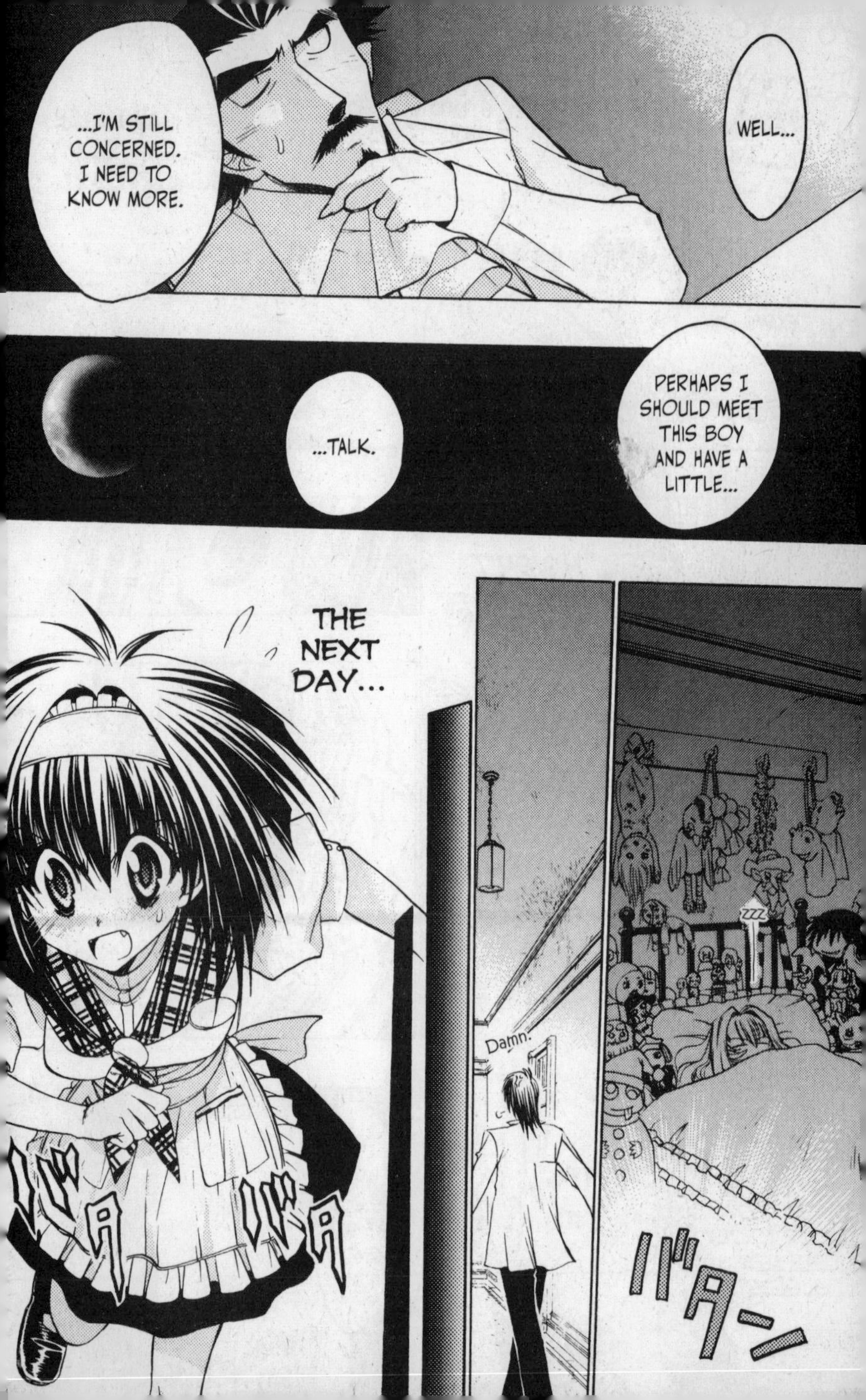

WELL...
...I'M STILL CONCERNED. I NEED TO KNOW MORE.
PERHAPS I SHOULD MEET THIS BOY AND HAVE A LITTLE...
...TALK.
ZZZ
Damn.
バターン
THE NEXT DAY...
バタ
バタ

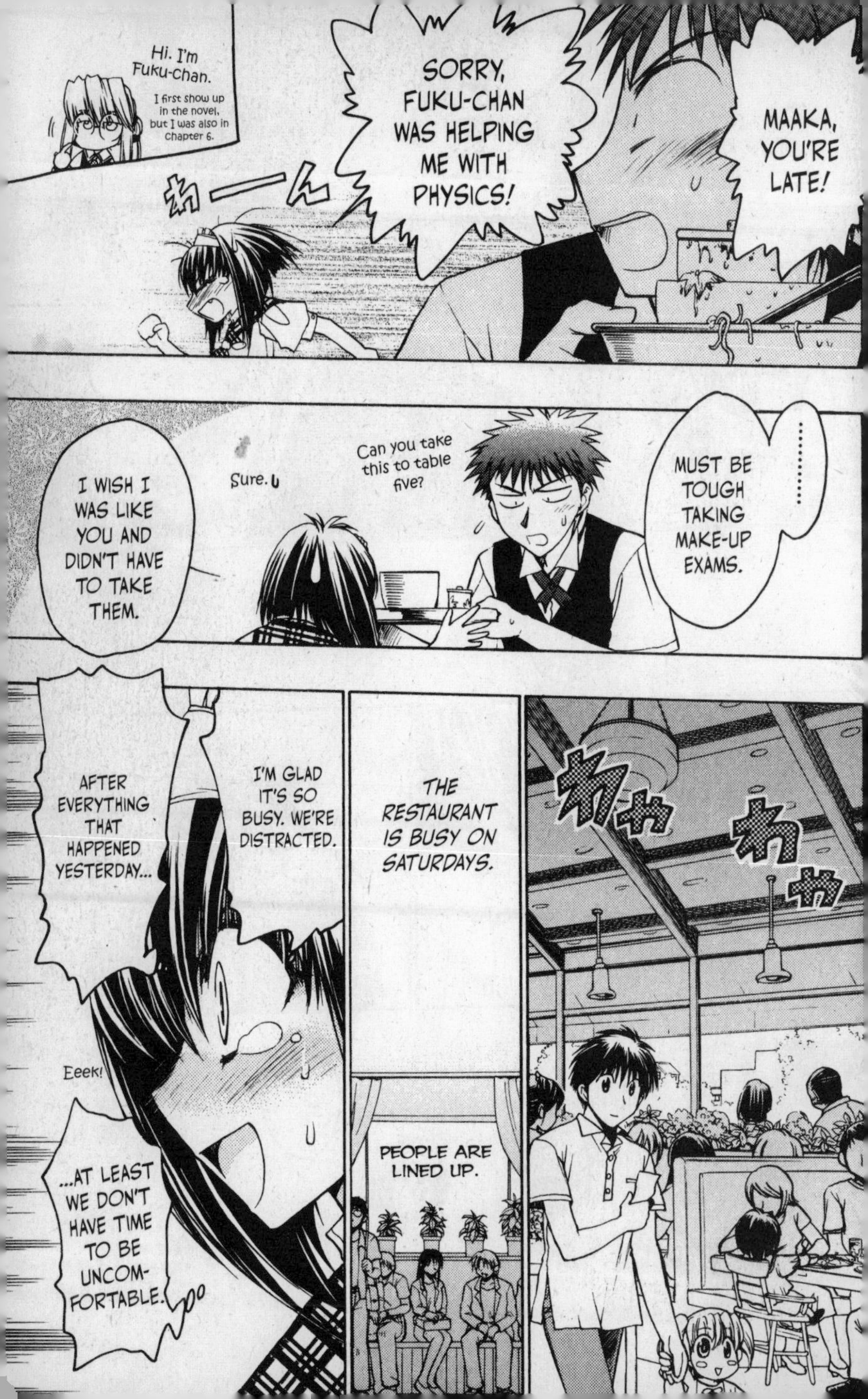
MAAKA, YOU'RE LATE!
SORRY, FUKU-CHAN WAS HELPING ME WITH PHYSICS!
わーん
Hi. I'm Fuku-chan.
I first show up in the novel, but I was also in chapter 6.
......
MUST BE TOUGH TAKING MAKE-UP EXAMS.
Can you take this to table five?
Sure.
I WISH I WAS LIKE YOU AND DIDN'T HAVE TO TAKE THEM.
わわわわ
THE RESTAURANT IS BUSY ON SATURDAYS.
PEOPLE ARE LINED UP.
I'M GLAD IT'S SO BUSY. WE'RE DISTRACTED.
AFTER EVERYTHING THAT HAPPENED YESTERDAY...
Eeek!
...AT LEAST WE DON'T HAVE TIME TO BE UNCOMFORTABLE.

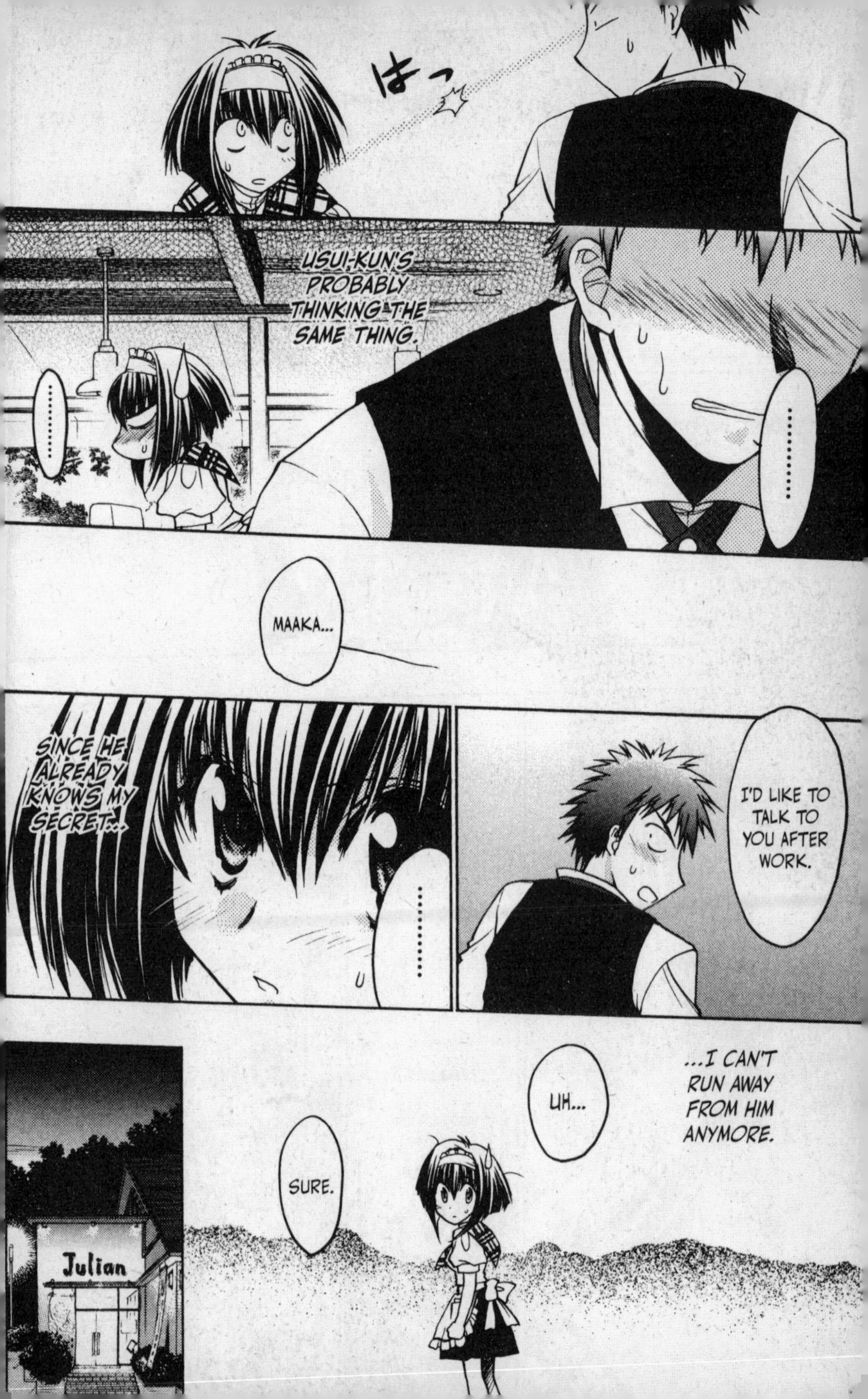
はっ
USUI-KUN'S PROBABLY THINKING THE SAME THING.
......
......
MAAKA...
I'D LIKE TO TALK TO YOU AFTER WORK.
SINCE HE ALREADY KNOWS MY SECRET...
......
...I CAN'T RUN AWAY FROM HIM ANYMORE.
UH...
SURE.
Julian

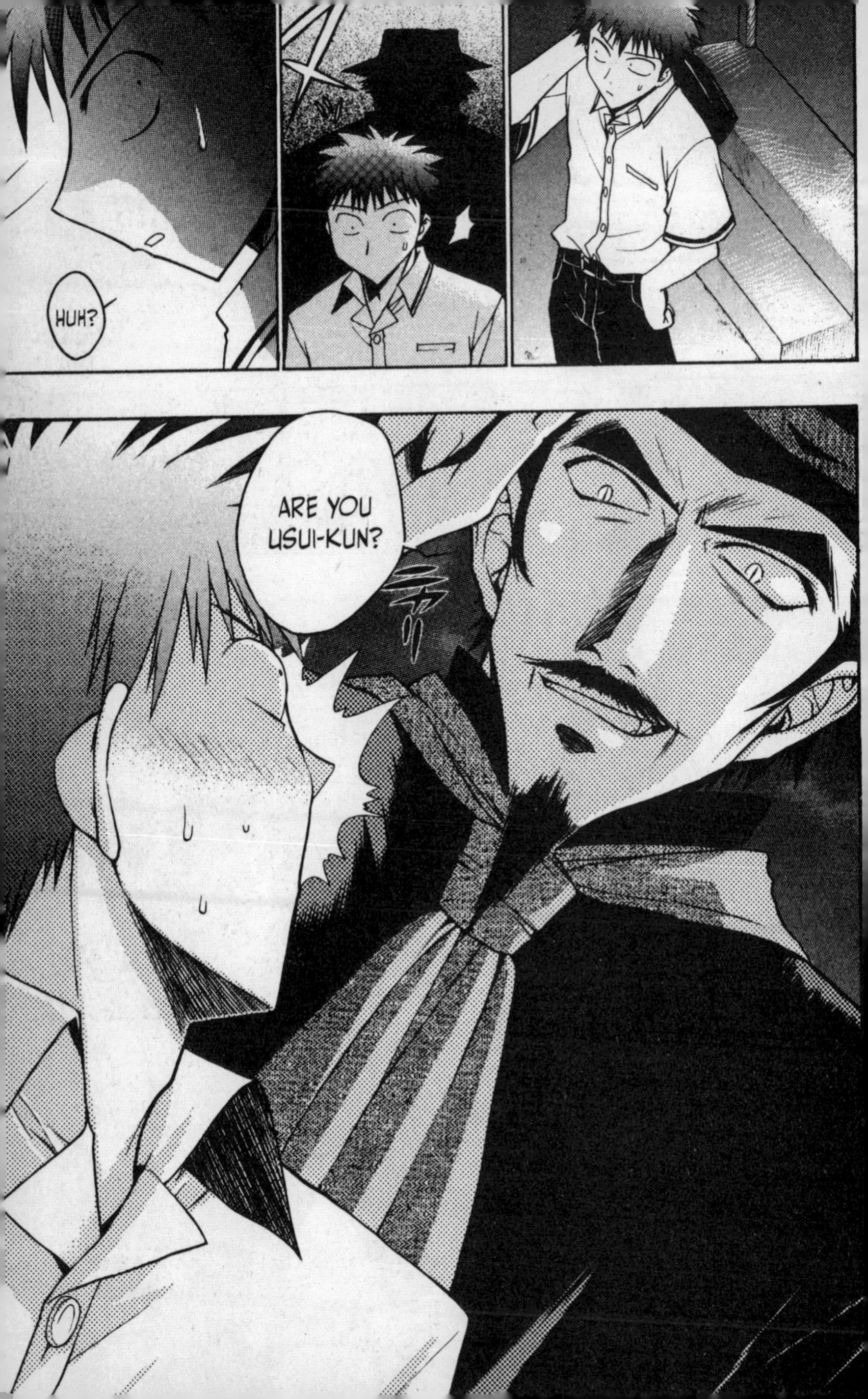
HUH?
ARE YOU USUI-KUN?

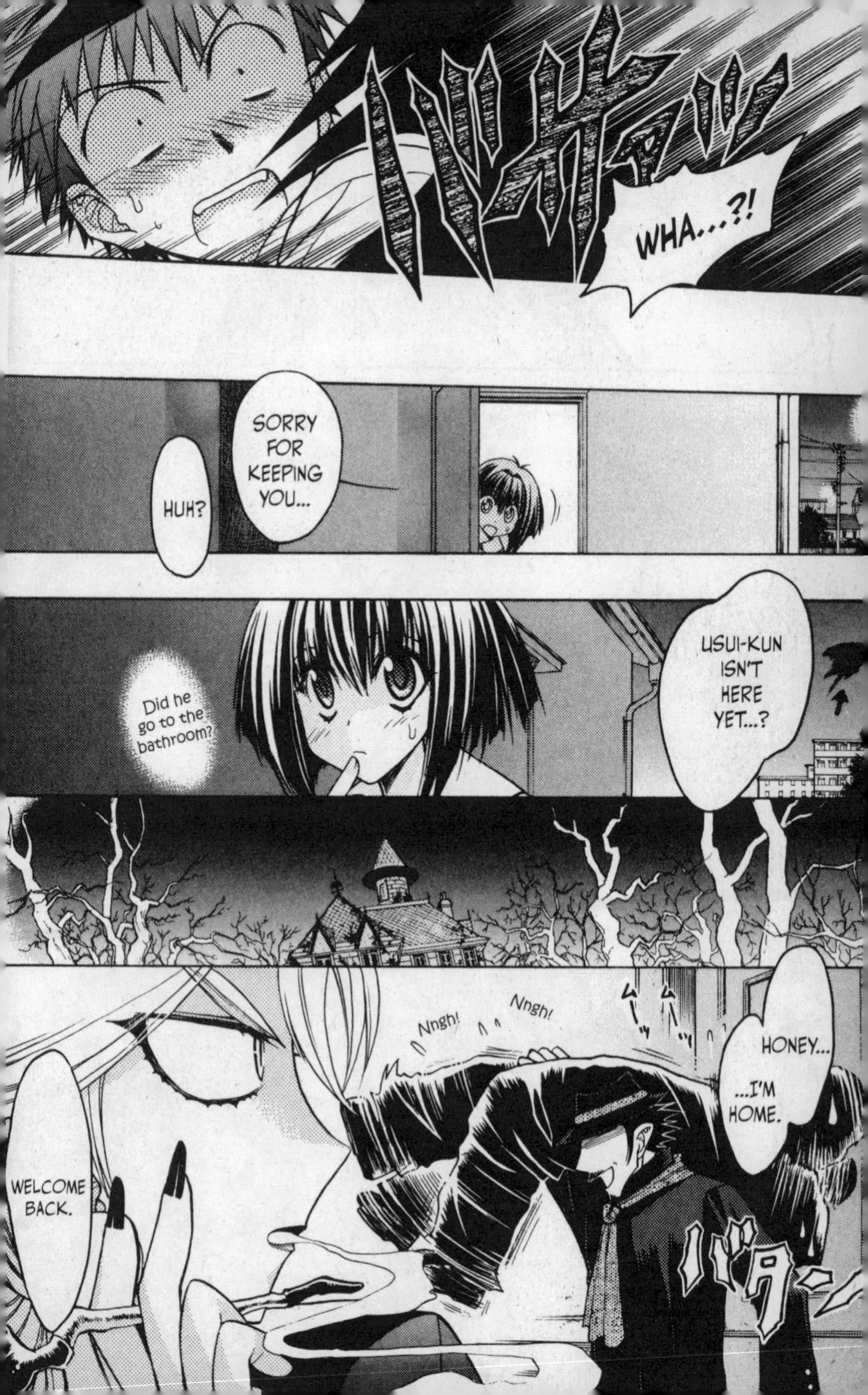
WHA...?!
SORRY FOR KEEPING YOU...
HUH?
USUI-KUN ISN'T HERE YET...?
Did he go to the bathroom?
HONEY...
...I'M HOME.
Nngh!
Nngh!
WELCOME BACK.

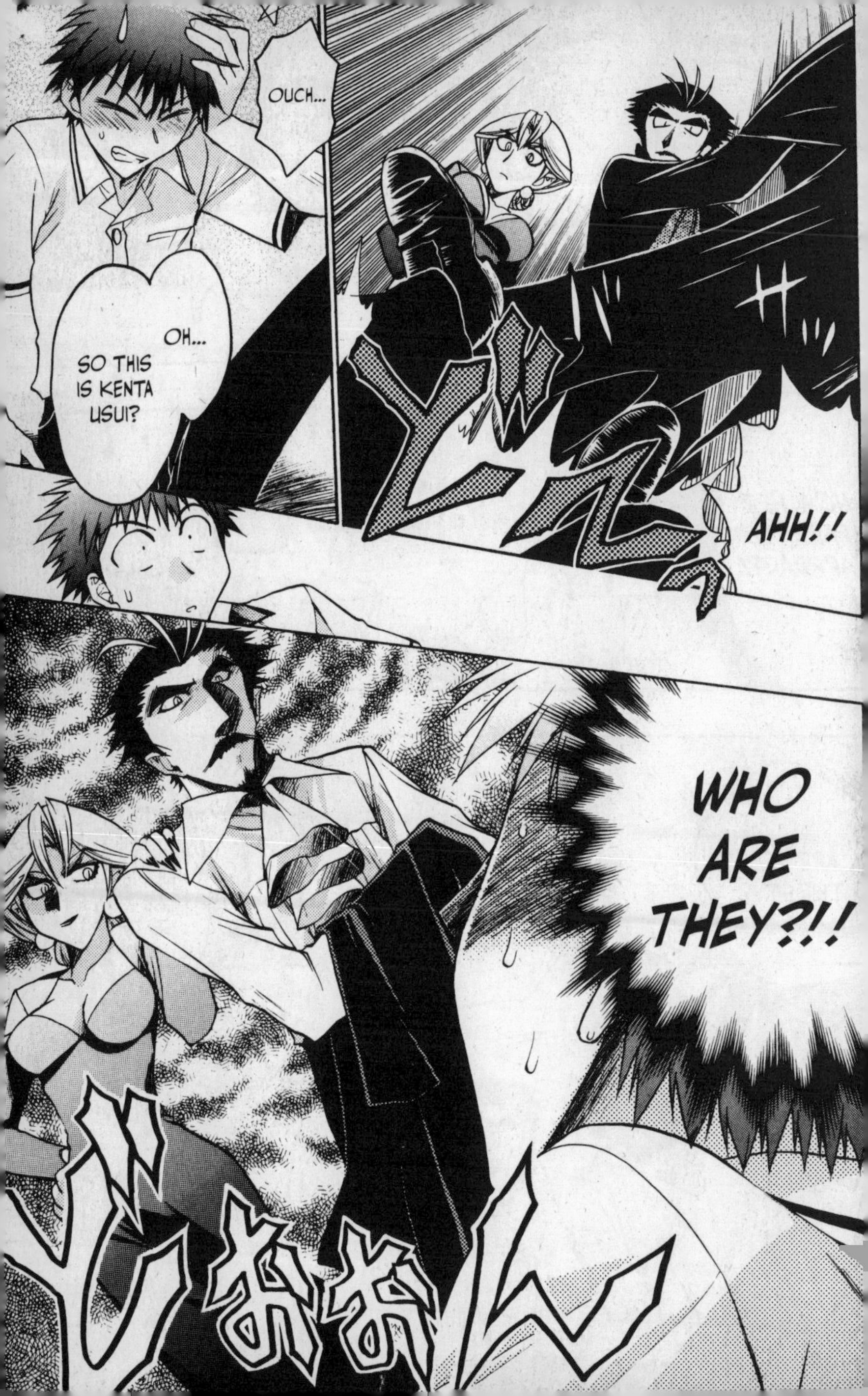
AHH!!
OUCH...
OH... SO THIS IS KENTA USUI?
WHO ARE THEY?!!

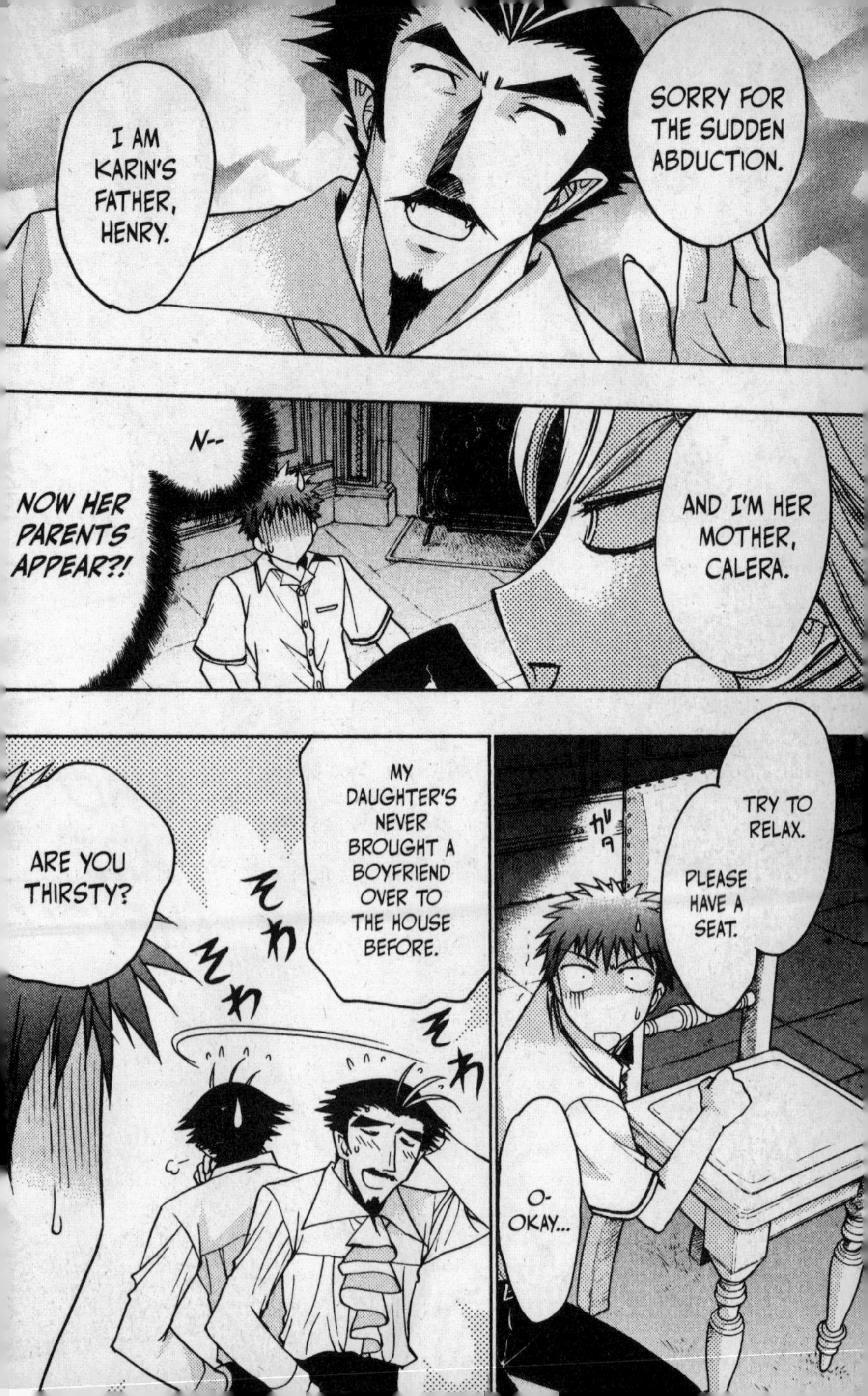
SORRY FOR THE SUDDEN ABDUCTION.
I AM KARIN'S FATHER, HENRY.
AND I'M HER MOTHER, CALERA.
N--
NOW HER PARENTS APPEAR?!
TRY TO RELAX.
PLEASE HAVE A SEAT.
ガタ
O- OKAY...
MY DAUGHTER'S NEVER BROUGHT A BOYFRIEND OVER TO THE HOUSE BEFORE.
そわ
そわ
そわ
ARE YOU THIRSTY?

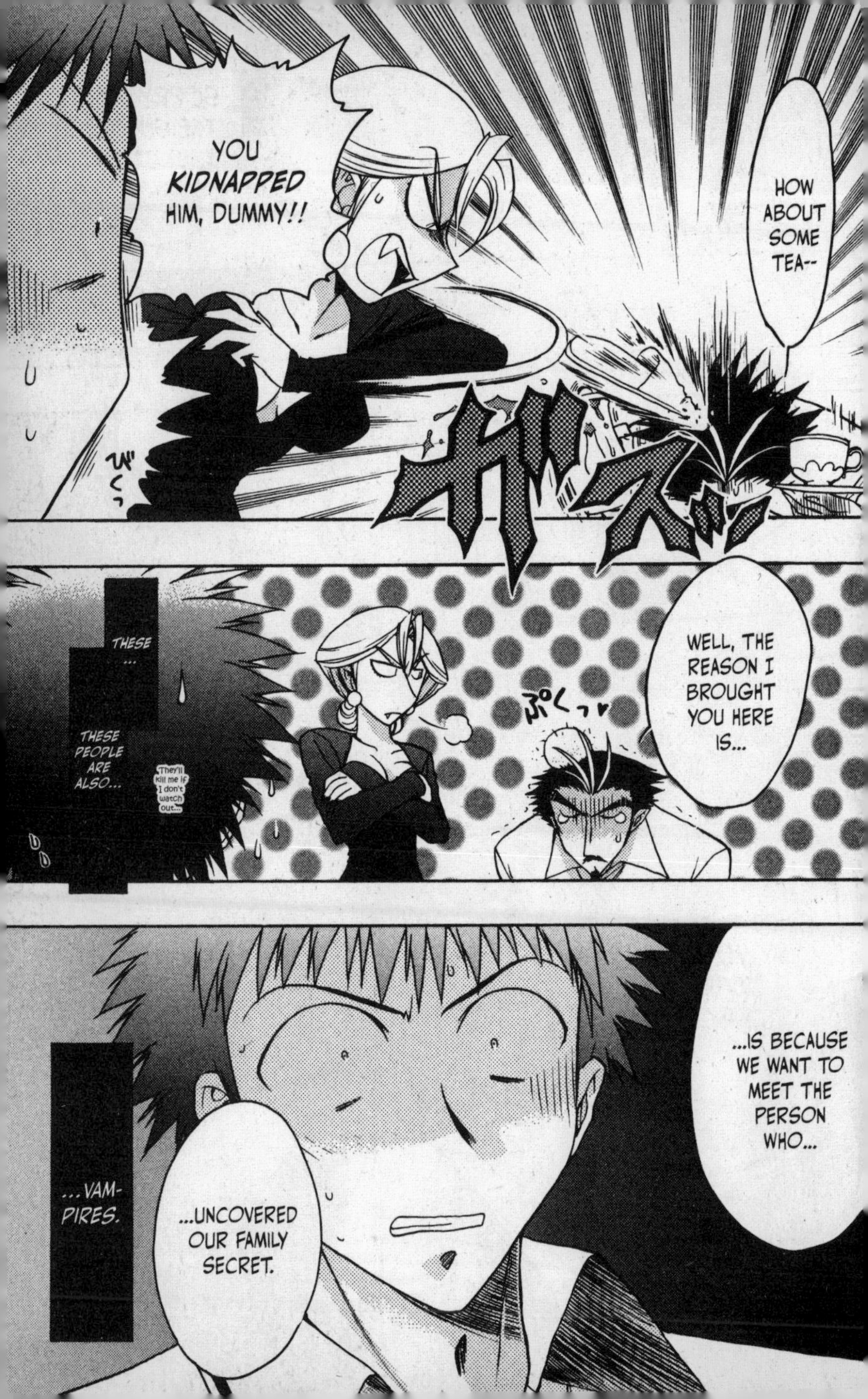
HOW ABOUT SOME TEA--
YOU KIDNAPPED HIM, DUMMY!!
びくっ
WELL, THE REASON I BROUGHT YOU HERE IS...
ぷくっ
THESE...
THESE PEOPLE ARE ALSO...
They'll kill me if I don't watch out...
...IS BECAUSE WE WANT TO MEET THE PERSON WHO...
...UNCOVERED OUR FAMILY SECRET.
...VAMPIRES.

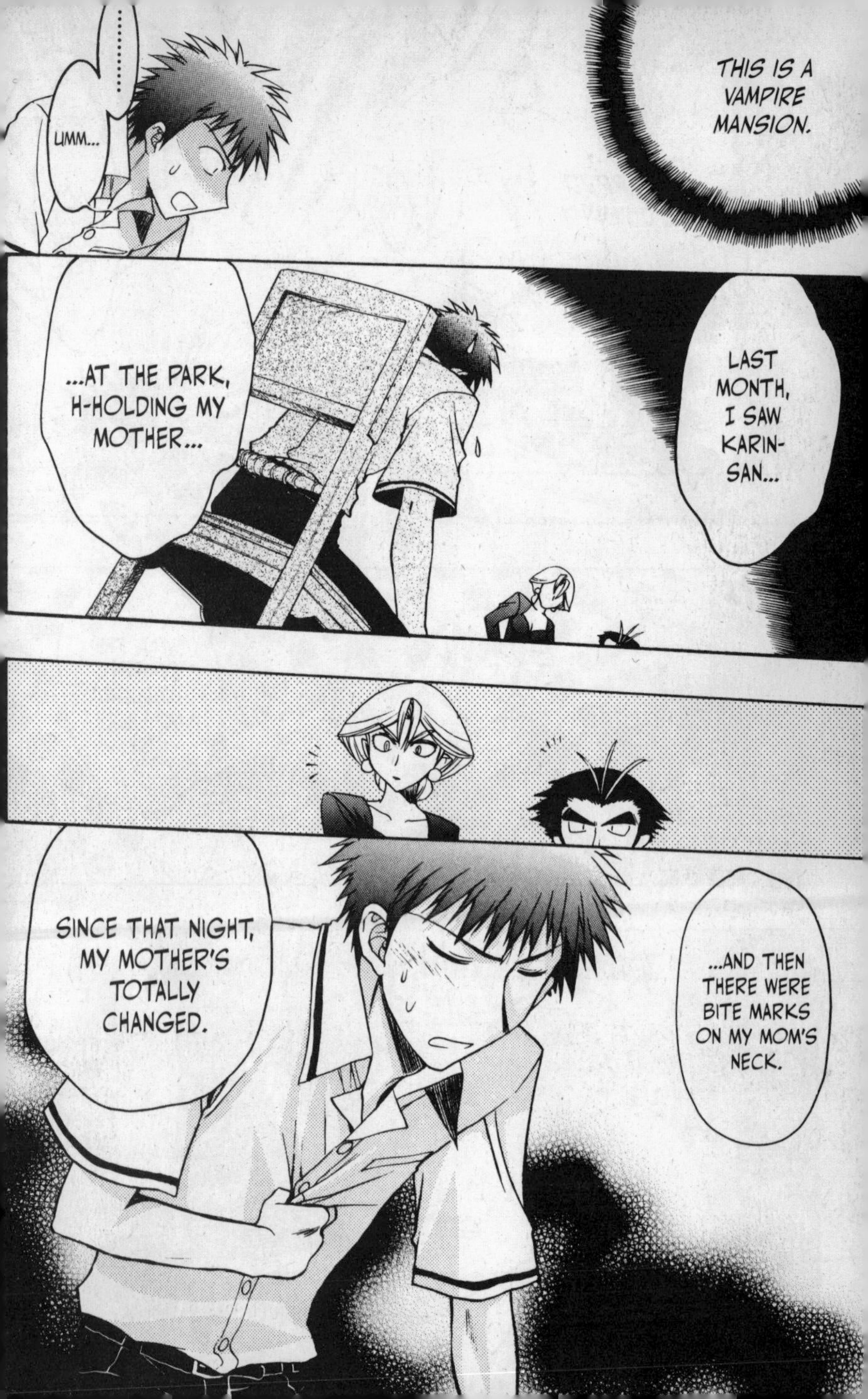
THIS IS A VAMPIRE MANSION.
......
UMM...
LAST MONTH, I SAW KARIN-SAN...
...AT THE PARK, H-HOLDING MY MOTHER...
...AND THEN THERE WERE BITE MARKS ON MY MOM'S NECK.
SINCE THAT NIGHT, MY MOTHER'S TOTALLY CHANGED.

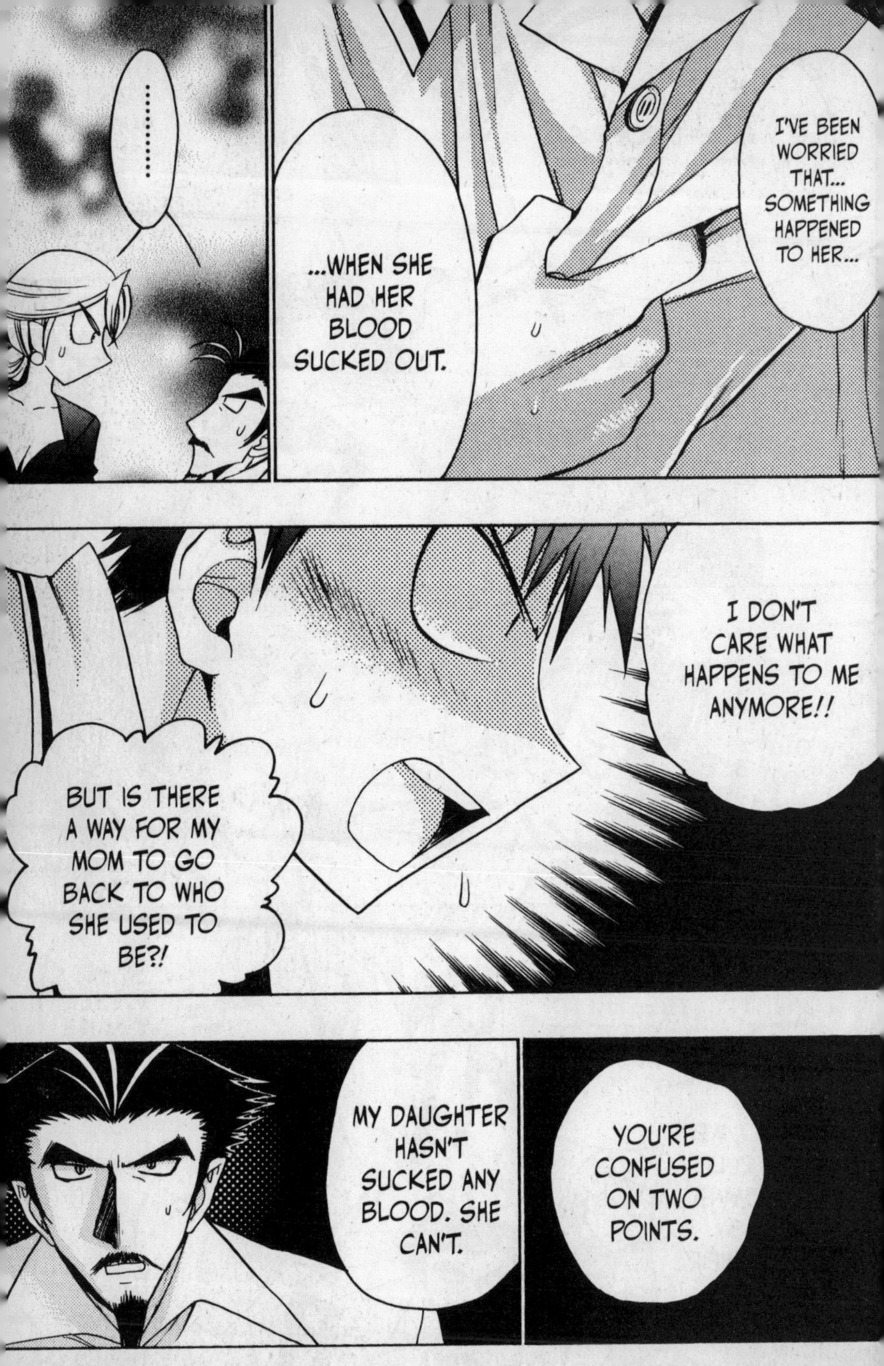
I'VE BEEN WORRIED THAT... SOMETHING HAPPENED TO HER...
...WHEN SHE HAD HER BLOOD SUCKED OUT.
......
I DON'T CARE WHAT HAPPENS TO ME ANYMORE!!
BUT IS THERE A WAY FOR MY MOM TO GO BACK TO WHO SHE USED TO BE?!
YOU'RE CONFUSED ON TWO POINTS.
MY DAUGHTER HASN'T SUCKED ANY BLOOD. SHE CAN'T.

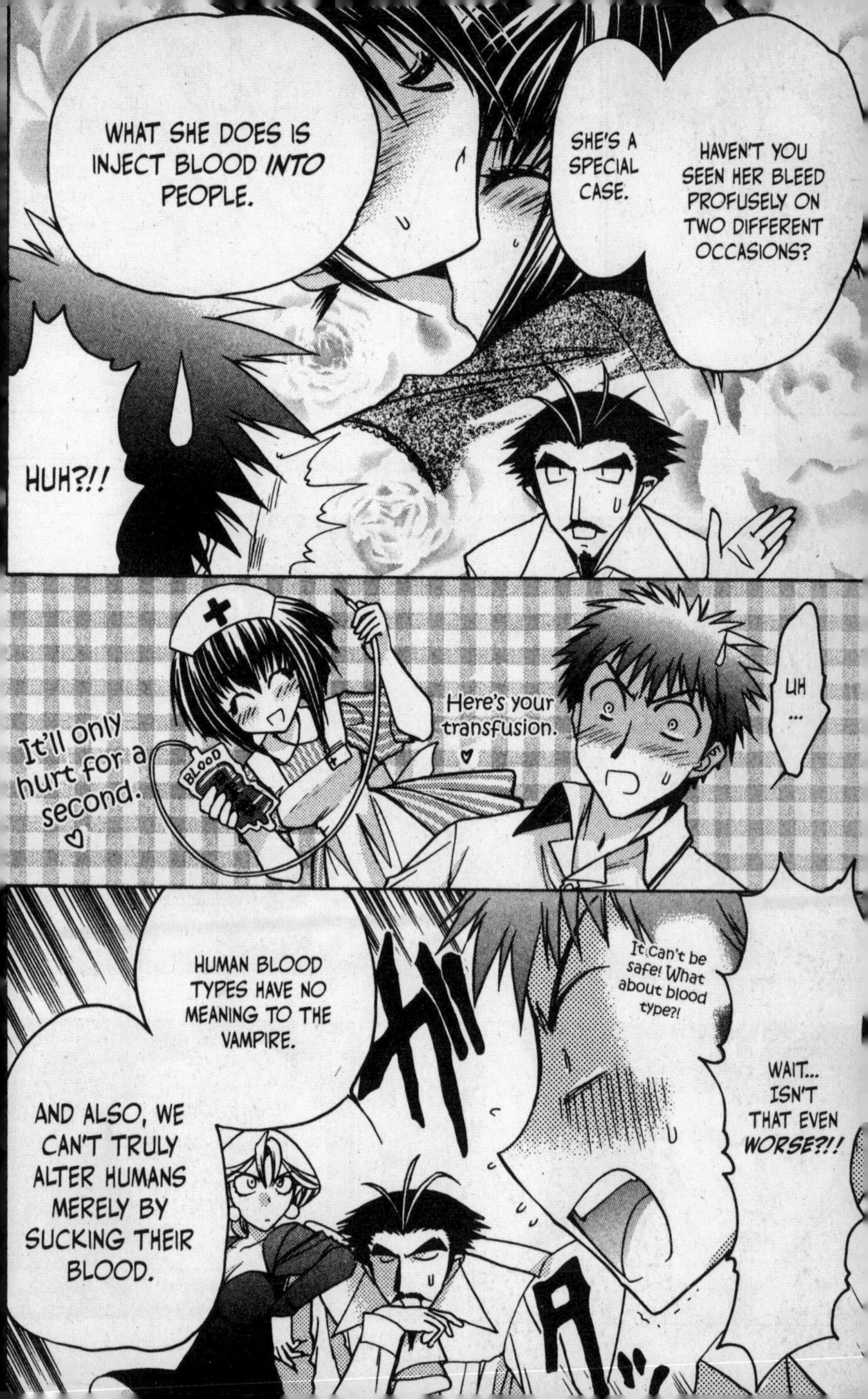
HAVEN'T YOU SEEN HER BLEED PROFUSELY ON TWO DIFFERENT OCCASIONS?
SHE'S A SPECIAL CASE.
WHAT SHE DOES IS INJECT BLOOD *INTO* PEOPLE.
HUH?!!
UH ...
Here's your transfusion. ♥
It'll only hurt for a second. ♥
BLOOD
It can't be safe! What about blood type?!
HUMAN BLOOD TYPES HAVE NO MEANING TO THE VAMPIRE.
AND ALSO, WE CAN'T TRULY ALTER HUMANS MERELY BY SUCKING THEIR BLOOD.
WAIT... ISN'T THAT EVEN *WORSE?!!*

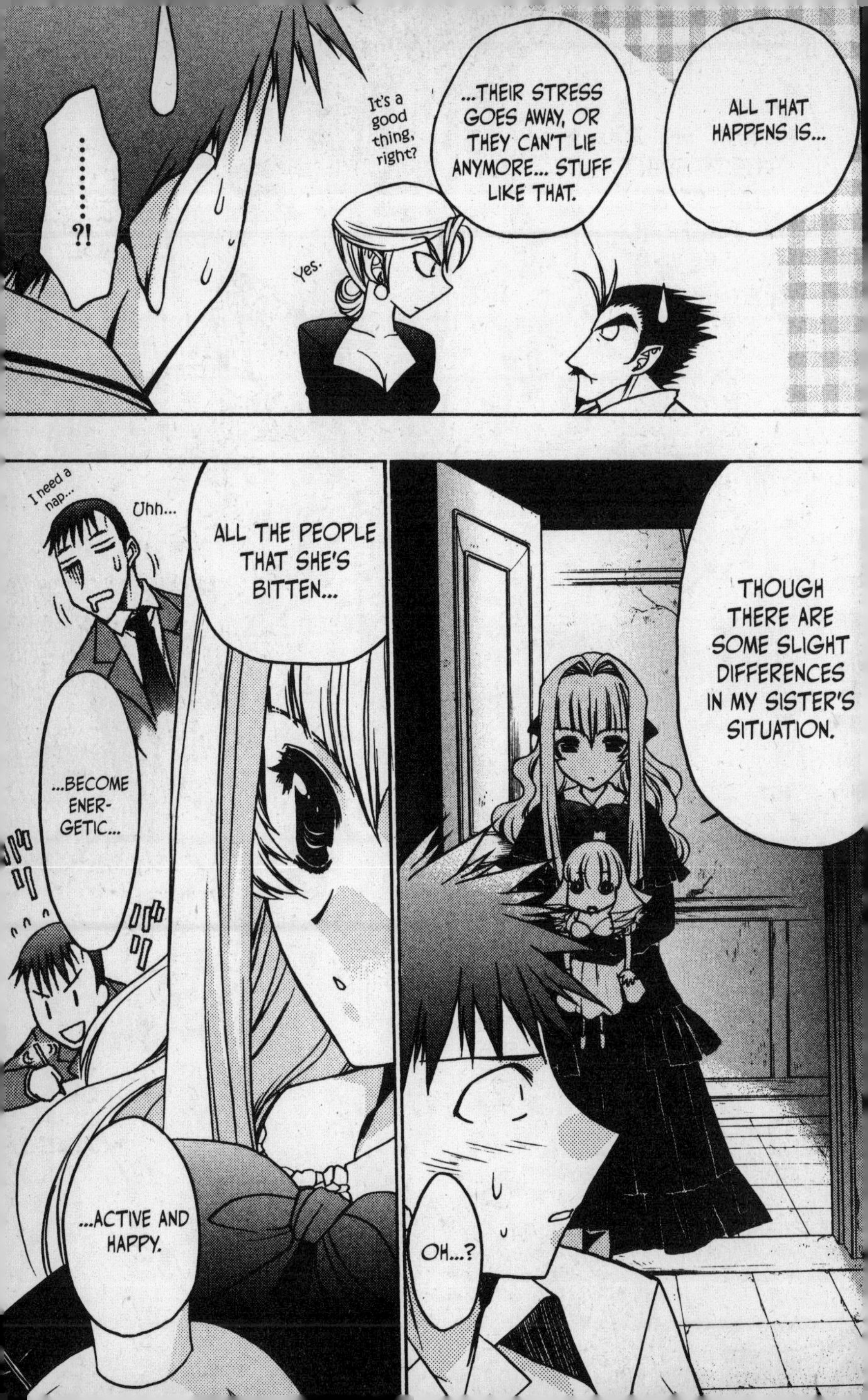
ALL THAT HAPPENS IS...
...THEIR STRESS GOES AWAY, OR THEY CAN'T LIE ANYMORE... STUFF LIKE THAT.
It's a good thing, right?
Yes.
......?!
THOUGH THERE ARE SOME SLIGHT DIFFERENCES IN MY SISTER'S SITUATION.
OH...?
ALL THE PEOPLE THAT SHE'S BITTEN...
I need a nap...
Uhh...
...BECOME ENER-GETIC...
...ACTIVE AND HAPPY.

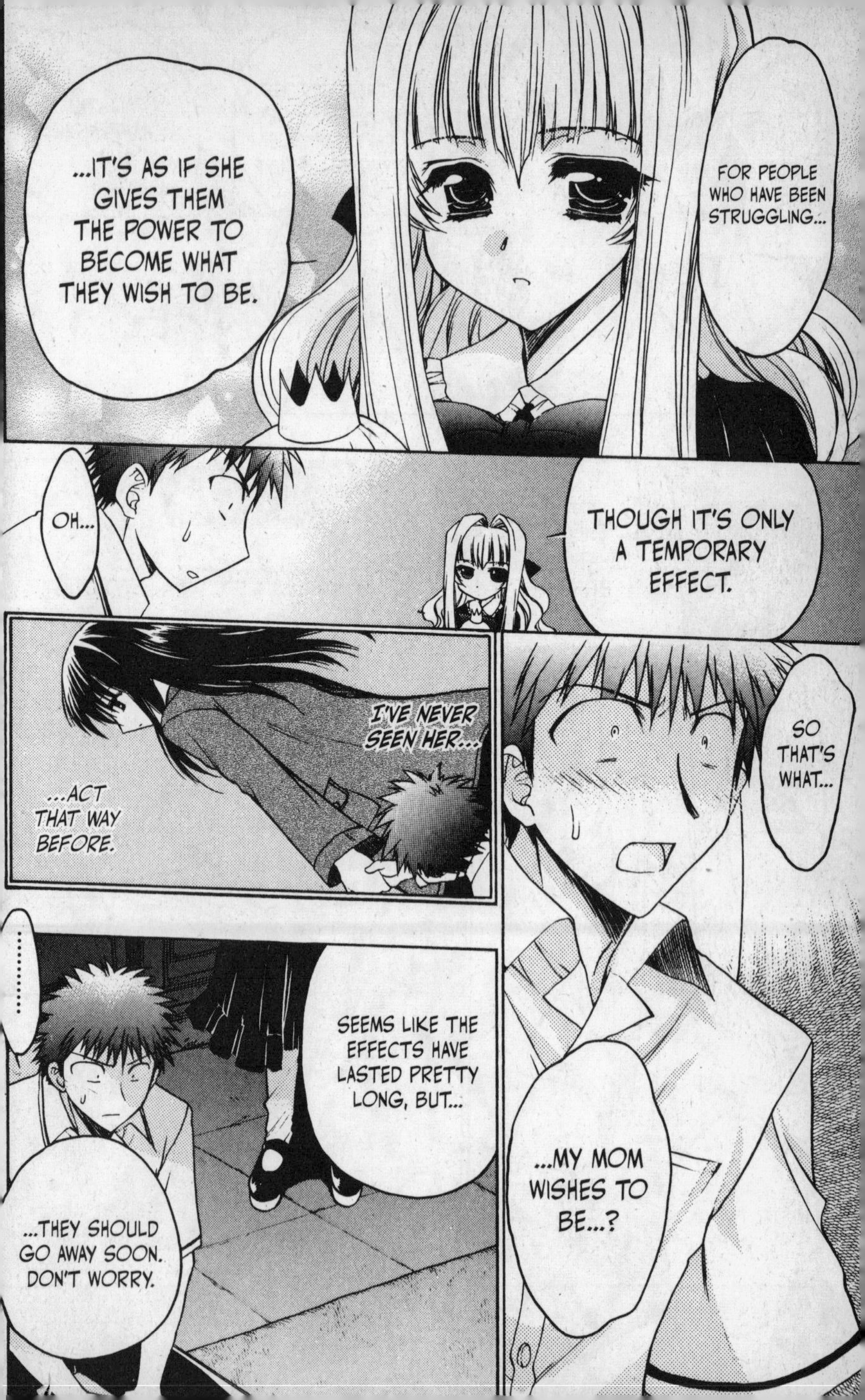
FOR PEOPLE WHO HAVE BEEN STRUGGLING...
...IT'S AS IF SHE GIVES THEM THE POWER TO BECOME WHAT THEY WISH TO BE.
THOUGH IT'S ONLY A TEMPORARY EFFECT.
OH...
SO THAT'S WHAT...
...MY MOM WISHES TO BE...?
I'VE NEVER SEEN HER...
...ACT THAT WAY BEFORE.
SEEMS LIKE THE EFFECTS HAVE LASTED PRETTY LONG, BUT...
......
...THEY SHOULD GO AWAY SOON. DON'T WORRY.

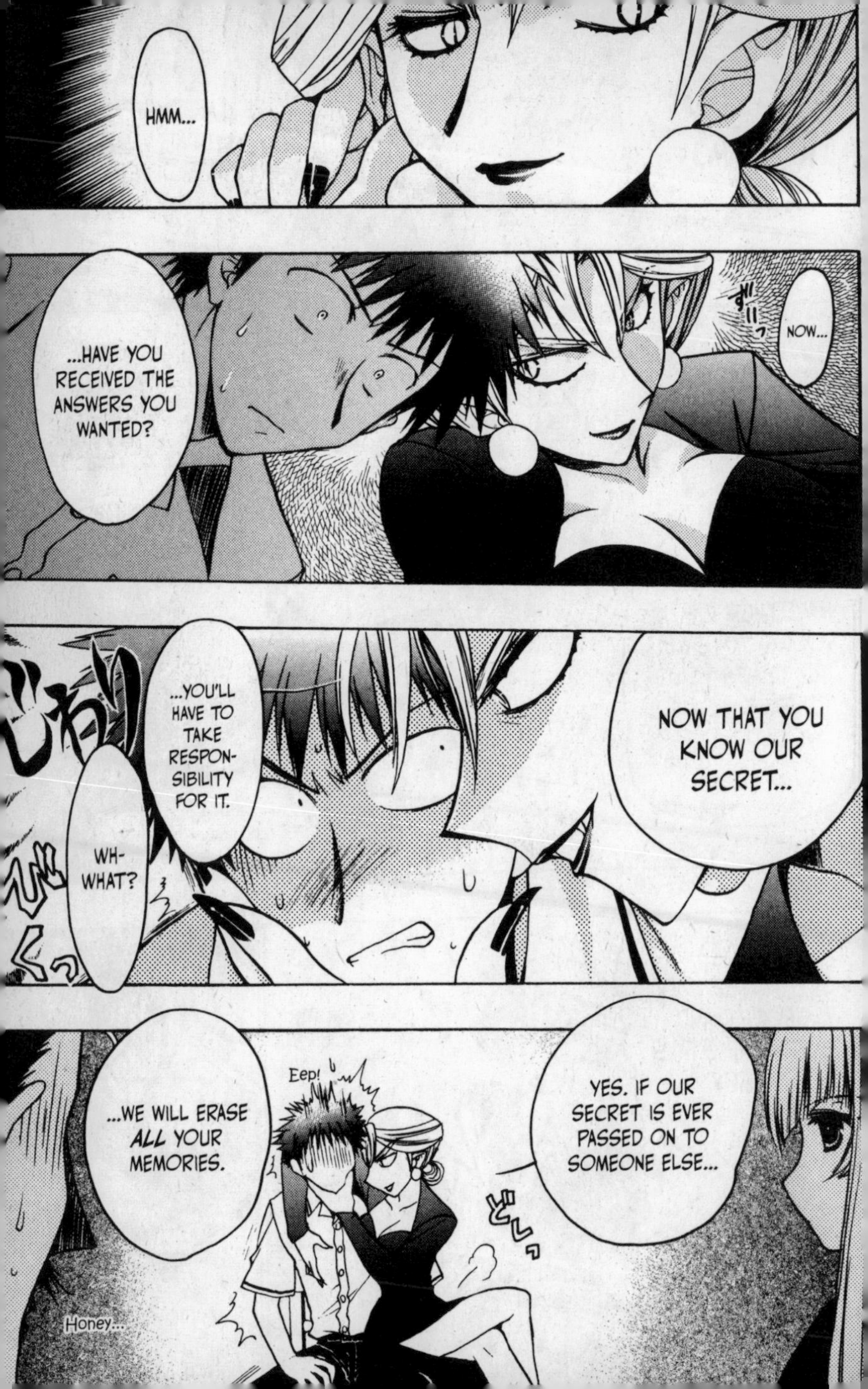
HMM...
NOW...
...HAVE YOU RECEIVED THE ANSWERS YOU WANTED?
NOW THAT YOU KNOW OUR SECRET...
...YOU'LL HAVE TO TAKE RESPON-SIBILITY FOR IT.
WH-WHAT?
YES. IF OUR SECRET IS EVER PASSED ON TO SOMEONE ELSE...
Eep!
...WE WILL ERASE ALL YOUR MEMORIES.
Honey...

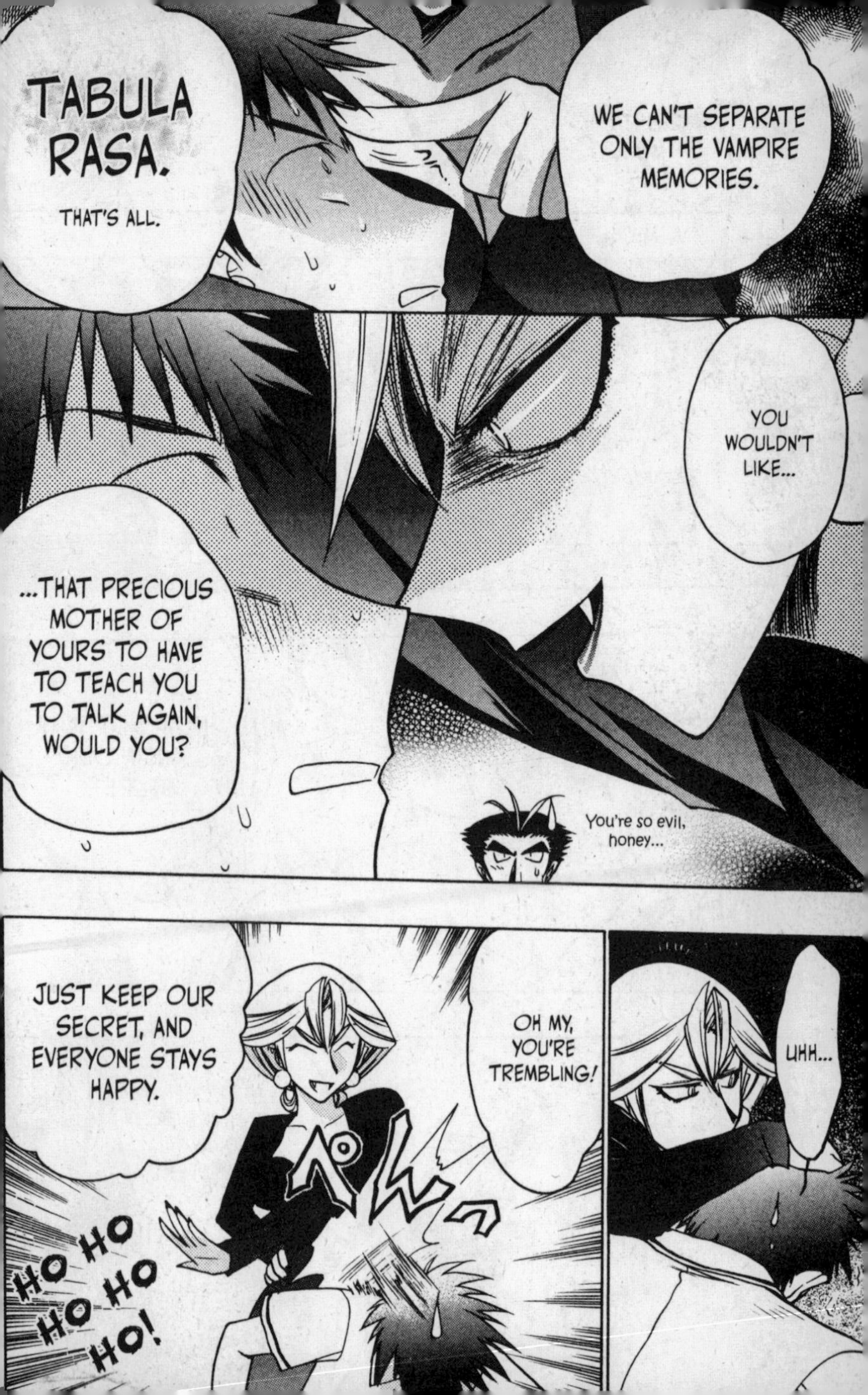
WE CAN'T SEPARATE ONLY THE VAMPIRE MEMORIES.
TABULA RASA.
THAT'S ALL.
YOU WOULDN'T LIKE...
...THAT PRECIOUS MOTHER OF YOURS TO HAVE TO TEACH YOU TO TALK AGAIN, WOULD YOU?
You're so evil, honey...
UHH...
OH MY, YOU'RE TREMBLING!
JUST KEEP OUR SECRET, AND EVERYONE STAYS HAPPY.
HO HO HO HO HO!

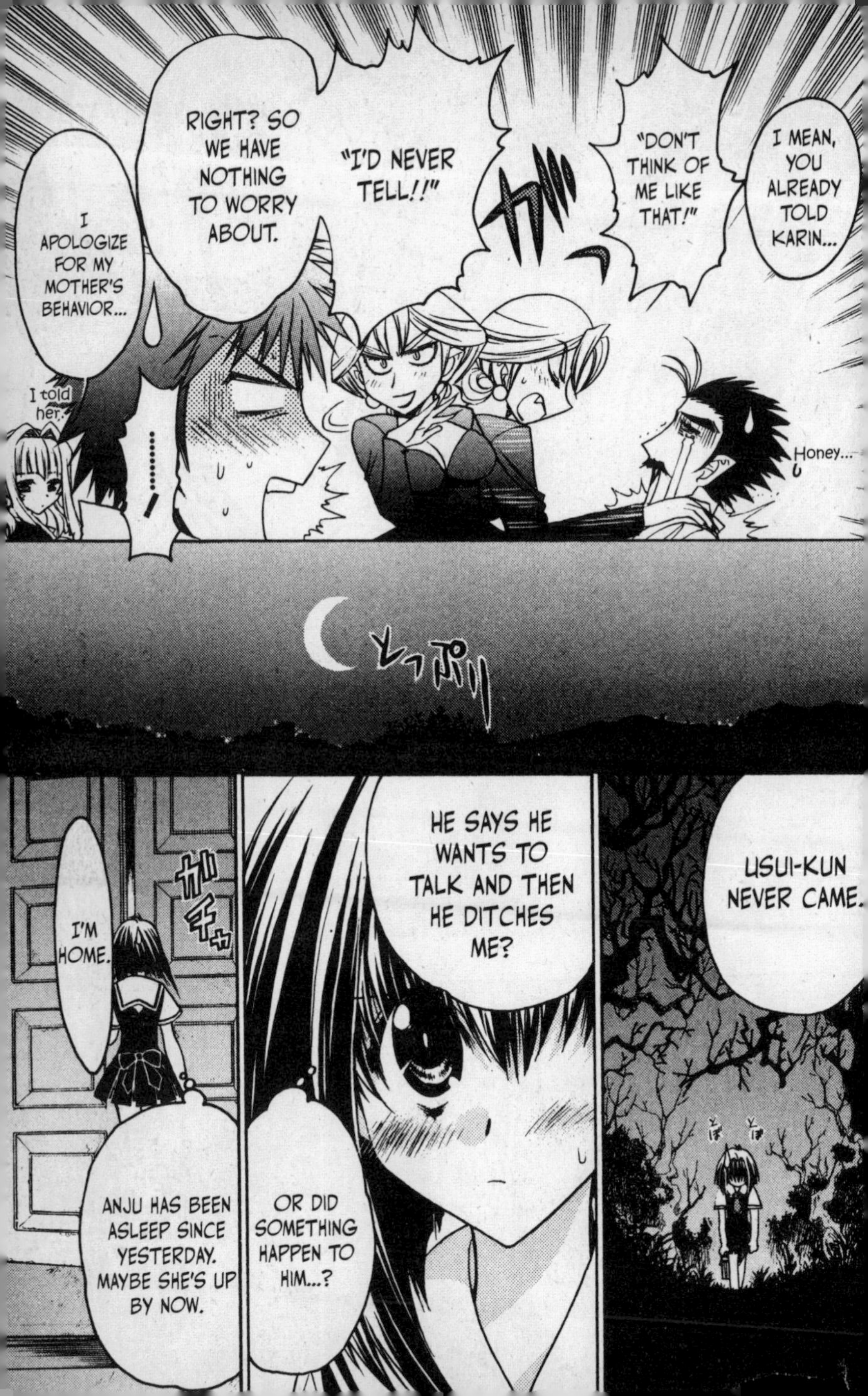
I MEAN, YOU ALREADY TOLD KARIN...
"DON'T THINK OF ME LIKE THAT!"
"I'D NEVER TELL!!"
RIGHT? SO WE HAVE NOTHING TO WORRY ABOUT.
I APOLOGIZE FOR MY MOTHER'S BEHAVIOR...
Honey...
I told her.
......!
とっぷり
USUI-KUN NEVER CAME.
とぼ とぼ
HE SAYS HE WANTS TO TALK AND THEN HE DITCHES ME?
OR DID SOMETHING HAPPEN TO HIM...?
ガチャ
I'M HOME.
ANJU HAS BEEN ASLEEP SINCE YESTERDAY. MAYBE SHE'S UP BY NOW.

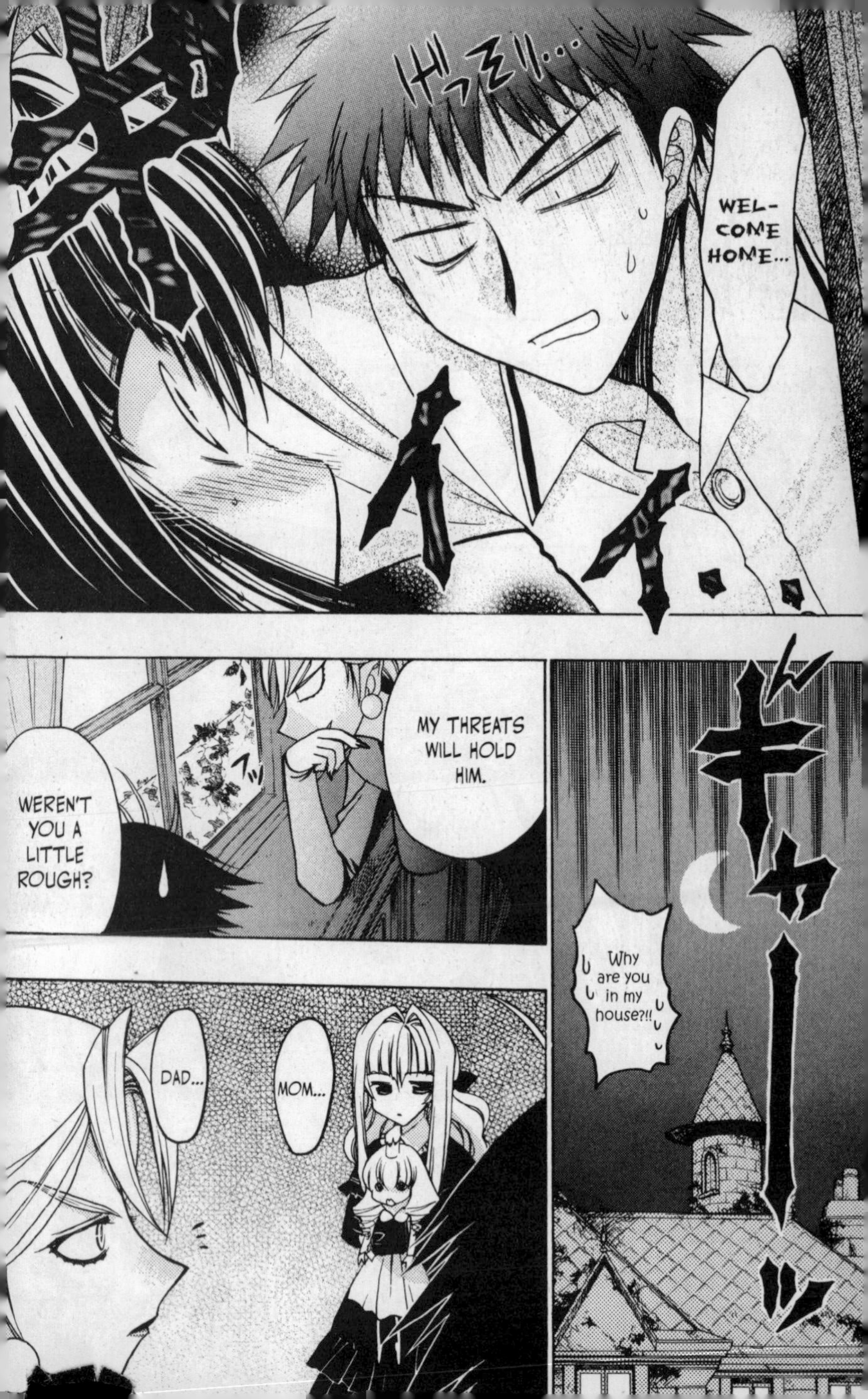
げっそり…
WEL-COME HOME...
ギャーッ
Why are you in my house?!!
MY THREATS WILL HOLD HIM.
WEREN'T YOU A LITTLE ROUGH?
MOM...
DAD...

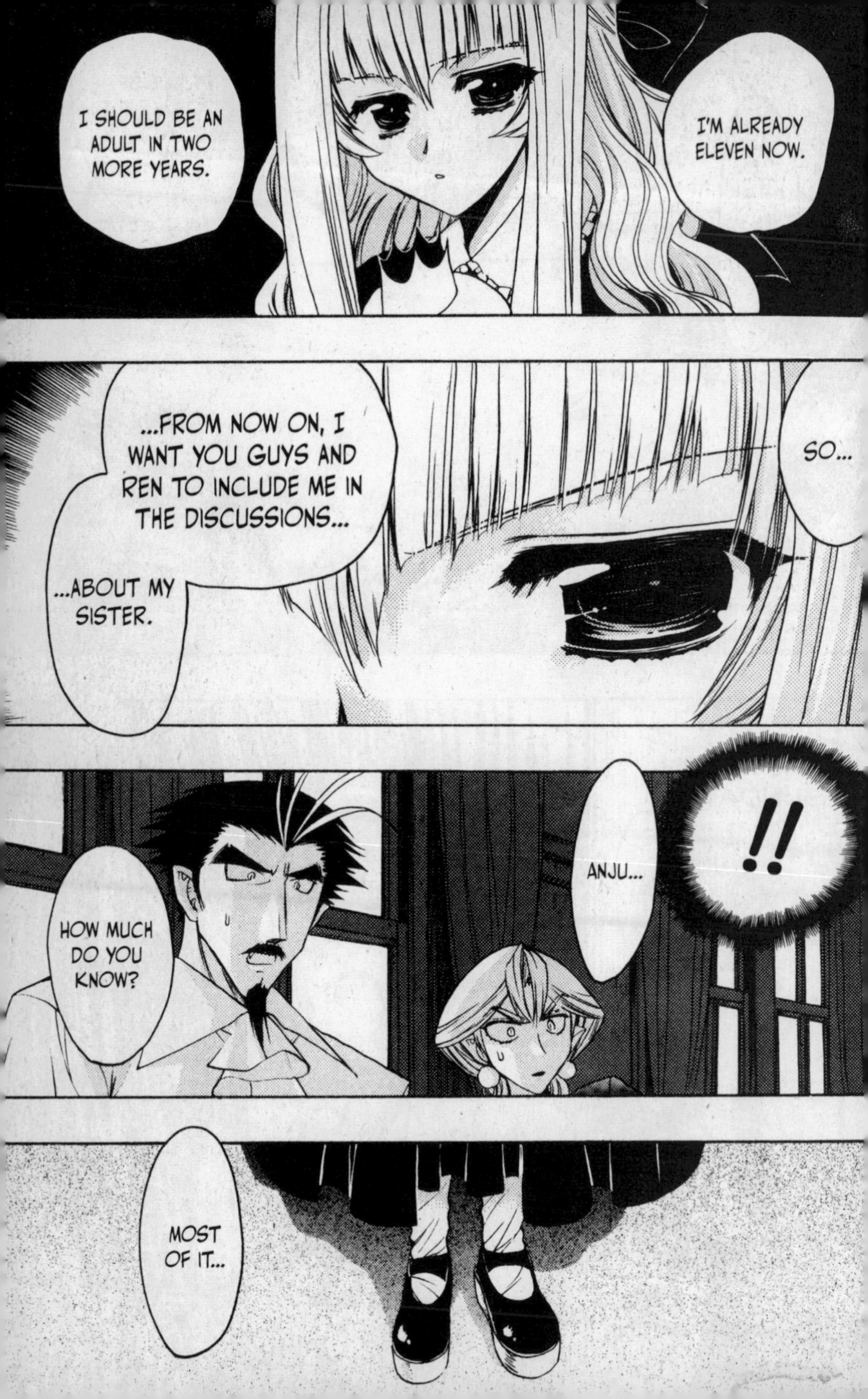
I'M ALREADY ELEVEN NOW.
I SHOULD BE AN ADULT IN TWO MORE YEARS.
SO...
...FROM NOW ON, I WANT YOU GUYS AND REN TO INCLUDE ME IN THE DISCUSSIONS...
...ABOUT MY SISTER.
!!
ANJU...
HOW MUCH DO YOU KNOW?
MOST OF IT...

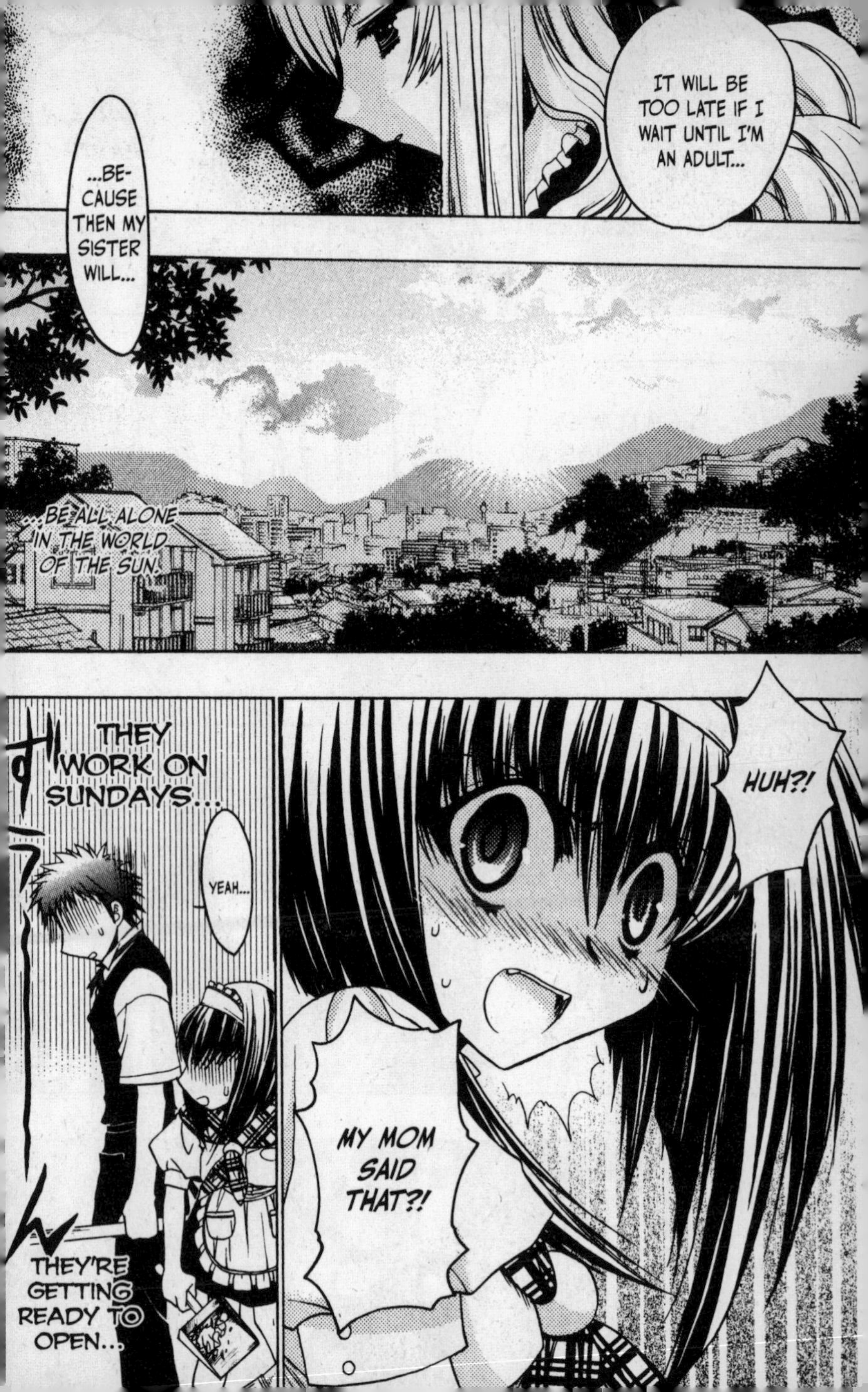
IT WILL BE TOO LATE IF I WAIT UNTIL I'M AN ADULT...
...BE-CAUSE THEN MY SISTER WILL...
...BE ALL ALONE IN THE WORLD OF THE SUN.
HUH?!
MY MOM SAID THAT?!
THEY WORK ON SUNDAYS...
YEAH...
THEY'RE GETTING READY TO OPEN...

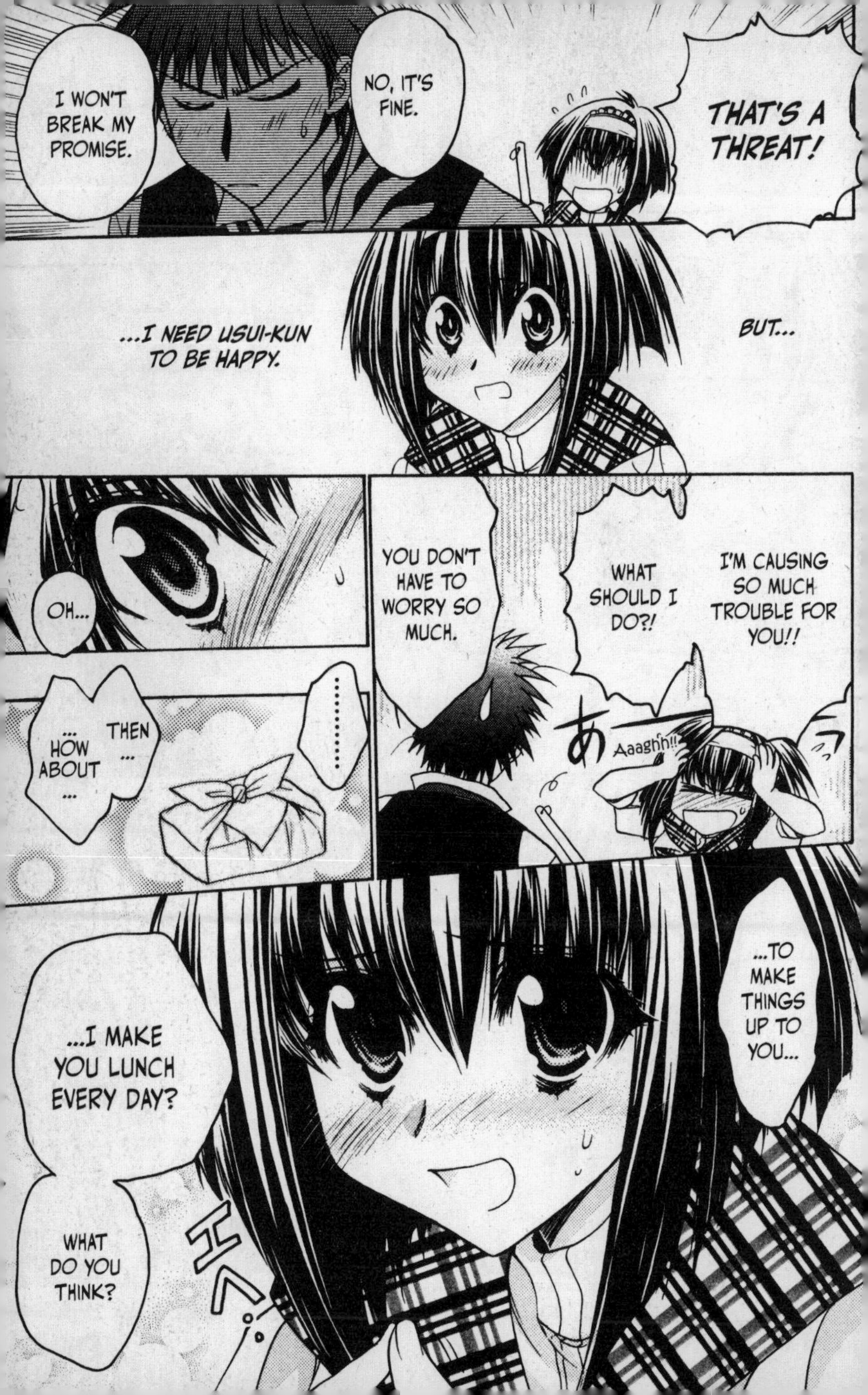
THAT'S A THREAT!
NO, IT'S FINE.
I WON'T BREAK MY PROMISE.
BUT...
...I NEED USUI-KUN TO BE HAPPY.
I'M CAUSING SO MUCH TROUBLE FOR YOU!!
WHAT SHOULD I DO?!
あ Aaaghh!!
YOU DON'T HAVE TO WORRY SO MUCH.
OH...
......
THEN... HOW ABOUT...
...TO MAKE THINGS UP TO YOU...
...I MAKE YOU LUNCH EVERY DAY?
WHAT DO YOU THINK?

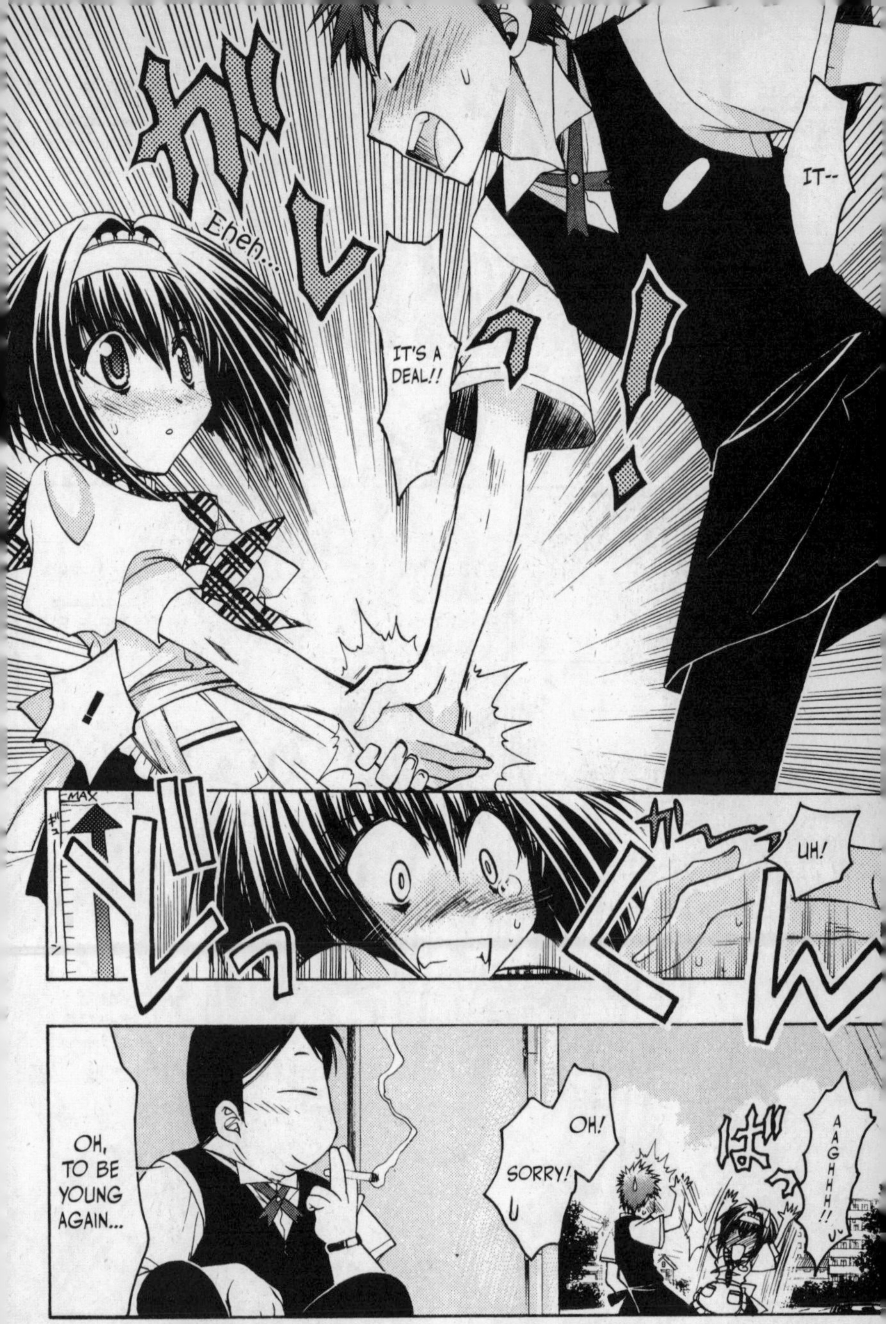
IT--
Eneh...
IT'S A DEAL!!
!
UH!
MAX
AAGHHH!!
OH!
SORRY!
OH, TO BE YOUNG AGAIN...

10TH EMBARRASSMENT END

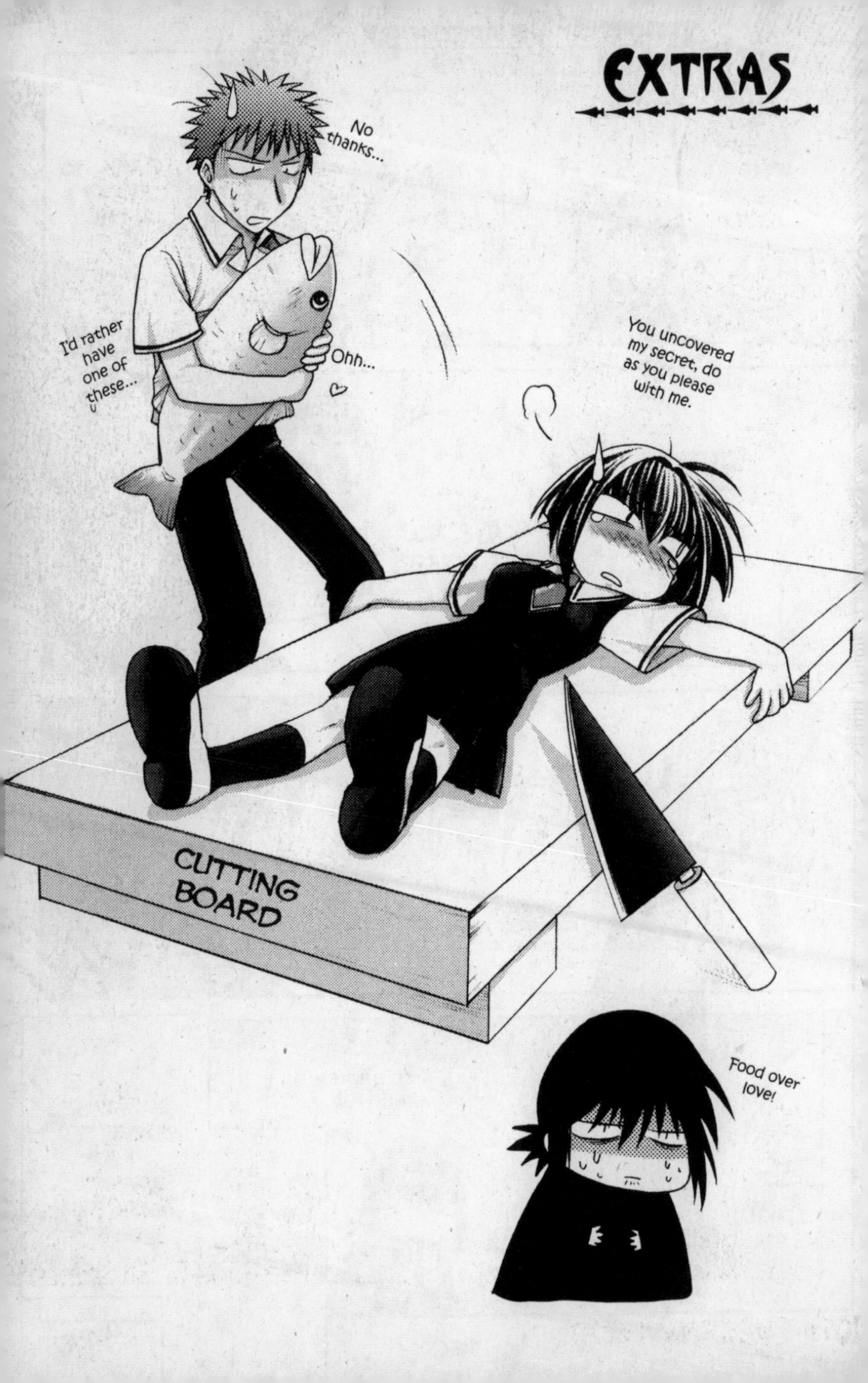
EXTRAS
No thanks...
I'd rather have one of these...
Ohh...
You uncovered my secret, do as you please with me.
CUTTING BOARD
Food over love!

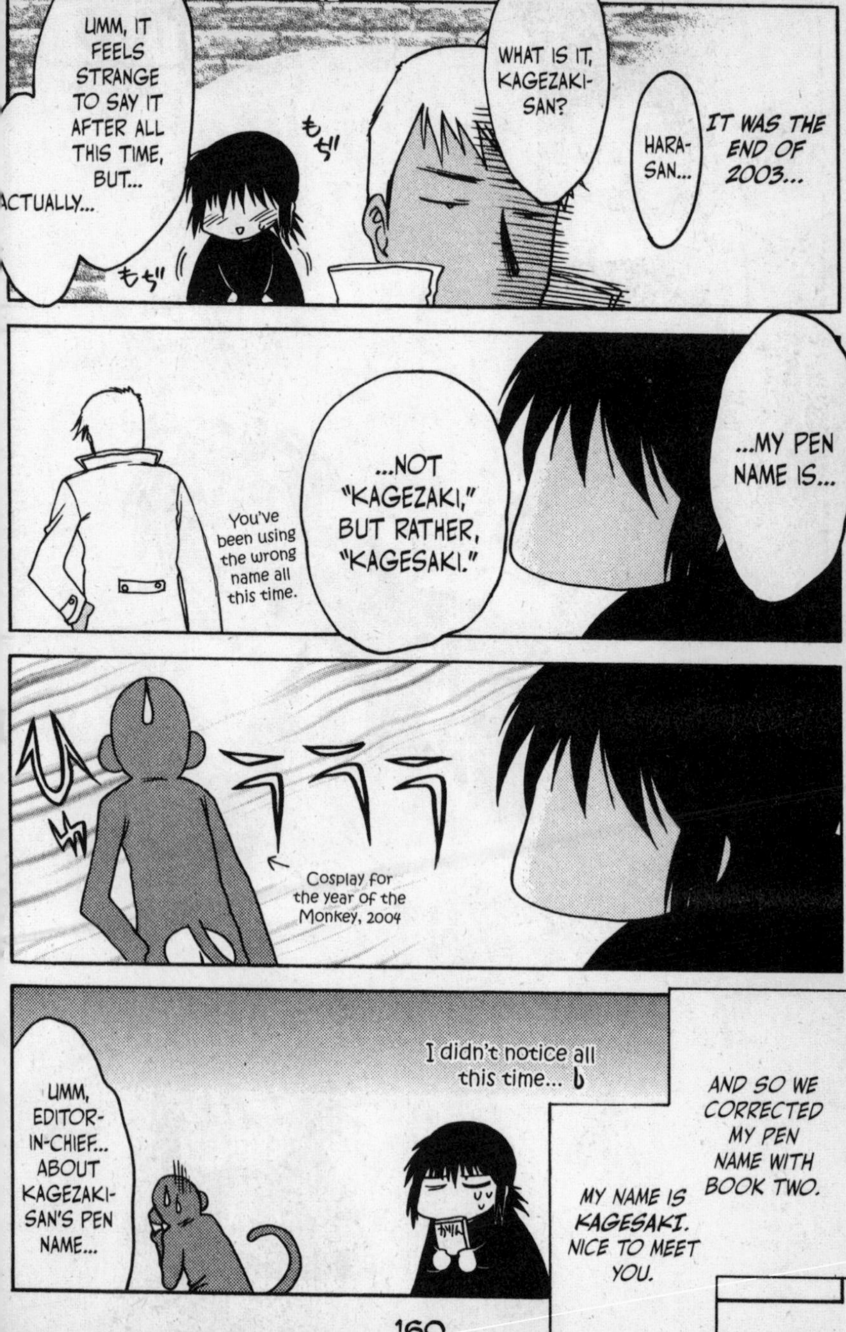
IT WAS THE END OF 2003...
HARA-SAN...
WHAT IS IT, KAGEZAKI-SAN?
もぢ
UMM, IT FEELS STRANGE TO SAY IT AFTER ALL THIS TIME, BUT... ACTUALLY...
もぢ
...MY PEN NAME IS...
...NOT "KAGEZAKI," BUT RATHER, "KAGESAKI."
You've been using the wrong name all this time.
Cosplay for the year of the Monkey, 2004
AND SO WE CORRECTED MY PEN NAME WITH BOOK TWO.
MY NAME IS KAGESAKI. NICE TO MEET YOU.
I didn't notice all this time...
UMM, EDITOR-IN-CHIEF... ABOUT KAGEZAKI-SAN'S PEN NAME...

AT FIRST I THOUGHT, "WHAT THE HELL IS THIS PERSON THINKING?!"

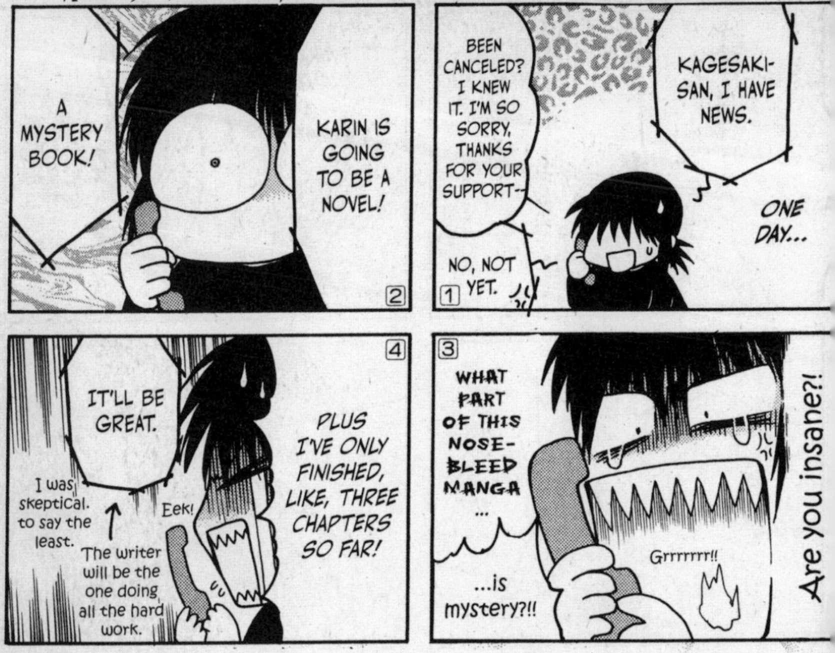
KAGESAKI-SAN, I HAVE NEWS.
ONE DAY...
BEEN CANCELED? I KNEW IT. I'M SO SORRY. THANKS FOR YOUR SUPPORT--
NO, NOT YET.
1
KARIN IS GOING TO BE A NOVEL!
A MYSTERY BOOK!
2
3
Are you insane?!
WHAT PART OF THIS NOSE-BLEED MANGA ...
...is mystery?!!
Grrrrrrr!!
4
PLUS I'VE ONLY FINISHED, LIKE, THREE CHAPTERS SO FAR!
IT'LL BE GREAT.
Eek!
I was skeptical. to say the least.
The writer will be the one doing all the hard work.

KARIN NOVELIZATION SNEAK PREVIEW

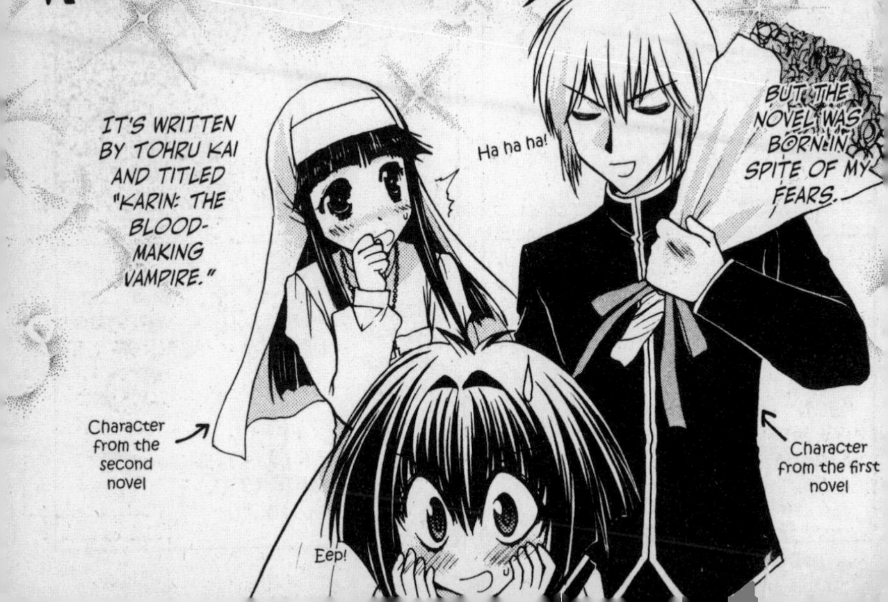
BUT THE NOVEL WAS BORN IN SPITE OF MY FEARS.
Ha ha ha!
IT'S WRITTEN BY TOHRU KAI AND TITLED "KARIN: THE BLOOD-MAKING VAMPIRE."
Character from the first novel
Character from the second novel
Eep!

CHANGING TRAINS IN AKIHABARA IS CONFUSING (JANUARY 2004...)

MUST GET TO NOVELS MEETING...
IT WAS A HORRIBLE RAINSTORM THAT DAY.
I SWITCH TRAINS AT AKABANE TO THE KEIHIN LINE.
THEN AT AKIHABARA...
...I TAKE THE SOUBU LINE TOWARDS IIDABASHI...
IIDA
AKI
...OR AT LEAST I WAS SUPPOSED TO.
I GOT ON THE WRONG TRAIN!
IIDA
AKI
HASN'T REALIZED SHE'S GOTTEN ON THE WRONG TRAIN.
THEN WHEN I GET TO IIDABASHI, I TAKE A TAXI TO...
COMING UP NEXT IS KINSHI CITY!
......
HUH ?!
TOOK ME A WHILE TO NOTICE MY MISTAKE.
......
AND WHEN I CALLED MY EDITOR TO TELL HIM I WOULD BE LATE...
KAGESAKI-SAN DOESN'T JUST WRITE KARIN... SHE IS KARIN!
...HE SUPPOSEDLY SAID SOMETHING VERY RUDE.
KAI-SENSEI

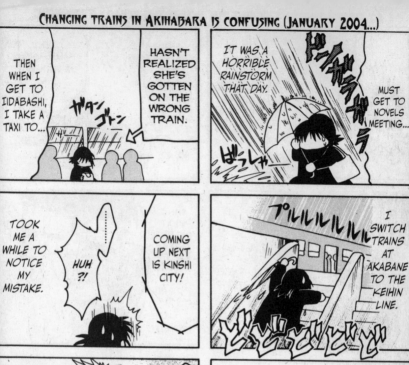

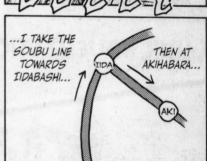

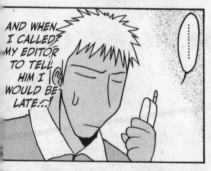

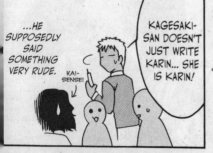

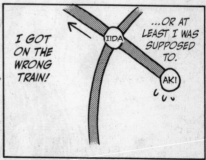

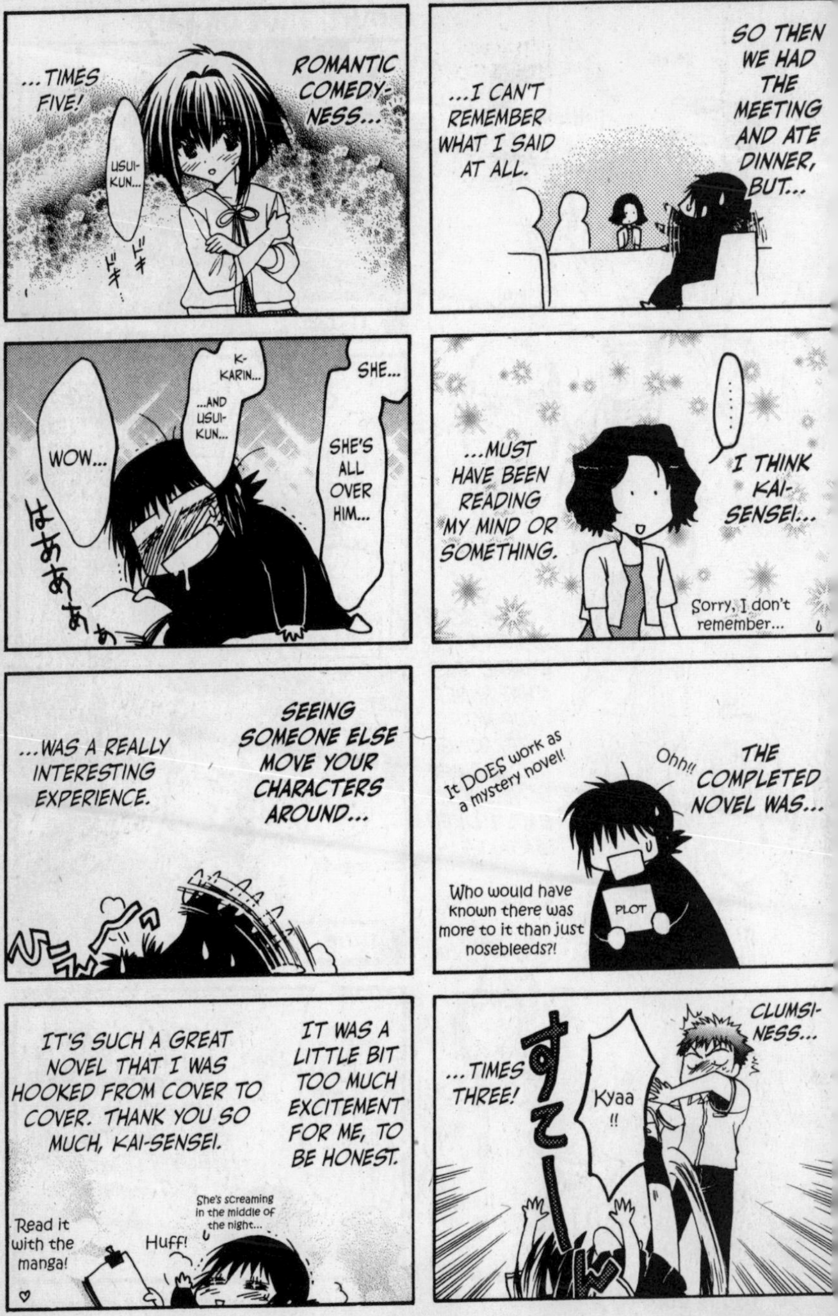
SO THEN WE HAD THE MEETING AND ATE DINNER, BUT...
...I CAN'T REMEMBER WHAT I SAID AT ALL.
I THINK KAI-SENSEI...
......
...MUST HAVE BEEN READING MY MIND OR SOMETHING.
Sorry, I don't remember...
THE COMPLETED NOVEL WAS...
Ohh!!
It DOES work as a mystery novel!
PLOT
Who would have known there was more to it than just nosebleeds?!
CLUMSINESS...
Kyaa!!
...TIMES THREE!
ROMANTIC COMEDY-NESS...
USUI-KUN...
...TIMES FIVE!
SHE...
SHE'S ALL OVER HIM...
K-KARIN...
...AND USUI-KUN...
WOW...
SEEING SOMEONE ELSE MOVE YOUR CHARACTERS AROUND...
...WAS A REALLY INTERESTING EXPERIENCE.
IT WAS A LITTLE BIT TOO MUCH EXCITEMENT FOR ME, TO BE HONEST.
IT'S SUCH A GREAT NOVEL THAT I WAS HOOKED FROM COVER TO COVER. THANK YOU SO MUCH, KAI-SENSEI.
She's screaming in the middle of the night...
Huff!
Read it with the manga!

NOVEL: TRUE OR FALSE

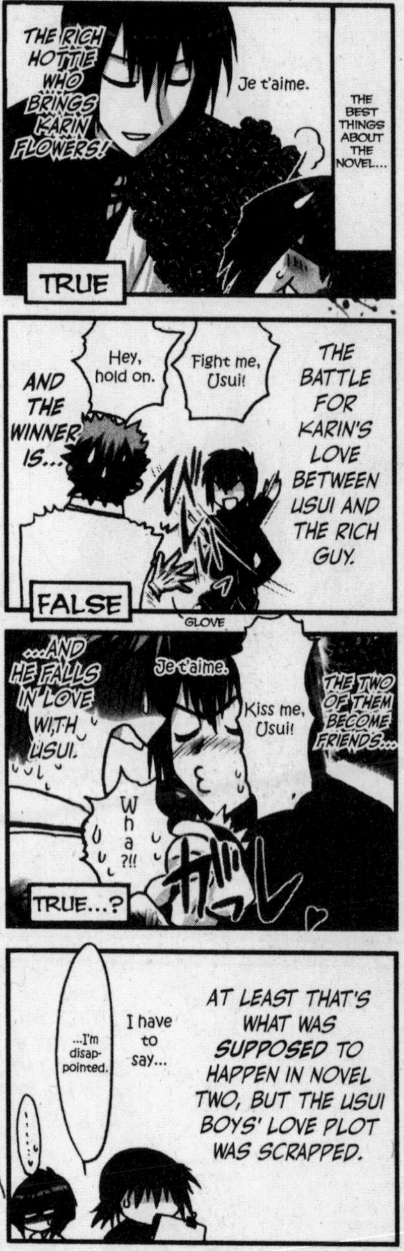
THE BEST THINGS ABOUT THE NOVEL...
Je t'aime.
THE RICH HOTTIE WHO BRINGS KARIN FLOWERS!
TRUE
THE BATTLE FOR KARIN'S LOVE BETWEEN USUI AND THE RICH GUY.
Fight me, Usui!
Hey, hold on.
AND THE WINNER IS...
GLOVE
FALSE
THE TWO OF THEM BECOME FRIENDS...
Kiss me, Usui!
Je t'aime.
...AND HE FALLS IN LOVE WITH USUI.
Wha?!!
TRUE...?
AT LEAST THAT'S WHAT WAS SUPPOSED TO HAPPEN IN NOVEL TWO, BUT THE USUI BOYS' LOVE PLOT WAS SCRAPPED.
I have to say...
...I'm disappointed.
...

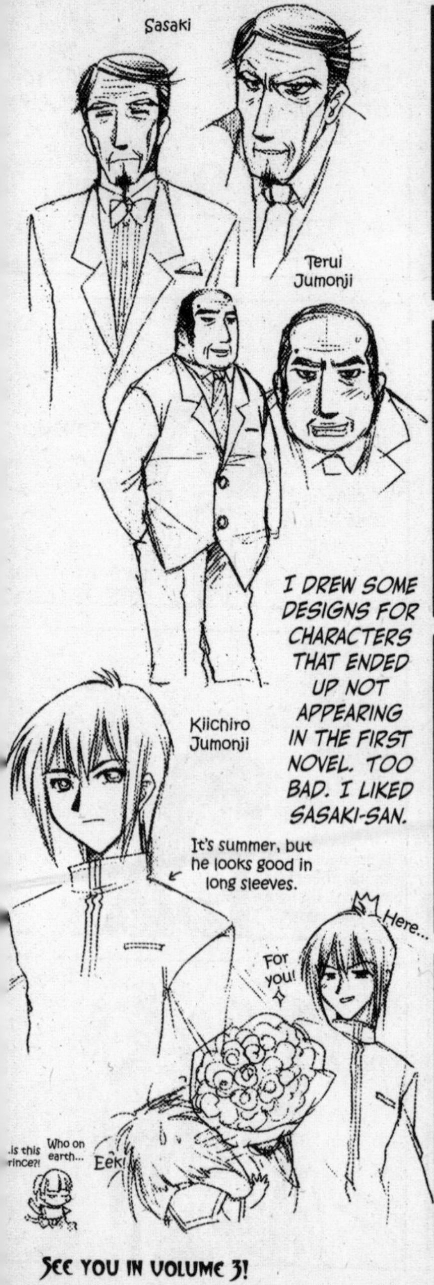
Sasaki
Terui Jumonji
I DREW SOME DESIGNS FOR CHARACTERS THAT ENDED UP NOT APPEARING IN THE FIRST NOVEL. TOO BAD. I LIKED SASAKI-SAN.
Kiichiro Jumonji
It's summer, but he looks good in long sleeves.
Here...
For you!
Eek!
Who on earth...
.is this
rince?!

SEE YOU IN VOLUME 3!

IN OUR NEXT VOLUME...

chibi Vampire
TOKYOPOP
Created By:
Yuna Kagesaki
3

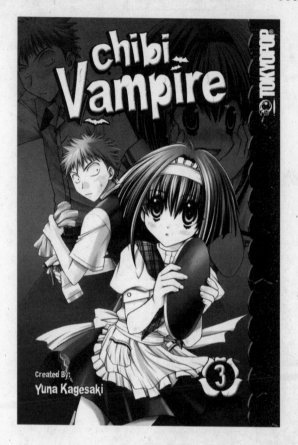

KENTA AGREES TO HELP KARIN STUDY FOR HER EXAMS, AND THE FRIENDSHIP BETWEEN THE TWO CONTINUES TO GROW. HOWEVER, AFTER MAKI CATCHES SIGHT OF THEM, THE RUMORS ABOUT JUST HOW MUCH IT'S GROWN BEGIN TO SPREAD. YES, SOMETHING'S IN THE AIR. IS IT LOVE OR... GARLIC? YOU SEE, KARIN'S TAKEN ON A NEW JOB SELLING CHINESE FOOD AT A JOINT THAT SEASONS EVERYTHING WITH GARLIC, WHICH WOULD BE A PROBLEM CONSIDERING THAT

KARIN'S A FREAKIN' VAMPIRE!!!

HELPFUL EDITOR!

FOR RESEARCH, WE WENT TO HAVE OUR BLOOD TAKEN.
IT'S GOING TO HURT, ISN'T IT?
MY EDITOR WAS REALLY NERVOUS.
MOTO-SAN
THEN ...
I'VE BEEN UP ALL NIGHT DRAWING. I CAN'T HAVE MY BLOOD TAKEN.
I'M ON MEDICATION, SORRY...
AFRAID OF BLOOD ...
SO HE HAD TO GO IT ALONE.
NURSE
BUT HE FREAKED AND PASSED OUT.
HUH?
WHAT'S WITH HIM?
MY EDITOR WAS WHEELED AWAY TO THE BACK.

It's always good to stay calm!

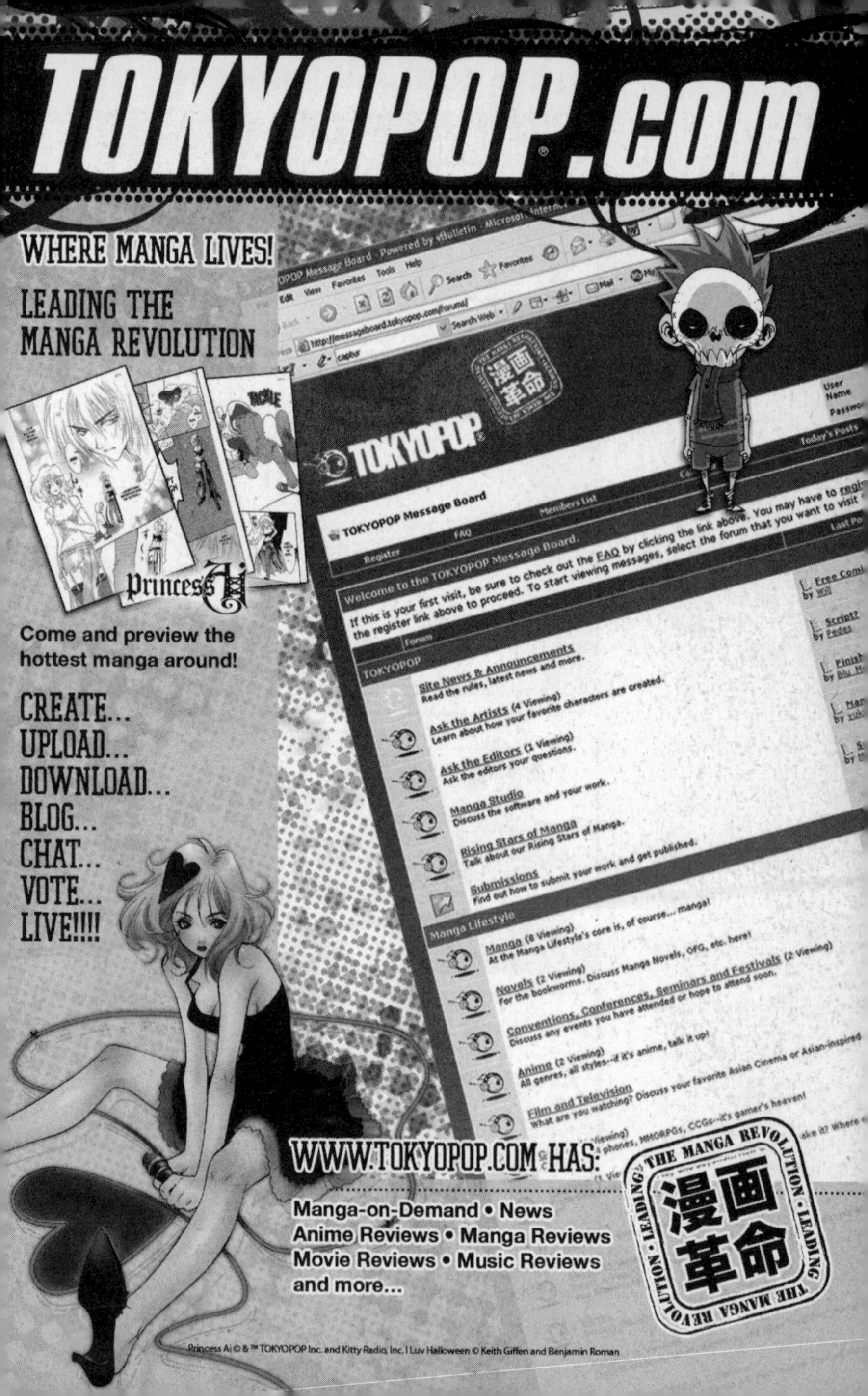
TOKYOPOP.com
WHERE MANGA LIVES!
LEADING THE MANGA REVOLUTION
Princess Ai
Come and preview the hottest manga around!
CREATE...
UPLOAD...
DOWNLOAD...
BLOG...
CHAT...
VOTE...
LIVE!!!!
TOKYOPOP
TOKYOPOP Message Board
Welcome to the TOKYOPOP Message Board.
Site News & Announcements
Read the rules, latest news and more.
Ask the Artists (4 Viewing)
Learn about how your favorite characters are created.
Ask the Editors (1 Viewing)
Ask the editors your questions.
Manga Studio
Discuss the software and your work.
Rising Stars of Manga
Talk about our Rising Stars of Manga.
Submissions
Find out how to submit your work and get published.
Manga Lifestyle
Manga (8 Viewing)
Novels (2 Viewing)
Conventions, Conferences, Seminars and Festivals (2 Viewing)
Anime (2 Viewing)
Film and Television
WWW.TOKYOPOP.COM HAS:
Manga-on-Demand • News
Anime Reviews • Manga Reviews
Movie Reviews • Music Reviews
and more...
THE MANGA REVOLUTION • LEADING
漫画革命
Princess Ai © & ™ TOKYOPOP Inc. and Kitty Radio, Inc. I Luv Halloween © Keith Giffen and Benjamin Roman

Jim Henson's RETURN TO LABYRINTH™

Jim Henson's classic continues...

The Goblin King has kept a watchful eye on Toby: His minions secretly guiding and protecting the child... Legions of goblins working behind the scenes to ensure that Toby has whatever his heart desires... Preparing him for the day when he will return to the Labyrinth and take his rightful place beside Jareth as the heir to the Goblin Kingdom.

That day has come...

...but no one has told Toby.

By Chris Lie
and Jake T. Forbes

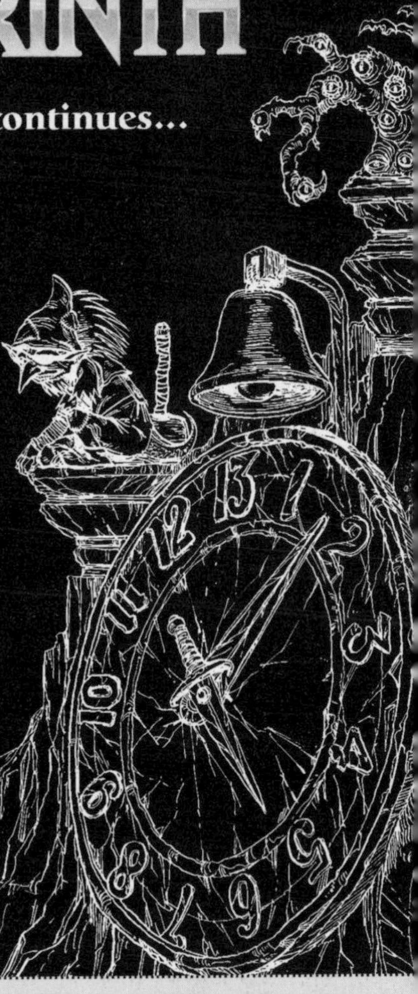

FANTASY

T TEEN AGE 13+

www.HENSON.com

FOR MORE INFORMATION VISIT: WWW.TOKYOPOP.COM

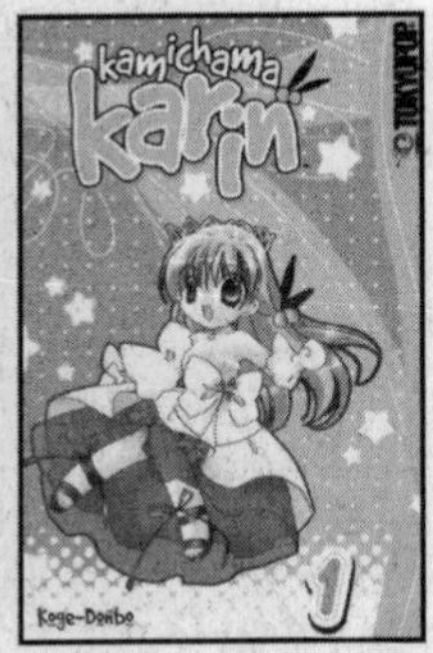
kamichama
karin
TOKYOPOP
1
Koge-Donbo

ROMANCE

Y
YOUTH AGE 10+

KAMICHAMA KARIN

BY KOGE-DONBO

This one was a surprise. I mean, I knew Koge-Donbo drew insanely cute characters, but I had no idea a magical girl story could be so darn clever. *Kamichama Karin* manages to lampoon everything about the genre, from plushie-like mascots to character archetypes to weapons that appear from the blue! And you gotta love Karin, the airheaded heroine who takes guff from no one and screams "I AM GOD!" as her battle cry. In short, if you are looking for a shiny new manga with a knack for hilarity and a penchant for accessories, I say look no further.

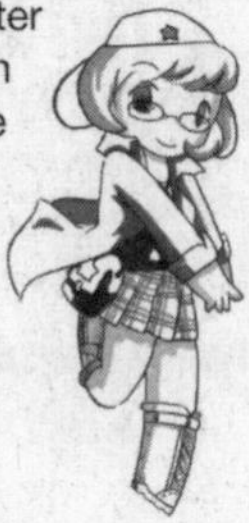

~Carol Fox, Editor

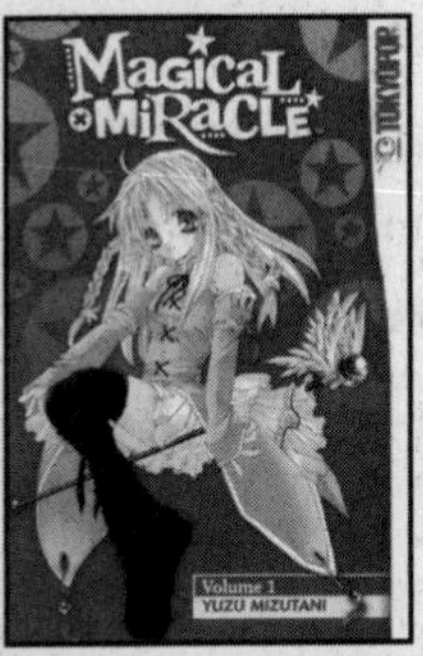
Magical
Miracle
TOKYOPOP
Volume 1
YUZU MIZUTANI

FANTASY

T
TEEN AGE 13+

MAGICAL X MIRACLE

BY YUZU MIZUTANI

Magical X Miracle is a quirky—yet uplifting—tale of gender-bending mistaken identity! When a young girl must masquerade as a great wizard, she not only finds the strength to save an entire kingdom...but, ironically, she just might just find herself, too. Yuzu Mizutani's art is remarkably adorable, but it also has a dark, sophisticated edge.

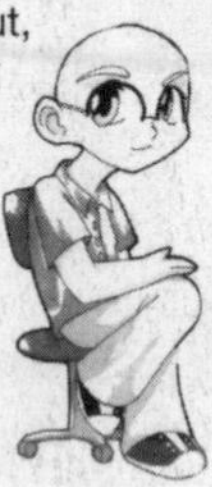

~Paul Morrissey, Editor

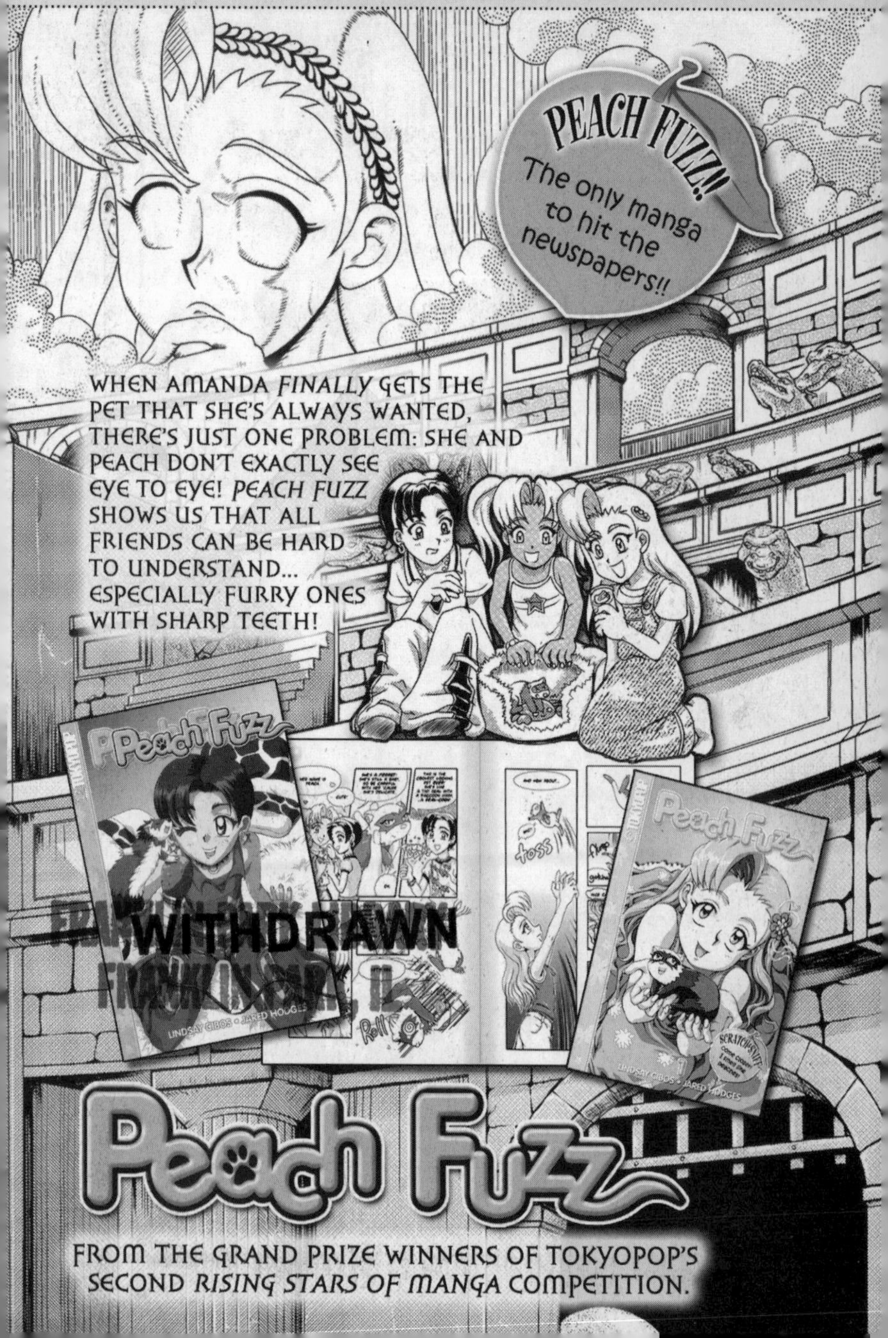
PEACH FUZZ!!
The only manga to hit the newspapers!!
WHEN AMANDA FINALLY GETS THE PET THAT SHE'S ALWAYS WANTED, THERE'S JUST ONE PROBLEM: SHE AND PEACH DON'T EXACTLY SEE EYE TO EYE! PEACH FUZZ SHOWS US THAT ALL FRIENDS CAN BE HARD TO UNDERSTAND... ESPECIALLY FURRY ONES WITH SHARP TEETH!
Peach Fuzz
WITHDRAWN
LINDSAY GIBBS • JARED HODGES
Peach Fuzz
LINDSAY GIBBS • JARED HODGES
Peach Fuzz
FROM THE GRAND PRIZE WINNERS OF TOKYOPOP'S SECOND RISING STARS OF MANGA COMPETITION.

PEACHFUZZ

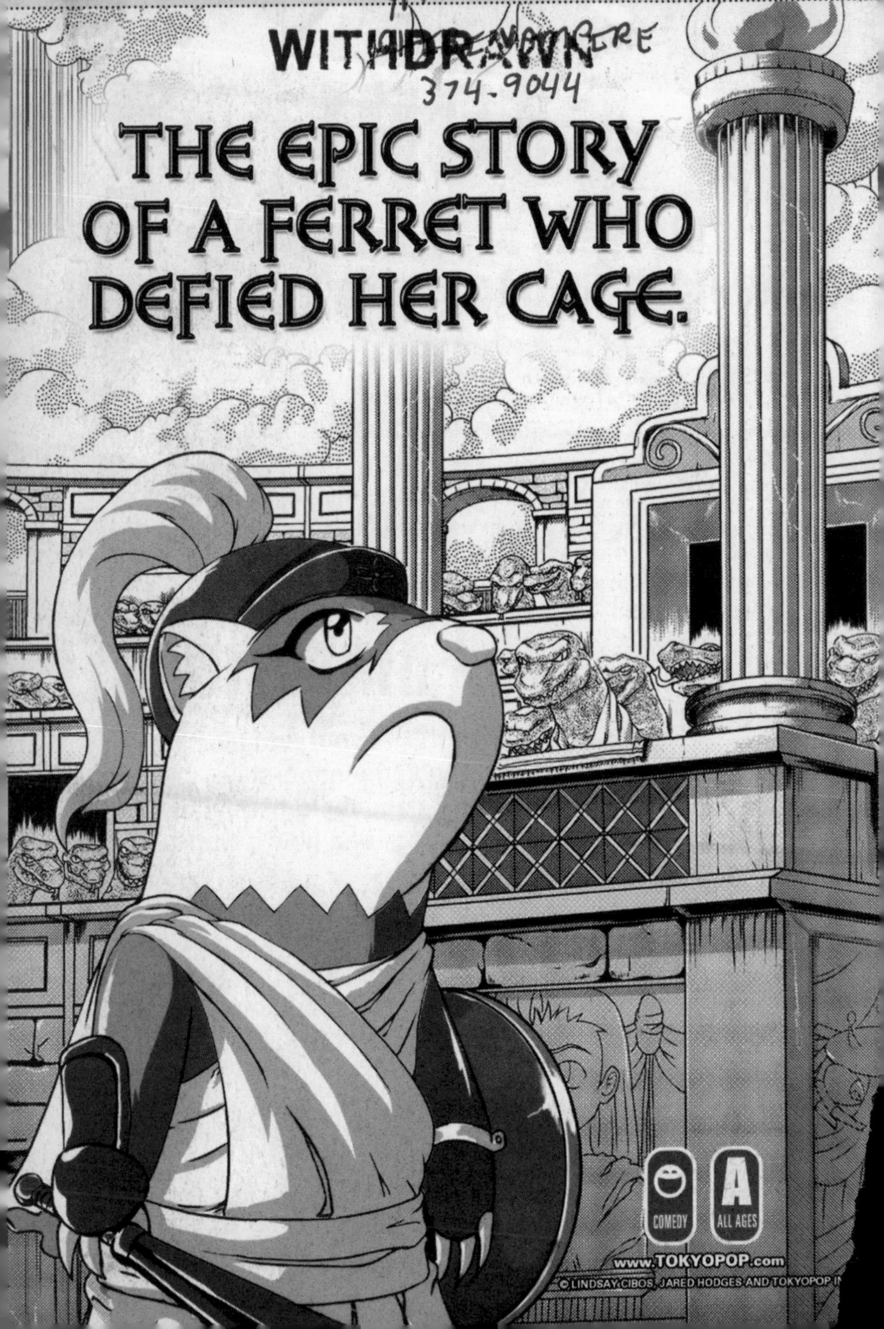
THE EPIC STORY OF A FERRET WHO DEFIED HER CAGE.
COMEDY
A
ALL AGES
www.TOKYOPOP.com
© LINDSAY CIBOS, JARED HODGES AND TOKYOPOP I

STOP!

This is the back of the book.
You wouldn't want to spoil a great ending!

This book is printed "manga-style," in the authentic Japanese right-to-left format. Since none of the artwork has been flipped or altered, readers get to experience the story just as the creator intended. You've been asking for it, so TOKYOPOP® delivered: authentic, hot-off-the-press, and far more fun!

DIRECTIONS

If this is your first time reading manga-style, here's a quick guide to help you understand how it works.

It's easy... just start in the top right panel and follow the numbers. Have fun, and look for more 100% authentic manga from TOKYOPOP®!

100% AUTHENTIC MANGA